Street Legal

Street Legal

Rafi Zabor

Terra Nova Press

NEWARK   CALLICOON   MATSALU

2021

ISBN: 978-1-949597-18-9

Library of Congress Control Number: 2020950615

published by:

Terra Nova Press
NEWARK   CALLICOON   MATSALU

Publisher: David Rothenberg
Editor-in-Chief: Evan Eisenberg
Designer: Martin Pedanik
Proofreader: Tyran Grillo
Set in Bembo Book

printed by Tallinn Book Printers, Tallinn, Estonia

1 2 3 4 5 6 7 8 9 10

www.terranovapress.com

Distributed by the MIT Press, Cambridge, Massachusetts and London, England

In Memoriam:
George and Maryam Steffen

One

Legalize it, and I will advertise it.

—*Peter Tosh*

1

EVEN BEFORE his eyes were open and without a clock Eli knew it was too early for this but he woke up to the Pearl Jam ringtone already sure who was calling. She'd been on his case a lot lately and here comes more. Dad gone almost two years and she still wasn't back to her old self. He rolled onto his left side, tapped the phone, put it to his cheek and tried to keep his tone humorous.

"Lea' me 'lone, Ma," he said, realizing as he spoke he was loud enough to wake Sukey, her body heat behind him as he rose on one elbow to get this conversation over with.

But it was Teddy. "Hey Pepina, this is Grandpappy Amos the head of the clan," using a code from some old TV show in this cracky old-man accent, any dumb cop could break it, let alone Poholek.

"Hi Granpop," Eli said instead of a few other choice words ready to go.

"I want you here by yestiddy," using that cracky voice heavier now. "I'm a'goin' crazy as a coot up here."

"Have yourself some Ovaltine and I'll get there in a while."

"Feed-corn crop needs lookin' after, Pepina. Feed-corn crop might be goin' funny."

"In a minute," said Eli, clicked off and settled his body back in bed. Sukey, quiet and breathing even, was pretending to be asleep or maybe hoping to get back to it. "Teddy," Eli told her anyway.

"I don't trust him," she said, rolled onto her side, her back to him, lovely square shoulders, delicate line of spinal bones. She didn't look pregnant from there and Eli tried to pretend for now.

"Baby," he explained, then the guitar riff from Not For You cranked again and he picked up. "Gimme half an hour, dude," he said, somehow knowing by the shade of silence on the other end that he'd been right the

1

first time and wrong the second time, no, he'd been wrong both times, wait, right the first time really—he was losing count—but he had to finish his line anyhow, "I'll be ready to check the crops in just one skinny-ass half hour."

"You told me you were quitting," his mother said.

Have to take this in the other room. As he left, Sukey rolled onto her back to give him the fish-eye but all he could see was the smooth tanned five-month mound that was still beautiful to him, her belly, which just went to show you.

There wasn't far to go in this tiny blue shack at the end of a driveway, though he didn't think it'd been built as a garage, the division into rooms was part of the structure and the low tilted roof cramping things close at funny angles. The DJ sound system almost filled the tiny living room, with the power amp hogging the armchair, which is what you get for trying to quit the skunk business and do something else, but try to tell your mother that.

"I don't care about the weed, honey," she was saying. "You know I don't object to it morally. I care about you getting caught, and face it, Eli, you're not a very good criminal."

"Be legal almost any day now, Mom."

"Not my point, and not today."

"Aarrhhh," he said.

"Listen to me, Eli. Stop what you're doing and listen to me."

He stopped what he was doing and listened to her. Then, thinking ahead, coffee and did Sukey put the leftover pizza in the fridge or did the bugs get to it, and another coffee in the thermo-cup to take with him in the car, put the back seats down and load the toolbox. He wondered if his mother could see the shape of Sukey's belly from all the way on the island off Seattle—she might be calling from the ferry, she liked to talk when she was already on the move—to right here in Eureka, Cal. She could be funny that way.

"What are you not telling me," she stopped her rap to ask him.

See?

Teddy's was outside town and in the woods with a dirt approach road up through the spruce and cedar, motion detectors and security cameras hidden in the trees, and the first thing you saw when you got there was the big deck jutting from the dark grey angular weathered woodslat structure that hung back and kind of hid behind it. Prow of a ship waiting for the flood. No, actually some kind of self-assertion, threat.

The world looked sharp today, in focus despite the not-so-great start on the phone first thing. Eli didn't want to jinx it but he could swear he was having one of his clear-brain days, got one every once so often, the planets or electrons in his head aligned and rotating just right for a change. Cool if it'd last awhile, get some hours in before, you know, things got less good again.

Eli pulled his Saab 900, faded blue paint with dings and scratches but the works still good, into the shade of the deck next to Teddy's red-dusted white Beamer and trudged up the noisy wooden stairs past the nothing ground floor to the spaceship-looking rooms where Teddy spent most of his time with the view on all sides through long windows. No idea what today's show would be until he saw the architectural model spread across a big new trestle-table in the middle of the living room and Teddy posed over it, hands on the top and too busy looking down at it, was the idea, to notice Eli coming in. If you wanted to build an old-time skunk dealer Teddy was the pattern you should work from, the shoulder-length dirty-blond hair parted in the middle hanging loose, the bony face and sharp eyes, buckskin-vested shirtless body skinny but tightly muscled, pecs and abs still etched at forty-what and a shiny silver and turquoise eye-thing hanging from his neck on a leather thong making like a pendulum because Teddy had only just settled on the pose while Eli was coming up the stairs.

Eli himself favored looking inconspicuous, if you could be inconspicuous at six foot three and a musculature he'd done almost nothing to earn and his drinking problem should have blunted even at twenty-three, but standing there a big kid with a blondish more-or-less crew-cut in T-shirt and jeans that said Marine Recruiting more than dope-involved professional. Eli liked looking trim and clean, but the difference between him and his boss was also a measure of their status in the industry, Teddy safe behind a curtain and Eli still out there in daylight, mostly.

"I'm still trying to figure out what other rides we could put in here," Teddy said without looking up from the maybe ten-foot-wide mockup of Smugglerville or Doper's Dream and one name Eli didn't even slightly understand, Vineland, because weed didn't grow on vines and was a bush. Anyway they hadn't settled on a name yet for the theme-park Teddy and three other local champions of the trade were gonna build because they were sure this is it, 2012: The Year Shit Goes Legal—personally Eli wasn't so sure—and once that happened there'd be no way to compete with the people already making it big in the legal trade, and then if you threw in the majors? Forget about it. Philip Morris had already copyrighted the brand-name Marley but Raleigh Inc. had beat them to a pack of Wailers and both companies had bought enormous tracts in the Valley planning on the time was coming soon.

"We got the car-chase track running through here," Teddy was telling him, "into the package-drop show but we can't use a real plane because the bundle might fall on a customer and kill him so we have to run a fake little plane on a wire—I *haaate* that—and he made us a nice Club Rave but we need some other shit. For one thing the chase car on the rollercoaster can't catch up. Has to be a way to gear it different so it can."

"How about a Bustorama ride," said Eli, "where you round the people up, cuff n'strip and cavity search, put 'em in cells and have guys in uniforms piss on 'em through the bars?"

"That'd work. Maybe all we really need is get 'em righteously ripped and have something soft for them to fall on—safety considerations will be of prime importance in this enterprise."

"Why would people come to you if they can buy it at the gas station?"

"Bro, would *you* smoke a Marley?" Teddy finally looked up at Eli to make a sourball face at the thought of it. "There's always gonna be room for primo artisanal weed with quality at least on the Häagen-Dazs/Mercedes-Benz principle of, like, you know, do a decent job at what you do."

Eli thought of all the extra product and tax regulations the industry would lay on the business if they tried to sell their own, plus the fact that old dealers like Teddy and them would never get licensed by the state, but decided not to mention it. "Franklin and the other guys have a Smugglerville model too?"

Teddy nodded. "Steiner had crews come out from the architects and set them up yesterday for all of us."

"You'll come up with outstanding shit inside a week," Eli told him.

"We could get people to load trucks all night but that might be too much like work." Teddy looked speculatively down at the model and lifted the roof off of Club Rave, dark grey shingles with a giant Gila Monster standing on it with its mouth open and a huge pink tongue hanging out one side. Teddy looked at it. "You think that tongue is anatomically correct?"

Teddy was good at talking like a jerk but he was a very smart businessman, which is why Eli stayed with him even with the lousy manners. If he was going to live and learn around here this was probably the best place to do it for now.

Teddy put the roof back on crooked. "Tell you the truth I'm not too happy with the design. Franklin thinks we should be working along the lines of a Wild West Show, you know, live action, reconstructions of famous busts and escapes. I think he's right but we have two other partners to deal with and Dodge and Windell got broomsticks up their ass. Listen."

"What."

"I want you to go check 6 North. Been getting reports about things happening up there."

"What things? Did you go up?"

Teddy did a long slow headshake, the silver turquoise eye-thing scraping across his hairless geometric pecs. "That's why you get the big bucks, Eli. People told me about lights, some kind of noises up there. Take a look, give me a call when you're in place. And send me pictures, close-ups of the plants, buds and leaves both. I want to see for myself when we should harvest."

"Three weeks from now, last time I looked," said Eli, already not wanting to go up there.

"Look again."

Up in the hills past Jacoby Creek Forest, Eli checked both ways up and down the two-lane greytop before turning onto State Fire Road 151. He drove in a couple hundred feet, turned the engine off and listened while the road dust caught up with him and spangled the air in front of his windshield, some of it settling on the hood. A quiet day in the forest, one annoyed caw-caw and the measured clap of a pair of wings leaving the scene but that's all. Now that Teddy's squinty eyes were off him for the day, Eli lit a short of middling skunk to get his maintenance buzz on and waited through it for the sound of anything that might have followed him, then cranked the car and drove, keeping it slow in second and scanning the trees for activity or any sign of change.

That was the problem being Teddy's Farmer John, or Pepina: you were the guy they busted, then if you did time you had to put your head down and keep your mouth shut and even then you always got fucked on the back pay and, Eli figured, if it came to looking after your pregnant girlfriend and soon her kid you wouldn't need a crystal ball. It's a dirty old world yes it is, and this was a professional niche he had to get out of soon as he could. The money and security were better than running a street operation and, okay, safer, but still. Transport was the thing to get into. Arranging it, not driving it yourself.

Another couple of minutes in, Eli saw ahead and off right amid the trees a young deer, totally gorgeous creature staring at his car with her large dark liquid eyes, holding still, holding still, then flick of an ear, making up her mind and bounding off, all four elegant legs simultaneous and stiff in that cartoon vault-hop they do, and it amazed Eli to see how she never hit a tree sailing through the air ten level feet each leap over uneven ground with her legs dangling and never lost her footing in the pine needles, her behind and upflicked tail ballerina-beautiful in goodbye, then *whooaah*, a big fallen tree across her path and without a misstep bunched her limbs and launched herself up waaay into the air taking a piece of his heart along and came down soft and perfect on the other side and kept going.

Go ahead, make my day.

Eli put the car in third and eased ahead a little quicker, the tools rattling heavy in the box behind him but who cared, quarter of a mile until he hit the old logging road on the left. He downshifted and took it, careful now cause the undercarriage could catch on something and rrrrip and even without that the road pushed one wheel up and dropped another in a trough, just killing his suspension. Really Teddy should lend him the Range Rover for these trips but noo, Teddy was paranoid about anything that might materially connect him to a crop, like everyone in Eureka didn't know already. Last time Eli asked, Teddy had said in a curlicue voice so

Eli couldn't tell if he was goofing on the word or just didn't know it, "But that would make me *vonderable*." And in an almost Bob Dylan voice, "Whynchoo trade your car in and get some kinda *truck*."

Should have answered, Because I don't want to be doing this *forever*.

Arranging transport, executive responsibility, less daily danger, a few grand a month, that'd be the life. If Teddy won't take me there then maybe Franklin, though Franklin has his longtime guy for that.

That is, if the whole thing isn't over and done with sometime this year or next with everything legal and the guys playing with rollercoasters and toy airplanes.

Then Eli saw it.

What the *fuck*? Lights and noises, did Teddy say? Someone had been up here to the off-road with serious machinery and done *some* kind of something. Eli pulled up short of the torn-up patch of road and rows of broken trees ahead and turned the motor off to listen. Trees ticking and creaking in a breeze, a passing insect whine and the little sounds of the earth working.

Eli got out with his phone in his hand, didn't shut the car door behind him, Teddy is definitely going to want to see a picture of this. He took one from where he was, then walked up and looked into the woods on the right.

You could say they had widened the path to where the crop was. You could say it hadn't bothered them one little bit to break young trees in half, crack them over with their near-white meat on show and dying now. Who did this, thieves? With big machines that dug huge tire-tracks in the dirt? What for? The crop wasn't ripe enough to steal yet.

Teddy was going to be a lot more than pissed off. Eli could hear it: "You shoulda been camping out in my property, *man*." So I could get arrested or they'd do whatever their thing with the crop was and maybe kill me doing it? You couldn't tell him that. Or you could, but he wouldn't hear it.

Eli snapped another couple of pictures but decided to take a look inside before he called Teddy or sent any snaps. He wondered if he should take a weapon with him, like a pipe wrench from the toolbox though really, what was he planning to do with that?

Eli set off on foot up the broken trail, eyes peeled, ears perked. The deer back there had been so beautiful he'd thought it was a guarantee, a signature of something, of Sukey's beautiful little rounded belly, say, and its future in the world, but that was foolishness and now the day was waiting for him in a different shape he didn't know yet.

He had an explanation ready just in case. I'm just here on a nature walk, mister. There's a den of foxes hereabouts I'm watching and um … but then, when he was halfway to the patch he saw wrong notes in the forest green ahead, metal, aluminum, something.

A few more steps and it was a cyclone fence. A lot of cyclone fence. Cyclone fence ten feet tall in two directions and still going when the trees closed in on it both sides, and they'd cut a few trees down to make the fenceline, professional job, no pulling up a fencepost here, they'd sunk 'em deep and poured cement. Teddy would have kittens. Teddy would have a litter of rabid puppies. Teddy would have several hundred screaming vampire bats flying out his ass. From the look of things, assuming it was still back in there, they had fenced the whole crop in, and now he noticed a license plate sort of thing clamped on the fence and he walked up to it, black print on white metal.

RALEIGH TOBACCO, INC.
NO ENTRY
NO TRESPASSING UNDER PENALTY OF STATE LAW
Permit # CA-1453-EP7

Get a load of this holiday snap.

Eli walked the perimeter a good distance in both directions, too long to go all the way around and no point to it, he'd scoped enough details and was ready to make the call.

"Whaaat?" Though Teddy didn't sound nearly amazed enough.

So Eli told him again, then asked him there were three ways he could play it, cut the padlock on the gate he'd found—he had tools in the car— or snip through the cyclone fence anywhere you like and slip inside, or climb the fence and look things over with no trace, all depended how much sign you want to leave, make the pick and I'll do it or, number four, I walk away and we talk about it.

"Climb it," Teddy said.

"No problem," Eli said, which was dumb. "I'll get back to you," which of course.

He was wearing an old pair of Timberlands, tan with yellowed white cleat soles, and it was no problem for someone of his size and vigor to get up and over. Why not sling coils of razor wire along the top if security was what you're up to, Eli had time to wonder as he clambered, slung a leg over, kneed up and dropped into a warrior crouch on the inside; then warned himself stop playing to the movie camera that wasn't there, like he was star of some show.

All quiet through the trees and Eli half-thought he could smell the crop ahead. Very shortly there it was and they hadn't rooted it up. It looked spectacularly green and healthy and smelled finely resinous and gave him an appetite for the output say two weeks from now but Teddy'd have to think through the complications of getting it out now. Grandpappy Amos the head of the clan and me just Pepina on the show, bless my lucky stars.

Then he was among the chest-high fronds, beautiful Purple Kush you could sing music about filling the clearing, the lovely green jagged leaves, buds starting to bunch but no way opening yet, fun for everyone, the sun pleasant on him and the plants the same. Before let's take pictures, checking his pocket, he swivelled his pocket magnifier out of its worn leather pouch to see how much glory's showing yet, early sign of rhizomes, hints of density and likely count. Eli wished his camera-phone had a macro function since that was what Teddy really wanted to see, buds up close, so Teddy really should come himself, when noises rose all around and up from under and it was like a dream, creatures moving to him through the undergrowth on all sides and scared the shit out of him and then he saw what they were and his heart fell and shut like a fist— where the hell had they been hiding?

A whole world of Eureka and Humboldt County cops was being born out of the greenery, two of them with service revolvers pointed at him to make the point. Eli's whole self and world were collapsing inside him, Niagara Falls, he was really radically losing his clear-brain day but had to keep thinking on his feet somehow.

"Hi," he told the encircling police, "just out here on a nature walk and look at all this stuff."

"Put both hands on top of your head and do not move," was all one of them had to say.

"Which?" Eli asked him, and the rest was routine, with sudden heavy gravity on him dragging him stunned and out of focus, almost blind, he wondered if he was technically in shock since everything inside seemed to be shutting down to sleep, and he didn't see Captain Bob Poholek until Eli and his police escort—their whole piecey world of belts, buckles, badges, patches, holsters, snaps, seams, firearms, cloth, leather, definitions, the dumbfuck precision of their way of dramatizing their picture of the world—had completed its process back through the woods and the padlocked gate now standing open, all the way back to Fire Road 151. Smelling the forest world the best he could because who knew when, Eli was making every effort to stay cool but it wasn't working, and Poholek in his blueshirt uniform but no hat, showing his balding blond hair and pale pasty face, standing back from the action, watching Eli as they eased him toward the police vehicle he hadn't heard get there and put a hand on top of his head to do that thing. Poholek's fleshy almost featureless face gave Eli no kind of comfort.

Because obviously Poholek had something in mind and Eli didn't know how to read it.

"Who can I give my car keys to?" Eli asked someone, anyone, sounding like a helpless idiot even to his own ears. "Is someone gonna take my car?"

What dawned on him too late, as they got ready to ease him into the navy blue Explorer with a star-badge painted on the door, was how Teddy had pretty much avoided looking him in the eye at his house earlier that morning.

But his question about the car keys brought Poholek over.

"I climbed a fence, Captain Bob," Eli told him, trying not to drawl sarcastically but not making it. Poholek was Deputy Chief now but had been Captain for years and the nickname stuck. "You got me for, what, *trespassing?*"

Eli didn't understand Poholek's movement right away, like maybe he was reaching for his walkie-talkie, but then that big white hand coming at him—not the fist but the palm open and the heel of it like a human stop sign—so fast he didn't have time to react and it hit him between his eyes face central on the whatsit of his nose, a lot like seeing stars, very close, but more like getting slammed stupefied before you knew what anything.

"Plus resisting arrest," Captain Poholek was saying out there as Eli sort of fell into the back seat and was also put there by some people with their hands on him.

"You break my fucking *nose*?" Eli wanted to know anyway somehow, careful touching it with his fingertips and seeing blood all over them and feeling it run down to his chin.

"Don't think so," Poholek told him. "Might've popped some splinters off the bridge. Resist arrest some more and I can push the whole thing into your frontal lobes for ya. Tell me the truth, Eli, don't you want the whole horrible nightmare of being you to be over? I see the way you live. I could help you move it along, get you there quicker. Die now, avoid the rush."

Eli decided it was not a good idea to talk back smart to him just now.

2

LINA CHASE took refuge with the Buddha and the Dharma and the Sangha but she was godawful at Tibetan visualizations. She'd give it one more try but would talk to Tony the Lama about it tomorrow and get a practice she could actually do. Of course Tony thought she needed all this apparatus to deal with her buried grief when in her own humble opinion her grief was already dealt with and she was kind of, fess up, happy with her little life alone, so he'd probably give her another complicated something-or-other she couldn't work with. She knew what Tony also sometimes had in mind for her, and even though on occasion she'd idly had it in mind herself they both knew they weren't going down the Eightfold Noble Path to that one.

A thread of smoke rising from the incense sticks above five white bowls of clear water in semicircular array, outside the wide glass doors the back lawn summer emerald in the sun, quiet little island, the house smelling like the fruitwood it was made of, just the faintest salt whiff of the strait from half a mile downhill and Nelson still alive in the photo on the shelf she should be looking at the *vajra* flag instead of, twenty-some years of a marriage full of struggle, close to breakup a few times, couple counsellors and spiritual teachers from two disparate traditions, and just about when she and Nelse finally had it working, looking at their second big good time at last, their two sons out of the house—one living an hour and a half away with a wife and her daughter and a teaching job, and Eli the problem child far enough away not to be a constant heartache— Nelson would lighten up on teaching and they could live on her annuity, then bing, the stroke, five hours of coma and out.

Take refuge with that and have a nice day. Well, hook up with a dashing six-foot-six-inch history professor twice your age at Berkeley then wait awhile and it can happen. Someone to look up to and, later, bury and grow wildflowers on top of.

He could have hung on paralyzed and speechless and drooling, spent his golden years in diapers eating through a stomach tube and pissing into a bag in a tilt-a-bed. Trust Nelson not to leave her with that, bless his cotton socks and size fourteens. Meanwhile here goes nothing one more time.

Lina closed her eyes and hoped her posture was properly upright and relaxed. The inverted red triangle was easy enough, and the inscribing blue square, though for a moment the yellow insets in its corners gave her some trouble because the other elements went out of focus when she fixed on them, and as for the green octagonal surround … It was the way a jungle cat working in a circus was supposed to feel with a chair pushed in its face, a tiger who could count to three but couldn't work out four chairlegs so had to start counting them again—she'd heard that's why chairs worked with lions and tigers. Lina got the general shape of the green octagon but whenever she tried to get a fix on the angles and how obtuse to make them … Now now now now *what* the hell was this?

Some obscure shape seemed to be coming at her through the scrim of her geometry problem and she shook her head to clear it out of the way—*bzzizzat*—and it duly faded, though once she got back to work on the green octagon—the tiny Bodhisattvas would have to wait because the angles refused to focus—here it came again, and despite her determined attempt not to see it the thing emerged into visibility regardless: a big blue Tibetan deity with four heads she could count facing the four cardinal directions with more heads stacked on top, all of them with open mouths showing bright white teeth and red gesticulating tongues, and like an aura around its body a whirl of arms she could not reduce to some sum total— in other words in old Tibetan *what the fuck?*

Lina opened her eyes, but as if in a dream she had many layers of eyelids and eyes behind them, and correspondingly many levels of waking, so that every time she opened another set of eyelids there the fucker was again no matter what the backdrop—alternately a stylized Tibetan mountainscape in primary colors or her own simple woodland home—baring his teeth and fanning his arms and also, not incidentally, presenting to her an extended blue lingam of alarming proportions. Thanks to her marriage to

Nelson she had accustomed herself to a formidable male member … but the point is it had never been *blue* so stop that reminiscence at once! She kept not running out of eyelids, therefore not returning to planet earth and her fruitwood home with emerald garden, and the blue guy seemed to want to arrange her in the receptive position she'd seen consorts assume on all too many tankas, seated on her bottom with legs spread to embrace the advancing blue male prick that the wrathful, no, let us say essentially *horny* deity, seemed determined to present—and since in this setup she appeared to have no operative will within reach, Lina drew in a lungful of breath and pushed out the most vociferous NO! of which diaphragm, lungs, throat, mouth and tongue were capable, at which point she heard it clang and echo in the long rectangle of her home:

"Fuck you and absolutely NOT!"

And she was back again, life on earth with a phone call to Tony the Lama definitely pending. The whole freaky episode, she calculated now that she was back in Pacific Daylight Savings Time, had taken three seconds tops.

Lina looked up and down the room, made a fist and thumped the floor to hammer the world back in place. Her heart hadn't recovered, though, and she needed to take it for a walk up and down the house if not outdoors. Stomping up and down her living room, past the view of her radiant garden and into the kitchen, then about-face back to the sofa area until she reached the television and had to stop.

She plonked herself down on the boxy off-white sofa.

Few people seeing her now would have deduced that she came from old San Francisco money—Italian, most of it legitimate since Prohibition, her father a piratical lawyer and a killer on the commodity exchange— and had grown up in two stately homes with summer places on the side, that her favorite of the horses was the wildest and most fractious of the family's three, Sir John Caramba, that she'd learned to hunt and shoot and had won a silver medal at the age of twelve, so of course by the time she got to college she married a communist so her life could go kablooey for her to land in this much crazy now.

Lina's mother's side of the family had come over on the cheap seats of the Mayflower and were distant relations of the Biddles; it was their surviving Anglo-Saxon brightening that kept most people from pinning a terminal vowel on the tail of Lina's ethnicity, though she herself had always viewed herself as an Italian chick of a certain kind, not hot enough for the movies but worth a look in real life even as she was crossing her forties, which might prove a crucial borderline beyond which the countryside was best not examined too closely. Her basic equipment was holding up pretty well so far, not that she was using it much. She'd meet a guy now and then, a maybe-good-enough, but as soon as she got the least bit alive to the prospect the foolishness was inescapable. All she had to do was think of herself telling a friend "Oh, I've met this *wonderful guy*" to hear how idiotic. Maybe it was I've got two sons, I've done my job and let's not fool ourselves, it's time to retire. How important could it be at this point really?

Anyway, there was no one in view she would walk a mile to see, though it was nice to know she could still attract a deity.

A girlhood reminiscence rose up unbidden before her: swimming in an Oregon lake one summer, wanting to dive to the bottom like the braver kids but taking in only a shallow lungful before heading down so that after touching the mucky bottom she was running out of oxygen on the way back, light-headed, began to panic, then saw herself breaking the surface into the world though it looked strangely dim, all grey, and when she took a big breath her mouth filled with water and she started choking, drowning. Fortunately she was only about one foot under and broke the true surface and coughed herself clear, but the important thing was that she'd hallucinated a detailed version of the lakeshore and the trees and there was a lesson in this … Where was she? Oh yes, the multiple-eyelid phenomenon just now, a similar thing. Damned clever these Tibetan Wrathfuls. Shall we begin again? I *will* do my visualization assignment, I *will* do my visualization assignment …

Lina closed her eyes and found the geometry remarkably easy this time: the figures and colors seemed already to be there, clear, the angles precise, the linearity reassuring, calming, so that when a blur in the imagined air started moving and she saw the first hint of blue whirling arm, a laughing mouth, a gleaming eye, she—

—but before Lina could jump up and insist You get the hell out of my house this minute! the phone was clanging like a fire-alarm bell loud and shrill as in grade-school hallways, which made no sense because she had a perfectly modern telephone, two of them and this was one of her two landline phones, a Turkish model that tweeted like a canary, a last remnant of Nelson she couldn't bring herself to scrap because it was so darned kitschy-fun …

Her hips were stiff as she climbed to her feet but she reached the dining-table before the bird could twirl the coda, then a moment of reflex fear before picking up, as if the call might be coming from Tibetan World, the theme park. "Hello?"

"Mob? It's be," said a voice she had to sort through to find him in the middle of.

"Eli? What happened, honey? What? I can't understand a word."

"Waitabiddit, I godda … take the cotton out of my nose. Done."

"That's better. What happened?"

"Shit, I'm bleeding all over everything," Eli said, and she heard him ask someone for a napkin but not the answer. Then Eli told her what happened, the story scattering forward and back but eventually she got the picture: only got me for trespassing but they want me to pay *bail*, there's gonna be a hearing later today, or maybe that's an intergation and tomorrow morning that's the important one, the one that counts, the bail one, *yes* it was in a patch of weed but I was only *walking* there—

"Who hit you, Eli?"

"The top cop."

"Were you resisting arrest?"

"I swear I wasn't."

"Okay," Lina said, assessing his tone and believing him on that part at least.

"All I did was climb a fence, a *tobacco company* fence, but they're trying to make something out of it, I don't know what but they're doing *something* and … I can't really talk here, Mom, but …"

"Let me make sure I've got this right," Lina stopped his recitation, "you want me to phone this bail bondsman whose card someone gave you and set up a wire transfer or a credit card payment right now when neither of us has met the man and we don't know what the charges will be in court?"

"W-well … I mean, accourse, *yah*."

It took Lina the better part of how many minutes to get her heart-rate back to normal and her hands shaking less violently so she could settle into the reality of what had happened to Eli and what might happen to him next, occasionally getting a few words in edgewise but not across. When Eli ran out of things to say Lina had got to the working end of her process and her voice was adjusted and the words came out in the correct order: "No, Eli, I'm not calling some Eureka bondsman I've never heard of—what's his name, Bobbs?—or wiring Sukey money, don't interrupt me, wait till I finish," careful to slide a factual, not a scolding note into her tone, "so you'll have to spend at least tonight in jail, honey, in part because," better not go into the particulars of responsibility and act and why, his mind will fog and eyes unfocus at the oncoming tsunami of ungraspable detail. After all these years and therapy what he still lacks most is a sense of act and consequence. He hasn't got the wiring for it and the work-arounds have to be rebuilt fresh every time. "Never mind," said Lina with a dying fall.

"You mean I have to sit … you mean I have to *sit*?"

"I'll get you out if I can, honey, but you'll have to sit tight till I drive down, and then we'll see what's going on."

"You're coming *here*?"

"As soon as I get off the phone I'll pack some things and get started so I can be there tomorrow morning."

"You're coming down *here*? Aww shit, Mom, d'you have to?"

"I don't see any other way of doing it."

"Umm … in that case … let me think … Um can you possibly get here like *today*?"

"I don't have a plane, Eli. I'm driving. And I'll have to cancel some appointments first." Her psychological counseling was pro bono or occasionally for barter these days but that didn't mean she could stiff her people. In fact protocol was stricter since the poor were truly vulnerable, not just in imagination: not long before quitting the group practice she'd had one client who was panic-stricken because she was down to her last eight million dollars and thought the walls were falling in on her. Nowadays her people's problems actually were problems.

Lina had left the paying practice after Nelson's death perhaps a little lazily in her mourning but also because in the last analysis she'd come to feel that mostly she was servicing her patients' vanity and illusions, and in consequence had lost the sense of doing honest work. Dad's annuity was enough to live on, so her sabbatical lengthened month upon month until it became oh gosh has it been a year already, what had she done with the time? She had played too much computer solitaire and could have meditated more often. And what else? "Oh," she suddenly realized, "there's something else I have to do first."

"You have to do something *first*?"

"Eli honey, get a grip. We've been through this kind of thing before— not for years, I grant you, and you've done real work and I acknowledge that, but here we are and there's someone I need to talk to."

"I only climbed a *fence*."

"I understand that getting arrested, even if it turns out to be only for trespassing, I know it pulls you back into a scary part of yourself, so there are two things you should know. The first is that I love you and I'm coming to help you, but you can't just pull my chain without claiming any of this as your own. I'm hanging up the phone now so I can get on the road to get there in time for the hearing tomorrow."

Then she waited, half-hoping he'd ask her to drive carefully, especially at night, Ma, but it didn't happen. Ah well, she thought as the hung-up phone stopped shaking and her hands, which looked like rakes to her, like forks, like claws, like rusting garden tools, still trembling slightly, here we go.

She hoped she'd be able to make that Seattle stop-off on the way.

Aha, I see, you're not accustomed to being *interfered* with, Tony would tell her if he felt he had to do his Lama thing, but even at the risk of being hectored and although the Seattle ferry went in the wrong direction and would add an hour to the drive south, she hoped she might find Tony home and friendly, saying Yeah, come on over, we can talk about this, you want some lunch?

"You sure you don' want lunch?"

Lina loved it that Tony hadn't lost his Jersey-Italian accent in the course of becoming holy. Sometimes he wore sports clothes but today he had his robes on, a heavy bearshaped guy, head freshly shaven, in a burnt-wine outer swath and an orange underlayer: ceremonial, but if you squinted your eyes when he spoke it was Tony Soprano in Himalayan drag.

Lina shook her head no to lunch. "Not sure I can keep anything down."

"I could ask Mira to pack something up for you, a couple a sandwiches maybe. Fresher than a roadburger."

"That'd be nice, Tony. Thanks."

She wasn't sure if Tony had noticed it, but behind him, through an anteroom and backlighted in a doorway, Mira was already on the scene, the less-than-two-year-old Valentino Marpa riding her hip and Mira's body canted anxiously, not secure enough, silly woman, to know that Lina wasn't competition gunning for a spot in the guru's bedroom. She was young and gorgeous, Mira, a lissome not so drifty blonde, ice-blue eyes, enviably long legs and torso, angular hips and the sun shining through her elegant almost floorlength linen dress, was she really buying Eileen Fisher? It could be a knockoff. Nice one though. She looked so good in everything.

"Baby do you mind?" Tony called over his shoulder, so he did know she was there, and Mira sidled off barefoot to the kitchen without a word. She was such a classic guru's-second-wife, a beauty hardly bumping thirty, Tony about fifty, the shakeup almost costing him his ordination but then they'd settled it.

"Stop," Tony told her. "Cut it out."

"I was only thinking."

"But pretty loud, pretty legible," Tony said. "Okay? So whaddayou wanna know?"

Lina had already told him on the phone about the apparition but it looked like he was going to make her tell it again in person. "I was doing the visualization practice you assigned me," she recited, "when all of a sudden this blue Wrathful Deity put in an appearance in my living room."

"*Wrathful* is really not the correct word." He pronounced it more like *wratful*, one or two Jersey Turnpike exits short of Dipthong. "Wratful is not the right word to use here. We may *experience* such a being as wratful when actually it is only there to break the conventional habit of our perception, y'know what I mean? The appearance of such a being prolly indicates you're up for some kinda change."

"And if I don't believe in such things?"

"Okay, you were doin' a visualization practice, you been around the imagery a lot, so when you had an intuition that something was about to go wrong, you didn't have to know it was about your kid, but the intuition showed up in that form. Like a metaphaw."

"Come on, Tony, I get that much myself."

"Yeah, but interpreting Eli's arrest as a punishment when it could lead to some kinda creative transformation for you both …" He ran his hand over his big shaven head. "Shit, I can't do this by the book." Doodis byda book. "You know how many times I got busted back in Jersey? And for a lot more serious shit than pot."

"You're telling me people can change."

"Yeah, that was the implication, but I wasn't there yet. You mind? Can I go on?"

Lina did the parody of a formal bow, her hands arranged in a graceful mudra, but couldn't finish it without laughing. "My son's in trouble and I'm doing schtick with you."

"Observe that," Tony said.

"Right."

"You sure you're okay to drive?"

"Absolutely. I was born on wheels. What did you get busted for.."

"That is not appropriate for you to know about your Lama. I got busted for every fuckin' thing. But no convictions. And I didn't kill nobody."

"Amazing."

"I must have been protected. I was such an assho—make that knucklehead. I was a knucklehead's knucklehead, a man among men."

"Tibetan Tony Torrezini."

"Used to be Tough Tony Torrezini. Some of the Tulkus tell me they're very familiar with my past incarnations and I have always been a very amusing guy the Big Boys cut some slack for, up to a point."

"So nothing changes."

"Everything changes all the time. Sometimes they talk about the slack and it's funny, sometimes it's about the up-to-a-point and they look at me hard, they, you know, squint. Nothing's permanent. What can I do to help you with your son? Call me anytime, day or night, I mean it. I'm up a lot at night, doin' practices. As for the so-called Wratful Deity, even wit your son's arrest included, try not to get scared, think of it as a sign of change, like someone bigtime showed up and is lookin' after you. I know you don't litrally believe in 'at, but looked at even as a metaphaw, what you call the transvaluation of values. It happens around here a lot, once you get into dis shit."

Southbound with the pack at a steady seventy-five and wondering if she should take the Interstate all the way or did she need a tour of the Oregon coast for her soul's sake, Lina ate the first of Mira's very nice roasted vegetable and mozzarella focaccias behind the wheel, careful not to drip the olive oil Mira might have drizzled on it just to mess up Lina's clothes and car. Or, be more generous, Lina bade herself, extra virgin could be standard practice on a Mira sandwich, and the lovely avocado slice is neither rotted brown nor underripe.

Only now, finishing this artfully composed item and reaching to the shotgun seat for the water bottle, did Lina realize that she'd gone through the whole Blueskinned Wratful story for Tony without mentioning its big blue appendage. Now really, why was that?

And she was sure about another thing for the first time: Tony keeping his heavy Jersey accent was at least in part an affectation. And a technique to ward off people who might want to holify him. Probably easier for him too, more comfortable, less work. We fall back on the things that worked for us when we were kids, even when it turns out that in life we turn out to be a Lama.

Driving south with gold deepening to copper outside she thought spontaneously, before she could censor it: Oh God Nelse, it's Eli. I still don't know what's wrong with him, explain it to me if you can, the doctors never got there. He's got a good soul, Nelson, you know that, but his rig was iffy off the bat even if we didn't see it at the start. Why does someone like Eli have to happen to someone like Eli? If you've picked up any fresh information on the other side please slip it under my door or whisper it to me in a dream. Tonight would be good.

Lina resettled herself in the carseat, irritated that Ford had overdone the futuristic cockpit aspect. She'd finally traded in the old Mercedes diesel for a new Focus and went with red even though it'd mean speeding tickets. It did what you asked but she missed that solid old Mercedes pleasure even though it had started costing her six hundred twice a year for parts.

21

Decent sound system, NPR when she could get it, country music when she couldn't, three Verdi operas in reserve on compact disc.

Nelson had been such a true believer. Couldn't be a lefty like everyone in Berkeley but had to join the Party even though he knew it was almost half informers, and when he got into Sufism the romantic Rumi-reading version wasn't enough and he had to convert to Islam and join an initiatic Order. Almost the last straw for me, moving East and that awful, bullying Turkish shaikh in Spring Valley. Funny that we came back West only because they made Nelse a shaikh and appointed him to a Seattle cabal. Also funny, in his latter years if you hit the right button he could still summon up a defense of Stalin, according to historical necessity. We were an odd pair of ducks but it worked more than half the time.

And Tony the Lama with his early life of crime. Maybe Eli would grow up to be a holy man too, a sainted Dostoevsky sinner? He was not from around here. Maybe he was from Up There somewhere and was working things out the hard way. Sure, that horse might fly.

Lina replayed the end of Tony's pep talk in her mind.

"How you think I made enough money to do Buddhism and raise a family? Two families, count my old folks and a couple knucklehead brothers back home, three. You see me out there on the street wit a beggin' bowl? I made my nut back east and invested smart."

"Didn't the Rinpoche ask you to give up your ill-gotten gains?"

"One, I already got rid of my most ill-gotten gains and two, he made a small exception in my case for the rest of it. Because, um, he determined that some of my investments were in the clear."

"And because your previous incarnations were so entertaining."

"That's what they tell me." Tony dropped his voice to get serious. "Look, unlike you I do have a moral objection to how Eli makes his money, because even including he can't do much else and this is practical, he's playing a dangerous fantasy, he likes doing the bandit, and it's gonna get him in trouble because basically he wants it to. Most likely, unless pot gets legal real soon he'll do hard time somewhere, but even if he doesn't there's a big false self, plus substance abuse and shit that'll damage him because basically he's looking for it to. So I do have that objection."

Gas gauge down, Nelson, and now that I mention it I feel a need to pee. After that let's get off the Interstate to the Oregon coast at Waldport if I back up a bit and Florence if I don't. Lina could whiteline it through the night and reach Eureka early, give herself time to poke around, but it wouldn't do to turn up frazzled and overanticipant. The coast would help, blue Pacific rollers, their white crests marching in formation to the pillar-shaped rocks that stood sentinel around here, and the colors warming, not yet her homeground's palomino light but on the way to it, seaside glory in shapes and tints until they fade, motor down the dark and find a Motel 6 in whatever stop-off turned up when her nerves felt the strain and her eyes got unreliable in the alternating dark and glare. Set the alarm for four hours' sleep. Three.

Sure she had money for a better place but always insisted on cheaping it. Motel 6, firm bed, harsh fluorescent light, hot shower, instant coffee.

Also a change of clothes come morning. She was comfortable driving in a saffron tank top and jeans hug-tight but lenient in the hips, but she'd get into character first thing tomorrow, her 50s-retro knee-length pleated navy skirt, offwhite linen blouse and winedark Jourdain semi-flats. The Liberty-print scarf and eighteen-karat helical slide could wait till she got to the police station to play the lady.

3

ELI WANTED TO tell people he couldn't help it. I can't help it! he wanted to cry out to them or just cry, because he didn't know how to tell them he couldn't help it. Not his mother, not anyone so they'd not just believe him but they'd see it, from inside *this*, the way he had to almost every day. He remembered when it started and he knew that it was glands, or do you say glandular, knew it before all those smart people did, and he still didn't know how to tell them. When the glandular thing happened about when he was twelve it was like, a little at a time and then surprise! a lot, like one part of his head switched off and another part of his head got turned up *loud*. I can't help it! Then they told him, you'll have to help it. You'll have to help us help you help it. That was one too many. It was clutter. Keep it simple: it's all my fault that I couldn't and still can't see a way clear enough through *and help it*.

This was how it thinks and feels in him, he would tell them and maybe they'd *try* to listen to the understanding he had, but when it came time to act, time for him to act in, the thing around him acted because the clock rushes up with yes, do it. And it's wrong, it's not connected, what is this thing, this thing that behaves no matter. It can't help me in here, it can only *do*. I didn't choose this!

Did I? Show me how!

★

"You bled all over the phone, dork."

"Lea' me 'lone, Ma," Eli told the guard, though wait a minute, a guy around here calling you dork is being gentle so don't wise back. "I had to pull the cotton out to talk to my mother and started bleeding again I'm sorry."

Eli was surprised he was still keeping it together. He'd been coasting for a good stretch, weeks, maybe months feeling strong and solid and unbroken as people took him for, but he knew how he was and that the world could flip on him like a quarter in the air from heads to tails and leave him where he couldn't keep track, total fear or sometimes blind chaos so he might do something and not know what it'd make happen outside him. But here he was in the pokey and his outline was holding up. Lucky but you couldn't trust to it forever.

"Look, man," he said, "now I'm bleeding on the blanket."

Didn't matter. Guy got him up and pushed him back to the sweat room, where Eli was surprised to see another guy sitting there with Captain Bob, the fuck. The guard cuffed one hand to the ring in the table like he'd try something if he was loose, and left. Who was this new guy? Eli had seen him around town a couple of times—it wasn't a face you forget: boney, stark, with a pushy forehead, slitty eyes, medium-brown hair parted like with a knife on one side falling in slants across his forehead—but hadn't figured him as a cop. His suit was blue with Western detailing on the pockets and lapels and he should have worn a string tie with it but left two buttons of his white shirt open showing a slash of pale hairless chest instead. What he looked like was a second bad guy in a spaghetti western or a junkie and he was staring right at Eli, if you could you call it staring with your eyes that narrow.

"How's your mother?" Poholek asked.

"Fine," said Eli. "I thought you weren't supposed to listen in."

"The walls," said Poholek. "Ears just grow on them. We use bleach and Lysol but they keep growing back."

"Can I have a paper towel for my nose you broke?"

"No."

So Eli sat there and bled while Poholek and the boney guy gave him the silent treatment, and wiped it away with his hand when it ran on his lips, then wiped his hand on his T-shirt. He could have snorted some of it back up his nose but it would get in his mouth and he'd have to spit it out on the table or the floor since there wasn't anywhere else and he figured Poholek would sock him again for that. So let Poholek and the other bastard see what they done to him. It was throbbing pretty bad up inside now and would probably be a killing pain tomorrow. The bleeding would stop eventually. So.

The boney guy shifted in his chair, reached back, wriggled and came out with a clean white handkerchief he held across the table to Eli.

"Really?" Eli asked, and the guy shook the hankie at him. Raising it to his nose Eli saw an angley blue monogram on a corner of it, figured out it was PKP. The guy nodded him to go ahead and Eli blew what turned out to be an incredible gob of blood and shit into it. "Thanks," Eli said, mopping up. If this was good-cop bad-cop it was a messy way to do it, and a laundry bill or just throw the thing out now really.

"Time to talk," said Poholek, and eased back in his metal chair, which didn't let him but he tried. Sitting next to PKP made him look fleshy, almost fat, actually until right this minute Eli hadn't seen Captain Bob really was getting a little fat. "You figured out by now Teddy gave you up, correct? Just in case, I'll tell you: Teddy gave you up. Would you like to know why?"

"Nope."

"Because all I had to do was threaten him with arrest a little itty bit and he sold me you. How does that make you feel, Eli?"

"How much is the fine for trespassing on a posted property around here? Let me know and I'll pay up."

"Ohh no Eli, we're not playing fiddly-fuck today. Teddy will testify in court tomorrow morning to keep himself outside. It's your patch of weed up there and he's just an old friend who maybe tolerates what you do for a living but is trying to put you on the straight and narrow."

"Someone's actually going to believe that bullshit?"

"It doesn't matter," said Poholek. "He'll say it and that'll be enough."

Eli's real feeling broke through when he asked Poholek, "What the hell you got against me?" Almost called him Captain Bob but held on and didn't.

"Absolutely nothing," Poholek told him. "I only got Teddy to sell you to me so I could get you to sell me him."

"Can you say that again? I lost track."

"Eli," Poholek said, leaning forward with his strong but actually kinda pudgy arms on the table, "give me Teddy's operation and you're free as a tweety-bird. I don't give a shit what happens to you, frankly, but out of the goodness of my heart I'll give you your stupid worthless life back if you give me Teddy's op."

"Tell me how much the trespassing fine is, Captain Bob. Teddy isn't gonna say an itty bitty word in court. He won't even go in there he's so superstitious. He's a very good friend of mine, and actually if I go to court I'll ask him to come along as a character witness even though he won't show up for me either. The fine can't be more than fifty dollars, right?"

"Eli," Poholek said, "are you really too stupid to know how much trouble you're in or how tightly wrapped we got you? This ain't about paying a little fine, you fuckhead."

Eli sniffed back up some blood and snot. "My mom's coming down and bail me out tomorrow morning."

Poholek laughed at him. "Your mommy's gonna save you? I sure hope she's got a lot of money."

"Actually," Eli said before he could shut himself up first, stupid, "she does have a lot of money so, like, go fuck yourself."

PкP looked at him different and Eli was pretty sure Poholek, turning a little red there, was about to sock him in the face again, but all Poholek did was push a couple of breaths out through his nose, press the buzzer and the guard who'd called him dork came in and took him back to holding. Where Eli thanked his lucky stars and hoped for the best.

Too much to ask for a clean T-shirt he was pretty sure. "Could you please get me a couple of Advils please?" Eli asked the guard as the guard walked out of sight on the good side of the bars. It turned out there were amazing things you could do just with bars. You could make insides and outsides that would take your life this way or that, but only one of each. Just the idea of that started something cooking in his stomach, and he could feel the fear-bubble underneath it looking for a way to get loose, come up and take him over. Eli started the work of pushing it down.

"You told me he was stupid," Kennis Pitcher said. "He's no Stephen Hawking but he's not stupid."

"What I told you," said Poholek, "is he can't think straight. He looks impressive but he's got a screw loose. You didn't see him long enough to hear it rattle and you haven't read his juvie record. I've had my eye on that boy for years. I have a lot of faith in young Elijah Chase, that he'll make the wrong choices for him and the right ones for us, Kennis."

"So you see him as the weak point of the turning world."

"Huh?"

Pitch sighed to have to say it.. "The point of entry, the little key you twist to hook up the first generation, the old hippy-dippy black marketeers, Swift and Franklin and them."

Poholek made a kind of grin. "You figure that out all by yourself, Kennis? You sure you ain't too smart to get here from the southland?"

"Got it one just lookin' in on some couple three weeks. Call me Pitch, if you'd be so kind."

"I like the name Kennis. I've never heard it before and I like the way it rolls. Listen," he said, hoiking his chair noisily around toward Pitcher on the concrete, "what do you say to fencing up another couple patches? Buy another few selected forest properties for the comp'ny, apply the pressure on the rest of the dealers, crack their system and then y'all can be free and easy in the county."

"Tell you what, you can call me Kennis if you don't say y'all. You don't do it right and it offends my ear. Also, don't you think that buying up everybody's skunk farms would tend to send them to my door with, I don't know, power tools or something?"

"Up yours, Kennis. How about it?"

Kennis Pitcher Jr. thought it was a good moment in which to be expansive, so he stretched his arms up high and wide, yawned and showed Poholek his clean and crooked teeth and stuck out his underjaw, which he knew was a scary thing to see, reminded people of a skull the way his skin stretched tight, then spoke English right and proper. "My principals in North Carolina would like to see how their first buy works out. My principals would like to observe local reactions to their purchase and refer the matter both to public relations and the legal team."

"Come on, Kennis, we all know you got no principles."

"Couldn't resist saying that, couldya? I'll pretend I heard it the other way. Muhrad Investments is legally distinct from Raleigh Tobacco, I am paid and funded via a chain of DBAs and cutouts you couldn't untangle in a court of law, but you're right, I have full liberty and discretion, up to a point, to buy properties here as I see fit—"

"The land prices I'm getting for you, Jesus."

"For which Muhrad Investments is duly grateful and will see you right at present and in the end, but it is my considered opinion and judgment, and Raleigh's too, that I should wait and see how you handle the current initiative and observe its workings-out before we, meaning Raleigh Tobacco doing business as Muhrad, invest another several thousand dollars of honest company money, not to mention our gratuity to you."

"You drug-addicted little fucker."

"Define your terms. Define drug-addicted. Also little, also fucker."

"I could break you like a stick."

"Maybe so, but what would it get you? On the other hand, abide with me in friendly fashion, brother, if you can manage to cool your head, and together we can serve the interests of American justice and private enterprise. It suits us both to sweep the landscape clear of dope-dealing hippy-dippy outlaws and it will do the State some service, and they will know it, if between us we can assure a smooth transition from the current higgledy-piggledy criminal and half-legitimate medical-weed misarrangement to the orderly legalization of marijuana in the imminent future. Very imminent future, if I may say so, in which you will be head of security in a major corporate enterprise that will make your golden years truly golden instead of sucking a big one on a *po*-lice pension. "

Poholek's cellphone must have vibrated on his hip because he picked it up, listened to a crackle of speech and said he'd be there in ten minutes.

Poholek stuck the phone back in its little holster and said, "Kennis, please get y'all the fuck out of my sight until at least tomorrow."

Pitch loved to hit the street in this town—Zowie, as he preferred to call it stead of Eureka—hot today, but walk out the door into the bright or dark in any weather to see all the people, not a single one of them smart enough to breathe if they had to do it for themselves intentionally. Plus in his opinion every last one, including Captain Bob who was crazy-sure same as the rest that weed was coming street-legal and sweet upon the air any minute now:

Years off at least, if then, and tightly controlled, if ever.

Back in Durham allegedly intelligent professionals in the head office and on down the firm were just as crazy-sure, and I say let em. Doesn't bother me atall, gives me something to do with my time and room to play. It's a mass hallucination. The same can be said of human life in general and this just proves it. I just wish they'd let me buy a few more patches so I can start to work private-like with the biggest local dealers.

Pitch put his shades on and frowned down the station steps at the angle-parked company-leased grey Chevy Malibu when he told them that a C-Series Mercedes would bespeak the seriousness of the enterprise though what he really needed was something that could offroad, even a little RAV-4 Toyota would do and maybe if he broke the Chevy's rear axle on a logging road they'd finally get him one—but *nooo*, we lease GM sedans, *commpanny pollicy*, at least they okayed his license and carry permit for the automatic in the back of his desk drawer because who knew with these people out here, and he'd left his Porsche back in Dixie because although it was a pleasure to drive and would play well with the ladies, once he got found out as tobacco-man in town he figured on someone keying his paint a couple times a week and maybe even giving it the gift of dynamite. For Wohelo means dynamite, among these Camp Fire Girls.

It was a too-short ride to his office so he zigged around town awhile in the hope of something cool but gave up. Muhrad Investments—Durham almost backward, a nonsense anagram he'd picked in part to freak people with the prospect of something A-rab come to town—lived up an external wooden staircase alongside a red-brown lapboard building over a health food store, convenient for sandwiches, organic coffee and women. Also cheap rent. When the mice came up even though he didn't store food the traps broke their necks and the office looked clean and tight: one big burled oak desk for him to sit behind, no secretary, AC on a timer, he had the key to the deadbolt and the windows were unbreakable plexiglass. Two green fake leather armchairs with brass tacks for business visitors, two-seat cloth sofa on the side, couple of lamps and a radio, enough. The only fine thing in the office was the desk, solid Southeastern live oak intricately patterned by Mother Natch, a real find in a quaint town up the Whatever Valley where they didn't know how fine it would look cleaned up, its working surface protected by a wide green blotter and his MacBook Air in a locked drawer just now and he took it home with him nights. Off-white stainproof carpet and soothing umber walls, good Scotch and artisanal bourbon in the cabinet, Chopin potato vodka and a crock of Genever gin in the freezer of the lowboy fridge.

Thank you very much, I think I will, this spud's for you.

He poured a one-potato two-potato cold enough to almost syrup and took it to his desk.

Pitch knew what would go just perfect with it, though take a note, he was getting further entangled with Poholek, a moron but dangerous, and should do something smarter with his stash. No point in giving the man leverage. He'd already let the man successfully irk him laying those you-alls on him when our boy from outside Knoxville had only a lick of southern accent and not deep south at that, loaded it lightly on his brush and sometimes applied it not at all or just as an undertrace of local color, hardly hear it but there it was, part of the impression he liked to make when he chose to make an impression at all, and that choice his alone. The cop had not the least suspicion of Pitch's origin or intellectual rank or how much of the world he'd lived in. Pitch had been expected, what, to aspire upward to Chilhowie Virginia? when all along he'd grown up on the good, southeast side of the French Broad River up against east Tennessee's holy Smokies that had given him a living spiritual grounding and perspective, indelible for him to this day, not to mention right through hazardous duty in Central America and the heaven and hell of his Paris years.

For the moment he opened, released the catch and pulled out of his desk the entire second drawer of three on the right, settled it on the carpet and reached way back to unstick the triple baggie ducktaped to the endpanel. No need to lock up while doing this, you could hear the stairs even with the a/c on full, which it wasn't.

In Pitch's opinion, Poholek had become a stupid man. They'd humiliated him for years and now he wanted his regular revenge. He was a robot, he walked straight lines, though give him credit, he was a goodsoldier type, and probably didn't get to kill enough people in the Marines, that was his problem and it wun't his fault, born too soon or late and landed in the service between proper wars: Grenada didn't count, neither did taking out Noriega, and the way Poholek told it he was there for Gulf War One but as a reservist got backwatered with logistics in Saudi and didn't see action. Rose to the top of the heap in the Zowie police and still had some operational smarts but just look at him. You could hear his metal footsteps coming down the mountain, hear his metal brain grinding out its sense of hurt. He's dependable, that's the upside. Dangerous, that's the down. An angry stupid man can surprise you if you don't stand watch.

Pitch himself had been in Army intel with the Connies in Nicaragua and that had been one whole education in itself, ending when he found it necessary one night in the big tent to use the .50 to mow down the locals he'd been working with over their pig and beans before they decided it was time to shoot him first—a matter of cocaine-money paranoia amid these alleged politicals. He walked away with everything in the tent a messy red abstract and his hands pretty clean, considering. Then I have no idea whodunnit sir, wink, and got not only an Honorable D but a secret medal from Papa Bush that was supposed to impress everyone and keep me schtumm and I thought was a joke in all respects, considering what the whole op had been like, apart from its educational value: all those guys with the food and stuff coming out of their faces and the other holes so I could walk out alive, a prospect I'd been working on down there, just in case, pretty much since jumpstreet.

Pitch opened up the big wrap baggie and untaped the next one inside it.

What he loved best about cocaine was the sheer heartlessness it brought him. Most jerks who used it—maybe not jazz musicians, who knew how it expanded time for them so they could blow without being rushed by bar-lines clocking in—the jerks liked the way it made their brains run fast, which showed you they couldn't tell blow from the speed dealers cut it with for the dumbfuck contingent, whereas he used to buy pure bulk once a month all the way up in Tacoma from a desk-jockey major at the Air Force base and never asked who flew it in from where but it was the finest ice Pitch had ever snarfed north of the border. Must be a lot of flyboys on it blasting through the skies in F-16s defending our republic to the last sonic boom. Is this a great country or what?

Nowadays he had too much bidness down here to get up there and cop, so he drove a little way into Oregon where a pair of old-school hippie dealers held up the ruins of a commune in the mountains west of Grants Pass and bought from them after making clear he knew what quality was and would pay extra and he got it. Pitch also'd been known to enjoy occasional pops of top-quality smack when he could find it but had decided it was a naff idea for the duration of the California gig. Well this part of it anyway.

He pushed the blotter aside, laid two modest lines on the polished desktop and took the silver straw with the lose-nothing nostril-cap from his inside pocket and fed his brain some coin of the realm.

Yes, yes, yes and thank you Lord. He rocked his head back. What a lovely word the Buddhists had for emptiness: *shunyata*.

Kennis Pitcher knew what the country-simple folks around here who played visionary in their bathroom mirrors thought they knew but didn't, that there *really was no self* at the center of your being—wasn't just a tasty concept, kids, but fact—self radically and literally not there and the truefound heart completely void, so clear that nothing in creation could fill it with its *maya* crap or leave its vain and pointless chalkmark. Pitch was perfectly tuned alone to the emptiness and fatuity of all begat and born human attempt. Buddha-Nature? He'd found it for what it was years ago and now what a blast to walk wide awake out your door in a world full of sleepers to see far and bright with means and privilege and with the inner equipment, the legit ability and the freedom, the inalienable *right* to get out there and dance between the puppets. When you can do that you own the joint.

Those old dogs in Asia knew what they were up to. If he bought a dog, a business-end Rottweiler with its vocal cords cut so there'd be no warning, he'd name it that: Shunyata. If he had another daughter— Céleste caught in her mother's BCBG bullshit hadn't sent him a word in years, by now she was just one more gorgeous piece of teenage Paris ass strutting her cocky bottom and perky tits on the grands boulevards who didn't know him from Adam Kadmon. If he had another daughter he'd call her Shunyata too, because when you come down to it, face the facts, love privileges no one really.

Pitch rocked his Aeron chair back and contemplated the world through closed eyes heartless to the core. Which of course made him super-attractive to women. All you had to do was cease to need and you could have. His cold heart was catnip, the vibe you didn't give a shit and could hurt them made you perfect. *I met this wonderful guy, Ma*, no, he wasn't really the kind of guy you told your mother. Funny thing though: he still thought sex was fabulous when he was having it, but betweentimes he'd begun to feel the appetite, the yen, the urge, as an actually unpleasant thing, an itch demanding scratch, an interference with the impeccable clarity of his will. Why didn't more people find it distasteful? Maybe they did but were afraid to say. Because it surely was.

On the other hand, when he had a girl howling and roasting on the spit what could be better?

Now that you mention it: coke and wrong-thinking had done for him and his little friend had perked up in his underwear, so he had to call his latest Betty-June, she should be at the gallery and maybe could get free, no one went there. "Hello darlin," he said when she picked up and gave the gallery name, the Dido, what was that about?

"What's up?" she asked him a little coolly it seemed to him.

"Whynchoo come up the office for a party. Got some treats laid out and it's the slow time a day, c'mon."

"I don't do office blowjobs, Ken." So there was no one in the gallery, talking like that, which figured considering the art was crap.

"Oh yes you do."

"The first time but not since, remember? Or do they all sort of blend together for you into one big suck?" Getting sassy now: he liked this one. Divorced brunette late thirty-some, no kids, smart-looking, fine-featured, liked to talk and act dirty but her flaw, a good one for him, she was a nervous type, highstrung, febrile. He was getting her into empirical areas she hadn't been to before and she didn't even see, yet, how far she'd come or where it was headed.

"Pretty much they do," he told her. "Don't you feel something spontaneous coming on?"

"Wine me, dine me, talk to me. Take me to dinner at the Belvedere tonight and we'll see. And that's not a promise."

The woman wouldn't take money but she ate like a thousand-dollar whore. Her bottom line was lobster and you should see her tuck into it. Then, later on at his place, a nice big serving of good ol' sea-cucumber, eventually with cream sauce … "Might-could do that, hon," he said, getting hot and pulsey and you could hear it thickening his voice, God damn it.

"I've got yoga class after closing." Yoga class, sweet Jesus, bend those thighs for *me*. "Call me on my mobile after. Seven, say, and maybe."

"Oh babe, you know you've got my number." Stop sounding like such a stupid horndog of twelve years old please.

"Yes I do," she said brightly, the latest and best in his Zowie string of Betty-Junes, wonder how much longer I can keep her. "You're such a prick, Ken, I don't know what I see in you."

"Asked and answered," he told her in court-speak, a prolepsis of tomorrow.

"*Bah*," she said, mocking the accent that sometimes snuck up on him without prior notice when he'd indulged a little.

So he wasn't getting his hat blown in his Aeron this afternoon and, shit, would have to walk his deep-down sex-surge and half a hard-on off since Pitch was not a man to waste his substance by hand. But first a word from our sponsor: he set out just two more lines—self-control in action—rebagged his baggies, reached in to tape them tight, pushed the drawer back in place, snarfed up and licked the desktop clean before going to the lowboy for another tot of liquid spuds and walk it up and down the office till he settled.

4

Deputy Chief Poholek didn't feel like driving so he picked up Hendrie in burglary—break-ins had been driving the county crazy since the non-dope economy tanked—and told him City Offices and take it easy, no rush. He hardly noticed the ride, tuned out, blank time, and had a headache at the thought of having to sit through Eric Olaffson, City Manager, for however long it took the man to say his piece of nothing. On the other hand, at least Olaffson had acted properly, bypassing the Chief, who used to be a man but was just gathering fat and dust and money these days pending his full pension and the dignity of nothing further. Olaffson had come to Poholek, as he should, with whatever was up.

And Olaffson was all happy to see him, it looked like, in his wood-panelled office, stars and stripes and California bear flag furled just so, big prosperous man filling out his suit and professional smile standing up behind his desk to gladhand Poholek hello. Wreathed. His face was wreathed around his sunburn smile, and there was red-brown skin cancer on top of his mostly balded head underneath the strands of reddish hair going grey. Big man physically, Olaffson, going heavy with the years but still vital. Prosperous asshole getting fat while everyone else et cetera.

"What can I do for you today?" Poholek asked the City Manager after getting through the hearty handshake.

"Sit down, sit down," hale fellow well met, "make yourself comfortable."

"Sure." Soft creaky leather chair. "What's up."

"Welll …" And then nothing. Help the man.

"You want to know about the arrest on the new Raleigh property east of Jacoby, right? Something about it is bothering you, sir. Have I got that right?"

"Welll …" Second go-round for that *welll*, and Poholek wondered if he'd have to start pulling teeth, but then Olaffson got into gear, up and motorvating himself back and forth behind his desk like he had someplace to go, which got his mouth working and it was pretty much what Poholek had expected. "What we want here, Bob, is as smooth and trouble-free a transition from the current situation to possible full recreational legalization of the um substance in the near future, and we're concerned, that is to say *I'm* concerned, well at least *interested* to know some facts about the arrest of this young man yesterday. Why are you making waves? We don't want waves."

"It was a simple trespass. We received notice from Raleigh's representative in the area—"

"This would be our Mr. Pitcher?"

"This would be him. We got word from Mr. Pitcher that someone was messing around up there and he was worried unscrupulous parties might be cutting up his fence for anti-capitalist reasons, so we sent a couple of cars and apprehended the alleged perpetrator."

"And that's all. You're not seeking further arrests."

"None. It's a simple trespass as far as we were able to tell so far."

"And there is no controlled substance inside Raleigh's fenced enclosure? I've heard there is some."

"Not that anyone has seen, sir," Poholek said, holding his ace-card tight. "It's just good property, good light, good shade, the right kind of soil. Raleigh knows what it's looking for."

Olaffson lifted the corner of a paper on his desk and pretended to examine it. "Then why is a bail hearing set for tomorrow morning eleven A.M.?"

"The young man in question vigorously resisted arrest, assaulting several of our officers and had to be restrained. He may be a little crazy. And a man here in town, said to be his employer but we're not sure, Edward Swift, has volunteered he wants to testify. We don't yet know if he wants to offer testimony on the young man's behalf or if he has a complaint against him, but in our opinion it would be worth getting him on the stand."

"You don't know if he's for or against? D.A.'s office hasn't vetted this person?"

"We have had trouble reaching him since this morning, sir, but we are confident he'll appear in court tomorrow."

"And you're not seeking any further investigation into any illegal activity up around there where you caught the kid."

"Absolutely not and we haven't seen anything other than trees growing inside the fence," Poholek said. He was glad they'd stopped circling and had reached a mutually recognized point: he and Olaffson were lying through their teeth at each other and grinning down the tide of mutual bullshit. Which was good: once we know where we stand we can get on with things. "The property in question has been used to grow controlled substances in the past and Raleigh is satisfied that it will serve them well in the legal future. And I look forward to that. It's not as if I feel humiliated eating the shit of these fucking dopers for twenty years—all right, ten or fifteen—and want to wreak revenge on their asses before everything goes legal and I retire with 60% and medical."

"No of course not."

"It's not like I've eaten their shit and yours, sir, for a couple decades instead of doing my sworn duty to uphold the law in these parts."

"Surely not."

"And it's not as if you and the administration are sitting on top of a ruined fiscal structure with logging and fishing fucked for decades and the only thing ticking over is the illegal trade in dopeweed so just to keep the town afloat, Cap, let it happen and keep off."

"It's not as if," Olaffson agreed.

"Since if it was I'd have a legitimate right to overturn the whole fuckeroo and throw all your asses into Q, and we both know I will not do that. So."

"So."

"So. Your behind is covered, you are outside danger from me and you have no reason to even slightly interfere with any of my operations. Sir. Would you like to know in detail how we've kept the Mexican dope cartels out of town? Hint: a sledgehammer was involved."

"No, I wouldn't like to know."

"But you're happy we do it and there's no beaners leaving corpse-messages in the streets of our fair city because three of their soldiers went home with their knuckles flattened and we don't have a shooting war here because we picked the right ones to do it to." Which was sort of true.

"I don't want to hear about it," said Olaffson, along with a wipe-away hand-gesture at his face, which was exactly what Bob wanted to hear from him and had had no doubt, really, that at some point he would. For instance now would be good.

"Three soldiers under Mexican management," Bob told Olaffson, "but without major family connections so they didn't come back at us with automatic weapons which can be a noise nuisance inside town limits. Meaning our intelligence operation was even more impressive than the physical interdiction, according to cause and effect and in the last analysis."

"I don't want to hear about it," Olaffson repeated.

"The upshot, sir, is that it's quiet around here and a safe place for Raleigh to invest in future properties, without which, let me remind you, since Philip Morris is buying their land in the Valley and lots of it, that without Raleigh operating locally Eureka will be out of the action and shit broke when the change comes. The upshot is I am looking out for your interests so just let me get on with it."

"Has Mr. Pitcher said anything about future purchases of property?"

"He doesn't talk to you? He's waiting to see what happens with the current parcel first."

"Which is just my point," said Olaffson, reinflating himself. "Don't try anything big in court, Bob. Don't rock the boat, that's all we're asking."

"The boat is exactly what I'm not rocking," Poholek told him, thinking You'd get rid of me if you could but you can't and it burns, don't it.

"One false move, Bob."

"I'll try not to make one, sir. And if I'm forced to make one I feel sure that you won't want to know about it."

This sounded like such a good exit line Poholek got up from the leather brasstacked chair unasked and headed for the door. "By the way," he said, holding the door open a tick, "you know a smartass around town name of Steve Hawkins?"

"The name sounds familiar, Bob, but no I can't say I do. Who is he?"

"Just somebody I'm keeping an eye on," said Poholek with a clever wink and shut the door on the wood panelling and flags furled just-so and official smiley shit feeling he'd played well and won it fair and square.

Even with top-quality self-medication Pitch couldn't get rid of that low sex feeling or his half a hard-on but he'd be damned if he'd be reduced to locking the door, pulling the shades and jerking off in his own office. Then he got the bright idea, let's jerk off in someone else's.

He phoned Ricky Burke in Durham, got his secretary and said yes he'd hold but not forever, hon. Pitch found the corporate pomposity of Raleigh Inc. howlarious, its roots sunk in slavery days whereas Philip Morris was the brainchild of a smart Vienna Jew with a large family and great cultural connections, but Raleigh? Oh come on now, illegal immies picking your crop and before that white trash like where I come from—sold my soul to the company store don't cover it, indentured servants under the yoke of money in the oven summer sun's more like it. I come from the kind of people you people wipe the shit off your shoes on. Just goes to show you genius can turn up anywhere, crapland outside Knoxville, short hop from the Smokies, last holy place in America, and here I am, complete.

"Dicky!" he cackled when he heard Burke's dull Yes on the line. "How's it hangin', bud?"

"Long week, Ken. How're things out there in Playland?"

"Copacetic. You sound bad. Everything all right at home, son?"

Richard Burke: what a funny thing: old college bud way back from Pitch's time at Duke, Burke a pretty smart guy but essentially a plodder, Pitch all speed and jagged edges, forked lightning in human form, and they'd become friends. Sort of. Pitch found Burke easy to impress and play and in his opinion Burke was at least halfway queer for him but didn't know it, and then all these years later and in a hard time he turns up ... Last straight gig Pitch had was in Tennessee, designed the newspaper office for a Memphis weekly, gutted the building, repointed the old bricks and let the light in, hired a guy to push the pencils and wield the T-square but basically it was Pitch's design, he had a gift for architecture but too late to go back to school and become official. The office was a big success and champagne all round but a month later Pitch had to break in and steal the computers for what he considered non-payment, easy-peasy since he'd designed the security system. After that some hard times, couple uncontrolled drug episodes, bad form, things slipping on him, about to get back into straight-ahead crime if need be, the odd stickup and thinking about going large again and try his luck with a nervous young bank teller gal if he could find one when, hanging around old Raleigh and Durham he happened one night into a little jazz club where Branford Marsalis was doing a trad gig unadvertised with some of his young students and there was Richard Burke, slogging down vodka tonics alone in a booth and Pitch felt a crack of the old lightning, the old flash he'd pretty much run the guy with when they were kids together back in school. Burke had put some pounds on but was still recognizable and when Pitch came up on him in the booth Burke took a second to reckonize him—hair thinner some and features harder-etched—and then got this confused look like he didn't know whether he was happy or wanted to run, but Pitch didn't give him the time. Wasn't hard to redazzle the guy with his fabulous Paris past in the film business and the picturesque wreck of a high-level cosmopolitan marriage to a family of cold-blooded mandarin Rive Gauche bonepickers, or the political campaigns he'd helped run, closer to the present his so-so adventures as a fixer at any number of American horsetracks—why he was back in Carolina actually, the hope of some high-stakes hijinks, maybe find a horse he could hold to ransom or a number of other tactics he was good at. But here was Burke, the top of his head grown smaller, it looked like, as the rest of him bulged down and went pear-shaped and kind of blushy but maybe that was the alcohol tonight. He looked glum, wife didn't want to come see Branford, looked like he was acting out an unfulfilled adolescence sitting there but no one buying in, the fantasy emptying like a bathtub with the plug pulled and him still in it.

Perfect timing. The gods were with him. Light in my darkest hour and all that. Well not darkest but getting dicey.

Burke was born to be a junior-exec and there he was with Raleigh Inc. and a wife and two and he needed a taste of the old excitement and it was enough to ease Pitch in the door. They had him licking envelopes and doing data but soon enough got a sense of his virtues and before long he was threatening indie farmers, infiltrating unions and workers' co-ops, busting bribetaking foremen and embezzlers, generally saving the company a lot of bucks and even doing some advertising for them, couple of clever slogans that went national, Raleigh round the flag boys, with a flag promotion, stupid but it played. Two years of this and he was in some money and bored out of his skull but it brought him this California gig

41

and the freedom that came with it since they needed a start out here and someone who could keep it hid, served them right for not diversifying like Philip Morris or what it was called these days, Altria, but they were sunk unless legalization came through and Pitch was the natural hitter to send undercover and set things up, get results carte blanche and deniable, just don't kill no one ha ha ha.

"Fine, fine," Pitch was telling Burke now. "The p'lice are just about working for us, some kid tried to cut our fence and they were there in a hurry with the handcuffs. That's how safe it is."

"And the state permit so we can get into the medical trade with this year's crop on that property, how's that coming?"

"It's in process and looks to be working fine," Pitch told him, which was true except insofar as it wasn't. What he wanted to tell Burke but couldn't was that even apart from state and federal legislative roadblocks the prison lobby was spending as much money in-state as Raleigh and Philip Morris combined, prisons the real growth industry in these parts and no way they were gonna let decriminalization through the legislature or what were they gonna do with all their buildings and construction contracts? Hand over fist out here, solid money, endless stock of mostly nigra perps on dope charges—people were getting high and enjoying themselves and this must be stopped do you hear me stopped. Incredible country the nifty fifty. Flyboys on pure blow armed unto megadeath, poison and prison corporations duking it out over who should punish people for their pleasures while the rest of the economy falls into the pit on top of the working people already in it, you couldn't make it up, a treat to be alive here and see. Life has been monetized and commodified, they've won with nothing left over. Whatever social movement I might have been a part of in my singular fucked up way, it has been defeated and it is done. Everything from here on is picking through the bones while the sky catches fire but at least the winners will win, until the world is reperfected without us, amen.

"See anything of ol' Branford lately?" Pitcher asked.

"I can tell you frankly," Burke told him instead, boring on the one point, "that absent a state contract for medical sales the corporation will not be interested in further purchases of land at this time."

"Yeah well."

"And I personally was against this buy. I didn't see the need for it."

"What is it, Ricky, you got it in for me or something?"

"It's not about you, Ken."

"Sure it is. It's always been about me."

"No. I didn't see a requirement in terms of policy. Especially with Obama, who knows why, he's busting more medical marijuana operations under Federal law than the Bushies ever did."

"He just wants to be America's first white president is all."

Got a teensy laugh but then Burke droned on. "What are you doing out there anyway, Ken? You're being paid a generous salary for doing what exactly? Are you doing any actual work these days?"

"That's rich. I been earning more than my keep. But you're right, I got nothing to do at present and why? For months your personal Smokey Mountain pirate sat on hilltops with binoculars scoping primo properties and tracking dealers to their patches who might shoot my ass if they knew, just like I did for Uncle Sam in Nicaragua with the Sandies on my ass. You climb any mountain trails lately and surveil major criminals without them seeing ya? I found Raleigh the best there is, ten properties in a row for starters, and you should thank me even though you only bought one measly. If y'all just followed up on my good work Raleigh'd own the fifteen finest properties in the county, which is to say the state, which is to say the whole damn country—y'all'd control the whole top end of the coming legal market and be sitting pretty on the biggest heap of gold since dragons did that shit in caves."

For which old Pitch would get, what, a gold star on his report card and a pinprick bonus come Christmas? Maybe another secret medal like back in Nica, ha ha ha. Whereas the truly frustrating thing about the dumbfuck dodos back in Dixie was that if Raleigh had made the intelligent business decision to buy and fence the properties he had scouted and mapped for them Pitch would personally control like 80% of the best Humboldt County crop of chronic by harvest-time. In other words *all the dealers would have to come to him.* He'd make enough to retire maybe even out of this one-horse country back to Paris long as some drygulching son of a bitch didn't ace him out, and he didn't think these local boys were sharp enough to get behind him when he wasn't looking.

"But noo, let's not buy up the fine *terroir* ol' Pitch found you," he told

Burke, "because that might be intelligent."

"I don't see why we have to buy it now," Burke said. "What's the rush?"

Which stumped Pitch a minute. "Well, Philip Morris—"

"Did all their buying in the Valley and don't have a man where you are," droning factual Burke admitted, so score one point there. "Look, Ken, you've still got them charmed, maybe a little dazzled, but it's tenuous. It's a kindness from me to you that I'm advising you of the need to produce a legal medical sales document licensing this one patch. Because you promised it, by the way, unasked. Without that it won't be long. They'll wind up your contract and call you home and your cover here at Raleigh will be thin due to non-performance. I don't know why I'm still protecting you but I am."

Pitch hated the sweat breaking out on him in hot little needles. "Well thank you for all the kindness, Ricky boy. Don't know what I'd do without it."

"I already regret bringing you into the company—"

"You *must* be having a bad week at home down there to be feeling like this, but I imagine it's good to get it off your chest, huh."

"Listen to me, Kennis," plowing on. "I'm telling you this because you're a clever guy, and despite my misgivings I want to give you a chance to produce something for us so you can come out all right."

All those years of his resentment just piling up and now he thinks he's got the edge on me. "Don't think I don't appreciate that, son. You just watch me. End of the month we're in bidness."

"I'll do you the favor of not repeating that upstairs so that no one holds you to such a schedule, but when this crop comes due ..."

"Gettin' it all worked out," Pitcher assured him.

"I wish I could believe you," Burke said. "By the way," sounding supremely like an office functionary, "HQ doesn't think it wise that you put Raleigh's name on Property One."

"Poetic license," said Pitch, wondering where Burke was getting his information he wasn't supposed to know about. "Something to warn the dealers off, juju so they won't fuck with it. Had the sign run up and slapped it on."

"You have exceeded your remit, and I suggest for your own sake, Ken, that you slap it off and put an official brand-name Muhrad sign up."

"But then the trouble comes to my door," Pitch told him.

"That's why you get the big bucks. Raleigh's name attached is not wanted in the current public relations regime. Take the sign down."

"That an order, sir?"

"It's both an order and good advice. You may choose not to believe me, but I'm still acting as your friend."

"You tired of me already, Dicky-boy?"

"A little," Burke said like it cost him something, the weary good man trying so hard. "I believe finally that yes perhaps I am."

"Well stay tuned, bud, the show ain't over yet."

But actually, Plan A looking fucked, Plan B said one patch wasn't worth teaming with a jerk like Teddy on but he hadn't yet worked all the way through extraction, getting it past Teddy and Poholek and out to the good old boys west of Grants Pass, though he had the shape of it in mind, a crystal working out the geometry of its laws then you hold it up in your hand to watch it catch the light. At least 500K for himself if he could pull it off, Pitch figured, not a fortune these days but add it to what he had in the bank plus if he sold the house in Durham against the remaining mortgage it'd buy him time and from the sound of things he might-could need it.

Pitch got tired of hearing Burke try to make himself significant so he said bye-ya and put the phone down, which is when he paused for a second to confirm his intuition that Eli Chase, dumb kid in the right place, could turn out to be the ticket to it and through it, so let's find out now what's happening to him and if it's good the kid was welcome to keep Pitch's monogrammed hankie, blood and snot and all.

5

Driving slowly south out of the town center and looking at Eli's neighborhood through the windshield, it was as if some great machine had scoured the earth clear of everything, drawn a grid and then a giant house-extruder had flown over plopping down new houses on small adjacent plots, the houses nice enough themselves, clean, blue, green, yellow, rose-color, contrasting trim and the lawns well kept, but nothing standing between them and the bare sky and it was as if all the detail and nuance and intimacy of life had been swept away and this was what was left. Lina loved California light but they had done something to it here. A few more trees would help, but they hadn't planted many. She couldn't tell one block from the next, they just seemed to go on and on, but she could follow the numbers and was pretty sure it was the next block, the gradual rise on the lowly rolling land, or maybe the one after.

On the other hand these colorful little houses weren't derelict or foreclosed and what if Eli was right and this was the dope economy protecting everyone around here from tumbling into the pit?

There it was, coming up on the right and she pulled to the curb with a view through the narrow grass alley left of the house to the tiny back-garden cottage where Eli lived with Sukey. Lina thought she saw a movement at the dark front window as she came out of the car and didn't bother locking it, then, yes, walking down the alley she saw Sukey appear, sort of shy and flinching in the doorway, a little wave and at first Lina thought Sukey was wearing something billowy against the heat—loose-fitting sienna linen atop a long blue skirt with faded golden moons and stars strewn across—but then Lina was pretty sure of the shape underneath the clothes and to protect herself from the wave of heat seizing her from top to toe she tried to see herself as Sukey must see her advancing alongside the house, motherly authority, the rule of law, the world about to show its heft—so please don't be dramatic, Lina, keep your impact low, there's enough in play already.

"Hi-i," Sukey managed to singsong.

"Hi Sukey," and drew near enough for a cheek-to-cheek mostly air-kiss.

"Would you like some lemonade?"

"Lemonade would be *perfect*," Lina purred, and they went inside, the cramped angular house not immaculately kept by any stretch but better than she'd expected. The question was who would speak first so neither of them did during Sukey's selection of two clean glasses with worn primary-color flower-prints on their sides, the clunking of the ice cubes, the pouring from a porous plastic jug of acidic lemonade that should be kept in what do you call that new non-toxic substance, *glass*, cool it Lina, and then, as they sat down with their glasses sweating on the mother-of-pearl-top kitchen table, Sukey attempted a start.

"Well, look, um, I know it looks a little bad, Mrs. Chase, with Eli in the dope business and in jail, and me, well I guess you've noticed that I'm a little …"

And then thanks be to God she couldn't keep it up and Lina couldn't either, a sort of bubbling-up past their stiffened jaws and the two of them without being clear whether they were laughing or crying, though it definitely started with laughter and spread from there, laughing then falling clumsily and because their chairs were too far apart, into each others' arms or at least against each other at the shoulders and transmitting what they had to via uncoördinated lurches and backpats, more perfect, even, than lemonade.

Lina was the first to detach and she did it on a laugh, wiping a possible tear from under one eye and saying, "Yes, there certainly is a bit of Tobacco Road to the picture, dear," and took a grateful sip of lemonade.

"The tobacco company?" Sukey asked her, and Lina realized she'd have to do a bit of intergenerational translation, looking at this now much more serious person in her life, *so young* though actually older than I was in the equivalent, but Eli's no Nelson Chase as was, so there: solid lanky girl, healthy sexual presence but already weathered looking, her slat cheeks and broad farmgirl forehead, the guarded grey wide-set almondine eyes and long straight strawcolored hair. Mostly Nordic or Germanic with perhaps a touch of Cherokee or somesuch. Reasonably intelligent, radically uneducated, a denizen of the new American wilderness now definitively launched belly-first into the unknown.

"All right," Lina said, starting to make order by placing her hands atop her thighs. "Your part of the story."

"Fifth month."

The Granny Lina race was on. Her first son Noah's wife had brought a prior daughter to their marriage but they wanted one of their own and there'd been hints on the phone that it might be on deck. "And whose idea to keep it?"

"Mine first but Eli was with it, he *is* with it."

"Quickly?"

"Right off the bat."

"Bless his pointy head. It's good to know I won't have to murder him today. Have you seen a doctor?"

"Not much. The free clinic twice. I'm healthy."

Okay, time to set her up with Fichtner. "Boy or girl."

"Girl."

"Boyoboy," said Lina. Girl was going to be harder for Eli to cope with, and even without that she was already biting her tongue in order not to say Look, I know Eli's gorgeous but you do know, don't you, that he has let us say a limited capacity for dealing with real-world consequences but whatever happens you will have a home with me whensoever you need it and for as long. Which was a lot not to say, though much of it so obvious it was being handled anyway on a rudimentary mindreading level abetted by eye signals and head feints. So Lina thought, though not sure how quick Sukey was on that kind of uptake.

"Are you and Eli, um, happy together?"

"*Yes.*"

That was enough talk between them, Lina thought, for her to pop the question, so she did.

"Oh, you know," Sukey told her, "he was going to tell you but like not this week, he'd get to it next week."

"Then next week became this week."

"He was afraid to tell you."

Bite your tongue again, he didn't want it to be real. But tell your mother and It Is Written.

Lemonade break, definitely. Take a sip and stop worrying about the plastic toxins. "Okay, please tell me everything you know about Eli getting arrested and by the way have they let you see him?"

It was more than a little confusing. On the one hand a misdemeanor trespassing charge, on the other a possibility that they were framing him on something bigger, probably to turn him into an informant. And not exactly framing either, since he was in the business after all. On the one hand misdemeanor, on the other a bail hearing and he was sequestered, Sukey hadn't seen him and couldn't call in, they'd talked on the phone but Eli couldn't-wouldn't say much right now, Sukey had spoken to the bail bondsman, had his card around here somewhere …

"And Eli's holding up?"

"A lot better than I expected, a lot."

"I think I should go talk to the bail bondsman."

"Marcus Dobbs."

"That's his name? Hilarious."

"I hear he's a good guy," Sukey said, but sounded dubious. "People say."

"It's better done in person than on the phone. Come with me?"

Sukey shook a briefly tormented head and Lina got it: she needs to face this piecemeal: all at once and it'll break her. Threats to her poised on every vector, threats to my son the same for me but I'm older and more broken in. Then the unprecedented fact that she's pregnant and everything in her life has changed, bodily and for good. Ah yes, I remember it well but Nelse had tenure and had only been in jail for protest marches.

"But you'll there be in court," Lina said.

A tense nod affirmed that she would.

Lina tried a move, reached out and grasped Sukey's forearms telling her, "I'm here and I'm on your side," but right away saw it was a mistake, too forceful, too direct a grab, Sukey flinching away from the presumption of trust, and Lina figured she'd have to stay another five minutes and try some inconsequential chatter, if such was possible, in order not to part company on a bad cadence.

★

Lina had readied herself for a pure slog of a day looking down the barrel of an unknown outcome, so the office of Marcus Dobbs, bail-bondsman, was such a pleasant surprise she had to warn herself not to build a castle on it. Gesturing toward the compact stereo unit playing on a side-table as she came in, "Is that the one he wrote while his wife was in labor?"

"String Quartet in D-minor, from the quartets dedicated to Haydn," said the presumed Marcus Dobbs, a truly lovely-looking café-au-lait man of thirty-what in a tailored white shirt and pleated offwhite linen slacks, rising from behind his walnut desk, "and I think, yes, Mozart's wife had a difficult labor with their first one and he sat outside the bedroom door and wrote this in order not to freak out. What an amazing man."

"Misplaced angel, in my opinion. Not from around here."

"Good an explanation as any. Can I help you?"

"May I collapse?" Indicating the customer chair.

"Be my guest."

The office was spare and clean and simple and Lina couldn't tell at first, apart from the grave and orderly Mozart, what made it so pleasant. Taste had been exercised but she couldn't find the fingerprints. The only extra item in view was a small Yamaha piano unit on black stalk legs up against a side wall, two small box-speakers mounted to it and a few pages of music manuscript aslant on top. She also had a problem not being completely taken with Dobbs, easily the most attractive man she'd met in ages and alas 1) too young for her, what must she look like to him at forty-six? and 2) her outlaw son's presumed bondsman besides, Eli's fate partly in his hands. "I'm Eli Chase's mother," she said.

"I guessed. Please call me Marcus."

"Lina. You're studying piano?"

"I write chamber music." Pleasantly deep and unaffected speaking voice. "Trying to."

Lina cocked her head, hoping she didn't look like a parrot. "And you're in the bail-bond business because?"

"Location, location, location. Eureka is a golden goose, and the work gives me time to write and study." Observing Lina trying to connect the dots, he added: "My father's a parole officer in Oakland. I grew up in the milieu."

"A-ha."

"Look, Mrs. Chase … Lina. It'd be pleasant to talk with you about music, but I know that you've got far more difficult things in mind, so let me say something that I hope will reassure you. You're unlikely to need my services today."

"I have money, that's not a problem."

Dobbs nodded politely at this irrelevance. "From what I hear from friends of mine in court it's unlikely that your son will require bail. Someone somewhere in the system is trying to make more of it, but all they've really got on him is a misdemeanor trespass. Statutory fine, double it if the judge has heartburn after breakfast, zero if he slept well."

"Eli *is* in the business," Lina told him, "I think you should know."

"With luck that's irrelevant for the present, and he's a foot soldier at best."

"Aren't they the ones who get sent up?"

"When they're caught with a truckful of marijuana, yes, but your son wasn't carrying more than a couple of jays in his glove box and they didn't even plant a few kilos on him for good luck. From their point of view it was a mistake not to."

"And resisting arrest?"

"He must have led with his nose. It's a wash, unless Deputy Chief Poholek has something up his sleeve. Which is possible, but I don't see it. Has your son been arrested before?"

Lina shook her head, "Not since he was a juvenile and never on a dope charge. Eli thinks his friend, his, um, employer, Teddy, may have turned on him though, and that Pollack is calling Teddy as a witness."

"Poholek," Dobbs said, then nodded. "I see. I don't think it's likely to play, but I'll be happy to come to court just in case. May I offer you a cold Pellegrino, and then you can tell me where your son lives, how much money he has in the bank and how old a car he drives. Just in case they try to make more of him than he is. You know who his P.D. is?"

Lina fussed a bit with the lip of her purse. "Someone named Culson I think."

"You'd do better with a head of lettuce," Dobbs said. "If money's really not an issue I can recommend someone, but as I say, I don't think it will much matter."

"Let me think about it. I don't want Eli serving time and of course I'd rather not pay bail, but it may do him good to worry for a bit. Can I change horses if we see they're building something up?"

"There should be time for that."

"Thank you for making things so clear and for being so very pleasant."

"You're entirely welcome. I hope the procedure will go as smoothly. By the way," he added, "I like the scarf. You're wearing it in court, I hope."

"That was the plan." Lina looked down, patted it and adjusted its helical slide. Oh of course: string quartets: I like the scarf: he's gay.

She looked up to see him half-bent to the fridge and its bottles of mineral water, narrowing his eyes at her in assessment, then a little uptick. "I'm not, you know," he said.

Flustered. "Not what?"

He shot her an Oh really look.

"Okay, you got me. Any chance you have a slice of lime to go with the fizzwater?"

"You're out of luck. Only lemon."

"No-body knows the trouble I've seen," Lina told him, then experienced a reflex worry that it was a misstep racially. Marcus's sonar did not beep back, and she drank down almost half her Pellegrino realizing only then how tired and tense she was.

"So, you like Mozart."

"Oh come on now," Lina said. "Also apples."

★

Out the door of Dobbs' office and a short distance along the sidewalk to her left, Lina found herself observed by a man about her own age in a loose-fitting navy-blue suit with countrypolitan trim and no tie. He was slouching on a new-looking grey Chevy Something, his reddish-brown hair hung lank over a bony face, his jaw looked weird, jutting, and it

52

seemed to Lina he should wear a sandwich-board hanging on a rope from his shoulders SEE THE SKULL BENEATH THE SKIN RIGHT HERE, fifty cents, a buck, whatever fare the traffic et cetera.

"I take it you are Mrs. Chase, Eli Chase's mother?" this person asked her. Faint regional accent, couldn't quite tell if it was South or West. Darting eyes that searched and assessed her quickly: not just the routine survey of tits, hips, and what could be made of ass and legs in such a skirt but seeking gaps through which to spy out her character and essence.

"You take it right. And you are?"

The man lifted a business card from an interior jacket pocket and extended it forward for Lina to ignore: this was not a man you wanted to look away from. "Kennis Pitcher," he said.

"Lina Chase," she said automatically.

"Raleigh Tobacco."

She had intended to walk past him to her car but this stopped her. "You're the one who has raised, put, whatever it is, you've got a trespass charge against my son?"

"Technically, I suppose I did, I do. It was more a police action and I went along with it in the interest of protecting my company's property in case your son intended to damage it. Now that I see that your son had no such intention I might be persuaded to drop the charge."

"I see. In exchange for?"

"Why do you assume right off the bat that I want something in exchange."

"You have that look."

"Aw Mrs. Chase, why d'you want to get me wrong right off?"

"In exchange for what," Lina persisted.

"Howbout," the man said, uncoiling himself from the fender of the Chevy, "the pleasure of driving you to court in my car here."

"My car's over there," Lina said. "And thanks anyway but I was thinking of walking to clear my head." Wrong thing to confess. This is not a free speech zone.

"May I walk with you a ways?"

"I don't see how I can stop you."

"Oh, you could stop me," he said, but once they were walking side by side along the pavement, beaten by the sun and relieved by patches of passing treeshade along the storefronts—hardware, coffeehouse, secondhand notions and antiques—he began speaking in a regular, unbroken rhythm, a reciting machine. "I've got nothing against your son now that I know he had no intention of damaging company property. It's rather that the deputy chief of police Mister Robert Poholek is kind of you could say eager to arrest some people in the weed business before its imminent legalization renders them safe from his intentions."

"I don't think legalization is all that imminent," Lina said.

"Oh really, why not?"

"Public opinion may have swung that way, but if it passes in a state referendum the legislature is likely to block it, and if they don't the federal government will clamp down, because if the great state of California goes recreational-use legal, that's it, the dam bursts and it all goes national, smoke all over the place and everyone out of their skulls from sea to sea. So there would be strong Federal interest in stopping that. Also the private prison lobby is putting a lot of money against the change and I don't think they plan to let it happen and lose all the cheap labor they've got inside. Capitalism works."

Kenny Whatsis looked sideways at her, a shard of gleam in his untrustable eye. "How'd you know about the prison lobby?" he asked her.

"I try to stay informed about the world I live in," Lina said. Okay line but pity about the sniffy tone.

Kenny What paused to look at her afresh. "God damn," he said. "An intelligent woman. I can't tell you what a pleasure it is to encounter someone intelligent in these parts."

She stuck her chin at him.

"If I want to have an interesting conversation around here I mostly have to talk to myself, and that gets eccentric."

"I'm sure you have fascinating conversations, Mister…"

"Pitcher. Pitch. Look, why are you getting on my case? I'm willing to drop charges against your son and let him walk out of court a free young man and now I come to think of it I might even be able to offer him a job that would remove him from the perils of operating outside the law, a consummation, ma'am, you ought to think devoutly to be wished."

Oh really, Hamlet: what's his game? "What kind of job might you offer him?"

"Why, a sort of expanded watchman job, the job of looking after Raleigh Tobacco property in the area in order to protect it from people who might want to damage or remove from it anything legitimately owned by the corporation. The property your son Eli wandered into yesterday is just, what to call it, a sort of pilot purchase in a general program. Raleigh is interested in buying up any number of parcels of state land that nonetheless have a proven record of being excellent *terroir* for *cannabis sativa*, Q.E.D."

"Because of the legalization you don't think is coming any more than I do," Lina said.

"We could be wrong," he said. "Anyway they think what they like back at HQ in North Cahlina. I'm just a humble functionary here."

In a pig's ass, Lina told herself so as not to say it aloud. "And you're willing to drop the trespass charge against my son."

"Let's see how things go in court, but yes I believe I have the power to do that even though Captain Poholek is feeling more ambitious. It remains to be seen if I'll have a free hand, but if I do, Mrs. Chase, it would please me to be of help to you and your fine son Eli."

Lina could not suppress a snort of laughter but then got back on track. "What does it depend on," she wondered, "your having a free hand or not?"

"On the appearance or non-appearance of a certain witness," he said, "and then upon the nature of this witness's testimony, should he appear. In my opinion he's a no-show and I can put Eli in the clear."

This conversation was some kind of refined tarantula quadrille, it seemed to Lina, with stingers poised at the ready. "Mr. Dobbs," she said with a backward hook of chin, "was of the same opinion. That this person wouldn't show."

"Mr. Dobbs is one smart brown cookie, and if I may say so, ma'am, you are quite the clever ginger snap yourself."

"It's kind of you to say so," Lina was fighting to resist a drop into a venomous parody of southern politesse, "but what I still don't get is what you want from me."

A crooked toothsome grin split his ghastly features. "Wait and see," was all he said, but then looked like he'd been struck by a fresh idea. "What's Lina short for?"

"Carolina," Lina involuntarily confessed, "despite the different e-sound," and then, as her mouth fumbled forward, she had to wonder how this creep had edged her into confessional mode, "because my father made his first good money in tobacco futures."

The creep's grin looked ready to eat her up. "What goes around comes around, don't it, on the wheel of karma."

That caught Lina's breath short. She came to a stop on the pavement outside a dry-cleaner featuring a loggy, rustic look upfront until you saw to the ranks of garments hung in plastic ghosts inside. "Very clever but not good enough. You're all theatrics and no facts. What do you really want from me?"

"See how smart you are?"

"Cut the crap, Ken."

"Okay. I'd like you to use your influence with your son—"

"He doesn't listen to me."

"I feel sure he does."

"Do you have children?" Lina asked him.

"Two daughters. In their teens. I adore them. We're very close."

"Yeah right."

"Okay, we're as close as we can be given they live with their mother in France who won't let me see them and anyway I can't get there often as I'd like." Lina nodded to indicate that she gave this small confidence a passing grade. "Say I hire your son, with your help, to protect a number of properties soon to be acquired in the area and to have the benefit of his expertise in the extraction of the crops therein, in order to supply the legal market for medical marijuana."

"To supply the legal market for so-called medical marijuana, which operates on a ninety-nine plant limit per property basis."

"Just so. You seem to suspect me of some kind of unlawful activity. It baffles me why. Mrs. Chase, I work for a major, respected American corporation owned and operated by the same family nigh on a hundred ninety years. In view of Raleigh's intentions to invest on a large scale the state of California is offering incentives and I am interested in employing your son for a living wage with health benefits for himself and for, um, any dependents who might, um, come along—"

Lina's spine snapped rigid as she realized that this bastard knew about

Sukey's pregnancy before she had, but the son of a bitch didn't seem to notice the change in her, he was hearing himself talk pure music.

"—because of his expertise and professional acquaintances in the field. There are any number of unscrupulous people round about who might view Raleigh's legal ownership of these assets as an offensive expropriation of their rightful property, and your son could be instrumental in making sure everything goes smoothly with these unpredictable individuals and their groundless claims, according to law, which is basically my offer."

"Sounds to me even more dangerous than what Eli's doing already."

"When we have the backing of the town, the state police," gesturing with open arms and upraised palms in the free American air, "and even if need be the National Guard?"

"You are a glittering snake in the grass, Mr. Picture," Lina said. This appeared to take him aback for a second, tops. "*Latet anguis in herba,* no pun intended on *herba,*" she added, but her too fucking clever smattered Latin didn't throw him either.

"Blessings on a good Catholic education. *Et in Arcadia ego,* baby." He came at her grinning through his crooked fangs and Lina finally got away from him back to her nice new hell-red car.

He didn't follow, and on the way to the car Maria Callas launched an aria in her shirtpocket and she recognized Marcus Dobbs' number—was he leaning out his door to watch?—and she got the jump on him this time by not letting him speak first: "The guy who picked me up outside your office? *No kidding.*"

And just as his kindness and courtesy earlier had smoothed the contours of her day, it was good, on the line or rather through the aether and from a satellite, to hear his warm familiar laughter coming at her now.

6

THE SUN WAS UP. Or was up some hour ago.

It's not my fault! I didn't do this to me!

Mom, Dad, both of you so wise and kind, I get that. But I did not choose this, to be in this, to be the no-help center of this, I don't see how this was my decision. Did you two somehow make it that way in me?

Can't one of you hear me and not judge it?

Sukey can. Sukey can so I must serve her back and then there's daylight possible. If I can't believe that then I might as well. Crumple. Collapse. Crumple into the dark. Is the dark intricate or simple? Am I? Until we know.

With a small dark human coming from there inside her there.

God help me. God, can I believe you? Can you reach me? If you are not, can not, I might die completely here. I believe you but I'm still helpless, help me, I must not let Sukey down and what's in her body, which is mine also, I must not let her down or let either one of them, God help me, be lost. Otherwise the winds of hell, something I heard Dad say not long before he died, those winds won't be more than I owe, forever. That's what I feel and it scares the hell out of me, at least I hope it will. I don't know what to do about it.

★

Eli got like no sleep in last night's cell and just when he was getting some early morning downtime they yelled him out of it and police-carred him cuffed and twitchy through stinging daylight to the back door of the court building and now this even smaller cell and wouldn't let Sukey send clean clothes so here he was T-shirt all bloody and other discharge, for breakfast a cheese-slice sandwich on lame white bread and instant decaf and the bridge of his nose throbbing like a motherfucker.

Poholek had dropped in to threaten him and Eli was pretty sure he'd get punched again but didn't so there was that. He said he'd sue Poholek for the nose and Poholek just snickered at him. Rat on Teddy before he rats on you was the tune and Eli didn't sing along even though Poholek went on about superviolent black-guy prison gangs who would find him pretty.

When he saw Teddy in court, depending what his face looked like when their eyes met, maybe, maybe. Or if their eyes didn't meet, if Teddy looked away, like he had Jesus was that just yesterday morning? Seems like forever ago. Eli looked around the bare grey cell. Fuck! How long's this gonna take? Maybe if he had a little private time with Teddy later he'd do to Teddy's nose what Poholek had done to his.

Big talk, but he felt a threat on his margins, the chance, the first hint he might come apart, seams, nerves, whatever he was made of.

So therefore the worst thing, his mother. Mother, mother, mother. She was coming *here*. Remember to call your mother. It was so unfair. Because your mother knows it all and has seen it all and is smarter than anyone and wiser than anyone too and she adjusts her voice to just your level when she talks down to you exactly like Sukey pointed out, softens her voice and directs it so as not to scare the scared little animal inside you, she *modulates* her voice and whole approach, and Sukey's right that Mom's an elevator that is so pleased with itself because it stops exactly at your floor, not an inch too high or an inch too low but just perfectly and it works so well its buttons shine and its rug don't ever need sweeping and it tells you which floor it wants you to go to and get off at. It runs so quietly you hardly even hear it coming. My mother the elevator. Sukey's smart. Sukey's known Mom, right, how long? and I've known her since, you know, and I didn't spot it, and Sukey did.

Mom was going to be there, in the court, if her car didn't crash and kill her on the way. Fuck!

And right then they came for him. Too soon! He needed a minute to—and as the two clanking guards lifted him by the armpits and guided him out of the cell one on either arm Eli saw the walls slipping and tilting and he knew what might be coming on. "Could you guys wait a minute and let me catch my—" nevermind down a corridor and he couldn't cordinate his perception of it even as he tried to remember everything he'd been coached and therapied through: how to track the real world and keep it in sequence so it didn't get impossible on him but he wasn't getting traction. "Could we go a little slower down here so I can—" but the windowlight was coming from the wrong direction and he couldn't make the walls and ceilings add up. It was slipping so he knew he had to switch to Plan B, which was above all just sit through it and Don't Do Anything, sit it out, wait it out, and whatever you do don't add extra chaos from yourself. Eli gave up trying to get a grip and best he could just let it happen without freaking.

But they came too fast and hard through two doors and the last one was the courtroom, which was way too large, the shape and dimensions all wrong for him, the colors jangling, the wood too much of it, where was the light coming from, faces faces faces but which ones knew him, the pieces of his sight zagging apart and this was the worst time for it to happen—it wasn't because he was scared but because they'd come for him in the wrong part of his sequence so he couldn't catch up—and he guessed the direction they were tugging him to stronger now had the chair he was supposed to sit in but he couldn't find it in his sight, it moved away.

Lina saw it from the gallery the instant they pulled him in through the doorway to the right of the judge's dais, staring up at a corner of the ceiling with his mouth open, looking drunk to an unschooled eye but Lina knew better and wished him Hang on Eli don't fight it and above all please please *please* don't fight *them*. Especially given how strong you are. Since she knew what she knew, seeing it was worse than the blood bruise spread across the bridge of his nose and under his widened eyes, midnight blue at the center then dark red wings outspread and the mess of dried blood on the front of his shirt, that cop had really whacked him one but Eli was strong as a rock and could take it. But his mind, we've worked on it so hard, *he's* worked on it so hard, he's won so much territory back from the chaos of bad wiring—she had to fight the impulse to jump and run to him over the people and the chairbacks, and she supposed it helped that Sukey was digging her fingernails into her right forearm and that her own voice, as she leaned to Sukey to stage-whisper, "Hang on dear this could be a rough one," came out sounding unhysterical and almost humorous as if issuing from a conscious and present human being and not a spirit being ripped in two like a bedsheet, which is what she felt herself to be this minute.

They pushed Eli down into the chair behind the defense's table with the lettuce-head P.D. and Eli passed the first big test and stayed put once he was planted. Count of five. Still there, big head and shoulders steady. My sons look like Nelson, solid Saxons who have never seen the Mediterranean or eaten an olive. Well, by now they've had a dip in the water but you still couldn't sell them a Gaeta or Picholine. Count of ten and he's still in place, Lord have mercy.

Lina detached Sukey's fingernails from her arm and told her, "There's a chance we might get through this."

After what had seemed to Lina the incredible noise of Eli's arrival but probably had not been loud at all, the officials of the court went on fidgeting and sorting papers, the judge behind his dais looking distracted or possibly only bored. Mediocre-looking duffer, robe and specs, a mop of unkempt hair that Lina figured for an affectation, as if he should have a palette in his hand, brushes instead of a gavel, a canvas instead of a courtroom. Probably a pretentious amateur. "Mr. Culson?" he seemed to say to no one in particular while looking elsewhere.

"Just one minute if it would please the court, your Honor."

This didn't rate an answer. Everyone seemed to be searching for the grocery list they knew they'd put down right here somewhere.

Lina stared hard at the back of Eli's large crewcut head, willing him to turn around and see her but it was no dice. Behind her the sound almost of a scuffle that was only dramatic whispering turned her to see the man she'd learned was Deputy Chief Pollack reading the Riot Act to two highway patrolmen, poking one of them in the chest and practically booting them out of the courtroom through the wooden double doors. This was good, this was good, they don't have Teddy, she hoped that's what it meant, but if that was the case why did the skinny-headed A.D.A at the prosecution's table look so unperturbed?

Because they might still find him.

Lina turned around again to scope Deputy Chief Pollack though she was told everyone still called him Captain, whom she was pleased to see looking rushed and unhappy, and she only now noticed Marcus Dobbs sitting inconspicuously at the far left end of the last row, practically in the corner. She eye-signalled him with a big silent ask and he indicated back Don't be seen communicating with me but I think we're cool, with a tiny hint of secret smile. This made her feel better but only until she saw Kenny fucking Picture sidle in and slink into the back pew nearest the doors.

His presence completed for her the grotesquery of the courtroom itself. She had expected the kind of nondescript bureaucratic space you saw in clips of televised trials these days, blank walls with random decorative flaps of cheap wood panelling, worn-out podia, bad microphones no one spoke into properly and not one trace of anything resembling the Majesty of the Law except a few limp flags and some garish bronzed bald eagle crucified to the wall behind the judge, but the actual place in which she found herself and into which they had commanded the body and soul and poor whirling mind of her mortal son was a crazy place washed onshore by some antic inappropriate whim of time's inscrutable sea.

For here in possibly the most economically devastated county in the Golden State were gallimaufried half the insigniae of its golden age: the dais and the balustrades murdered out of giant Sequoia, atavistic pure land-of-endless-plenty conspicuous consumption, the walls a hideous mustard and the gewgawed windowframes gorgeous redwood too, giants pulled down and bent to petty human service beneath the tinny ticking clock of human time. There must have been redwood chairs for the major figures once, maybe the judge still had one back of his robe, but they'd worn out she guessed and this was what was left of the gold rush of the grand old days when grab the land manifested God Himself and His Intention for the country.

Eli's head had turned, not all the way yet but he was starting to look around and his motion seemed steady. All her sight was on him so she didn't know who had announced out loud, "Is Mr. Edward Swift present in the court?"

"Who the hell is Edward Swift," she whispered to Sukey, stupidly, since she got the answer as she pronounced the syllables of his name.

"Teddy," Sukey said. "I think his family's in the meat business."

Swift? If it's the same Swift they were in the meat business like Raleigh was in tobacco and Chrysler was in cars. It absolutely figured, it was classic: family money bankrolling the black sheep, the miscreant, the vain little creep, the insolent petty privileged devious little kill-my-hurt-child purely evil tiny twerp.

"Once again, officially," the bailiff announced, going once, going twice, while Lina's heart hung there in the auction, "is Mr. Edward Swift present in court?"

Poholek was furious out the back door in search of the chariot of the gods, Marcus steadfastly did not turn her way or emit a single filament of interpersonal signal-smoke, and she had to force herself to look at the snake Kenneth Picture and he was already grinning directly at her from his distant pew with his smile of crooked fangs.

Lina faced front as quickly as she could and there was her son's Godmade face looking at her. The moment was too rushed and intense but she tried for an assessment: normal human helplessness and fear, not the blank chaos that hid in circuitry Eli hadn't been provided with or connected up, parts of the brain that hadn't learned to talk to each other inside its fragile shell. Her heart going like mad Lina put everything she had into her face without the least idea what it looked like and beamed it straight at Eli, who just then shifted a degree and put the same wide eyes on Sukey.

★

Better, better, still scary at the edges but he was remembering to breathe slower, deeper, don't rush and it was getting a little better.

He was settling down but it was still hard shit to follow. Whereas-whereas and given this and given that and especially apparently no Teddy present, there was a lot of paperwork to shuffle, this condition, that sub-condition, some more whereas, then everyone rattling through their papers, getting lost and asking for another minute if it please the court, Poholek back in the room sneaking forward to *whisper urgently* in the skinny teacher-looking prosecutor's ear and the prosecutor not responding, this pretty much had to be and even might be good but Eli was still having *some* trouble keeping himself here in time and space, this time this space, even though a birdie told him he could ease up and loaf now if he could manage it, looked like he might be covered. Tried, couldn't, oh well, it's happening pretty much without me and we'll see.

Trespass, resisting, anecdotal evidence, medical examiner's report, there *was* no medical examiner's report, why was there no medical examiner's report, corporation property, not exactly corporation property, no controlled substances present on the scene—*excuse me? what?*—the suspect carrying only a misdemeanor quarter-ounce but well-known to be an affiliate or employee of, can the District Attorney produce this individual? If not, I move to …

Compared to movies and TV these people didn't know their lines or where the camera was. And the room kept disengaging, losing touch with Gravity Central. A little. Not always. Hang in there, dude, you might get outside this clench of a room alive and soon.

Lina had to hand it to Kenneth Picture, he had subtlety to him as he wound his way forward through the chairs to the prosecutor's table and bent to speak in the man's ear, and when he withdrew to the rear of the room it was as if he'd never passed through, never bent and spoken, never even flicked a glance en route at Lina. This was a person who moved in invisible ink.

Nevertheless, it was written, a minute later came a gap in which the D.A. stood up and may it please the court announced that "in the interest of all parties and of the business of the court the complainant Muhrad Inc. has dropped the charge of Criminal Trespass against this defendant."

The judge looked pissed off because of wasted time, and the lettuce-head P.D. fantail-dropped a sheaf of papers to the floor climbing to his feet to say, "In that case, your honor, pursuant to, um, the defense moves that all charges against the accused—"

The judge slammed the placket with his hammer. "So ordered. Court is adjourned until two this afternoon and I will see counsel in my chambers. That means both of you," then a humble-grumble continuance under his breath that did not sound like a compliment to anyone involved.

Calloo callay!

Eli wasn't sure he heard it right and then he must not of, because the same two guards were coming for him and he felt frozen in his chair, he didn't want to move and they were reaching for his armpits again exactly like before and he pushed one guard's reaching arm away with his elbow, the left one, then he was either getting up or they were pulling him up and he got the guy on his right with his other elbow and was just about to get his feet under him solid so he could operate fully when a noise started coming at him from behind and scared him half to death, but when he turned to see it was his mother coming through the rows of courtroom like something out of a nature documentary on TV—here we see the mother animal rushing despite all danger to protect her young offspring, and before he had time to take another breath or figure which next move to make she had her arms around him pinning his arms to his sides and hanging on like Hulk Hogan but trembling and digging her face into his chest and muttering something he couldn't hear into it.

There was other noise, and the gavel banging, and his mother hanging on until the waves receded and the guards backed off, then his mother pulled her face out of his chest and bellowed a hoarse "THANK YOU" in some direction or all directions and then to him quietly, "If I let you go can we leave? Look, here comes Sukey. Eli, can I let go now, can I let go so we can leave?"

7

Lina suggested a victory celebration at any place they chose, sky's the limit and she was buying. Eli was buttoning up a blue plaid shortsleeve shirt and had dropped his bloody T-shirt on the marble floor of the vestibule. Lina picked it up and crumpled it tight and held it in her hand. Eli seemed to be coming around but his hands were shaking. Well, so were her own.

"I've got a clean pair of pants in here too," said Sukey of her shoulderbag, "or do you want to go home and wash up?"

"I'll put 'em on when we get to the bar."

"*Restaurant*," Lina said, then when she saw the two of them glare at her, retracted it: "No, you're right, I said wherever you choose, you're right."

"Actually I'm really starving," said Eli.

Lina choked back her amen cadence and said, "Let's get the hell out of here, I need a drink."

Outside, Deputy Chief Poholek had posted himself along the portico on the right so they could see him stare bullets at them as they went down the stairs to the freedom of the street and off to lunch.

Lina would have been up for the Belvedere, well-named with its fine ocean view and food that looked better than it tasted, but Eli and Sukey directed her through streets she didn't know to what she supposed was some kind of bistro lodged in a blue-panelled house among trees on some outflung arm of town. It wasn't busy and they took a table on the side terrace in the shade of trees. Eli's redwinged nose still looked horrible but Lina was getting used to it. They ordered drinks from Hi-I'm-Deedie? and when they settled into them only Sukey looked happy with what she had, a Margarita. Eli sucked up his vodka rocks so quickly he was able to order another before Deedie disappeared around the bend but told his women, "Actually I'd rather chill with some weed."

Lina's antennae went up: Sukey thought Eli had a problem with booze and not with smoke so he'd thrown her a sop but what he really wanted was to get plastered. Lina thought his problems with both were about equal except when his yen to binge booze went haywire.

"Actually," Lina said, sipping her much-mocked summer usual—tall glass of single gin, double tonic, dash of bitters, ice—to such dull effect she wondered if she should have ordered a double everything, "I might want to join you in some serious drinking."

"You? You're kidding, Ma."

"I don't *think* I'm kidding," Lina said. In fact she wasn't sure if she was telling the truth or just trying to cozy up.

The youngsters ordered fancy Frenchified sandwiches on lengths of toasted miche and organic frites though Lina would have splurged for anything, and she went with a quarter of cold chicken, not bad, side of salad, good local sourdough and a second tall cool g&t that began to maybe hit the spot.

When they got back to the bungalow Lina declared herself in desperate need of a nap and the youngsters said Yeah us too, followed by a lot of Alphonse-Gaston about who'd get the bed, capped by Lina saying, "Remember, I have to sit up when I sleep," which was true, a breathing problem, so she went outside and pulled the flimsy orange-strap chaise longue into the shade of the back of the house, where she listened to Eli and Sukey going at it loud and hot on the other side of the wall, feeling complicated emotions, but didn't wait for them to finish before needful sleep took and slowly let her fall.

"Come on down the office, Bob," Pitch said into the landline phone on his American Oaktop.

"Not a good idea today," Poholek said. "Maybe not any day from here on out."

"After our débâcle in court? Don't let it worry you."

"No? Anyway no way am I going to your office and compromise myself in public sight."

Followed a series of alternatives with Poholek not liking any and finishing with, "Come on by the station, that'll still look legit."

When Pitch got there a Uniform led him to the interrogation room, where he was left to stew for fifteen minutes—not so stupidly he had brought a copy of the Portland paper and idled through the sports section specifically because he didn't give a shit who'd won—so that when Poholek finally made his entrance Pitch was able to look up and ask him, "Planning to put the screws to me, Cap? You better brought some tools."

"Ha ha very funny. Just tell me what the fuck you did to me in court."

Pitch aimed his jawbone at the mirror. "You sure no one's behind that with a camera and a hard-on?"

"Absolutely sure," Poholek said, hoiked a chair noisily from the table and sat in it across the table from Pitch.

"All righty, what I did for you in court this morning was something you might call a favor and bring me roses or a drink."

"How's that, you little fuck."

Pitch blew out air. "You're not kidding? I really have to explain it?"

"Pretend you do."

"When did I tell the D.A. to drop the trespass charge? When it was clear you couldn't get hold of Teddy no matter what. Which meant you had nothing, so I thought let's not fight an untenable position plus make everyone happy. Good for the company and good for you."

"How was it good for me."

"Because right now you don't have Eli to turn against Teddy or Teddy to turn against him but I'll make friends with Eli soon as his momma leaves town and offer him a job as watchman on the patch. Steady, legal work, hire and salary, cash on the barrel when his girlfriend's pregnant and he can't take a dope bust. Only way we retain him as an asset or to play against Teddy, which is still the aim in view and good for us both, correct? Round up all them varmint dealers starting with Teddy Swift. Eli might-could be a little peeved with him right now, plus we have Teddy's crop to drive Teddy crazy with. If you know some other new and better way just tell me."

"We have Teddy's patch," Poholek said, as if he warn't sure no more.

"Point of fact, Bob, Raleigh and Muhrad Inc. are the only legal owners of what once was Teddy's crop and the only way *we*, meaning you and I, have Teddy's patch is I'm a nice guy working with you hand in hand and will get you hired as head of Raleigh security when everything goes legal. Bob, are we working together here or not?"

"That's what I want to know."

"What don't you understand about what I just said? There's no other option."

"Are you sure you know everything about *my* options, Kennis?"

"If you have something you should tell me. You should've had Teddy in custody from the gitgo, and you didn't tell me what you had and didn't and you let *me* down."

"Don't tell me how to operate my office, Kennis. We went after him as soon as we had Chase but he was already gone."

"Teddy's a wily little shit when it comes to self-survival, ain't he. You should've busted him the same time as Eli, by the clock—or sooner, when Eli was driving to the patch."

"We didn't have probable cause."

"Fuck that, you could've logged the times different. What happened to your sense of tactics, assuming you had some?"

Poholek had to think about it before telling him, Pitch guessed, because it was oh-so sensitive info-wise: "We had Teddy's domicile surveilled. The place was pegged on all four sides."

"But he pulled a rabbit."

"He got out," Poholek admitted. That's how long it took to get him to cop to something, anything.

"So let me sum up here, Bob. Things got fucked up today but thanks to my prompt action when Plan A crashed we still have an iron in the fire and I'm gonna hammer it soon as his momma goes. Eli, I saved you from the evil trespass rap and your girlfriend's got a bun and I'm offering you a job."

"Raleigh'd pay a jerk like that?"

"When their property's been invaded? Crop's worth most of a mil so they'll pay to make sure no one steals or burns it before they sell it to the medicos."

"They'll pay the guy who broke in?"

"Who better? And you think I plan to tell em?"

"They'll find out."

"I been making a good living for years from the folks in Carolina, Bob, and if Raleigh finding out worries you the least little bit I'm prepared to pay Eli Chase out my own pocket for the what, three weeks before the crop is ripe? If I've got him I've got the crop safe and *we've* got a hand on Teddy. Worth every dime, wouldn't you say? We both wish we could have some property belongs to all the major dealers, Roger, Windell, Franklin, but we don't."

"If … we can bust Teddy … with a solid case against him," Poholek said dumbfuck slow.

"You can use him to take down the rest of the dealers," Pitch finished up the thought for him rather than wait all day. "So, is there anything else I can do for you this afternoon? Because if not I'd like to head on home, cool myself off and get ready for a fabulous fucking dinner date."

Pitch got up and Poholek let him walk out, certain that Poholek would now sit there at the table in the concrete-block room thinking the whole thing through piece by piece with his guts grinding and wouldn't find a gap in the wall of Pitch's argument or see anything other than his own pasty face in the big two-way mirror.

The sage can dive into the sea of events and disappear without a ripple.

Waking to late afternoon light for a moment Lina thought she'd fallen asleep in her own back garden, but the saggy nylon straps and the creak of lightweight aluminum disabused her and gradually she placed herself back of Eli and Sukey's shack with gin still working lightly in her and heavy lifting just ahead. The fond dream of her own garden had been born of her wish to put the oncoming talk behind her as finished business. She decided to start things off by sending out a comic vulture croak, "Eliiiiiii!"

"Yah!" from inside the house.

"Bring your mother a gallon of ice water!"

"Yah!"

"Never mind I'm coming." Up from the contraption on stiff complaining limbs—*bad* gin, *bad* gin—and into the cramp-ceilinged bungalow they always kept too dark. Eli and Sukey were at the dining table looking freshly showered and shampooed after a vigorous bout and the bird with blue heart and red wings spread across Eli's nose and eyes looked almost decorative now that the threat was past. One phase of the threat. Which was Lina's necessary starting point.

Even so it took a while to get to it—sleep all right? want a shower? like some ice in that? a beer?—and when Lina finally lowered her voice from the trivial to the unavoidable Eli and Sukey squared up their bodies in rough unison where they sat. They were a gorgeous couple, beautiful but unknowing, and that laid a primal power on her. Lina reselected her vocal tone and began.

"Let's ... just ... talk. No conclusions, no decisions, just a look at the current situation so we can see what's what."

"You're such an elevator, Mom," Eli told her, and since this made no sense whatever she decided to pretend he hadn't said it. Even though she saw Sukey pass her son a tacit little nod.

"I think it's gotten very dangerous for you here," Lina said. "Maybe too dangerous, under the circumstances."

Eli came out with some kind of dumb-cluck hyuh-hyuh but then laid a fact on the table. "It's never been exactly safe, this life here."

"I *know*," hating the insistent italic in her voice though she wanted to push a solid point across the table. "But it's different now because ..."

"You haven't lived it, Mom. We have. It's always been a pisser. I been the Farmer John watchman on a bunch of crops and we're *always* the ones who get busted. And I didn't."

"But now you *have* been busted."

"A trespass. A nothing. Charges dropped. You were there or did I miss that?"

Let me get my ducks in a row. Let me show you where the pieces are on the board. Let me ... Lina was getting nowhere with the runup so she barged in. "Sukey, you're five months pregnant, and you've both decided to go ahead with it. A new life. It's brave and wonderful and I'm here to help you. Let me finish. It makes you more vulnerable since you have immeasurably more at risk than before, and just now Deputy Chief Pollack's got a bead on you—"

"Poholek's an asshole and he's always been on my case," Eli said, and Lina wished Sukey would put her oar in and say wait a minute.

"All right," said Lina, "he's an asshole, but he's also dangerous, and something's changed. You're going to have a child to take care of, and maybe legalization's coming in."

"That makes everything easier till it happens," Eli explained. "After that we might have to figure something else out, but for now we're extra cool."

"So why did they arrest you up in the hills yesterday?"

Lina watched Eli's forehead fail to compute, but he came up with a better answer than she expected: "Because Raleigh's in town and wants to throw its weight around."

"And have you met, I keep losing pieces of his name, the guy from Raleigh Tobacco, Kenneth Picker?"

"Who?"

"Stringy guy, wears a western-style suit, he was in court today, lanky brown hair, face like a skeleton, he came to see me, he knew where to find me before—"

"Him? He's from the *tobacco* company?"

"Yes, and he might be more dangerous than Pollack."

"He's from the *tobacco* company?" Eli couldn't seem to get his head around it. "I saw him in the—" Eli said, then buttoned up, and in the gap Lina saw something horrible: Eli's penchant for the wild guy, the outlaw, the brilliant schismatic, which he himself was not but dearly wished himself to be. Eli had seen that creep and instinctively *liked* him. Because he looked like the way out of human nature and Eli desperately wanted to find that door.

"You saw him where?" Lina asked.

"Around." Eli doing some inept lying here. "Saw him around town."

What was he covering up? I mentioned the man's name and Eli didn't know it. "He's an extremely creepy guy," Lina said, marking time, hoping to get a look in.

"So? There are a lot of creepy guys around."

"This one is aimed at you and so is Pollack." Lina was getting a grip on her voice, levelling it, more matter of fact, less emotion. "Aaand …"

"Look, here it comes," Eli said with a confidential nudge to Sukey, and Sukey nodded knowingly back.

"This is my proposal: if you leave Eureka and come up to the island, I'm prepared to support you through the pregnancy and the birth, with housing and better medical care than you'll have here. If need be, I'll live in the cottage in the garden and you can have the house. It's your life, not mine, I know that. What I'm trying to do is protect that life. Your two lives and the life of …" A sudden suspicion. "Are you sure it's a girl? Have you had a sonogram?"

"No," said Sukey, finally emitting a syllable. "But we know it."

Lina bit her tongue and managed not to say anything to that. One other interpretation of Sukey's little new-agey statement: she had the power in the tandem. Eli's grin looked particularly passive, almost shit-eating just now.

Here passed a protracted silence of their beauty and unknowing, a seamless compound of the innocent and the smug. Finally Eli had a question, which he actually worked at, bless him, to make less sarcastic than it started out. "What would I suppose to do with myself up there on the island?"

"You'd have to get at least a part-time job."

"Flippin' the giant blueberry pancakes at Jensen's? You think someone else'd hire me? They saw my teens up there, fuckup drunk, arrested for disorderly, back from reconstruction camp then putting on another show? I can't live there."

"That was then. You're a grown man now, Eli."

"The elevator's out of order," he told Sukey. "The elevator isn't working."

"Eli," Lina said, "that's the second time you've mentioned an elevator and try as I may I haven't the foggiest idea of what you mean."

"Foggiest idea. Try as I may. That's great stuff, Mom."

Lina could only blink at this and feel immensely, heavily tired. "I don't know what you mean. Please explain it to me, Eli."

"You always come to just the right floor. Not the one above or below, and you stop just right, perfect level."

"I don't know what you're referring to, but is that a complaint?"

"You come right exactly to where I am."

"Like coming to court today, ready to bail you out?"

Eli shook his head no. "And you didn't need to."

"We didn't know that in advance. Anything might have happened. I came, I was here, I was ready. And you're complaining about that? I should have let them lock you up?"

"Why do you make everything so hard to say?"

"You called me and asked me to come. You asked me and I came as quickly as I could."

"Right to where I am, level, so when you talk down to me you hope I won't notice that you're talking down to me, but you are."

Could you have a splitting headache without the headache part? "No," she said, "I still don't know what you mean." The elevator idea didn't sound like Eli and Lina wondered if Sukey had coached Eli on it so she could keep her own trap shut. Lina hated the bargain-basement mother-of-pearl tabletop in this kitchenette, the aluminum ridges binding its sides, the cramped angled ceiling, the way the house was set so that not much sunlight got in the narrow windows that needed cleaning and the lights weren't on.

"Maybe it's something you do with your patients, I'm sorry your *clients*, Mom, but you can't do it with me anymore. I can see the buttons and I know when the door's about to close and what floor you want me to go to."

Lina tried to swallow down and stomach the enormity of the offensiveness, the most appalling part of which was that maybe they had her dead to rights. "Do I really do that? Is that what I do?"

Eli was kind enough to shrug and say nothing further, but Lina watched Sukey forming the statement, could see her take some rehearsed perception and reframe it toward the newmade context and Lina wished, oh wished, that Sukey wouldn't come out with the probably unanswerable banality, but Lina was sure she would, and paused to listen, wishing she could replay for Sukey her heroic crashing like a madwoman through the courtroom to wrap her arms around Eli before he could slug the bailiffs, but Sukey pronounced the words to her *mother-in-law*: "You're so controlling, Mrs. Chase."

Despite the solid thunk of failure as the vault swung shut Lina had to say it, "Please just *think* about coming up to Washington, to the island."

They were so purely beautiful, these two, in their fair young skins, the third one inside Sukey spinning hers as Eli once spun himself together out of Lina-stuff inside Lina, and they had closed themselves against her.

8

When Poholek got home Marion was at her new default position, sitting in front of some crime show on television with a drink going, not her first, a vodka-something because there was the jughandled tank of Smirnoff on the coffee table next to a bowl of melting ice and a big plastic bottle of tonic at her feet. Looked like she was out of lime now, because there were a couple of squozen rinds on the ovular rag carpet. She looked washed out, pale blond going grey and her features sliding slack when once upon a time … No point in stirring those ashes, Bob thought.

"Honey, I'm home," she told him.

"I know it."

Marion clicked the sound off in case they had anything to say to each other. In the beginning theirs had been a marriage of opposites attract, the college liberal intellectual, the real-world cop starring as life without varnish, and the electricity of the differences had kept them zazzed for the better part of twenty years. They had learned a lot from each other until they didn't.

Onscreen a sweaty perp was being interrogated by two cops, a TV show or a movie, Bob couldn't tell. The cops and the perp were doing it wrong, unreal. He'd served five years on the big-city Oakland force before moving up here and he knew.

"Do you think they're going to beat him up, Bob?" Marion asked him, so she was the cop now and he was the perp. "Is that what you would do?"

"You know I don't do that kind of thing, Mar," he told her.

"Except when Mexicans come to town and move into an empty house."

"Who told you that? Who the fuck told you that?"

"It's different," Marion said, not looking at him, "when it's Mexicans."

"We didn't know if they were dishwashers or that was their cover and they were fronting for a cartel. And we had to find out. We have to tolerate the local fucking dealers but we can't have Mexicans leaving post-it notes on corpses all over the burg. You got to stop that before it starts. They were stealing electricity from the mainline."

"So you brought a sledge hammer and used it on a man's hand."

"It wasn't supposed to happen that way. Young guy on the squad got excited … Who the fuck told you? I want to know who told you."

"I heard it was you with the hammer."

"Who told you that?"

"You're supposed to say no it wasn't." Marion gazed straight aheadish and waved a hand in the air.

"No it wasn't and they were stealing electric from the mainline and maybe posing at Magnolia's and the Belvedere and could have been fronting for the cartel."

"So no more knuckles for them."

Bob froze for a moment in which he believed she was fucking someone on the force and he'd told her something but then Bob dismissed it. She wasn't interested anymore and she wasn't that interesting anymore either. But she was good at hurting him with the defeat of his life where it hurt him most. But where was that exactly? Was it indoors here or was it out there in the world?

Marion took a long sip of her melted vodka tonic and nodded at the television. "I think they're going to start beating up that poor little guy any minute. Do people still use rubber hoses or phone books or is it all from the hardware store? Hammers, saws."

"You used to be a lot subtler with your punches, babe," Bob told her.

"You're not paying attention so I have to turn up the volume. Just in case there's something left in there listening. Some people would say old Bob is gone, but I think there's still," she took another drink of her drink, "*hope* may be too strong a word for it, but whatever it is," waving a limp celebratory finger alongside her head, "I haven't given up on it yet."

Doesn't look that way from here, Poholek didn't say out loud because what for.

He went into another room and sat down. It was the bedroom, on the bed, maybe a bad choice but at least she didn't follow him in there to arrest him at the scene of the crime. The spark wasn't what it used to be even before they didn't have to cut her breast off for the cancer, just take a couple of pieces out, but when Marion finished with the rays and chemo it was pretty much over. Not just that she lost her looks, which came later. She said she didn't own her body anymore, it had been invaded and altered, she didn't know whose it was now and she couldn't put her name on it or will it to do things. Three years of this. And he had managed their situation well, almost no screams and accusations, not a single slap either way, and if she had to drink to medicate herself that would have to be a possible adjustment because the psych people hadn't turned the trick.

Not fixable till retirement, when if he didn't take the head of security job with Raleigh they could travel and see beautiful places to get her some back from what she'd lost. Which he worried was a pipe dream, a lie he told himself. Or he could split off a piece of his pension and they could go their ways. He owed her that much. His life, the way he'd built it, without her, would have been a no man's land. She had filled it while she could.

She came to the bedroom door, leaning in it with the light behind her like something from a movie, and his scariest thought was that sometimes she was trying to bait him so he'd put her out of her misery.

Before she could start in Bob spoke up, "Would you make me one of those you're having, and then we can watch the picture together and I'll send out for dinner?"

Magnolia's sent enough ribs for four people with cornbread, blackeyed peas, yams and collards and Bob ate a lot because it soaked up the vodka he'd been keeping pace with Marion on. She didn't eat enough, but sharing drinks did get them laughing during dinner, about the time trout fishing with Jan when Bob had finally taught the kid how to use the flyrod right and he caught this big trout but then fell into the stream. They'd made a party out of it, jumping in with their clothes on as if to save Jan from drowning. What a day.

"The best thing, Bob, you were always so anal with your gear but you didn't mind that everything was in the drink! You let it happen. Amazing."

"You're right, I just let it go."

"Because usually you're such an asshole."

And the happy story had another knife in it, since Jan made UC Davis but was doing mediocre and Bob had his suspicions as to Jan's personal habits there. Keep it up and he might pull Jan out of there from those people, straighten him up at home or in a boot camp and if he wouldn't enlist in the armed forces get him a job with the Eureka force since there wasn't anything else around and Bob could keep an eye on him.

"And your fishing gear wasn't damaged, Bob. You got it all clean and safe, right, see?"

Sometimes he wondered if she had another cancer coming, which'd be one way out, if that was what she was hoping for deep down, to finish this. He watched her getting tired at the table till she said she would take a little nap if he didn't mind and went off.

"Don't worry, I'll clean up," he said over his shoulder as she wandered through the bedroom doorway.

Everything would keep okay except the greens which would go soggy and you could reheat the ribs in the oven if you laid them in a rack and put just a little water and maybe a dash of bourbon in the bottom of the roasting pan, for the fumes.

He washed the plates and stowed the food in the fridge except the cornbread. He put a dish towel on top of that and poured himself a Maker's Mark. Checked his watch: too late to call Burke in North Carolina but he had three cellphone numbers for Teddy Swift and even though he felt a heartburn coming and could've paused for Pepto he used his station mobile to leave pretty much the same message on all three: "I'm not out there looking for you, Ted, you can come on home now. Things got a little fucked up there but I'm not mad at you and we got another go-round, I'm ready to offer you a chance if you're up for it, you could even outsmart me and win or I could win or we'd both do okay. Give me some other people and you can go scot-free. Tobacco's got your property fenced in but there's a way you can get your goods back. Won't guarantee I won't try to catch you at it but here's your out. Eli Chase can take a fall for all I care, he was totally ready to turn on you, but what'd make me all the way happy is you get me Franklin, Windell and Roger Dodger, two out of three'll do and I'll show you how to do it. Come on home, and if you got balls enough to stay a free man come down the station and talk to me. Come on in and talk to poppa."

Teddy picked up the middle of the last call. "Why should I trust you one damn inch," was his opener.

"Because if you don't I'll have you do state time for the Raleigh patch and that's a promise. How can I put this."

"Play ball with me or else?"

"Works for me. Come in tomorrow afternoon the latest."

"Nah. I like it where I am."

"Try not to be tardy, Ted, tomorrow's the last day before I shut the door on you. Batter up."

After the cramp-roofed enclosure of Eli's Eureka, Lina drove north on the Interstate toward Oregon beneath a high evening sky swept clear of cloud, still bright above earth's lengthening shades. A scattering of drivers had turned on their headlights in the coppered underglow so they wouldn't forget to do it later and Lina joined the pack, why not. The highway air was vile with motorbreath so she had the windows shut, AC and filtration humming and the Gobbi/Karajan *Falstaff* on although, preoccupied, she barely heard it and wasn't feeling very jolly. Lina enjoyed driving even if her new red Ford didn't have that overbuilt Mercedes purr, the cruise control was set at seventy, level with the traffic, but she was tilting lousy.

Maybe what she should have done was say goodbye to Eli and Sukey, drive off but take a room at the Victorian and think about picking up on that discreet call-me gesture—forked fist, thumb at his ear and pinkie at his lips even though phones these days were mostly small flat things—Marcus Dobbs had flashed her on her way out of court with Eli. Hotel room and Hello Marcus, let's meet for dinner, thank you for your help today and let's discuss the case.

"Hello, Marcus?" Lina spoke airily to the landscape beyond the windshield. "I was already on the road home when it occurred to me …" She sounded as transparent as a schoolgirl and she reconsidered.

Such a call would be completely unambiguous and not only cast her as the older woman making an unmistakable assignation, but as an older white woman making a call that cast him as a young black stud ripe for service, and as beautiful a man as Marcus was, sharp and humorous and possibly even talented with quartets, she had never been built for quick starts, still less one-nighters on the way out of town—brass tacks, sticky sheets, what's the time, I really must go, an insult to them both in their essentials.

"Marcus," she said throatily, then made several faces to rub the sound of her voice away. It sounded like the growing heat in her … loins, let's call them.

Although to tell the truth she felt like it, yes she did, and even now, sixty miles up the highway, there was time enough to turn around, go back and get a room then make the call, so famished and desperate a move that whatever sweetness followed would end up in the dirt. She felt low enough, or almost low enough, to try it.

But that wasn't the real source of feeling so lowdown, it was a daydream, an attempt at a connection to distract her from Eli and Sukey's gobsmacking unkindness to her, and beneath that Eli's damnfool vulnerability in an increasingly sinister Eureka—not just a matter of her battered feelings but possible life and death and prison for him. How many people were aiming at her flesh and blood? Two she knew of for sure and Teddy a probable third, but the first two were scary enough, and Eli's perfect blindness to present danger was all too familiar from his adolescence on. He wasn't stupid, he just didn't have the kit.

Flesh of my flesh with a portion of my soul alive in him. According to some accounts she almost could believe in, she and Eli had agreed to this connection before the curtain went up: two timeless individuations shaking hands, okay, let's play these roles when we get there. May be. Whatever was ultimately real or not, the threat to Eli made her want to scream out loud, and it felt as if the car was rushing her toward a vortex of loss poised on a horizon dark enough to swallow her, headlights and all.

Turn the car around, get a room and call Marcus. Save me, Mister Man.

"Marcus, I thought I'd give you a call to ask if you might …" It was the worst of her three attempts, with the desperate throb blatantly audible.

Lina turned off *Falstaff* because even though it was a comedy it partook of the Italian melodrama that was still too much a part of her despite all her training. She'd been holding steady since Nelson's death but just this minute felt the possible crumbling of her defenses, her psychological expertise, the battlements she knew how to man and armor but had learned as she grew older not to trust in any ultimate sense, in part because Buddhist practice had brought her to a more substantial accommodation with the radical impermanence of every mortal trace and thought, against which emptiness all defense was silly and unskillful pretension. But it wasn't a concept or a meditative state now, it was real and a threat, it was life in the raw and she was losing the empowering angle of insight she was supposed to possess.

Out here in the bareness, the *shunyata*, she wished compassion for herself as she would for any other living creature caught in partial light and unstoppable time.

She had driven blindly through a whirl of thought for the last fifteen minutes hardly seeing a thing, not the road, not the other cars, and as she came awake Lina also realized that she had not consciously noted the transition outside but it was almost full dark now with a half moon rising in the east like a railroad lantern held just atop the low hills on her right.

There was a time of early Buddhist non-attachment when everything looked simple enough to see in this conceptual-meditative frame and she'd thought of Eli, all right, I can't do anything, can't save him, if I lose him, if he dies, that's how it is, I accept it. At the moment of the thought it had been so convincing, Lina believed, that she hadn't quite suspected that her brandname newfound stoicism wasn't real, and would thaw and run at second blush.

She remembered the fierce maternal deathgrip she'd laid on him in court that afternoon. There you are, that's you.

"Sorry Marcus, just calling to say that I won't be calling …"

The car was heading north toward home, and to shake the alternative from her body Lina shivered her head and limbs where she sat, got rid of most of it but still had to stretch her mouth open and howl at the top of her lungs in order to see straight ahead with any clarity.

Tony didn't like doing therapy-consultations, preferring to repose in the suprapersonal stability of the dharma, but when she got home she'd phone him, ask for help, and make clear that this time she really needed his guidance and it wasn't about meditation technique or any of that, she had problems and they were personal and she needed a hand.

At the Belvedere they ordered surf and turf, lobster fra diavolo for Betty-June and for him prime rib *saignant*, blood rare just short of purple, and although she was one of the most refined-looking women he had fucked at least since France, she put her wild-woman look on at the table in upscale public Zowie, little black dress plus string of pearls across her elegant collarbones as she ate and it nearly freaked him out to see her sucking down a curve of claw-meat grinning wickedly, tossing her head so her hair flew, the woman high on tangling with a danger-man and letting loose that low throaty laugh of hers, too loud and sexy for in public, drawing the notice of the dinner crowd though he wasn't sure she picked that up or cared, even though she owned a local business and needed to sell things to these people who if they knew less than shit about art might-could know how to read a woman losing her *pudeur* and a lot else along with it. It occurred to Pitch that maybe he had taken her too far too fast. Or even that because of him she was dosing herself with he couldn't tell what yet.

"People are looking at you," he told her.

"Let them," she laughed. "I'm out with my outlaw and enjoying it."

"I think you should cool it."

"I think it's hilarious I can make you nervous. In public. It's impossible in private but in public you're full of secrets you want to protect. Makes you funny. You could use more funny."

"What are you high on? You haven't had that much wine. What are you on?"

"Maybe I had to nerve myself up to go out with you. God knows there isn't much in life I have to nerve myself up for anymore, but you qualify. You should consider it a compliment."

"You're making me nervous."

"I get my kicks where I can find them," she said.

That was at dinner but now back at his place he was a lot more interested in what her newborn wildness would let him get away with, starting with her peaches let me shake your tree.

Pitch's bedroom was a turret room with six windows up a wrought-iron spiral staircase from the rest of the second-floor apartment—good isolation, people couldn't hear much noise—in a gingerbread house, rent paid by the company, painted lilac with blue trim and a slated grey roof in a quiet part of town, and the special feature of her breasts, medium-small perfects holding up very well and firm but not too firm, were her nipples which were pinkish even though she was black-haired and not young and were always, even when unstimulated, pretty much erect, their tops flat and textured like little corks and sensitive to his leastmost tongue or touch, but her special feature overall, in the wavery light of two fat white floorstood candles, on a long lean body something like a dancer's though the musculature less exacting, she did yoga, was the blueblood network of veins, so close beneath the pale skin you'd think so thin you could sip blood from them with a touch of your tongue if you wanted: intricate fatal veinwork, blue conduits up under her jaw even into her cheeks, a web that blended beauty with a mortality so obvious the kick was new to him, her body an exquisite momentary thing bent beneath him now, arched between this living moment and almost corpseness. This appealed to him. He lowered his mouth and sucked, then moved over and licked the other nipple across its top, texture against texture and her tune spun upward, twisting stranger though not deeper, up there vocally, more human and female, less animal than the other lower chugging thing he'd also moved her into. It was nice he could bring in other notes and harmonies.

They'd been going at it, bareback with an IUD since the blood-tests came up fine last month, for maybe half an hour now and he had his cock up her cunt and two fingers he'd juiced from her cunt up her ass working in a circle, and this had taken her from the croon of normal fucking into harsher sawtooth belly-deep breath, hoarse coming in and going out so that she started sounding like her real name, not Betty-June but Anne Dujardin, donkey from the garden, *heee*-haaw, *heee*-haw, which was kind of embarrassing so he gave her his tongue to suck and she wound her own tongue greedily around it. When after a while he took it out and stuffed it in her ear to fog her schoolgirl mind, she had switched to a kind of feline uvular gargle, a *ghghghhgghhh* he'd never heard from her before and he loved it because it was so graceless, his two fingers up her ass pulling that generative second-chakra energy down to shake her at the root not doing her any favors, really, since that kind of chi didn't belong there even if she didn't know it, even with all her yoga, but it got her rocking deeper than she'd ever gone with anyone ever, he'd bet. He had her almost completely commanded now.

Pitch kept working it, his pace medium slow, steady, sliding cock and circling fingers, his cock rubbing against his fingers through the thin slick membraneous flesh between cunt and ass that was driving her away from here into strange noises and who knew what in her head and her body shaking, but he was afraid she'd think that the feel of his own cock against his fingers through her flesh was what turned him on and since he wanted to keep the power on her he got his thumb inside her cunt to work the membrane between fingers and thumb and moved his cock to the roof of her cunt and if he got her body angled juuussst right then pushed her hips down, up top he'd be set almost perfect to give her G some nice lonnnnng rubs full stretch with that thing God gave him—there it was, she began to shake all over, body arching rigid, going, going, almost gone, so it was time to pull her back from la-la, hooooo, *ghghghhh*, *haaaw*, wherever.

He'd been training her, been bringing her along and opening her up one stage at a time and now they were getting near her limit and she was over it, gone from him, therefore … The first time he started hurting her it was spread her arms wide with his hands then dig both his thumbtips hard into the *mons veneris* in the drumsticks of her thumbs until it hurt her bad enough so he watched her head and face come up, pure shock heading for anger, so he eased that off and kept fucking her and went back to working her ass until her eyes started to roll and he recrucified her and dug his thumbs in again, and gradually she got it: the two-hole fucking— he never put his dick in the back door, didn't like the feel of it, made him think cloaca—taking her out of this world then the pain bringing her right back into it, the combination stronger than either, two worlds fused together in her till they broke her open, which is what he was looking for.

Thumbwork wasn't enough anymore of course, they'd moved on, you had to keep it building and it was a matter, really, of logistics. There she was, hoarse breathing, mouth open and bared teeth clacking as she bit the air. He thought she was too vain of her features to take slaps in the face, much less the punches he'd landed on other women, so with his unsoiled left hand he found a soft spot on the right side of her abdomen, wrapped his fourfingers into her back and sunk his thumb into her like a claw, digging into major organ-protective nerve country with the thumb pressuring her liver and fingers behind getting at her kidney, just a little, and within instants there they were again face to face eyes open to each other in consuming alchemical fire, he watched her eyes as her breath stopped cold with the shock and pain and she screamed a little to get her release but she knew what she was doing, knew the way of it by now and held most of that scream inside, constricted, veins popping, sweat on her forehead, eyes wide on his, she was all the way away and also right here, pain and his strong hand holding her in the balance, not the rolling-eyes-and-gone look now but her entire soul on fire, in the fire, he watched her eyes and face and saw that she got it, she got it, she got it and was with him there, right there. Next thing on the menu now that she understood the principle of the thing, but not tonight, he'd start strangling her on and off to bring on vaginal convulsions and punch her in that slender little archframed belly she was vain about, solar plexus, punch her breath right out of her and see how she dealt with that.

The sex had gotten where he wanted it: they weren't even people anymore. *Gaté, gaté*, they had gone beyond, *parasam gaté*.

He held her there hissing and writhing for as long as he thought wise, hurting her a little worse to keep her there while the rest of her went away, then finally took his pincer hand out of her rear and the left one off her belly to go into long slow simple fucking so she settled into cooing like a soul relieved, the sweetness of two fellow beings who'd gone out and now'd come back. See, the fire was the water was the fire, the fire and water and mud and shit of their human origin, they had passed through it together, and the relief for him was the news, again, as he had his privileged moment of seeing it before life closed back in on him, that he had always been a pure spirit and he had always ever only loved and only did it in the world's absolutely intensest way, and that knowledge and experience was present between the two of them right here and now in this.

When he saw that he wasn't going to come, that he was running too deep a tantric continuity for it to reach him over a distance he didn't want to travel now, it was either she could suck him off or he'd take a break and come back for seconds, or on the other hand could go pure and retain the prana for himself, though he wasn't sure he felt like that tonight.

When he slowed, stopped, and began to withdraw she kind of sighed and said in a kind of human voice, "Ohh you didn't even come yet," and put her hand around his thing but he took it off him. "You don't want me to get you off?"

"Get me off?" It was amazing how little they understood, even when they'd been through it a little, which is why they were poor dumb Betty-

Junes and weren't him. They still thought the world hung from the fatal cliff of some impoverished strictly momentary *gasm*. This when he'd just given her a continuous rolling one for half an hour or so, with short breaks for pain, and now we were human again and talking normal just the way we did before. Still, "What'd you think that was?" he had to tell her. He slid off and lay down sideways. "That was plenty good enough. In fact a tiny liddle bit better than good, wun't you say?" He almost wanted to tell her that she'd been amazing to watch but he couldn't, wouldn't, that'd give away too much, to call her amazing. "You were a lightshow, babe," was as far as he could go, and even that was further than he wanted.

"Uh huh?"

"And I ain't done either. Just want to take a break before we go back in and get some more of the feast."

That throaty laugh of hers again, mouth open and throat working like a songbird's, but she looked drunk. Which reminded him, but he let it wait a minute before mentioning it.

"You know," he said, "tonight's our best so far and we ain't finished but," and started trying to tell her, it wasn't easy, about her behavior at the restaurant. "It's fine in here but out in public people are looking at you, the way you act."

She had a different laugh for him this time, not the throaty one but with an edge, some mockery in it. Hickory hockery mockery dock.

"I'm only lookin' out for your interests," he said.

"Really," she had to get her breath. "It's a little tough to believe it of you, Pitch, and even a little charming, but it's kind of funny to find a corner of your character where you're a more than a bit of, well, a *prude*." That edgy laugh again, it wasn't funny, it was mean. He might have to hit her, without all the buildup rigamarole.

"Prude?" he said. "I think we might be in need of another counter-demonstration here."

"Don't get upset, Kennis, it's kind of touching, in a way."

He got up from the low bed and stood above her in the semi-dark and candleflame. "I'm gonna take a leak and wash your asshole off my fingers so you can suck 'em when I come back and kiss your titties, *âne*," and as he headed for the stairs she was laughing a third, more friendly laugh this time and was safe again for now.

"Ever the gentleman," she said, still laughing, as he started down.

This was getting about as good as it gets, but the bad part was that pretty soon next up—she didn't see it yet but he did and she would— she'd realize how degraded her position was, how degraded she was in her position, rolling and moaning, turning on the spit over the coals and can't tell sex from hurt till she was truly lost, not just in hot nighttime episodes but full time and for real, even out in daily daylight, big surprise, she hadn't known it wasn't just for burning heats racing to the edge and over but getting permanent in her, and once she saw that she might hang in there for a time but ultimately in not too long she'd end it. He'd never found a woman who'd go all the way there with him and he knew this wasn't Her again. He'd almost got there with a man down in Nica, that was a wild time but it broke that man and damn near broke me and he died, besides which I'm not that way, only down there that time it happened to work, and hard, very hard. Sad to say, the womenfolk, even the real ones, not just Betty-Junes but even the real ones always did it, go so far but always encountered that last little fucking limit, always stopped short of going beyond dimensions, absolutely nowhere and all the way in the truth of it. Then they quit and leave me, every time.

Sukey got up to puke around three in the morning and when she came back to bed smelling of sweat and toothpaste they lay on their backs side by side looking up through the ceiling at whatever the dark world above them was holding ready.

"You think she might be right?" Eli asked her, hearing his voice waver as he picked up the conversation they'd had before turning their backs to each other and twitching off to sleep.

"She could be," Sukey said.

"You understand how hard it'd be for me to live up there?"

"I think so."

"Not only her but the people who've known me forever the wrong way, all the old places, the whole old scene."

"I get that, but she might be right about how dangerous Eureka is right now."

"She'd make me get a *job*, and it'd be a shit job not enough to keep us. We'd be completely dependent on her for everything. That's the way she does her thing."

"And there's a lot she wouldn't let you do."

"Yah. She'd use it."

"But that might not be so terrible, Eli."

"You sounded like her right there. It might be fucking awful, a real dead end, just dead, nothing doing, totally, for us both." Specially if she starts getting *you* to sound like *her* more, he did not say. Which, he realized it, which definitely she will, if she goes under Mom's influence for any length of time.

He expected Sukey to say something for or against Seattle, it didn't matter which, just the sound of her voice would do, her voice rubbing against his voice in the air, the sound more than anything they said together, the comfort of it, but it wasn't there, she didn't say anything and it was quiet.

"How's this," he said. "I'll hang back a few days, see what happens and who does what, Poholek, Teddy, that tobacco guy I saw at the police station. If it's bad, maybe we could go up there and live on the island, but only for a *little* while."

"Is there any way we could do it not on your mother's property?"

"She won't give us money we could rent another place with. Not right away, not until, you know, you have, we have, the baby." Why was it so hard to talk sometimes when other times he could talk just fine? "She might help us get started, then, or, like, just before that all happens, but not until." It sounded so unreal, actual baby actually coming, his.

"Eli?"

"Yah."

"Do you have any idea, is there any way you … This is happening in *my own body*, my whole *me* is changed. I mean it's natural and all and in some way I already know how to do it but it's freaky when your own body is being changed because there's no distance and it's *you*. Not to mention my whole future out of my hands for years and years, but the strangeness of the body thing. Is there some way you can understand that?"

Eli waited before speaking, wondering if this was smart or completely dumb and he'd get pounced on. But it was real and it was all he had, so: "One time when I was sixteen I got drunk and fell off the roof of a friend's house and broke my arm …"

"Eli …"

"No, listen, let me finish. The thing was, the way I fell I was going to land on my head and probably get killed, because it was the driveway, it was paved and I was falling from third floor level pretty much head first, but drunk as I was everything slowed down and *as I was falling* my mind got incredibly clear and somehow I had the time to twist my body so my head was away and my left arm was stuck up in front. I heard the crack when I landed and I knew my arm was broken, but the thing was that while I was on the way down and after I hit I was calm and knew that this was it, I could die but I had that clear moment to choose in and there was enough time, like someone just stretched the time and gave it to me and I made the change and fell on my arm and not my head."

The room was quiet again. Is that what they meant by Pregnant Pause?

"And my arm was broken and there was blood spreading under the skin there but it didn't stick through my skin, so it wasn't compound, which was good."

"Um."

"All right, maybe it's kind of off-track, but there's something in it, I had my life all together in one spot, yes or no, in a second, you know? It may sound dumb to you, Sue, but it's not, and it's what I've got to understand what you're going through with. That's what I've got that kind of applies."

"Okay. Thank you."

"For trying?"

"Uh huh. But I also mean it."

Quiet again, but neither of them turning over on one side to go to back sleep yet, or the other way to face each other and you know what.

"I think I might pay a call on Franklin."

"Who you should've been working for already," Sukey said, not vague now.

"Well, Teddy got me started—"

"And he almost got you finished." Sukey thought about what it meant to be protected. There hadn't been much of that since she'd left the not-so-great plains and her nightmare of a family for the wild west coast and sometimes it was there in Eli's voice and the warmth and strength of his body and his arms around her and sometimes it wasn't and it scared her shitless, like all the lights in the world could be turned off on her while a wind outside was rising. When Eli was good he was the kindest man she'd ever known. But the facts: here she was, a kid with a kid on the way and her lifelove a half crazy manchild in the dope business with people after him and it was getting hard to find the words and talk to him. "Maybe … at least your mom's heart's in the right place and she really loves you."

"I can't live there," he said and turned over and away. "It'll kill me."

"Right. I know, I know."

Two

Fire on the Mountain:
Perseverance brings good fortune
To the Wanderer.

—*I Ching*

1

ELI HAD GOOD DAYS and bad ones. Sometimes the world had too many things in it to keep track of and it swung out of focus, but today was one of his strong clear ones and if he knew how and why he'd bottle it and take a drink when he needed to make it happen. He felt like a walking tower, not because he was six foot whatever and strong but because partway he was the human Eli everyone knew and saw and could talk about or to but also he was this larger uncontrollable thing everyone was afraid would break loose because he loved it, and sometimes had a brilliance on top of it sweeping the darkness like a lighthouse but he had learned to listen when people ganged up to tell him he didn't have that part of himself together and that it damaged him and could hurt people outside him too. And sometimes, though not lately, he had seen the damage. Which was fucked up, that he couldn't get to the most important part of himself without crashing into the wall that told him You've messed up your chance one more time, you have to stop. These people weren't kidding him or working up a bad story, they cared about him, they said they really cared and they did care and even loved him. Which didn't mean it made everything suddenly easy or fixed it. He was a power in the world but he wasn't running it, it was running him, unless he didn't let it.

Sometimes he knew he wasn't anyone at all, just a house with people walking through and he was pieced out as all the people. Faces appeared and disappeared in the stream of day and night according to no schedule he could work out, so he was supposed to be responsible for all this? Or, an old idea he'd had sometimes in his teens when the trouble started, he was an angel who wasn't supposed to be born as a person but here he was, a buracractic filing error he had to live out best he could.

He'd felt the walking tower lighthouse thing as he went around town the last few days, worried about toppling into the little storefronts on the street like cheap movie sets but he had to watch out for them, he'd learned to control it enough not to break them and the weirdness was just some feeling left over from being in court. That had been hell but he was back in the world now, a little unsteady but definitely there.

They told him it wasn't bodily dysnormia but something different they didn't have a name for. Well, he didn't either.

He had to be watchful because when you came down to it he knew he wanted to let it loose, that was his condition, or it wanted to let itself loose and it wasn't him, be careful with alcohol first off because of Sukey, but a little weed was all right because Sukey didn't care too much about it and Mom wouldn't know up in Seattle, but what no one understood is that even without stuff, the power was poking his outline from inside with that energy he couldn't help loving, he'd had therapy but was never really ever rid of it and one of those fuckers said he'd never be. Actually they were wrong about that. He was going to get it right but he didn't know, yet, when that would happen for him.

It'd be best to lay back and chill for a week but Teddy wasn't gonna be paying him anything, Eli didn't even know if Teddy was back, Teddy wasn't answering phonecalls and Eli figured it wouldn't be very cool to go up to his house and talk to him if he was there, Teddy might go batshit on him before Eli could knock him out. So Eli'd been walking around town vibing out the territory like a water-finding rod even though he already knew the place, waiting for the moment to get inserted—he could be superstitious, waiting for the moment that said yes, go, now, it's time—and there were two people he wanted to see and he decided Kennis Pitcher at Muhrad Inc. first because it was legal work, on the books even, and he'd drop in on Franklin later. Roger Dodger and Windell could take a leak. They weren't much.

On the phone Mr. Pitcher had said Eli, who still had his PxP business card but had lost the hankie, hey you can come by anytime, but when he started heading to Pitcher's office Eli had a bad feeling, so maybe the moment wasn't right, or could be it was a bad idea, so he took a walk in that part of town, thinking he might run into Pitcher, which would take care of the problem out of his hands, but didn't see him and had to wait for the better feeling to come around again and say Yah, let's do it.

The landing was a few two-lane switchbacks down through trees from Lina's island doorstep then a short ferry ride across the placid water, the snowmass of Mount Rainier hanging sky high in azure southeast in a dry summer for so wet a part of the country. Lina got out of her car and walked to the rounded bow and leaned on a bollard to watch the water come dark and unruffled as a lake, she realized, because that's how she wanted to see time coming at her now and it wasn't, so she sat there and forgot to watch the water until the horn blew and she got back in her car to wait for the ramp to come down and the drive from Fauntleroy to Gig Harbor.

Gig Harbor still looked like a picturesque fishing village from some angles, white clinker hulls and a forest of masts metronoming in the cove, but was more of a posh Tacoma suburb now, since the second bridge to the city was built and opened five years back. It wasn't her habit to linger in the tourist traps, though sometimes she'd break for a dozen local oysters and a cold glass at the Coastal on the way back if the visit had been rough. The women's prison, something they didn't show you on the postcards, was a five-minute drive up the peninsula from the harbor, and today she took the curves with more than usual on her mind: still depressed three days back from California, she had to remind herself in a dire internal voice to give Nikki Jackson her full attention before getting into anything else with her. By which she meant: information.

Nikki was serving her sixth year of a statutory twenty for being stupid: two old falls for her heroin habit leading to the fatal third in which, hooked up one more time to a bad man with a stash, she was along for the ride—unknowingly she said and Lina mostly believed her because by then Nikki probably wasn't knowing much—that turned into the armed robbery of a convenience store with her alongside the guy holding the gun and getting his picture taken. Armed robbery, at least Lingo hadn't shot and killed the man, only got him in the shoulder. The judge's hands were tied, went the phrase.

But Nikki had been exemplary inside what was not a bad facility, considering, a lowbuilt rambling modern installation with less than eight hundred in the general pop where the flagship program was Pet Partnership and where Nikki had graduated last year from medium security to low, completed her GED, become more than just computer literate and an expert ornamental gardener and landscapist and also, yes, got friendly with some of Gig Harbor's nicest families' golden retrievers and chocolate Labradors, and having hit rock bottom and gone twelve-step had genuinely rehabilitated herself according to rules she would know how to follow later. Nikki also loved babysitting any one, you name it, of the eleven little babies behind bars with their moms and the babies liked her too. Superintendent Parnell might even recommend her for limited work-release soon and had in fact put her weight behind Nikki's appeal currently crawling half-crippled through the back offices of the court system but not dead yet, to get her work-release for a weekend or two at least, then see.

Lina was counselling her as part of her pro-bono docket and would testify for her in court if it should come to that. Nikki was deeply serious about what it would take to get out, and Lina had bonded with her on that project.

Not too many cars in the lot today, apparently mostly staff, so Lina parked closer than usual to the low buildings that fronted the place and gave nothing away and said high school more than state pokey. Heading for the entrance she squared her shoulders and shucked off her gloominess to put her gameday face on, good cheer and glad to see each individual one of you as she passed through security, gate, wand, a perfunctory pat-down since they knew her, Hi Patricia how's the backache and what mad thing did you do to your hair, Shequonda Eveningstar?

Redheaded obese Belinda Getchek rotated in her chair behind the u-desk and phoned Lina's name ahead and told her that because of the low visitor volume today Nikki could meet her at the outdoor tables, you can go there and wait if you like, oh, a cup of tea with us? It can be arranged and there's a lemon in the fridge.

Tea and chat took enough time for Nikki to be waiting for her at one of the long picnic-looking plastic-top tables under the wavy fibreglass sunroof in the sideyard along with a scattering of visiting spouses and families, Nikki looking as serious as always, or was the word intent, long mid-brown face with prominent cheekbones and grey eyes that stood out in her face almost as if they were blue with a clarity that held you. She was thirty-five years old, hadn't lost her looks despite her life, cut her natural hair medium short and had made everything about her look tamped down and rigorously under control.

Lina sat on the bench across from her and Nikki beat her to the professional punch: "Tell me how it went with your son Eli in California."

"Oh Jesus," Lina said, and they were off. Lina knew how to work the levers, what to say and what not to say, but the reason things worked between her and Nikki was that when you came down to it they plain and simple liked each other, the sense of sisterhood wasn't pushed or faked, we all feel a little trapped in ourselves sometimes, with or without a wall and a razorwire underline. But Lina was determined not to be out-Lina'd by this woman, a manipulation to be resisted, first principles. "First tell me if there's any news about your appeal."

"The answer my friend is blowin' in the wind," said Nikki, grinning, rehearsed, but still didn't blink or take her eyes off Lina's. "Otherwise, you want me to do the list? I had a big argument with Georgia, almost a breakup but we're over it, anyway who's gonna break up in a place like this, if you got something you know to hold on to it unless you really stupid. Otherwise no big bumps, work-release is still hangin' there, no promises but it could happen soon they told me … Is that enough? Come on, tell me what happened with your Eli."

Since she'd already told Nikki on the phone about no bail and charges dropped, they were into detail that made telling the news a more demanding venture, with confidences that had to be kept from Nikki, more a matter of emotional tone than information, for the sake of their necessary professional interface. On the other hand, Lina did want practical advice from someone in the system and formerly in the life, so she wanted solid reportage even if it had to be paid for by confidences in exchange.

When Lina got through the story as well as she could, Nikki made sure to put on a still more serious look than when discussing her own case and told her, "Get your son the fuck out of that town, Doctor Chase. Whatever you have to do."

Lina lost her composure by giving Nikki a pass on calling her Doctor and by dropping her forehead into her own open hands. "I know, I know."

"I'm not gonna get started on scenarios, what the cop would do if if, what's the story with the dealer Eli was workin' for," Nikki said. "That'd be just one more conversation at the coffee station about some movie, you know what I mean? I'm no better at that than any other person, though if there's something I'm absolutely sure about it's watch out for the dealer."

"Teddy?"

"I know it's only smoke and not serious shit, but these people are always vicious bastards, which is why they do what they do as a profession. This guy knows Eli knows he gave Eli to the police, and you say he's from family money? Jesus keep me safe from that man."

"That could be," Lina said, thinking that with all due deference to lived experience this sounded like coffee-station movie stuff, and Nikki's clear grey eyes had begun to stare, a sign, could be, that she was into dramas of her own, "but that's not how it looked to me when I was there."

"The sheriff and the tobacco company guy, huh. Thing is, they're in positions, they have structures, whatever it is they might do it's likely to be slow, but Teddy? He knows Eli knows. This man is in scorpion mode." Nikki snapped her fingers almost violently at Lina but was careful to keep a distance from her face. Even so it got a warning hand from Shirley Benton in full security rig at her station by the double gates and turnstile. "Like *that*. Guy like him it don't take half a second to snap. Please first of all tell your son he sees him coming go the other way, don't wave back, don't get talkin' with him phone or in the face, nothing either way. That's for starters, and just generally get him out of there, he's the weakest piece on the board, you know that."

Nikki was supposed to be good at jailyard chess. Lina took a moment to look her in the face and nod while asking herself what's in play here.

"I think I'd like my cigarette now," Nikki said after a time. "You did remember to pack, didn't you?"

"Of little faith," said Lina, and dug for it in her bag.

It was a routine that they didn't talk while Nikki fed her habit as if she needed to keep a corner of lesser addiction alive and well, also pretend she didn't smoke during the week, but this week's smoking silence was a fraught little cube of air. Nikki's world was one of trouble-management and clarity of will 24/7 but this week Lina had brought her own requirements.

Midway through her Pall Mall, Nikki spoke up. "Tell you what really worries me. The move is on, everyone talkin' bout it and I'm scared to death they'll privatize this place before long. They'll triple us up in cells and convert activity rooms to dorms and feed us our own reprocessed shit for lunch. Make us work too, building some kinda shit for slave wages for the system. And personnel, the guards? Forget it, once the jail don't have to deal with the union and they can hire cheap it'll go all to hell in here."

"Is it happening?"

"Everyone expects it."

Just as everyone in Eureka expects pot to go legal any minute now. A coastal condition, everyone living on an edge of their own conception, a community of edges, a non-community of strictly personal cliffs and fears and falls. And of course The Big One always latent, possible, a Richter jackpot that would send us all sliding into the sea.

"Everyone expects the privatize including me, but I do not intend to spend my days worrying even though I'm worrying. Can't waste the time I have on that." Nikki looked down at her half-done cigarette. "Don't even want to finish this thing." Bittering her lips she stubbed out the remainder, then carefully field-stripped it and looked at Lina up from under a rucked forehead. "If it don't pay the rent I don't have the time to think about it. If it don't pay the rent I just leave it there. That's so simple even I can live it. Know what I mean by rent? Because everything on earth we only rent it."

"I haven't heard it said like that," Lina decided to say.

"Write it down, Lina. Write it down and tell them it's from me."

"Do you want to talk about your fight with Georgia?"

"Ar-gu-ment, not a fight, and no, not really."

"What was it about?"

"Nothing. Not enough. And so stupit it made me wonder if it's worth living with her like I am. I don't want to talk about it."

Lina eased her through a difficult fifteen minutes, hard stuff about Georgia and the rest of her personal life, unsparing, back to family system and early history, but at the end she asked Nikki to remind herself how the relationship with Georgia had helped sustain her, specific instances at specific times, and how even if her needs had changed that didn't mean that the relationship had to go. Nikki stayed in good-patient mode throughout, listening politely until Lina dropped it.

Then they took a breather, and Lina made early fidgets toward departure: car-keys, wristwatch, tucking a length of hair behind her ear. "Nikki, did you mind my asking you for advice about Eli?"

"Is that what you did? I didn't mind atall."

"Is it all right if I ask you again if anything changes, or even if it doesn't?"

"You know where to find me, phone privileges till 7 PM and anytime you want to take the ferry don't be a stranger, I'm right here."

"Thank you."

"Anything else you got on your mind just let it rip … No, what I want to say is, thank *you* for coming, you know that. You ready to go now? You can stay awhile if you want but I feel kind of talked out."

"I'm driving a little way south to visit my number one son."

"Ahh, nice. Family. Tell him Nikki Jackson says hi, because she does."

This guy Kennis Pitcher might be working for the big tobacco company but he was an exciting, edgy guy, and somehow that calmed the edges of Eli's world. Pitcher looked relaxed and cool in his office, leaning back in his desk chair with a glass of some fancy bourbon and a couple of ice cubes swirling in his hand but you knew the guy was wired inside. He'd offered Eli whiskey and though Eli had a bit of dry-mouth at the invitation he said no, and Pitcher didn't seem like the corporation type at all, even though Eli didn't know too many straight corporation types, you know, just generally, from some movies. Pitcher was explaining how Muhrad alias Raleigh Tobacco was going to sell Teddy's former crop to medical marijuana shops and clinics and Eli believed about half of it. This was so cool, especially if he'd be working for a legal corporation in case things got funny, which he thought they might.

He still felt self-conscious, though, about the colors Poholek had spread across his nose and eyes, the wine-color gone, dull blue and a sick yellow like bad boiled egg on his face. He kept trying not to put his hand up there to cover it, and kept finding his hand there, like trying to cover it.

"Aren't the medical weed suppliers mostly all little backyard and growroom operations?" Eli asked, to see if he could put a wrinkle in the guy. "Not that everybody pays attention to the ninety-nine plant legal limit exactly, but *small*."

"Sure, but this is natural capitalism," Pitcher said, "the way it goes, natural growth: the grocery store goes under to the supermarket, the little hardware store to Do-Rite or whatever and the beat goes on."

"But is that good?" Eli wished he had more of his dad's political talking points down for this, but he didn't.

"What it is, Eli, it's inevitable."

"But state law," said Eli, pushing to see where the reality line really was, "still puts the limit on how much you can grow legally, ninety-nine plants."

"We've applied for an exemption in view of how much legitimate taxable income we're going to bring to California, which has fucked itself for property taxes which is why it's going broke even though it's rich, and I think we're going to get it in time to harvest. Now … we'll have to hire some people to pick our patch. *Raleigh* has to. What was Teddy's usual practice?"

"People he knows, also hires some AIDS patients who need money for their meds."

"We wouldn't have to do that, of course."

"Teddy called it community outreach. And hiring those people was good, it helped them out. There were rules of course, like no open sores, no Karpotsi's thing."

"Sarcoma. But you can't just run an ad in the papers for those people."

"Teddy knows everyone personally. He's a startup, a buildup, over the years."

"But Teddy's out of the picture."

Was he? Eli wondered, and didn't say shit.

"If we were to hire up a harvest, Eli, could you run it? All of it, top to bottom, I'd supervise and check you out, of course, but hire and fire, transport, logistics, the works. Could you?"

"Sure," Eli said, wondering if he could do it without asking Teddy for tips, or hire any of Teddy's people without Teddy coming for him with a hatchet.

"And if we had to keep it quiet?"

"Why'd we keep it quiet? You're street legal, you got all the papers, right?"

"The application procedure for statewide medical sale just might not go through in time for harvest, the way it's coming up so fast this hot dry summer. It's complicated paperwork and a pain in the ass talking to stupid timeservers behind government desks, so we might have to do it on the quiet and store everything until the situation settles."

"You might have to do it on the quiet." Which started Eli thinking hmmm.

"And store it. It's perfectly legal for us to own the land and what's growing on it is growing on it, Eli, but until the papers come through and the last asshole affixes his stamp it's not legal for us to sell or even hold, so even if we did sell a little to a few established shops ... Let me be perfectly frank with you, I'm having some trouble with your pal Captain Bob Poholek. He could come down on us if he feels like it. He doesn't care that we're doing everything in our power to be legal. Plus the federals, they like to bust medical weed operations on their own whack, don't even have to consult the locals or the local legal situation, soo ... could you manage the logistics if we had to do this thing discreetly?"

"What are we doing here. You *are* the tobacco company, right?"

"Raleigh true and blue. I can show you my contract."

"Yeah but what are we doing really?"

"The legal scene is unsettled, it's chaotic, growing medical weed being legal in the state but transporting it never and selling it sometimes not, and all of it's against federal law, so it's an irregular situation and we might have to improvise a little."

"Mister Pitcher, Mister Pitcher," Eli said laughing. He was getting smart again, after days, since getting busted and feeling stupid. Things come and go and here it was again. He was getting smart.

"It all depends how things work out with the legal medical arrangement."

"But if it doesn't," Eli said, "we 'improvise.'"

"Like Charlie Parker."

"Who?"

"Old-time jazz musician."

"Like Satchmo Armstrong?"

"Not as old-time as that. So Eli, do you and I have an arrangement here?"

"I have to think about it, Mr. Pitcher."

"Sure. It's not as if I don't know you'll want to talk to Franklin Bass." How'd he know that? "I wouldn't bother with them other two. You do what you have to and come on back. Just remember I'm offering you legal work, everything on paper, salary on the books if that's the way you want it even though I'll be paying you out of my own pocket for the start."

"Because Raleigh has slow procedures," said Eli, still trying to lay a hand on Pitcher's slippery facties.

"Because Raleigh has slow procedures and it's a hot dry summer and time is on the march. But we'll have a notarized contract, you and Muhrad Inc., with a copy you can take home and frame, six hundred dollars a week plus benefits."

"You know I'd make ten times that being Farmer John for Teddy just on this one patch."

"Six a week, benefits, plus you don't get arrested and a hefty bonus after we sell it to the medicos, all of it in ink and sealed with wax if you want. Now, you sure you wouldn't like a taste of this Basil Dearden?"

"A small one," Eli allowed, his chest lurching for it and his saliva glands starting to water up either side at the back of his tongue.

Pitcher went to the cabinet. "I recommend a little water with it or one small ice cube to open the flavor."

"Ice," said Eli, his voice coming out a little croaky.

When he got the drink he swirled it the way Pitcher had, then took a sip. It was whiskey, he didn't know how much it costed but it was still whiskey, which was not a good taste in itself, just one you got habituated to. Then one second later it tasted really incredibly good to him.

"Like it?" Pitcher asked.

"Y'know, I know people doing so-called medical sales in weed dispensaries and clinics where people come in with a note they have restless leg syndrome and need to get high, they're good old heads playing the game and I could talk to them for you. They're licensed and everything, but you know it's only a cartoon."

"But they couldn't handle quantity, for instance Teddy's whole crop, could they? They're too legaled up and regalated to move."

"Enough of them together could."

"Well, that might be a little ad hoc, excuse me, too improvisational and piecemeal for Raleigh to do as a corporation, it's not how that scale of business works. It'd be too loud too. Too many people talking."

"So who the hell w'we be selling to exactly?" Eli had only about half-finished his glass of Basil Hoozis but it was getting to his head. Careful what you say now because this guy might be a snake full of shit. He sniffed the whiskey as if there might be something funny in it. "You can't deal that kind of quantity and be legal," Eli said. "Far as I know."

"That's my end, Eli. Raleigh is a global tobacco company investing in the future economy of California. Allowances will be made. I've been in the process of setting it up for some time now, but tell you what, go talk to the people you know, see if we can work with them too."

Eli felt a quick momentary belly-flutter, the startup of a fear that could take him whole and tilt the world and fuck him up, but he managed to push it down and out of sight this time. "Because it'd be all right if you, if we, um, 'improvise' a little," he said, his tongue thickening in the middle of that speech but basically okay.

"Another old jazz saying: it ain't whatcha do it's the way whatcha do it."

"I don't know what that means here."

"Think about it and it'll come to you," Pitcher said.

Eli sniffed the funny whiskey again, then drank it down because he was pretty sure it was what had helped him push the fear back down. "Can I have another one of these?"

It was a beautiful day for a ride in the country, Bob Poholek thought five hundred feet above the peaks and forest slopes of the Coastal Range, worldsworth of intricately figured Godmade green, sometimes swooping down for low sweeps over the treetops and early in the day a couple of landings to check acreages of weed almost ripe for harvest, up there with Major John Emigh, a man he'd said at least hello to for years, former United States Marine, glory be and luck of the draw, combined special agent and pilot with the DEA in the specially modified OH-6B a long shot better than the copters the county had, with a high-resolution belly camera, an extra pair of rotors for faster quieter running even if that didn't make it a black whirly of paranoid local legend, and best of all a configurable GPS screen on which Emigh had already corrected old weedpatch markings and added outlines to the map of the patches Poholek had scouted and shown him today. Just about everyone down there was growing something, but now they'd pretty much mapped every major patch of Humboldt County contraband, framed and charted and ready for printout and handout and let's do the op.

He and Major Emigh enjoyed excellent operational rapport even if Emigh played the protocol of rank a little heavy, and if the hippybillies down there heard them drone over and had phoned in some sense of their flightpath to KMUD in Garberville to broadcast as warnings between rock songs who gave a fuck? Especially a flying fuck. We are charting the major growers here, and we have got them down. They could have asked me a long time ago, but okay, that sucks but we're doing it now.

"I just want to be sure we're clear about the Raleigh patch," Poholek said into the orange foam mic-pod suspended in front of his mouth from the helmet as they flew.

"You know as far as the Agency is concerned," Emigh's crackling voice came to him through the inside earpieces, "it's still an illegal grow."

"Even though Raleigh legally owns the land, I understand that, but why piss them off when they're gonna invest so much money instate one day soon?"

"Once again, that's not the Agency's concern, Bob. Officially if California legalizes we don't give a shit, and unofficially we can burn up growth on all the land Philip Morris buys in the Valley if they plant shit till federal law says otherwise."

"Or Paraquat it."

"The Agency no longer uses Paraquat. Turns out it's a serious toxin."

"I know that. Figure of speech, I meant, and anyway you'd never notice brain damage on these people they're so far gone already."

"Seriously lethal lung and liver toxin, Bob."

"And a shame you can't deploy it. I just want to be clear about leaving the Raleigh patch. I mean, please burn the shit out of everything else, but leave that one for me to make my case with."

"We do not have an authorization for that, much less a go-ahead, Bob."

"Two weeks," and Poholek cursed the pleading tone looping back to his ears through the circuitry. "Three weeks absolute tops and if we leave the one patch standing we can have all them fuckers concentrated in the one spot to grab the only game in town, plus we do it without irritating certain commercial interests with lobbyists all over Washington."

"I understand the principle, Bob, and I'll push it ahead best I can, but I'd like you to please cool down some. I can not promise you anything at present. There's procedure and authorization to deal with and you should have come to me sooner with your information."

"Yeah sure, right, uh huh." It seemed to Poholek that the slanting down-dive to the right Emigh poured them into just then was meant to emphasize the point of who's who around here and maybe make him sick to his landbound stomach and shut him up, but he held on. "Situation is very fluid here, Major Emigh, I even had a setback the other day in court."

"We heard."

"But now we know what we got to go ahead with—once they harvest this year's and move it this time it's all over, the world changes, it's crazy-legal and it's done."

Emigh righted the helicopter and flew in a straight line ahead to Japan eventually. "Listen up and then forget I said this: the Agency has its own plans for this year's crop, and the Agency is grateful for the comprehensive information you've provided, and for that reason and that reason only it is barely possible that I can convince people in the time available to dovetail our operations with what you would like to achieve."

"Fuck, Major, come do it with me. Could be the last roundup before everything goes whoops and we'd love to have the benefit of your resources. Just look at it how sweet it is now we have this halfway legal Raleigh patch to work with."

"The property's legal, not the patch. Ninety-nine plants okay, but the rest is still to be authorized. If."

"If all that's left is the Raleigh patch, the major dealers will be humping each others' asses to pick the shit, so we can pick up sticks and bag 'em all. You and a few friends will be welcome at the feast. These people have got to go. Including the Raleigh guy." No reaction. "Pitcher. I'm talking about Pitcher. He's crooked as shit."

"It's possible is all I'll say," came Emigh's voice. "Possible. Just. Not yet. Don't get your hopes up."

"Ultra-important no word gets back to Town, County, the mayor, manager, chief or anyone on my force. They think the economy's gonna collapse if the trade gets hit."

"We understand the principle."

"Very important there be no leaks down the chain of command."

"Piece of advice, Bob. It doesn't help your cause to piss me off with comments about how I handle my responsibilities in re chain of command, all right?"

"Major, please, fuck's sake, I was talking about the people on my own side here."

"You have already communicated that security situation. Now it's time for radio silence. Absolutely last thing I will say on the subject, otherwise I will throw you right out of copter just to get my peace of mind: I can not say yes or no to your specifics at this time but I will try to help you if you keep clear of being a pain in my posterior until I can get it done. My personal opinion, you have a good idea working. I wish I'd known about it sooner, okay I didn't, no blame. It may be we can produce some if not all of the conditions you'd like. Another thing I did not say just now: there are people who want to teach Raleigh Inc. a lesson by taking out their paid-for patch and burning it."

"Aw shit."

"But I am against them and others are with me too on that."

Poholek waited for Emigh to continue—it'd seemed like the start of a real story, after a lot of pulling rank on him most of the day—but there was just rotor roar and the occasional tick or beep from the complicated instrument array foregrounding the still-spectacular view.

"How come," Poholek asked Emigh, "what I don't get is why the Obama admin is so hot on making weed busts. You'd think—"

"The joke around the office is he wants to be the first white president of the United States."

"Hey, that's good," laughing to show he appreciated departmental humor and hadn't heard the line a hundred times already. It looked like talk was over, so Poholek settled in to enjoy this flyby of the view.

You didn't live in this part of the country if you didn't go loose with wonder at the green of the Coastals and the rolling blue flag of the Pacific even if you were what they called a po-lice, and this high flight in a federal copter brought some of that worn-down wake-up sense back to him from the too much paperwork and official office bullshit of his profession and the soft collapse of his life with Marion, brought back how much he truly hated the brainfucked drawlers, the dangling human weeds who fouled this place with their smoke and wasted human substance, sick enough to bring a nation down and spoil its glory to almost nothing, their stupid lives not worth one square foot of all this splendor. Just let us live in it unbothered, was all he asked. Take one good look and it shouldn't be so fucking hard to understand. And look at what they do to it, these organic hippie types scarring the land bare with the worst pesticide runoff of anyone because they're only just scrambling for the buck and don't give a fuck what they do to the land really. They're so dishonest.

"Time to head back," said Emigh's voice inside the helmet, "and I'd say one more thing if I was sure you weren't going to get all crazy on it."

"Go ahead. I promise."

Emigh fist-thumped his shoulder as the copter started the long curve on course back to base. "You're trouble sometimes but you done good work here. You had to eat a lot of shit over the years and you could use a change, I know it. Don't lose the faith, in other words ...Well, keep the, you know."

Emigh wouldn't say it but the obvious unspoken words were *Semper fi*. Poholek's heart swelled up knowing that was what he meant. It was gonna happen, it was real, it would happen and they'd do it together like brothers. "Let's live it," Poholek said.

"We will do our level best."

2

THING IS Eli'd always *liked* Franklin Bass, always been *comfortable* around Franklin Bass, like now smoking primo very easy Redbone Hound, just a touch, sharing a skinny with him on his second-floor deck, all these guys had decks but Franklin's came with a view of the ocean from the sandspit north of town with a comfy breeze easing in from the gigantic blue and two cold Coronas beading on the table, which was why he had to be *careful* around Franklin Bass. Too easy to fall into it with him, too *charming*.

"You don't want to be workin' for that creep, do ya?" Franklin asked him. "Comp'ny corporation creep at that."

"I just took a bust and was lucky to get off, and he's legal, I saw the papers."

"Work for him you might take another couple busts and see you in the *daily* papers, mon."

"He was the one got me off those ones, dropped the charges."

"So he can always drop 'em back if it suits his mood. What are you gonna do for that man? He can't sell Teddy's shit and if he does Teddy will come out and kill *you*. Some people, not me but some people say Pitcher's just a front, a narc. Things so fucked up it's not impossible. Meanwhile our local legals with they medical skunk boteeks, they mostly lookin' to bulk up the bidness to sell out to people who can play the bigtime market and that means your boy Pitcher. They lookin' for cash for value and that mothafucka gone laugh in they faces and pay dem wit tree-dollar bills, mon."

Franklin, who was a Jamaican-born guy from San Francisco some people said was really a Brooklyn-born guy from Brooklyn, had a cool deep black-guy voice he played in different, what do you call them, keys, and cool dreads parted in the middle to go with the voice, not furry funky

Rasta locks but the kind that looked braided but maybe weren't, shiny but weren't oiled, fell away on either side from a part in the middle of his head to his jawline with a couple of turquoise and cowrie shells in it—a handsome man, coffee-black, fine long features, looked after himself, light in his eyes and Eli liked his talking grin.

"Meanwhile Teddy and me and Rodge type of people, State of California won't be givin' us no license in the new regime, so we make do best we can."

"Hey, Franklin."

"What."

"Did you get one of those Smugglerville theme-camp models they sent Teddy?"

"Uh-huh and I broke it up, used some of it for kindling and threw the rest of it back of the shed. So never mind that, it ain't gonna happen, whereas I have something real in mind for you," Franklin said, "a nice little pocket in the action I can only tell you so much about today without at least a little bit of yes from you in front."

"But you'll tell me *something*, right?"

Franklin looked right and left along the cove for punctuation. "Even before this new shit happened I thought you were giving loyalty to the wrong person with Teddy."

"He brought me up in the business."

"He kept you *down* in the business. You should've been off tenant farmer sharecropping year before last, campin' out in the man's weed like with a sign up sayin' Please arrest me Mister Man. I'da had you managing transit by now." And raised a signifying eyebrow for the camera and held it there, which worked well he had such definite sculpted features, eye, nose, the way his mouth was modelled. "And I know that's what you want to be into."

"You have that for me?"

"Limit to what I can say, Eli. Limit to what I can say, be-cause," playing a little tune with the word, "I'm doing something a little different this year and I have to keep it close."

"Different."

"A minute, Eli." Franklin got up from his slatted deck chair and stretched his muscles, a runner's body or a swimmer's under a loose red and green woven vest and cutoff jean shorts. "A minute. Ah will thinks on it," putting on the accent, and went off barefoot into the house for Eli to watch the ocean and suck up the last hot pull of Red Dog, toss the microroach and take a sip of beer and enjoy his head.

Inside the house Ziggy Marley switched off in the middle of a line and different music came on, an icy muted trumpet against synths and a lopey backbeat, an *insinuating* sound, and Eli figured Franklin would be coming back outside in a new tone, but then he didn't come out and Eli had too long to sit there.

And had the feeling, not the same feeling but close to what had bothered him at Pitcher's office, of being played, but he expected that with Pitcher, he didn't know the man so it was all right, only this was his friend Franklin and it bothered him a little.

Then he heard a door creak open and Franklin's toilet flush. See? He wasn't hiding on you for effect. You have to be careful with your head.

Franklin came back out, squinted once at the ocean to make sure it was there and sat down without even looking at his beer. "This is what I can tell you now," and right, his tone had changed, same as the music. "I got a spot open, this minute as we speak, it's open for you but I can't hold it open too long and there are others who might want it. I like you, Eli, I trust you to get a job done. Your head may be screwed on a little funny if you don't mind my saying so, but I like your heart, I don't mean soft feelings, I mean the loyalty you gave Teddy even when you shun'ta, and the way I've seen you work."

"Okay."

"I have a definite feeling that this will be a different year this year. More than a feeling. I have people in the police tellin' me things."

"You've got a cop?"

"I got better than a cop, Eli. I wouldn't trust a cop. I got cleaning ladies and janitorial staff, and not only do they collect papers from the trash for me but no one pays them any nevermind, cops keep talkin' while the niggas and Mescans come around with they brooms and shit—*invisible people*—and from what I hear we're headin' for the last roundup, podnah. Teddy and Roger and them been worrying about it but they too stupid to do anything but what they doin' already, anyway I haven't seen them do a got-damn thing except dream pothead dreams about a theme park for the kiddies, and yes I got a model of it too but I took it apart and thew the pieces down the basement. I have made some plans and I have made alterations in the way I do my business and I have recently lost faith in a formerly responsible person, someone I will not work with anymore, or any of his people either, so in this radically altered situation I need someone I can trust and I trust you that much."

"Well thank you."

"There is a station to be manned, and it's not here in Eureka. It's not even in California." Eli could see Franklin stop and think again, how much to say. "There's a house for you, all paid up, beautiful place, big, nice neighborhood, walled community, if you want it and we agree on things, in Seattle—"

"*Seattle?*"

"Yes, that does mean you'd be in transport."

"*Seattle.*"

"Arranging it, not driving shit around. Other people do the perilous work and I need a man up there in that house to coördinate the shit. I know that's what you been lookin' to do, so here it is, your lucky day."

"That's not why I … *Seattle.*"

"I know, you used to live there, that's a plus, know your way around, have friends there, that's good. So you can figure out we're movin' north, but what you don't know is the radical degree of difference regarding every aspect of the logistics, and that is all that I can say to you unless you join up. I believe that a ton of shit and hellfire is comin' down on everyone who will not wake up and look around, and I believe I have finessed my operation to the other side of that."

Franklin was talking like a mastermind in a movie, his brilliant genius plan, a big secret, revised transport headed north and Eli wondered if that meant hashish instead of bud, maybe even dab and shatter, which please put behind me Jesus, I don't need that much wreckage, but less bulk to move for even more money, and Franklin had found a market maybe up in Canada where hash is a thing, because sure as shit there wasn't much market for it even up in Wawa. It could work, but move up to the capital city of my bad luck *Seattle*? This is so fucked up. "Uh huh," Eli managed to say.

"You notice, Eli? You and I just smoked a little weed, something on the mellow side, Redbone Hound, but we're not rockin' back and laughin' our asses off how silly the world is in that fine old teahead way. You might think that's cause we been talkin' bidness but think about it, how many laughs you heard around town these days? Good old knockback pothead humor, you'd think it's less financially dependent but you don't hear as much of it as you used to, right? This is not an amusing time."

"You're right."

"I'm damn right if I do say so. This is not a happy time in a happy country and I believe that what kept everybody smilin' when they talked, smilin' in the street hello and talkin' with they friends, it was be-cause there was money in their veins supplying they arms and legs and heads with blood, but they were country-simple, mon, and din't know it was money smilin' *them*, laughin' *them*, tellin' them the joke of the day so they could go and tell they friends about it. That money has been gone awhile and it is not comin' back and now they begin to know it, not all the way, just a little, feelin' some small discomfort. That's true for everyone in this land. You know it. And in our personal industry the change is comin' whether California legalizes or not, and I see a lot of problems ahead of legalization, let me say."

"So do I."

"Because you have had a wake up. Your nose still looks like shit, mon, ugly lookin' bruise, is it broke?"

"Couple little splinters knocked off the bridge, I saw the x-ray."

"You gonna look a little different when it's done, not an old time boxer look, but different, a little thicker up there, not as fine. Might work for you, you're a man, it's all right to show where you been. You have the time to see Cap'n Bob's fist comin' before it hit you?"

"Had maybe half a second." Eli couldn't find a moment to say it wasn't the fist but the flat of his hand, the heel of it, but okay, he didn't see how the difference mattered to what Franklin was telling him.

"But you saw it comin' and it was the news. It was the news saying welcome to the world to come. Do I really have to explain you this shit? While we were out here enjoying the weather and all the pussy we could fuck people with money were workin' 24/7 and they bought everything including the ground we're standing on. You didn't know? Now here's the news, one chance if you take it, between me and you, the last free enterprise before a world of shit comes down on us perfectly legal signed up slavery. They just time for you to wise up and get out the way of a big fist comin' out the world at your face one more time. Or you and me could make us some mo-nay instead. So Eli, you want to come work for me or not?"

3

IT WAS A LONG DRIVE to Kwakanikuk because of all the inconveniently configured water in the region, the dangling-finger disconnected peninsulas and inlets requiring almost interminable drive-arounds on too-distant bridges, and sometimes you had to put your car on more than one ferry to get there, all the way to the small back lawn of this slanty whiteboard house under perpetual repair at the end of a dirt road about half a mile in from the water, where Lina got the news and found her life changed yet again as she watched her elder son Noah play with the beautiful four-year-old girlchild Laila he had inherited when he married her mother Shirine, a golden half-Iranian woodland creature with new life inside her that wasn't showing yet, this dear Lord grandma Lina year, her eyes tearing up while she told herself it was only the sunlight and the length of her travels.

The amazing thing, sometimes, was not the world of miscreant complication whorling around Eli but the regular-guy nature of her firstborn son, emerging from her and Nelson neither especially an intellectual nor an instinctive gut-level rebel, not taking that sort of predilection from Dad and Mom, though he was conventionally countercultural for his time and place and generation, but such an essentially good, normal sort of human person, becoming a man now as he walked, blinking at first but with increasing certainty, out of the wanderings of adolescence into marriage, family, work, beloved by his students at the Waldorf School where he taught since back east he'd been educated by the Anthropops, short salary, school in trouble and just this month cutting his health benefits for next year—she'd write him a blank check for emergency use—fixing the house up with his good hands and tools, just like his dad, to take a slice off the rent, and now this, biological fatherhood, life without pause unceasing, form after form, mind upon mind, appearing and appearing, radiant in the radiance of the world.

Now Noah looked up at her from his golden play in the light with the dreamchild Laila, his already receding darkblond hair shaven almost to the skin showing a shape of head and jawline that seemed a perfect average of hers and Nelson's without recapitulating a single recognizable feature either way, though there was a curl of mischief in that smile she would peg as hers and which made at least the lower part of his face, for the moment, into an echo of her own.

"Howdy, grandma," Noah called across the spangled lawn, laughing at her. Yes, she had a son who said Howdy sometimes even not when joking, and here came Shirine nudging the screen back door open with her upraised shoulder, careful with her tray of glasses and pitcher of fresh lemonade while the Pinot Grigio Lina had brought rechilled in the kitchen fridge and she would need it.

Girlchild Laila looked across the sunset lawn at Lina now, golden face in a spill of sungold curls, and sent out as emissary a happy giggle that had nothing to do with calling Lina names or laughing at her caught in time, and it was as if all three of these people were advancing on her through the late afternoon dazzle in a lifegiving pageant from which, in all this lancing sunlight, there was no place for her to hide or turn her face away as, no other responses left her, unstoppable tears rushed from her burst heart like life continuing and irresistible, Eli included, up through the petty hydraulics of her eyes to spill out like springfed freshets of natural water.

She would sleep here tonight and with luck wake up in light as rich as this come morning.

"It's about fucking time," Poholek told Teddy Swift, back from the hippybilly wilds of whatever part of the forest of his criminal fantasies, the homemade movie he starred in in his mind, standing right in front of Bob this seaside nightfall.

"You're sposed to have me bagged and barred by now, ainchoo?" the little wiseass said.

"Ah why bother, Teddy-boy, you're done, your goose is cooked, man got your land—"

"Not all of it, Captain."

"Don't count on that. You hear any helicopters in the sky while you were out there? People making plans for you up in the blue, looking down at you from clouds, eye in the sky and I don't mean just us local laws who are pissed at you anyway. Poor Teddy Swift, if only he'd played along and come to court."

"And what, watch you turn Eli Chase on me? No tickie no thankee."

"Saw me coming, did you?"

"You're easynough to spot."

Poholek had called this meeting away from the station-house and they were up a dead end with a stand of trees between them and a stretch of seacoast rock as evening fell, and it pleased him that Teddy'd shown up with no apparent trepidation that Poholek might arrest or shoot him on the spot on general principles and as a fugitive from justice. Which was tempting, and Teddy showing up renewed his trust in human nature ha ha ha, but it was too dicey for uncertain gain while there were other options still in play and you could push here, push there, look for the outcome, everything working your way because you were in the best, not to mention safest position.

"I might allow you a free hand with that pissant Pitcher," he said.

"Because why?" Teddy's angled face said in the thickening dimness as a big wave crashed home at the edge of earshot.

"Because frankly he's become more of a pain in the ass than you are, and I'd rather see you collect the shrubbery than him have it. *If* you can take it from him, that is. I'm not sure you're good enough. You don't take it, I might just cut and burn you both out."

Teddy was looking at the pistol riding Poholek's hip, Glock with the fifteen-shot mag, the holder strap snapped in place below the hammer. The thought must be crossing his mind: dead-end, unpeopled, dusk. Teddy was wearing a long unbuttoned black overshirt covering his buckskin vest and Poholek, his trained and instinctive eye, had spotted the shape of the thing Teddy was wearing under that shirt against the base of his spine. He might use it to defend himself but would never pull first, not in a million. And if they did get into it, hey, the fool had come here armed with something he owned and his prints on it, Poholek would simply *breeze* through the inquest, sir.

It was win-win out here with the sound of the seashore in late dusk.

"I know for a fact," Poholek told Teddy, "that the pissant Pitcher is a heavily medicated individual, and I mean apart from whatever illegals he's on. I mean medicated, I mean significant periods of his life spent hiding under tables and shaking all over."

"Oh?"

"And I'd say that an individual of his type might be susceptible to persuasion. The man's all nerves and his self-assurance is a skinny sheet of paper."

"Oh?"

"I'm only saying," said Poholek. "I'm not you, but if I was you I'd give the man a little push and see which way it tips him over. I think he's a nothing and you can take him. And I would thank you for removing an irritant that digs into me right where I sit and it's hard to reach."

"*Remove* him?"

"Oh for Chrissake I'm not suggesting anything violent or lethal. I'd just like to see him disempowered, and if you can do it you could-might have your product back. The city fathers don't want to see you busted, they gave me hell on shitwheels after the courtroom flop. Town's broke and they want all you big growers' money circulating, the people you hire, the money they spend, it's all the town's got these days. Wasn't for you guys everyone'd have to move out for nonpayment of rent. California won't go recreational-legal for years yet."

"And I'm supposed to believe you."

"What you got to lose you ain't lost already?" Open-hands gesture of nothing to hide in the darkening seafresh air. "Suck it and see."

Tony and Mira lived rent free in the carriage-house of a half-timbered Tudor-revival hulk built by an old-time lumber baron, now owned by the Foundation, on a quarter-acre plot technically across the southern border of posh Montlake but still breathing some of Seattle's more rarefied air, the kind of neighborhood where they didn't mind Tibetan prayer flags if there weren't too many of them and they'd let you build an ithyphallic white stupa in the backyard if it wasn't higher than your roofline and didn't show from the street. Tony tried to be a regular fella but sometimes felt like shaving his head, sometimes like wearing his robes when he mowed the front lawn, and although the neighbors were clear that he and his wife and kid lived modestly in the carriage-house, they'd been inside the big place on get-to-know-us open days and had seen how the lumber-baronial dining hall had been transformed into a cavernous blood-red room with golden trim, an enormous gilded smirky Buddha Tony wouldn't have chosen to head the room, and probably too many tankas featuring bigtoothed blue and red guys dancing up and down on the corpses of their demonic enemies and waving their many arms, sticking their tongues out their many mouths and their wangs up the yonis of their ecstatic shakti consorts—you could talk to people about the symbolic nature of the representations, the polarities generating the universe, positive and negative charged particles and even, with an eyebrow, the big bang, but it was hard to bring the interpretation off in an enormous room in which an ocean of unmitigated hemoglobin red flooded the eye from every available surface and there were all kinds of objects—prayer wheels, bells, vajras, symbolic battle axes, ornamental spears—that were not normal accoutrements in the other Tudor-revival homes of the neighborhood. Lapsed Catholics did better with it because they were used to imagery wall-to-wall but regular unlapsed Christians had problems because they found the iconography kind of radical. And people didn't notice the peaceful compassionate Green Tara goddesses much. Their eyes went right to the hot stuff, the wrathfuls, the demons, the trampling. It was understandable. It was another version of what people liked to watch on television.

"We try to keep human sacrifices to a minimum," he'd joked with visitors a couple times, "and the dead guys symbolize illusions."

Buddha-mind all-cognitive at the center, ringed by heavens, hells, glutted appetites and hungry ghosts. Gods, demons, personifications of abstract principles riding through clouds on the backs of blue mules: Tony could have done without a lot of the trappings even though they lit him up—we have the rest of human life in common and it's simple, we're all pretty much alike: sometimes he thought he oughta give the robes a rest—but it was the Foundation's call and the Rinpoches felt at home when they came to stay in the guest rooms upstairs when there was a conference or an intensive. This summer was almost nothing doing till

September but the autumn was booked with conferences, ceremonies and retreats: someone musta consulted an astrologer or an oracle.

He was wearing a blue polo shirt and chinos today and feeling nervous about Lina's visit, half-hoping she'd be late or would phone to say something had come up and she couldn't make it.

He'd never had to deal with Lina Chase at the level of personal problems outside prevailing Buddhist practice, which was good because it kept their relations from getting too personal, since face it, if he hadn't happened into Mira—if Mira hadn't turned up for a meditation workshop like a young Botticellina stepping ashore from a scallopshell, shortly accompanied by a precognitive flash of their future, um, conjunction—if not for that, Lina, a woman almost his own age, already been through everything, wouldn't need a basic education in how life goes, probly understood in her bones by now that whatever advantage life had ever handed her was temporary, plus wouldn't want to have more kids with him and was Italian to boot …

These reflections by way of readying himself for Lina's visit. In a previous go-round of troubles with her son Lina had formed a stoical-compassionate compound response from which she would do what she could for Eli but if he was determined to fuck his life up beyond what she could help him with she'd detach, wouldn't tear herself to shreds over what she couldn't fix or prevent. But it sounded different this time. It sounded like a lot of old baggage rattling down her chute, a load of stuff all her smarts and practice couldn't get a handle on, and getting into personal nitty-gritty with her worried him, no shit.

Yeah, they gave him a Lama license but no way was he free from normal human foolishness. And he'd seen a few big guys tumble, Trungpa Rinpoche back in Boulder with his two or three daily fifths of Scotch to maintain himself through the pain that hit him soon as he took his robes off, put on a suit and started living right up the middle of the modern world—and had accomplished important things in it: Naropa, the hookup with the Beats, pretty much paved the way for Tibetan Buddhism in the States, and for a finish popped on a ten-gallon hat, dowsed for oil wells, hit 'em and put the money where it'd do the Path some good. The booze for the stress of what Trungpa chose to do had killed him young, though. What a guy, not Tony's teacher by any stretch but an exemplar in some respects. Easy on the costumes and rituals, for instance, even though the Tibetan line was strong in that: great color sense, reds and golds, not to mention actual Tibetan faces, if you had one, radiant despite the tons of shit and history. Plus the pictorialism and sense of ritual were catnip to old-school Catholics. Just look at him, for instance.

Before planting his Jersey feet solidly on the eightfold noble bricks, Tony'd spent time in Swami Muktananda's circle, totally cool Hindu guru who looked like Thelonious Monk underneath the robes and flowers and tooled along perfectly okay for decades till he became an old man who discovered a yen for teenage girls and for whom, therefore, certain arrangements had to be arranged, at which point, yeah, it got a little strange around the ashram near Benares, especially after word came down it was time for certain individuals to be carrying Glocks and Louisville Sluggers, and Joe Don Looney, former New York Giants halfback who'd been too much for the Giants and too well named even for the NFL, was put in charge of the enforcement squad. Tony's last day there he finally got into it with Joe Don, had to knee him in the balls and when they were down in the dirt almost bit his nose off to escape that scene alive and on the run, tighter scrape escape than it had ever been in Jersey—how about that—through the trees to the road praying for a hitch to town and swearing next time it wasn't gonna be anything like this no more.

Not that he should flatter himself, he'd been recruited by Looney for an enforcement role and it shamed him to admit it but he'd been young and unformed and a Giants fan and *he'd felt the pull*, only something saved him.

So maybe he had better qualifications than most for counselling Lina on her outlaw son who was some kind of holy innocent only he was in the skunk business. So why was he so worried today? Maybe he'd luck out and she was nervous too and wouldn't show.

But the doorbell rang on the dot and it was her.

They had a moment in the doorway, fumbling their hellos for a second while Tony saw her looking different, less a matter of her looks than aura, not that he saw auras much, so maybe what he meant was a sort of emotional disarray he picked up on before clocking any of its tells.

"Hi Tony."

"Hey. Sh'we go siddown in the garden?"

"Fine."

"Anything to drink?"

"Got any cold fizzwater?"

They collected bottles and glasses from the carriage-house fridge and took them outside.

Tony didn't have as many precognitive experiences as he used to when he was a kid starting out but when they happened they still ran true to form, usually but not always featuring a woman and a bed. In the one with Lina the bed was unclear, cramped inside a closet or something, but naked Lina underneath him radiating reddish waves of light was clear enough, and Tony was struggling not to be compelled by it, trying to be a little wise and take it as a warning, which is probably what it was. Red light: stop.

Look what happened to Macbeth. Best information, ironclad guarantees on the future, everything working out as predicted and, thinking of the Kurosawa version, a fast arrow through your neck for the finish.

Point being, short of true awakening everything was just more dream so don't get caught in it. You know this stuff inside out so pay attention, Tones.

Must've been a hell of a day for Mifune on the wooden castle set while they shot a couple hundred arrows right at him, props but they could still take your eye out.

Tony and Lina sat down at the white bumpy-glass-top umbrella-table at the back of the garden against the tall ranked poplars a topwind kept asking to bend and sway and they did it.

"Is Mira around?"

"Playdate with Valentino Marpa."

"For infants? What do they do, goo at each other?"

Tony nodded. "Last time I went to pick Val up from one of those, first thing I saw when I came in the door was three toddler girls on a bench in the entryway like a display, hands down the front of their Pampers masturbating pretty much in rhythm. Their other hands, sucking their thumbs, they had both ends working."

"Girls are precocious, it's an educational experience for your son."

"Very much so. Good preparation for what he'll encounter in years to come … All right," Tony said, "tell me how it went down there in, uh, Eureka."

Lina went into her story and he listened and her pain about her son hurt him. He had never seen this intelligent, accomplished woman so torn up. Which just went to show you, it was always possible, it was never far, thou comest when I had thee least in mind, you fuck.

After Lina finished once, then twice, then a third time to make sure she had omitted nothing important, Tony sat quietly with it for a minute and Lina let him. Teams of honeybees with their heads pushed down past the petals, and an occasional bumblebee plundering the back doors of the blossoms, were stitching the day together in the bordering flowerbeds, piecework and on the margins but it kept life going for everyone, no exceptions. A honeybee lives about six weeks, Tony marvelled. Think of being a bee.

"I'm afraid I'm going to lose him," Lina said. "Jail or worse. All too possible. I can feel it looming."

"What would you do if you could do anything?" Tony asked Lina, and took a sip of Ferrarelle water.

"I'd pull him out of California and make him live at my place, give him the converted garage in the back garden. With Sukey."

"But you can't."

"Even Nelson couldn't control him once he got going. Look, Eli started out a normal kid, normal enough, then got terribly vague in middle childhood, we didn't know what it was but as soon as he hit puberty everything went flooey. Suddenly he had a lot of power and not only no way to control it but whole areas of perception and cognition blanked out. Almost no sense of consequences. The blank was so complete it was obviously structural, not psychological in origin. It's his wiring."

"Your professional opinion."

"My professional opinion plus tests. When he hit fifteen and got in trouble with the law we were able to get his sentence suspended so he could go to one of those boot-camp operations. Later on he worked hard in therapy, against the grain, not easy but he tried. He made progress but the root problem's still there. When he's not on a binge he's big, charismatic, gorgeous—"

"A mother's objective opinion."

"He looks big and strong and people are drawn to him. He's drawn to the outlaw life, where they think he's the rock of Gibraltar, the perfect go-to guy, but whadda they know? They're out of their depth and so is he. Things will go wrong, and when they do he'll be headed for prison and the waste of his life. Or or or the loss of it. He needs to be protected and I've reached the limit of what I can do for him."

"And he won't come up here."

"There isn't enough chloroform in the world."

"What was the charge on the first-time sentence you got suspended."

"A couple of his friends boosted a car for a joyride. A firearm was discharged."

Tony tried not to grin but couldn't help it. "Sorry," he said. "Small world and so fort. You'd think kids'd find new stupid shit to do, but no."

"But you never did time, not even juvey time, you said."

"Not even boot camp. I got off, y'see, because it was friends of mine who stole the car, not me."

"Just like Eli, then. An innocent in bad company."

"Yeah, sounds like exactly the same thing. Eli's friends shot the gun off too, huh, not him."

"Eli shot the gun. There was a witness."

"Some old snoop."

"His hands tested positive for, what is it, cordite?"

"What'd he hit?"

"A Stop sign and a bedroom window."

"There's the difference right there. Back in Jersey me and my friends hunted grocery stores after midnight. And hit em. And ran inside for beer and laughs. Listen, serious a minute. Are you asking me for advice because of my former unworthy activities or in my capacity as a teacher of the dharma?"

"As a man of both worlds, I guess."

"As a teacher of the dharma there are some long Tibetan prayers I could teach you phonetically, don't look away, why're you looking away? You don't want that kind of help from me? I assume you're already meditating in the middle of this, and if you're not you should, and you're so smart on the psychological level I don't know what kind of advice I could possibly give you in that area."

"Just talk to me. I'm stuck and I need someone good to talk to and you're it. My former colleagues in the practice are nice people but what do they know, they haven't lived enough … And you start telling me phonetic Tibetan prayers, long ones … "

"Pretty long."

Lina dipped two fingers in her glass of Ferrarelle and dabbed her forehead. "You remember, don't you, that things got started with Eli this time when I was doing that visualization you gave me and I, um, encountered the Wratful Deity—"

"Why're you pronouncing it like that?"

"Like what?"

"Ratful."

"Because … Never mind. I was ready to look at that figure not as wrathful but as transformative, and that was fine, Tony, until everything started transforming. I don't want Eli transforming into dead Eli, or career prisoner Eli."

"Which is why you were warned," Tony told her. "You wouldn't have been warned, see, if there wasn't a constructive point to it. Think it through."

"But if you're asking me to have some kind of faith in supernatural beings … I can't do it, it's not my thing."

"Even when you've seen one."

"I'm steeped in the imagery. I've been visualizing it. So it comes. That's all."

"Fine, it's a personification. You're right. Question everything, don't take nothin on faith, but you have to know there's compassion in the universe, as a reality, as a power. It's up to us to verify it in our own lives. Blue skin or not, whatever, compassion is paying attention to your case." Tony rubbed the top of his head. "I sound like a shithead preaching the rulebook. I don't like doing it. It's okay with some people but not with you."

"Great," Lina said, but dropped her forehead into her hands. "Eli, Eli. Tony, what am I supposed to do with him?"

"We're working on it," Tony said.

"What would you do if it was your son in Eli's situation."

No hesitation: "I'd drive down there, bop him on his head, tie him in a croaker sack, bring him here and lock him in the basement."

"And his pregnant girlfriend?"

"She could have the best guest room upstairs. The Green Tara."

"I don't have a basement or an upstairs," Lina said. "Or enough muscle. Even Nelson couldn't push Eli where he didn't want to go, and Nelson was no wuss."

"I know, I met him, remember? Not long before he."

Tony looked around the yard, the splendid lawn, the stately house, then the whitewashed plaster stupa, the swaying poplars, as the wheel turned and showed its pictures. The pressure on him was that this woman really needed his help. Not someone else's. His.

"I could go down there," Tony found himself saying, "and lay some tough love on your kid. The Buddha, the Dharma and the Mafia, which I never officially was part of but so what, I been through enough."

"Are you saying you'll do this?"

"I'm just talkin' here, I'm just proposing this to you as an idea, and it'd be up to you too, obviously, to say yes or no. But in principle, it's possible, yeah, I might."

"It's a long way to go," Lina said in a small voice.

"I got an acolyte'd be happy to lend me his Porsche, one of the nice new ones ain't even ugly anymore, a black Carrera, be a nice drive down in 'at."

"What is this, the movie version? Tough Tony to the rescue?"

"Maybe a little. But maybe I could help. Also it's a break, a change of venue, there's an old friend I could visit down that way, but gimme some credit here, basically I'm tryina help you out."

"And you'd get through to Eli because of how you've lived? The tough guy gone straight, also sort of holy."

"Not too holy."

"In Eli's mind, I mean. He's been looking for a hero since Nelson died."

"That could happen," said Tony, thinking Whoa, this is going too fast and too far and doesn't sound realistic, really, and she has to be wondering what's happening here too. I should be feeling relaxed and unattached, not getting lost in the story, not desiring a starring role. "But it's not my intention to be his hero," he said, making a mess of it now for sure, "and it prolly wouldn't be the right thing in any longer run."

"I'd take short-term help, no question."

"Also, if I go down there, I'm just talkin, maybe I could make an impression on these people who are a danger to him." He was at a loss to know what kind of conversation they were having, as if his past and present were wet paint, different colors sloshing together. Careful now. Why leave your place near the center of the tanka for one of the cheap seats around the rim?

"What," Lina asked him, "you'd lean on 'em a little? You're starting to worry me, Tone."

"Either I'm making an impetuous mistake of some kind or it's necessary. I can't tell which. It's confusing."

"Some spiritual teacher you turned out to be," Lina said.

"I know, I know. Aha, here comes Mira and my kid."

"Saved by the bell, huh."

"No, actually I don't think so."

Mira, coming up the drive alongside the house with Val harnessed asprawl across her chest might not have recognized Lina right away because it took her a moment to unpack a patently insincere smile wide and white enough to be visible from a distance: note her excellent dentition. At first it looked like she was coming all the way into the garden, but now she pointed awkwardly over her head to indicate that she was going inside the house and they could join her if they wanted. A pretty graceless shot at escape.

"Let's go, I guess," said Tony, "unless we're not finished here."

"Do I have to deal with Mira right this minute?"

"No, you get a pass. Go on up the drive. Phone me tonight if you wanna talk. Phone me anytime."

"And going to Eureka? You'd do that?" She looked up now. "I'd go with you, that is, if you wanted."

"Let's think about it and see how it sounds in the morning." Tony couldn't help it, his body went warm and his little friend threw half a party in his pants. "Might, might not. You all right for now?"

"A little better, I think," Lina said, and rummaged up her car keys from somewhere in the bottom of her bag, always going somewhere, she told herself, but all her motions were starting to seem pointless and repetitive and unproductive, mere shufflings in a world that was emptying out fast.

"This is hard, Tony," she told him.

"I know it. Drive carefully, awright?"

What Lina knew without a doubt: flesh of her flesh, soul of her soul, she was going to lose her son. He would be pulled out of her body again, this time by hard uncaring hands.

4

Eli was sitting around the office over the health food store with Kenny Pitcher, town getting dark outside the windows, sipping good whiskey and signing agreements that weren't quite contracts, but what the hey, seven hundred bucks a week legal on the barrelhead and a big bonus to come after harvest, he put his Hancock down feeling safe for a change, responsible, with the baby coming and all. Not only was life getting steadier, more stable, but looked like it might be entertaining again too, because Kenny Pitcher was an entertaining guy.

"I used to have stronger shit than whiskey in the office," Pitcher told him now, "but on consideration of the security basis I decided that ship has sailed across the ocean blue."

"To China."

"A slow boat to Japan. And Yucatan. Full of Coca without the Cola."

"What a shame it had to go," Eli said.

"Alas and who gives a shit," Pitcher asked him, using that funny half-Southern accent thing he did, wordplay, sometimes with an intellectual sound, sometimes just Alas and who gives a shit, the alas part intellectual, sort of, then the rest of it street, or country. Entertaining, as Eli had put it to himself, but the part he didn't like is that he could feel himself getting stupid again, as if Pitcher's intelligence kind of took away his own, stole some of the oxygen in his head, which was funny because when he was deciding what to do, Pitcher or Franklin basically, he'd been thinking clearly again, seeing things and people the way they were, with insight, except Franklin wanting him to move up to Seattle fucked up the view. Even though, as he'd told Pitcher, Franklin was throwing in a walled house in a gated community up there and, he said, ten grand a month for starters. Great money but Sukey didn't trust it, so.

On the other hand Eli also had that good, almost perfect alcohol feeling now, just the right balance between being awake and being fucked up off your head, the feeling you could ride for miles if you held it right there, hold that pose, say cheese—actually cheese was a sickening thought just now …

Eli heard the sound and looked up, the door of the office opened, Teddy walked in. Eli felt much less fine in like half a second. Teddy was doing his usual bare-chested thing but had a long black shirt on over the rawhide vest and he looked kind of wild but Eli couldn't figure out what he was stoked on even though it was kind of obvious he was stoked on something. Eyes like knives, Teddy looked at Eli sitting on the sofa next to the liquor cabinet then at Pitcher behind his fancywood desk with the complicated curlicue grain and Pitcher didn't look too disturbed, still knocked back in his complicated black office chair with a glass of whiskey and ice in his hand.

"Motherfucker," was Teddy's hello. "You not only steal my patch, you take my best boy."

"Good to see you, Ted. One, it's not your patch anymore and Eli's not your boy, people don't talk like that anymore, he's a free man, and even though you're being impolite I'll invite you to join us in a sociable glass of whiskey if you like."

"I'll permit you up your ass," Teddy said.

"Eli?" Pitcher asked. "Maybe you know, maybe you can tell me what that means? Permit me up my ass. I don't know what that means. As a statement, it doesn't appear to mean a thing. The offer of a whiskey— only one I'm afraid because you look a bit unstable and I don't want to unbalance you—one generous measure and then you can go, still stands."

"Oh I *know* you're afraid," said Teddy, but then backed off unsteadily because Eli stood up from the sofa and Teddy probably could tell that the size of Eli's anger was filling the whole room up to the ceiling into the corners of the walls to the cornices and probably even through the plaster. "What the fuck happened to your nose, man?"

Eli lightly fingered the bruise still spread, but fading and without any purple-red in it anymore, across the top of his nose and below his eyes like half a mask. "Captain Bob happened to my nose, *man*, and I've been wanting to see you ever since I found out you turned me in to him." Eli made a fist of his right hand and left it hanging at his side but tried to make it clear he was measuring the space between himself and Teddy and didn't feel even slightly rushed. The room was his, that's how big he was. "I think I owe you one, I think I should happen to your face the way Captain Bob happened to mine."

"Boys, boys, not in the office," Pitcher said, but no one was listening to him. "We should have business to discuss here, Teddy, you and me. This is a business office. Like, grow up."

"Who said I turned you in to Poholek?" Teddy asked Eli.

"Poholek."

"And you believe him?"

"I remember the way you didn't look me in the eye at your place before you sent me up there."

Teddy looked away this time too. "Well you were gonna rat me out in court too," he said.

"I wasn't gonna say word one about you in court," Eli told him, hating the hint of emotional bleat in his voice. "All this time and you don't know me even slightly. But now I know you."

"This is unproductive bullshit," came Pitcher's opinion from behind his desk. "We have legitimate, well, mostly legitimate business to talk about for our mutual benefit, fellas."

Eli brought his fists up belly high and took a solid step toward Teddy who was behaving funny, stepping back and fumbling around behind his shirt and Eli didn't understand why Teddy wasn't putting his hands up to defend himself, give himself a chance, but then saw the movement come out from behind Teddy's back and the flash and it was Teddy's big old Bowie knife weaving the air between them, the chrome blade heavy enough to chop down to bone on you anywhere and break your small to medium bones: the thing was like a cleaver, and Eli stepped back. Eli was still large, he was still filling the space, but the room was too small for him and Teddy's knife and there was nowhere to go in it, and why was Kenny Pitcher laughing from behind his desk?

"You call tha' a knoife?" Pitcher said in a pretty good Aussie accent from that movie whatsitsname, Crocodile Jones. "Tha's not a knoife. Now *this* is a knoife," but he didn't have a knife, Eli looked over and he didn't have anything beside the whiskey and it made no sense that he was having a good time watching this, the combination of knife and stoked-up Teddy and how small and cold the room was wasn't even slightly funny.

But at least Pitcher'd gotten Teddy's attention. Teddy was looking away from Eli at Pitcher, and Eli wondered if there'd be a moment for him to step in and pop Teddy on the jaw and drop him, because Teddy with a big knife in a small room was likely to go very bad so let's take the knife out of the picture. Eli was hoping to have that feeling he'd had sometimes when time slows down and despite everything that's going on you have enough of it to move between the dots and get where you have to go while other people are slo-mo, that's what he needed here but he wasn't sure it was happening, and if you weren't sure it was happening then it probably wasn't happening and you shouldn't move as if it was happening, but Eli couldn't tell for sure.

"That's right, *man*," Pitcher told Teddy, "look right here," which Eli liked because Teddy did keep looking at Pitcher, which might be enough for him to take a step inside on Teddy. Teddy was a wiry son of a bitch with quick reflexes, Eli had loaded trucks with him and though Teddy didn't have much meat on him he was strong as shit. Eli was stronger, though, and had the weight and reach on him and the time thing felt like it was starting to happen and he figured he might be able to use it and deck him. The booze he'd already drunk was helping with that too.

★

"That's right, *man*," Pitch said one more time in order to keep Teddy's attention. "You didn't come here to scare Eli with that thing. You didn't know he was here, you came here to scare *me*. You want to get your patch back and now that it's mine I'm willing to work with you. Put that knife away and let's talk about it."

"It's not your patch, it's mine. I planted it, I tended it."

"Actually I did that," said Eli, but they weren't paying attention.

"All you did," Teddy said, and he hadn't put the knife away, "was put up a fence."

"And legally bought a piece of property from the great state of California. You forget that."

"It's my fucking patch!"

Pitch took a sweet sip of whiskey and grinned his favorite show grin, the sharp one. "It's not *your* patch it's *my* patch? C'mon Teddy, that sounds like It's not *your* toy red fire engine it's *my* toy red fire engine. Is there something wrong with you or are you only stupid? You lost the round. The patch is mine. I can work it on my own, but lookit, might be better if we come together on it. Teddy, put the knife away so we can have an adult business conversation. Eli, pour this man a glass of our best bourbon. Teddy, put the knife away. Eli, stop looking at me funny and pour the man a drink. Teddy, put the knife away. Oh for fuck's sake, no no no, not the liquor cabinet."

Pitch watched Teddy step past Eli, haul his leg up and put a boot to the liquor cabinet, bottles and glasses falling off the top, ke-rash, and who knows what breaking inside it. Pitch was glad to see that at least his new employee Eli Chase had his priorities right and was trying to catch the toppling bottles, but Teddy booted it again and wood and glass were smashing.

Teddy came away from the broken cabinet and started making menaces in the air with his knife, Pitch didn't want to take the trouble to figure out from which movie. Eli was edging along the wall to the office door. Hold on there, Eli, we can't afford to lose you right now. You could be an important part of the picture.

"Teddy, you really are an asshole," Pitch said. "The liquor cabinet. I'll have to sweep up all that broken glass, you know. Little bits of it'll get stuck in the carpet, a real pain in the ass, and that was good liquor, cost good money. And look, you got your pants wet. Come on over here," he said, "I've got something I want to show you," and started rummaging around in the center drawer of his desk.

"Oh I'll come over there all right," Teddy said, waving his big chrome-bladed knife with the scored burnt bone handle, and now Pitch saw that the blade actually had the name B O W I E sandblown on one side in case someone didn't know the legend. He figured Teddy didn't really want to hurt anyone with the thing, just scare him off the patch, but Teddy could make a mistake with it and already wrecked the drinks cabinet and was acting too stupid to deal with and besides that he was just generally beginning to get in the way of business and piss him off.

Still rummaging inside his desk, Pitch said, "Too much crap in here.

I really need to keep a neater desk, can't find what I want when I need it. Look, while you're waiting why not take a chop at the desk with that thing, I'd like to see how the wood holds up."

"Oh I'll chop more than your desk for you, motherfucker," and cranked the knife above his head to ready the blow.

"Just the desk, thanks," Pitch told him, the blade came slamming down on the edge of the desktop and it went even better than Pitch had hoped.

"OWW!" Teddy said as if he was filling a word balloon in a comic strip and dropped the knife as the shock of that rock-hard live oak hit his hand, probably worst in his wrist, Pitch figured, coming straight there from the blade.

"Twaaannng," Pitch sang out for fun.

Eli was coming across the room looking to get to the knife from wherever Teddy'd dropped it, and Pitch felt a moment of alarm, saw a dangerous and more to the point a pointless struggle coming out of that. "Eli," he said, got Eli's attention to wave him off enough for Teddy to bend down and get his knife back, straighten up, rub his wrist and call Pitch a fuckin' asshole, which is the thanks you get.

"That's aged live oak," Pitch told Teddy. "I thought there was even a chance you'd break the blade on it. Tough stuff."

"Fuck *you*."

"Why don't you jump up on the desk, Teddy, so you can get at me with that big blade of yours."

"Good fucking idea," and Teddy obligingly jumped up on the desk, agile lad he was, and stood on it waving the knife in the air, a little incongruously but still making his movie, which just goes to show you how bad taste is eternal.

Pitch had finally gotten past the paperwork and the stapler and the pencils to the back of the drawer and had his hand on the Smith & Wesson knockoff PPK, state license, carry permit, one in the chamber and the safety off, that is he hoped it was in the off position, memory can play tricks. He felt for it with his thumb but crap in the drawer got in the way. "C'mon, Teddy, you just going to stand there waving that thing or are you gonna take a swipe at me? Eli, I hope you're watching this."

Eli seemed paralyzed, which was better than him running out the door.

It was like hunting bear, Pitch felt, or hunting some animal that could do you harm, hunt it with bow and arrow, put your life on the line, give the critter a fighting chance—high-powered rifle with a scope from a quarter mile on a big buck elk more majestic than any mere human could ever be, please someone shoot me that hunter. You had to give the animal a chance, and this was the moment Pitch was giving Teddy, also if he drew the safety might be on, and that would turn the lights on for Teddy and he could take a second chop before I can reset. There, that was decent odds enough for fairness' sake.

His hand was still in the drawer and would take time to pull out. This was the moment in which he would do nothing in his own defense. One chop of that blade, Pitch knew, could sever every muscle in his shoulder, and if Teddy should go for his neck with it, well, bye-bye love.

Pitch looked up at Teddy. "Here's your big moment, Ted. What're you gonna do with it?"

What Teddy did with it was lean down and take one big swipe at Pitch and in the moment there was no way to know if it was for real or show, live or die, and Pitch felt the breeze of the big blade as it went by his face. The face: Pitch hadn't thought of that: could cut my jaw clean off or crush my cheekbone and cut halfway through and as for a head blow, well that could well be splitsville …

Pitch pulled the gun out of the drawer and had to consider where to shoot Teddy, and he couldn't take his time because Teddy'd seen the gun now and was likely to really chop him any second, of course he could also jump away off the desk backwards, depending on how well and what he was thinking, and then we'd see: might even still talk business but frankly after this bullshit with the knife and busting up the liquor cabinet Pitch was disinclined to do business with the man.

It wasn't as if Pitch hadn't killed anyone before, but it had been a while, and besides, this time he had to figure out how it'd go down at Raleigh since he was a businessman now. They'll probly be pissed off enough to fire my ass if I so much as kneecap Teddy, which would be a fittingly painful experience for the jerk, they'd be pissed off at me never mind I was defending an—okay, deniable—affiliate of the corporation protecting legal corporate business operations from an attack by a deranged drug criminal. I could pop him in the thigh to stop him, and if I hit his femoral artery that'd be too bad, he'd bleed out, and I don't care what anybody thinks of me but I am not gonna shoot him in the gonads, that would be just nasty, though now that you mention it … I could gutshoot him and dial 911, see how it works out at the hospital, take it out of my hands and put it on the paramedics how soon they get here whether he lives or not.

Fuck it, thought Pitch, and it was like spinning the Wheel of Fortune, he looked up at Teddy, let the gun find its own spot, even though he'd decided on the leg he up-from-under shot him in the chest, the safety'd been off after all, the entry point about diaphragm-high below the breastbone, that bullet should be heading up into the organs, heart, aorta, vena cava, or just the lungs take your pick, depending. Teddy popped backwards off the desk with his arms out and an Aaarghh to where Pitch couldn't see him, but Eli had jumped up and was shouting something hysterical and wide-eyed.

"The fuck you are," Pitch shouted Eli back down and pointed the gun at him. "You're not leaving, you're my witness. This man was attacking me with a Bowie knife and I defended myself. Sit the fuck back down!"

Eli went back to the sofa and sort of fell in it even though there was broken glass on it.

"Find a bottle that ain't broke and take a drink," Pitch suggested as he got up from his Aeron chair and came around the desk to look down at Teddy, and it was a funny thing, blood all over the place but he didn't hear the sound until he saw Teddy lying on the carpet clutching his chest and rocking sideways: yep, a sucking chest wound, the guy was certainly a goner, a lung and possibly also the heart, but every dog must have his day. Pitch reached for the phone to dial 911 and, fuck, that's when Eli Chase bolted from the sofa and ran out of the office without giving Pitch a moment to consider shooting him in the ass to keep him here as a witness. Fuck! The cops'd be here and that kid was gonna be hard to find as teeth on a chicken.

Pick up, pick up already, then the operator's voice announcing.

"Yes, 911 Emergency? This is Kennis Pitcher of Muhrad Enterprises in Eureka, I've just been attacked in my office by a man with a knife and I was obliged to shoot him in self-defense. Please get an ambulance here pronto, I believe there's still a chance to save this man's life."

After he'd given the address and repeated it and promised twice not to leave the scene he had a look around the office and saw it wasn't busted up enough. The possible loss of the liquor cabinet had gotten to him at the time but now he saw there wasn't that much damage, it wasn't even slightly dramatic except for Teddy, whose breath was still rasping in and out of his mouth and his chest at the same time, blood bubbling on his lips, so while he had the time for it Pitch went around the office kicking chairs over, breaking the standing lamp against the wall, and he wished he could do some damage with the knife, hack the walls up or cut up the cushions on the sofa and the chairs, but getting his prints on and off the knife was not a good idea.

When he was done he looked around, small town, no great distances, the med center not far and still no siren, very inefficient system, saw the damage he had done around the room and the smell of broken whiskeys and decided it was good.

5

Eli didn't bother calling to tell her, of course not, no, Lina had to hear about it on the eight AM two-minute local news segment of Morning Edition on KUOW, coming awake to the story as the voice said that in Eureka, California—the mention of the town lifted her head from her mug of French-pressed Peet's Vienna Roast—a reputed figure in the local marijuana trade, Edward Swift, had been killed in a shooting incident last night, and Lina's blood ran freezing cold and her body hot with the fearful certainty that Eli had done it, revenge for Teddy setting him up with the police, therefore flooding down upon her the functional end of Eli's life and freedom, her own peace of mind and life and conscience for the remainder of her poor time here on earth. Lina staggered slightly on her feet and was it possible that she was going to faint or something? so that she almost didn't hear that the shooter was Kennis J. Pitcher, said to be the representative of an unnamed tobacco company who had not yet been charged and may have acted in self-defense, press conference at *eleven AM this morning*—the English language slipping even on NPR as Lina's breath heaved out convulses of relief—which led to a sidebar about the possibility of legalization in the autumn and the commercial plans being made by—

Once Lina was breathing properly again she was so full of rage at Eli for not having called her that she couldn't correctly punch the numbers on her telephone and when she remembered he was on auto-dial couldn't remember what his code was. Once his line was ringing … ringing … and then she didn't believe it, she was getting his *voice mail*? … her second uncharitable thought was that if she had her druthers it would have been the other way around, since in her admittedly subjective estimate one more or less Teddy Swift wouldn't make much difference to the world

137

whereas the elimination from it of Kennis J. Pitcher would be a distinct improvement. "Eli, pick up the phone, this is me, I just heard the story on the radio, call me *immediately*—" which was when the phone in her hand started ringing at her and she almost jumped out of her chair before realizing that it was Eli phoning her back on call-waiting.

"*Eli*," she told him before he had a chance to say hello, "why the hell didn't you call me? "

"I'm *all right*, Ma."

"Why did I have to hear this on the radio, why didn't you call me?"

"Because, look, I was never in any danger, but the police came and they had to take my statement—"

"What?"

"—and by the time I got out of the station it was too late to call you, like middle of the night, almost morning."

"Are you out of your mind? Why did the police want a statement from you? Did you—"

"Because I was there," in the tone of one explaining something to a stupid person.

"Because you were *where*?"

"Jesus, Mom," eye-rollingly bored-sounding, his assumption that they must have mentioned it on the radio because, after all, it was him, "I was there in the office when Kenny shot Teddy."

"*What?*" Kenny, Teddy, he made it sound like a schoolyard dustup.

"Listen, Ma, I'm all right, I'm not intricated in any way, I was the witness, so they had to take my statement."

"What were you doing *there*?"

"I was, like, signing contracts and stuff with Mr. Pitcher—"

"You were going to *work* for him?"

"Well, like, *yeah*, at the *time*, but not *anymore*, you know? Anyway I was signing papers and having a drink with him when Teddy came in looking pretty crazy and …"

"You actually saw him get shot? Eli, what are you feeling?"

"What do you think, I was completely freaked but then I spent like half the night at the police station and after a while I got used to it and then I started getting really really tired. Maybe that was shock, like, *finally* setting in."

Lina tried to think what to say about Eli getting over seeing someone killed in front of him. "Eli, you saw Teddy murdered right in front of you …"

"Well yeah, but it was kind of self-defense, Teddy had a Bowie knife and …"

Lina listened with such intentness to the story that she couldn't follow it, was barely able to connect one of Eli's sentences to the next, while the news that Eli was not criminally implicated told the limbics and hydraulics of glandular relief to flood her body and soul with something that simultaneously made her sleepy and had her hands trembling so wildly they looked like someone else's hands overacting in some old pre-technicolor black-and-white movie.

She only came awake from this post-traumatic or shock-induced semi-stupor when Eli said something about …

"I'm sorry, Eli, can you repeat that?"

"Yeah, so, like, I'm moving up to Seattle."

"Eli! That's great!" I can make him safe! "I just have some cleaning out to do in the garden cottage and I guess I'll have to buy a double mattress for you and Sukey—"

"Mom."

"—or for the moment we can bring in the one from the guest bedroom, you can do the heavy lifting when you get here because I'm not going to drag it—"

"Mom."

"I can have the place ready for you by tonight, when are you coming?"

"Mom, you're not listening."

"What do you mean I'm not listening?"

"I'm not moving to your place, I'm moving to *Seattle*, there's a house and everything in Madison Park."

"How can you afford to live in Madison Park?"

"It's part of a job. I've got a job. I'm working."

Lina's mind was working only slowly, though: a job, a job, slow on the uptake to realize it was just another something in the dope business, okay, we can deal with that later and don't come down on him now because at least it's getting him out of Eureka where someone was about to kill him and then arrest him once he's dead. "*How* much a month? You're kidding!"

"No, that's the great thing, Mom, I won't have to get my hands dirty with product, it's totally, totally safe. Mom, I'm finally handling *transport*."

In the tone of someone who'd just sold his screenplay to a studio for a million. Lina's hands were still shaking while the rest of her flooded with increasingly equivocal relief, and although it felt as if she'd been through a couple of complete lifetimes in the last five minutes she still had to wonder if it was possible that "Frank, no I shoon't say his name on the phone" was really going to pay Eli between ten and fifteen thousand dollars a month, depending, to live in a gated community in the poshest part of Seattle just to talk on the phone—"and Mom, the place has super-secure phone lines and cable, a pool table *and* a hot tub"—every couple of days.

★

Lina waited until nine AM to call Marcus Dobbs at his office, left a message and didn't hear back from him until past ten, with the slow movement of Schubert's String Quintet playing in the background that he switched off as soon as she said hello.

"I hope you didn't mind waiting," he said, "but I didn't want to call you before I could get solid information from my friends at police HQ. First thing I should tell you is that your son is completely in the clear."

Lina breathed out not just breath but the last cargo of her mortal tension. "You're sure."

"He gave a complete statement to the police that held up under hours of questioning, he was a good witness, and the most important thing as far as I'm concerned," Marcus said, "is that there's no sign of Kennis Pitcher trying to put anything on Eli. Because I wouldn't put anything past that son of a bitch, excuse my language."

"Is Pitcher under arrest?"

"I believe he's still held for questioning, but from what I hear he's unlikely to be charged. Eli's statement confirms his claim of self-defense, and so from what I hear does evidence at the scene, and best of all, Mrs. Chase—"

"Lina," she said almost helplessly, feeling that twang for him where it counted and shouldn't be there right now in medias this.

140

"Best of all is that the extremely unreliable Mr. Pitcher has every reason to be grateful to Eli and make sure he comes to no harm."

"Yes," Lina said, feeling one notch more secure but Pitcher scaring her no matter what, that man ticking through the underbrush anywhere near me or any kin of mine like a bomb just waiting. "When are they going to let Pitcher out?"

"Probably later today, maybe tomorrow. They'll take his gun away as evidence and suspend his permit, and I think he can expect to lose his job with Raleigh Tobacco if he ever really had one. My guess, unless the police want to keep him in town pending further investigation or unless, say, the DEA wants a word with him, is that Mr. Pitcher is not long for these shores."

"May the devil let his servant depart in peace," Lina said.

"Amen, sister. So, does that make you feel a little better this morning?"

"It does. Thank you. How are you, have you been well? Forgive me for not asking sooner, my manners today …"

"Completely understandable under the circumstances. In confidence, let me tell you that I have personal reasons to want to see the back of Kennis Pitcher."

"Civic duty?"

"A friend of mine … an ex-girlfriend, someone I'm still fond of as a friend," with an emphasis that seemed in part directed at Lina saying, yes, I am hot but unattached, people are so funny, "has been involved with him for the past few months and I've been concerned for her well-being."

"I hope she'll be all right," said Lina, awkwardly, her voice bucked by misplaced sincerities.

"Oh I'm sure this will be the end of the affair … It's hard to get unstuck from him but this should do it. She should take a vacation somewhere until he's out of town."

"Speaking of which," said Lina, "Eli's moving out, coming up here, I mean this direction, a place in Seattle."

"*Good.* Because what I also hear from my friends among the police is that Eureka is about to become an exceptionally perilous place for anyone in local agribusiness, let us say."

"I don't think he's out of agribusiness, though."

"Let him be in it anywhere but here. Even before this I was pretty sure

141

there was going to be a sweep, but now, after this shooting, the scandalous local situation, the economy, the halfway legal medical trade, the do-nothing Johnny Laws … the sooner your son's out of here the better."

"I think he'll be on the move as soon as he can go."

"Unless the DEA wants to get something out of him, leaving the state shouldn't be a problem. If he runs into difficulties have him call me. I'm sorry that his departure … um, removes any reason for you to come down for a visit."

"You smoothie you," said Lina, suddenly reverting to a young girl in a soda shop pleased to be flirted with, but this quickly turned into a burst of intense wholly mature heat, and she felt as if she were projecting herself through the phone line with a welcome home baby—a shock of excess she tried to put down to the extremes of emotion she'd been whipped through this morning, Tilt-a-Whirl and Cyclone and a book of tickets to the other rides. She tried to keep her voice from buckling as she said, the hussy, "Well, Marcus, you never know. How's the music going?"

How lucky had ol' Pitch been?

Let me count the ways.

Which was good to pass the time in this here holding cell.

One, his first supposition when Eli hightailed it out the office door without the benefaction of a bullet in his ass was that Eli would disappear into the woods or ocean waves and would not be found by the enquiring minds of the police, thereby leaving Pitch up Shit's Creek not only without a paddle but with Captain Bob Poholek, than whom he would rather have no company at all just now, thanks, for company; but Eli Chase, bless his pointy head, had only run to cuddle away from the exposed terror of the world with his pregnant Betty-June at home, where the law found him presto and brought him to the station to tell the whole truth or most of it.

Two, Pitch told himself, Eli didn't try to play the position against me, which he could have done, bless same pointy head he probly din't realize he had my yoomagais in his hand and could've squeezed 'em hard. Not that Pitch had given Eli any reason to do so, but you never knew, he could have tried to protect himself by telling a tale against ol' Pitch. But didn't.

What was three? He forgot, but there was way more than just two lucky things working his way now.

142

Also good was Poholek's slip of the tongue somewhere in the gutter hours of the long interrogation during which ol' Bob tried to nail ol' Pitch's pelt to the station-house door even though Pitch'd been so good to him: when Poholek must of been tired he let slip, "When I sent Teddy to you this wasn't the outcome I was looking for," as if to say Old friend I was wishing you no harm by sending you an armed and dangerous hopped-up dopehead who'd been cut out of the deal, "I just wanted to give him a push and see which way he'd tip over."

Also good was Pitch managing to bite his tongue that instant and not say all outraged What! You *sent* him to me? So much better to look like you already knew the facts and thus obtain a fix on the matter without tipping your cards to the drygulching son of a rabid tit-hangin' country bitch across the table.

"Sooo," old dog Poholek kind of howled like a mournful bloodhound, "you're tryin' ta tell me Teddy Swift just ambled into your office and pulled a Bowie knife on you with intent?"

"I assume you have young Eli's statement and have examined at least the photos of the crime scene, how he busted the place up on me." It was going to be a long and wearing night and probably morning too but unless Eli flipped on him they didn't have a thing and Poholek knew it.

In retrospect Pitch was losing count of his blessings, but one more was the frustrated and tired Poholek making the mistake of also telling him, "Your old friend Richard Burke back in Durham, I imagine he will have lost the last of his motorvation to want to keep you on the company payroll now."

The new information that Poholek had been in touch with Burke— which suddenly made sense of all the cynical suspicious unfaithful bullshit he'd been getting from little Richie on the phone, which was not a part of their old-time established universe of discourse—sucked an enormous big one but was good to know, because it's always good to know, plus he'd be back in Durham sometime and would settle up with Burke then.

They'd taken away his watch along with his belt in case he wanted to hang himself and time it and there was no clock in the cell but a small high-up window was showing the merest early hint of rosy-fingered dawn and no matter how they tried to draw this sucker out on ol' Pitch it wun't-cun't be all that long before he breathed the bright air of American freedom, then had a look around at the world and decided what to do in it next.

"Okay, now that you're in with me I can tell you," Franklin said. "To get out from under the world of shitfire comin' down I've made the move from selling bud to running—wait for it—*hashish*, and before you say no one wants it I found a market for it in Canada, where people are more sophisticates."

"Oh man that's brilliant," Eli told Franklin, trying hard not to smile too much and give the game away. "And it makes transport easier even though it's longer ride. A lot less bulk, man that's smart."

Eli thought it was okay to let Franklin enjoy his own smarts, which he was doing.

"But what about the problem of it drying out, Franklin? When'd you press the shit? Few months later it loses half its kick, um, potency."

"One of several innovations I have made is finding a smart boy genius who figured out how to infuse hash oil and other natural essential elements into the shit so it'll hold up for a whole year between harvests so far at least and still counting. And innovations, that's only one. My genius boy has also improved the potency of shatter, mon, pure hash oil in plate glass form, the strongest ever by like a factor of five, ten, fifteen, take your pick, it's atomic."

"Jesus keep that stuff away from me," Eli said.

"You mean you have your limits?"

"It's one thing to love being fucked up but that stuff's too far, I go batshit crazy and lose all function. And you made it worse?"

"But you can move it, right?"

"No problem. I'm not even tempted."

"But tell me, did you actually see Teddy *die*?"

"I saw him get shot but I was out of the room before he, um, went," said Eli. "Can we not talk about it?"

"What I want to know is that cat Pitcher coming after all of us for some fucked up reason or other?"

"Teddy came into his office, already pissed off about the patch and wired on something," said Eli. "Then he pulled his bigass Bowie knife, you know the one? first on me and then took a whack at Pitcher with it. I'm not sure he was actually trying to hit him with it but he was a dangerous and crazy man and the room was too small for it."

"So Pitcher just popped him."

"Teddy was standing on Pitcher's desk swinging down on Pitcher."

"Holy shit. And Pitcher popped him."

"Yah. Now can we please stop talking about this please?"

Calm sea today from Franklin's deck, blueglass under burning summerlight and just small white lips of wavebreak, maybe too calm, meaning a storm on the way but the cool thing, keep your eye on the water just past today's low surf and you catch the curved black back and sharkfin of a dolphin rising clear from right to left, then four or five or maybe even eight of them working through the water, their hoopy backs breaking the surface hooped and turning, the fin cutting free then disappearing so that each one looked like the top, the visible part of a wheel, and each wheel was a part of a giant many-geared mechanism of dolphin-wheels turning systematically inside the ocean, and it occurred to Eli that this was pretty decent weed and finally he was relaxing a little after a bad night and morning.

"What is this shit?" he asked Franklin, passing him the burning remainder of what was left.

"Purple Martian Moonblossom," and Eli had to figure out if that was supposed to mean anything at all, unless it came from Mars which it didn't. Maybe the effect. So this wasn't information, just a name. Gooood homegrown Humboldt County shit, a little slow to get to you but then it packed a woozy.

"You make hash out of any of this?"

"Gabbalabba maggalaba boo," Franklin seemed to tell him, only much much better, which meant are you kidding? it would kill whole peoplefuls of people if you, if you. Wheels of dolphins doing their hoopy thing in the water of the world, but the air up here was hot and the sea over there so blue and cool. Which was the difference. Extremely.

"Oh man, is it all right if I go inside and lay down? I think I have to go inside and lay down."

"Remember to call your mother," was the last thing he either heard or didn't hear Franklin say. Damn, did Franklin lace this stuff with … *lace?* No, it was, "Remember *not* to kill your mother."

He was walking indoors on long funny legs, he saw the figure in the carpet, geometrical, he saw his own figure on the sofa below the window open to the beach, safely closer than the floor, safely closer, and he fell into it because it fit perfectly because he didn't have so too many geometric angles, except for except oh no as his figure tilted sideways like a whatsit, on a tilter, lilter, filter, quilter …

★

"All right," he said to Franklin after he woke up way too late in whatever house this was, also room, the ocean either on his left or right or on his both, that can't be right. "No more smoke and now you tell me."

"I make the best Jamaica Blue Mountain coffee and I'mo get you some," Franklin said, and he also had the best laugh, which is why he used it, not too much, just the right much of laughing.

"I'm sceptible," Eli told him, which sounded like what heee, then he forgot.

★

Next time it was almost night and definitely time to talk.

"You with me?"

Eli's mouth was very, that special kind of dry, but "I am with you," he could say, slowwly because his jaw all slow elastic, and he hoped it was so, because now Franklin began to lay it out.

But, "Did you say something about coffee a minute ago?"

"A minute," Franklin was laughing again. "Wasn't a minute ago but, yeah, I'll make you some."

Eli fell asleep again while Franklin was in the kitchen.

★

"No, this isn't usual," he had to tell Franklin, who he was afraid might lose faith in him. "It's like, I saw Teddy killed and it took a lot out of me and when you gave me that Blue Martian—"

"*Purple* Martian Moonblossom."

146

"—when you gave me that Purple Martian to smoke it all just ran out of me and I must've really needed it and some *rest*. I am not this uncool normally, I promise."

"If I didn't already know you …"

"Man, that's coffee," Eli said in an old-style television voice his dad sometimes used after taking a sip, but Franklin didn't get the joke. It really was good coffee, though, and his brain had mostly stopped smooshing all over with the Purple. Just a little tilt and whirl in the center of his brain was all. "All right, man, *diga me*," he said, pleased that he could sound cool in Spanish.

It turned out Franklin had been busy. It turned out that the boy-genius who had figured out how to preserve hash by oil-infusion plus making dab and shatter even crazier-making had also invented a portable battery-powered separator-drum machine, you could carry the whole works in a backpack and put in skuff and buds and leaves and it would screen the trichomes out with the selectivity and resolution of a Mila P500 or even better, but Franklin's people were being subtle and traceless, paintbrushing the precious little bumps off the buds and leaves and only then refining them, Franklin said. "Pure intoxicant and nothing but," Franklin told him. "And when I say nothing but, I mean no big picking operations, no trucks, no convoys. What I mean is no catchee."

Franklin had a dozen separator rigs so far and a squad of trained operators.

He wasn't talking like a movie mastermind anymore, he was talking practical accomplishment, very realistic, so realistic he started to remind Eli of his dad, more about the task in hand than how smart he was to be doing it, the kind of intelligent sense Dad made, only the subject was different: "I had let's say an intuition that it'd be wise this year not just to go all the way to hash and dab but especially also do some early picking, so what I did was plant a whole lot of small patches on south-facing slopes, totally unknown beautiful little primo patches, ripe already and I've had my people up there with the roller-drums and that part of the harvest is complete. I've even had some people inside the Raleigh patch already, finding early buds and divesting them of their lovely little titties and not leaving the littlest bitty trace behind."

"They didn't get busted?" Eli asked him.

"You were set up, mon. Teddy set you up. These people are hikers with backpacks and none of them has a local reputation and they're in and out." Franklin looked both ways before crossing. "I've had them inside Roger Dodger and Windell's patches too already, suckin' up them chomes."

"Is that cool? Roger and Windell, man …"

"Yes that's cool because those patches will never come to normal ripe and harvest this year, the man is coming. I am stealing nothing from no one. What I'm doing, factually, is preserving the fruits of everybody's labor, I'm saving what has been grown." Franklin didn't have any of those accents now. "I am preserving the environment. When it's all done I might even give Rodge and Win a taste, a kind of service fee, thank you for your work but you were too stupid to save it from the man so I did, here."

Eli really had to think. He wasn't sure about Roger and Windell would ever get that charity taste. And what if the man didn't come with wind and fire and big machetes? What then?

"It's like when Jackie Robinson came to play in the majors and he was so good he burned everyone up, all they could say was That's right, let a nigga in and he plays like one, thing he's best at is stealing bases. But what Jackie Robinson was doing, he was revolutionizing the game and so am I."

"Jackie Robinson."

"I'll show you some Youtube, Jesus, where you been."

"And you need me because?"

"I don't need you, I want you, Eli, because my main man in Seattle, my hub of transport, I had to let him go."

"What for?"

"Watchoo think? Man was stealing from me even though I paid him better than fine. And time being what it is, there's not enough to find out who is doing what and who among his people might hold a grudge enough to rat on me, I had to let all *his* people go and they were handling my transport. Besides which," Franklin made an uncomfortable gesture with his head and neck, "the guy I fired kind of, um, disappeared and some of his people think I did something, which I didn't even though a fuck a lot of money was stolen from me, so his people are not to be trusted right now. So, you know Teddy's people and there's no more Teddy, right?"

But, Eli wanted to say but couldn't find the place for it, Teddy's people weren't safe to work with him, Eli, that is: some of them spooked, some thought maybe he had something to do with getting Teddy killed or if not they thought he was, like, unlucky. So he and Franklin were in almost the same condition, which was funny, not ha-ha but the other kind.

Franklin kept talking. "And we won't need all of them because my specialists already done most of the selection. Transport gawn to be simpler because we eliminated the problem of all that bulk, but I still need a man up there to coördinate and I'm glad to put you there because I know your heart is good."

Meaning also, same-old same-old, I'm the guy they catch if we get caught. "Thank you." So, what he'd have to do with Franklin, which he didn't wannoo because he liked Franklin but, was make like a human who got his script in the mail like all the other people who studied their lines and knew where to stand and when to say them. He didn't want to do this to Franklin but he didn't see what you supposed maybe would call an alternative. Having to do it hurt himself in a place he couldn't reach except by doing it, so therefore he would.

"It's a beautiful crib in Madison Park, mon, wait till you see it, semicircle drive inside a stone wall, iron gate, surveillance cameras, alarm system, great views, beautiful rooms. It stays in my name, well actually my company's name behind a couple of cutouts. What I have to put in yours so you have skin in the game is I have to transfer title of the Recreational Vehicle to you, because it's no more trucks and vans full of gone-off fruit to hide the smell, it's one bigass RV with the wall panels hollow and we fill it full of quintuply vacuum-baggied bricks no dog can sniff of the world's most beautiful hash I'd run up against even the best historical Nepalese, mon, anytime."

"Nepalese, whoa."

Franklin made his face unassailable. "Better than. Believe it. Plus the killer candyglass."

"And I'd be driving?" Eli had to make absolutely sure he would not.

"No you'll be *arranging* it. Have you not been listening, mon? You'll be arranging it, by which I mean you have to find me the straightest-

149

looking drivers in the world, nice middle-aged married couple say, someone nobody stops on the road, you'll arrange that and be there at the hub to supervise further transit and distribution. You know the people, right? There is going to be bucks to go around, this will be a real job, I wasn't gonna tell you this but okay, last year I wasn't ready to sell hash in bulk, the market wasn't prepped and I wasn't sure security was up to speed, but I made the hashish and stored it, which is how I know my boy's oil-preservation technique works, try some and it it'll rock you like a motherfucker. Got it stored in a tannery I own up the Klamath River, you ever see a leather tannery? You have to see it, big water-driven wheel, the funky cowhide smell getting cured, chugga-chugga-slosh and I'll give you a wallet after, or a vest, a briefcase, or you want a pair of fitted buckskin pants? You probly seen the Bassworks label around the shops, that's mine. The tannery is historic and authentic. So there'll be plenty work for you, this is not a part-time job and I hope you're up to it … Now in the old days, by which I mean last year, we used the Seattle house for storage and that could be dangerous for the person living in it, but this year we are so compact the house is gravy. Your gravy, Eli, just for doing the job. We can rent you a little off-premises storage facility, be all we need, but if you want to use it for small-size private sales I'll give it to you cheap, right? so—"

"I don't, I won't. Been there, done it, nevermore especially since, you know, Sukey and a baby coming."

"Okay, then after Seattle everything goes to Canada. Just tryin' to turn extra income your way if you want it. You know all Teddy's people, right?"

"I know the good ones and the bad ones."

"Well let's take some the good ones if you don't mind."

"Why does it have to be, um, *Seattle*?"

"My good idea for a few years now, the scene is looser up there than here, they might even legalize come this year's referendum, and we already have the house. Police all over the highways south to S.F. and L.A. and the main roads back east, don't matter what's your detour they're on the eye. Check my losses against anyone else's. Much easier to ship north, been proven, and much less risky do it all in one. There's too much pressure this year, and some of our people already suspect some of our other people and us. Send a lot of little vans out, dangerous, they catch one and squeeze hard, someone squeaks and there goes the whole organization and me too. It's time to do like my man Mark Twain tells it, put all your eggs in one basket and *watch that basket*."

"They're already growing a lot up north, though."

"They are not growing primo Humboldt County bud with their grey weather or in their basements with the lights on. Or pressing it into the world's greatest longest lasting hash, bricks you can build a house with and gold windows of dab to end the world with. This is the diamond mine. No one can touch our shit, am I right?"

"You are right."

"So, Eli, we don't spit in our hands and shake on it because that's gross, or whatever magic evil-eye shit Teddy did, just tell me, I've said it all, are you doing this with me?"

"Oh yeah, was there any doubt? Yes I am, it's great, absolutely yes. One more thing," he raised the cup, "when they legalize recreational use …"

"Man, they never gonna legalize that for years. They do it in a state and the DEA says nuh-uh you busted anytime it wants. That's bullshit you can get away with in Colorado maybe but this is California large. You can't operate in a environment like that here."

"Okay, but *if* they legalize and you're out," trying to keep it light and friendly now, though it was a little lame to say, "you should go into the coffee business. This is good."

"I am *already* in the coffee business. Who the fuck you think imports this shit?"

"That mean enough for me to have another cup?"

"Go in the kitchen and pour it for yourself. You family now."

6

IT WAS TRICKY. One thing he'd forgotten, it was a long time since circumstances had compelled him to kill someone, is how once you got started you developed a yen to keep going, so satisfying like, nowadays, in a video game to just *eliminate* any irritant that pops into view. So unless you wanted to give your will permission to go wild out there and do something it was time for a bit of whoa there fella.

For instance Marcus Dobbs, just on the principle that he used to be fucking Betty-June-Anne and now that she was sure to leave ol' Pitch after the shooting and almost as sure to go running back to that brownskin boy and tell him tales about yours truly, so definitely, on principle, Marcus Dobbs, but then in practice wait a minute. And he wanted that one more time with Anne he was pretty sure, now, he wasn't going to get unless he *made* it happen, one more last big time with some piece of him up every hole except her nose so she was rolling and howling beyond every human and animal borderline in the land of pure unnamable fuck from before things became things and people became people and he wanted, big change here, making himself vulnerable to her this way, he wanted her hand up his ass too, as much of it as she could grease up there, so he could be dragged with her down into the shit-tasting root of all things, rolling and rasping in fathomless undertow, all the way down in it lost to normal human mind, and then he'd start punching her in that finemade blueblood face she was proud of and let's see what happens, then.

On the other hand that would be risky if he was still full of kill, if he still had the yen he could take it too far, zing over the line without noticing it until too late. *Oops*, with a disposal problem after.

Anyway most likely he wasn't gonna get the chance.

Therefore the word was cool it, Pitch, let things settle and see what you

152

have left when things stop rocking on their bottoms. Not much, was his intuition, which meant this would be a time for him to start improvising quick as Charlie Parker. He'd expected to have a stronger position to play, with the Raleigh framework backing him, but now he'd have to make his move from the invisible. He was good at that, he'd been good at it before and hadn't lost no capacity for it since.

So all right, time to face the music, sitting in the fuck-turret of his cool apartment with the windows open to early evening light, sitting up in bed with his left hand on the balls and sausage in his pants with the top loosened, pick up the phone and get the readout from that pathetic turncoat Richard Burke.

Pitch thought it best to cut directly to the chase: "So I'm fired, huh."

"Not yet," Burke told him, a surprise. "What management wants is for you to close down your office, finish up any outstanding details and come back to HQ."

"So they can fire me there." He gave himself a squeeze inside his pants and it responded.

"That's not clear yet, but, okay, most likely, yes."

"What about the patch we got fenced in here?"

"It rots where it stands. We're not concerned with it. What we have to do is hold down the scandal, the violence, I mean for Chrissake you shot that guy. Even you must understand that that kind of thing is bad for business."

"Heroic Raleigh Employee Shoots Crazed Drug Czar in Self-Defense. That's a headline." Another squeeze.

"You probably think it's an ad campaign."

"It's a lot better than what you've got."

"And what's that?"

"Raleighs Give You Cancer but a Pack of Wailers Will Make Dying Sweeter Going Down. We'll Kill You But We'll Also Get You High. Seriously, Rick, you think y'all have any PR or ethical standing? It's a joke. You're transparent, there's nothing but moneygrubbing while we kill you. At least I *did* something."

"You sho'nuff did, Ken."

"Don't give me none of that phony cracker jive. I defended civilization, such as it is in this fallen world, against a ragtag bunch of outlaws."

"You were attacked by a *bunch*?"

"I was attacked by a representative. I am Wyatt Earp. Best Raleigh can possibly do under the circs is go with the story. Kennis Pitcher, American hero."

"You're out of your mind but I'll put it to the board."

"More of your famous bullshit fair-and-even-handed act, but now I find out you been telling tales to Deppity Chief Poholek, cutting my balls off while I'm trying to do right for the comp'ny out here in the wildaness."

Richie made a phony sigh to demonstrate his patience and forbearance. "I didn't call Poholek, he phoned me up a couple of weeks after you got there because he found you a mite strange and squiggly."

"And you told him I was twisted like a pretzel."

"No, I stood up for you." Still keeping to his weary honest act. "I told him you were an old friend and on the up and up. *He's* the one that began supplying me with contrary information I found rather troubling, for instance the mostly incomplete or possibly forged paperwork submitted to get into pharmaceutical supply and the lack of response from the state re exceeding the legal grow limit."

"You try dealing with that bureaucracy and ten different contradictory orders of law, it's legal to grow but not to sell, and which local judge is sitting where and what he have for lunch the Tuesday he hears your case. Poholek in particular has got a fixation. He thinks everybody done him wrong and he's the last man standing in a rotten world."

"Not how he struck me, Ken."

"Then you weren't paying attention. He's a true American hero, for an asshole. When did I start losing you, Rick?"

Burke sighed again but it was just a staged public sigh intended for the cheap seats. "I can't remember. In fact it's hard for me to recall what you used to have on me."

"Want me to tell you?" Pitch ran his thumb lightly over the mouth of his cock, gliding on a newcome trace of liquid slick.

"What, that you were smarter, quicker, more charismatic, had the drop on me from back in college days at Duke?"

"Don't let yourself off easy, Ricky-boy. What I had on you, what I always had on you, was that you were queer for me."

"Oh please."

"Not even pretty please. You wanted to suck my dick and kiss my balls and didn't know it. Didn't let yourself know it, but that's what it always was."

"That's disgusting, Ken. Even for you, that's disgusting."

"Look in the mirror, Ricky-boy. You already know it." Pitch pulled his hand out and licked some pre-ejaculate off the pad of his thumb. Amazing how he tasted like Anne pussy, which is maybe why we hit it off so well: chemistry, pH, she's mild for a woman of her coloring.

"I don't see the value in continuing this line of talk—" Ricky trying for a point.

"I bet you don't."

"—so let's stay with the facts for the moment: wind up the office, we'll give you a week to deal with your rental and belongings, return the Chevy to the local dealership and we'll deal with the unpaid portion of the lease, then come home on the company ticket for a talk and we'll see. I've lost patience with you, but I'll tell you honestly and against my own interest that the board isn't there yet, they don't know you like I do, so you might have some play left."

"That means ten days?"

"A week. Surely you can do the office and apartment closure simultaneously. How much contractual work do you have outstanding for Muhrad? Can't be much. You just bought the one property. In fact you haven't done much of anything, really."

"I was *preparing*. I prepared a lot at significant personal risk of a kind you've never put in play for anyone and I was waiting for the go-ahead from central. Give me ten days and you got a deal."

"A deal? We're not making deals, we're winding up your shop and reeling you home before you do more damage. I trust you've kept away from the television crews."

A dash of motion outside the windows caught his eye but it was only a crow landing in a tree across from his house and Pitch did not believe in omens. It was a crow, and shortly he could expect a caw to claim the territory in glossy ignorance of larger concerns anywhere operative.

"The teevee people are all over town and would like to be all over me but I have given no interviews—"

"They got your perp walk on tape, though, it's a hit on CNN."

The crow said *Cawwww, cahwwww*. Old McDonald had a farm.

"Not one word, Ricky, have I given to the press. Looking out for the compny's interest like always."

"Some job you've been doing."

"I like to think. But the disrespectful way you been talking to me, maybe I *could* use some face time with the cameras."

"Don't, just don't. If you want any kind of future at Raleigh, don't. And frankly, what does it matter, if you stay for seven days or ten?"

"It doesn't. I can stay the fuck out here on my own money long as I feel like. I'm gettin' fired anyway and I like it here on the blue Pacific, but it'd be nice to have the office and especially the car, and ten days should be just about enough for what I have in mind."

"And what is that," Burke said wearily.

"I will huff and I'll puff and I'll bloww your house down, little piggy."

Well, that was bullshit but he had to say something. On the other hand he still had the only keys to the padlock on the fence of CA-1453-EP7 that Jack built and time was a'wastin. Eli Chase was lost to him but there were still the good old dudes up around Grants Pass and they knew how to pick and pack and move bulk product.

And on yet another hand, if he did go back to Raleigh-Durham, Ricky Burke, thanks to his confidential colloquies with Poholek had earned a visit and some form of special treatment that hadn't quite come to mind yet in the mists of future time, among other scores to settle here and there.

There were always little tension-times, tag-ends of old-school unresolved issues, of authority mostly, between father and son, but in general and in bulk Marcus enjoyed his dad's visits up from Oakland. Marcus owned the ground floor of a well-made California lumberland oldie with big oak beams and fixtures, plenty of room, good light on a leafy street and a six-foot Yamaha baby in the living room, its glory and limitation how fat and monochrome its tones were, a good one though Marcus would have preferred a Steinway only he couldn't find the Steinway of his dreams so why bother and the prices were ridiculous. What he should do is move up to a full grand and do it *this* year, seven foot, eight foot, ten foot *bunch*. It could be justified: he'd had a few performances on the conservatory circuit and published a small book of Preludes, Etudes and Nocturnes for piano quartet via a Midwest university press, plus a Sonatina he was happy with, and a chamber group was talking prelims about a concert tour and a first recording. It was just the beginning even if it was coming relatively late—if anything broke he'd have to work hard as hell and learn everything he'd put off about orchestration for years, don't think about why—but that it was coming at all to someone essentially outside the accredited system and its ladderworks of influence and sinecure, not to mention happening to a dark-skinned individual though that wasn't the kind of obstacle it used to be, in fact if he pushed a little more music out there he could be up for a MacArthur Genius because those people, bless their souls, seemed to like the Negroes and were eager to uplift them and had made some let us say premature bequests and Marcus wouldn't mind one.

Stop dreaming. You make a living and you have free time and a decent piano so thank the Lord.

"Want another beer, Dad?"

"I'm fine," his father said, swirling the bottom of his bottle, wouldn't drink from a glass when one was offered, a shortish brown man looking young and fit at sixty though with a potbelly and some of his hair gone in front and back. The usual amused look in his eyes, man of the world, man who'd conquered the piece of world he chose to live in, a place you had to be tough in, face-forward to the penal industry, dealing with career monsters much of the time, huge hulking mostly black men who wanted to beat the system any way they could and this stubby little man knew how to put a collar on them, turn them into friends you could invite home, some of them, to meet the wife and the growing son because you wanted the boy to learn the world the way it was—dangerous game to play if you didn't know what you were doing and were a fool. But Dad wasn't one and they didn't mess with Dad.

"Tell you what," his dad said. "Bring me a cold one and let's listen to one of yours on the hi-fi or you can play me one on the piano."

He was being kind. Marcus didn't write his dad's kind of music. Lionel Dobbs' roots were in Motown and other soul music, Aretha and before that church, and when it came to jazz it was the older cats from Ellington and

Basie's heyday, then Horace Silver and Jimmy Smith and the Messengers and Bird, Miles not so much and he stopped short at middle-period Trane. Which was okay with Marcus, a man can't be everything all at once and his dad had done a lot.

Marcus himself was happy to be composing in a polyvalent time and felt particularly pleased that it was kosher to write strong melody again, so he could be, I don't know, post-Impressionist, post-Soviet, post-Britten—he meant it was possible to write the music as he heard it in his head without a knot of worry and still get dissonant and difficult when the muse suggested it. And even snag a grant or two. What to play for his father now? Maybe the slow movement from the Sonatina, or he could improvise and pretend he had composed a blues. It might have been easier if he could have been a jazz musician—though how easy is that?—but it turned out he liked to ruminate, think things through, take his time and only then put down a phrase of notes.

"I'll get you that cold one," Marcus said, and when he got up so did Thor from beside his father's armchair, and Thor's toenails followed him clickey-click-click on the parquet from the living room into the kitchen. "You thirsty too?" He bent to pat the dog's big head and got a wider eager grin and dazed brown eyes in response.

Thor was a somewhat thickset brown-on-brown Doberman who scared the living let's say daylights out of everyone who met him until, gradually, they saw that he had the affectionate manners of a puppy. What they didn't know is that Thor was also a complete professional whom "skizziks" in a commanding voice would bring to the ready stance, shoulders squared, snarling with fangs exposed, enough to stop most comers trembling in their boots, then if need be "pooters" to send him in for that horrible Doberman bite in which the jaws clamp down then grind the flesh sideways, shredding blood vessels and meat—and "palookas-o" for over a hundred pounds of living rocket with teeth up front into the throat and that would finish any human.

Marcus poured a fresh bowl of water and Thor seemed appreciative and noisily lapped it, though he was always a happy dog who liked the people he knew and was ready to like other people unless directed otherwise, and then it wasn't personal it was business. Thor couldn't have been too thirsty though: he followed Marcus with the beers back into the living room, then resettled alongside his master's armchair and grinned around the room, pleased to belong.

"You should get yourself a Thor, the business you're in," his father started in, and here we go. His dad's voice was often a notch louder than most people's, as if making a definitive announcement of some kind. To Marcus it showed his class origins and his sense of how far he'd come, out of the Abyss of the Niggers as he called it in unguarded moments, to owning his own home in uphill Oakland, treating people fairly, perhaps especially including parolee denizens of the Abyss, raising a son into higher if less funky life-options, and who honorably had looked after his wife during the hideous pain and subtractions of her cancer—his announcer's voice showed legitimate pride in what he had accomplished and become, and Marcus said amen, but it was also true his dad didn't like being disagreed with and could be a pain.

"Dad, we just get potheads up here, pacific doodlebugs with nary a bone in their heads."

"Yes, as we saw in that wonderful shooting incident the other day. Doodlebuggery at its best, good country people, a Bowie gainst a Niner. Listen, I could leave Thor with you for oh let's say a month and see how you like it. I go see parolees with Thor on a chain leash and they give me nooo trouble, never. He likes you, he's happy to see you again, look how he follows you around. And you might think he needs a lot of activity but he's cool just sitting around the office he has such an even temper. He's even a little lazy if you let him."

"I'd have to work out how and when and what to feed him—"

"I'll leave you the whole system on a sheet of paper, tell you what to buy."

"—take him out to shit."

"Well of course you do. Even you still shit sometimes, am I right? He's good company and then he protects your ass in times of trouble. Take him for two weeks and you'll want one of your own. I know police dog trainers back home in Oakland, the best."

"I don't think I need Thor's professional services, Dad, if you don't mind."

"You cannot defend yourself in a tight situation with a string quartet."

"Has it been tried?"

Then he was saved by the bell, one short and even let's say hesitant ring, followed by a polite knock upon the oak. "Minute," he told his father.

When Thor started getting up to accompany him—he had the protective instinct bigtime—Marcus flashed his dad a look and Lionel only had to say "Stay" one time.

Marcus opened the front door and it was Anne Dujardin in a little black dress, no pearls this time, collarbones still fine and delicate without need of ornament. Also: no bra necessary, he could not help but notice, for the fine and modestly upstanding.

"I know," she said, "I should have phoned."

"Not at all, not at all, come in, I'm pleased to see you." What he was pleased to do was search her face for damage. She seemed stressed, still a beautiful woman for her age but kind of wired today. "My dad's here, visiting from Oakland," the social obligation helping him through the moment, "and I'd be pleased for you to meet him."

They were through the square oakwood arch to the living room and the problem was that Thor had risen to meet and greet the newcomer, up on his impatient toes and stepping in place eager to be introduced, and Anne had gone rigid.

"No no no, he's just a puppy," said Marcus, and rising from his armchair his father came out with an imperious "Thor!" and what pleased Marcus best, once nerves and dog were settled, was how quickly Anne recovered her poise and began to look comfortable with his dad.

"Lionel," his dad explained.

"Anne," and the three of them stood there with Thor watching them from a distance until Marcus told her that he and Lionel were drinking beer but he had cold Sauvignon Blanc in the fridge, and Anne said that would be lovely, and Lionel had read the vibes between them enough to say, "I believe I know when it's time for me to take a walk around the block or, er-uh, a whalewatching ride on of those boats from the harbor, back in a couple hours …"

"Not at all, not at all," Anne and Marcus hastened to assure this borderline rude individual, so they sat around the living room for ten minutes exchanging polite inanities and bits of routine personal history until Anne was able to ask Marcus if she could speak to him alone for a minute.

"I'll take a walk," Lionel volunteered, but was beaten back.

"We can go out on the deck," Marcus suggested, and that was fine with Anne.

"Thor," his dad said warningly as the couple started for the back of the house, "*behave* your ass now."

Once they were outside, a small pineboard deck with a couple of canvasback chairs overlooking the immaculate lawn and Marcus leaning awkwardly on the teak rail, Anne felt free to show her distress, pacing up and down the boards and knotting her face up, heading partway up the road to Dora Maar.

"If it's about Kennis Pitcher," Marcus told her, "you can say anything at all to me without worrying that I'll judge you or be critical. You're my friend."

"God, Marcus, it was such a sick relationship. I don't know how I was dumb enough to get into it but boy I'm glad it's over."

"So am I," said Marcus, and waited for the rest.

Anne put her stemware glass of pee-yellow wine on the railing and taking her hand away accidentally knocked it off onto the plush green grass.

"Never mind," Marcus said.

"Marcus, he actually *killed* that guy."

"I heard."

"*Killed* him. Not that I should be surprised after what I've seen. The man's a psychopath, sociopath, whatever they call it."

"I always liked the old word, and that was my estimation of him."

"He has no real feelings. He's not human."

"If only that were true," Marcus said, and immediately regretted the comment. This was Anne's time to talk, to unburden, and he was scoring interpretative points as if on paper.

"He killed that guy and I, I you-know-whatted all naked with him, and he *killed* that man."

Marcus wanted to say something about too much information but he managed to say no more than, "Yes."

Anne tried to do something to her face with her hands but couldn't swing it. "How *could* I? How could I? I must have been out of my mind. What happened to me?"

"But now you're back. Hello? Now, you're back."

"Marcus I want to rush into your arms but I don't dare to after, after what I've been … next to." She started moving, just the first twitch, as if to rush him, and one of his hands flickered upward in a reflex, and he saw that the gesture hurt her because she understood that it was meant to prevent an embrace. Especially because before that he'd almost palpably felt her more or less undressing him with her eyes.

"Let's just talk," Marcus said.

"How *could* I?"

This was going to take a while. "Wait here. I'll bring you another glass of wine." Better, he'd bring the bottle.

On his way through the living room he saw his father theatrically twiddling his thumbs and examining the ceiling while silently mock-whistling some tune or other. Sometimes the old man could really overplay his shit.

On the way back with the icebucket and a pair of glasses, he saw his dad bent stroking Thor's velvet brown ears between thumbs and fingers and the dog grinning with his tongue out one side. Not for all the world would Marcus be a dog. Human consciousness with all its options, not easy but definitely the life to live, nice work if you can get it, and here he was, complicated and tangled in it.

Back on the deck he saw that Anne had recomposed herself. He poured two cold stemmed glasses and she accepted hers with a ceremonial sip that just touched her lips. She stood by the railing but did not lean on it, her back to the lawn, sunlight catching in her hair. She looked very pale and for a moment Marcus had the illusion that he could see her blood pulsing through that network of blue veins that had disturbed him at first but then had become beautiful in their visible mortality, the frailty of flesh rendered into a late work of mannerist art. If that's the way you had to put it.

He sat in one of the deckchairs so as to be the still point in the scene.

"I didn't mean to get hysterical on you," she said. "This is what I came to say." A touch of fingertips to her temple to brush away a lock of hair that wasn't there. "I broke up with Kennis, *of course*, which was about to happen anyway, and I haven't seen him, I've refused to see him, but he's been on the phone with me and you're one of the people he talks about."

"Oh?" A sip of wine he didn't want, to fill the space.

"He shot and killed a man, he's sure he's about to lose his job with Raleigh and he won't leave town because he's after something or someone."

"And he's been talking about me."

"Among others. He's going nuclear. I think what he's after is money tied up in Raleigh's property in the mountains, you know about that?"

"I do."

"But why I came to see you is that he wants revenge from somewhere or someone, anyone, he's angry with a lot of people and might strike out in any direction, I think he doesn't much care which. I think he's delusional about what's been done to him and what he can do, he's in tentacle mode, thinks he can take on eight people at a time if he feels the need."

"Did you talk to him about me?"

"Um, at the beginning, in a general way, you know, ex-lover, recent."

"How much did he want to know?"

"Only a little too much. It didn't seem bad at the time because I didn't know how creepy he was. He led me in one step at a time to his creepy little world. The way you boil a frog starting in cold water so it doesn't know what's happening and doesn't jump out of the pot?" Anne shuddered visibly but Marcus pretended to himself he hadn't seen it. "It was something like that," she said.

It was a most unpleasant thought but he dragged his question into place on the simplest story line: "Was he jealous of me, of us, in the past?"

"I would have said no more than normally but now, after what I know and what he's done, I'm not so sure. Sometimes he's super-obviously a dangerous guy because he likes to play the role, which it turns out might be what he really is. I had no idea, I thought he was, you know, presenting. Other times he's very smart and hard to read."

"Why would he be after me and not you? Anne, what you're telling me makes me worry about you, not me."

She worried her forelip with her underteeth. "I think he's already hurt me as much as he wants to. He likes it that way. He doesn't have to do anything else. He won, so I'm done."

There was an abyss hidden in that sentence but Marcus didn't want to look into it. His gathering protective urge was enough compulsion to deal with for now. He tried with difficulty to remember what had broken up his relationship with Anne. Part of it was that she didn't want children, part that at forty she was borderline for that anyway, and part, for him, though he didn't like to admit it as a factor, was that she'd probably be losing her exquisite looks over the next ten years while he'd still be young, besides which black don't crack. Tough to look at but let's be honest.

There had been some reservation or objection from her side too, but he hadn't understood it. Something to do with her being so high-strung, but he didn't know specifically what it was. He was pretty sure it wasn't race, but you never know about that for sure.

"So you wanted to warn me," he said, but that train had already jumped the track while he was thinking and had fallen off the roadbed.

"I've missed you," Anne said. "Really missed you. Intensely."

"For how long?"

"Awhile, but now very much. Is there any chance?"

"Not this hot on the rebound from that guy, no."

"Meaning not now but possibly after a time?" Trying to fuss with her hair again.

Reluctantly he said, "Yes, I might. And you?"

"Without a doubt. In a New York minute."

Which gave Marcus pause. He wondered how straight he could be with her, and decided that this was as good a time as any to test it.

"One thing that worries me is that you're attracted to a bad guy like Pitcher and also a black guy like me, so that maybe part of what it's about for you might be some kind of transgression, something in your psychology that's not worked out."

"I don't see you as a black guy," she said.

"As what then."

"Are you kidding? I see you as Marcus."

He nodded. "That could be all right."

"I'll tell you what gives *me* second thoughts," said Anne, and now it was his turn to be looked at steadily, and for a flash he loved her for this, her bravery amid a tangle of wired nerves. There was also Lina Chase, hot stuff, bet she felt his heat coming down the phoneline at her last time, but it could only be a fling, heat that'd burn out once it hit the facts.

"Would you and I be together somewhere else?" Anne asked him.

"That's what makes me stop and think."

"What do you mean somewhere else?"

"It's a small town for people like us, not too many of us around, so possibly we could just be, you know, convenient."

"People like us?"

"Educated. Intelligent. Artistic."

"You're right," he admitted. "The circle isn't large."

"But you shouldn't draw the wrong inference. I'd love you if I met you anywhere, New York, Paris, Rome. I know it."

"You just used the love word."

"Oops." She swallowed down some of her wine a little fast, maybe for show.

"Would you be willing to have a couple of beautiful brown babies in the world I could show my dad?"

"With you? Yes I would."

"That's a change."

"I've had time to think."

Marcus's turn to drink too much wine in one go. "Hrrrum, well, hhrrmm, you've certainly given me a lot to think about, young lady." Horrible tone and choice of words, even as a jape. His dad's voice, sort of, with the jokey part of it out of tune.

But she got that sly humorous look he liked in her, lighting up those fine features, first flash of it during this majorly tense visit. "Well, sonny, the moving finger writes, so don't think too long or you might miss it."

Been through the wringer but still could flirt. That's my gal.

★

His father was looking way too pleased with himself when Marcus came back after showing Anne the door and she'd gone through it into the gold of fading day. They had hardly touched each other, which was strange. He had lightly touched her finely wrought rightside collarbone on parting, which was stranger. Maybe because they were both of them just that volatile. Their old mutual energy had leapt from her collarbone through his fingertips right into him. Or, you know, keep it cool because the old man's here. What if he wasn't?

"I'm not gonna to say word one about that nice lady unless you ask me to," his father told him when he got back.

"Yeah, right."

"She's not comfortable around black folks."

"She's comfortable around me."

"She's not comfortable around working-class black folks like for instance I could mention your daddy."

"She doesn't have much experience, she owns an art gallery."

"Well that would explain it."

"I thought she did fine. And some of it was about your dog. She's good people, Dad, she'd come around." There might be advice needed here, ask the wise old man, but getting it would entail telling Dad that Anne had been mixed up with the shooter, and once he opened that one up he'd never hear the end of it, the rest of Dad's visit hell on wheels, plus he'd end up with that lug Thor on his hands, son I brook no opposition you take him, that man is out there and he don't like you, so no, Marcus wasn't going to ask.

"I know what your mother would say, rest her soul," Lionel was sure.

"She was always the race lady, but that was never your thing, Dad."

"Oh, now and again, now and again. I have some old feelings, I was just never too doctrinaire."

"You played the other side of the fence once or twice."

"Not while your mother was alive."

"Anyway, Anne and I are not involved."

"Fiddle-dee-dee."

"We *were* involved."

"Foodle-dee-doo."

"She just came by because she had something to tell me."

"Stop hocking me a chainik," his father told him.

"What?"

"The Jews say it, it's Yiddish. It means stop selling me a teapot. Damned if I know what it means but now you can have the benefit of my unsolicited opinion."

"Oh no."

"That is the finest woman I have seen you with, and by fine I do not

166

only mean she looks good, which she does. She's a nervous type and probably demanding, she's used to money but doesn't have none now and will want to be cared for and looked after, but that said I like her character. Only thing against her she's a little old for you by I'd say five years."

More than that but let's not mention it.

"And that marbly blue-veined thing is kind of strange."

"You get used to it. It becomes attractive."

"Makes her look like a fine French cheese."

"She's of French descent." Christ what a stupid sentence that was.

"She want children?"

"Please don't start in."

"Does she want children like someone you know wants grandchildren? Considering her age, one child might have to do, specially if he's a boy, your mother and I did all right with you as an only and I could live with that."

"We're not having this conversation, Dad."

"Maybe you're not but I'm diggin' it. And when it comes to grandchildren, would that fine woman enjoy them in a shade of brown?"

"Dad, if you want to enjoy the rest of your visit …"

"Oh it was a little boring there for a while, for instance I thought I was gonna have to listen to some of your music but now I'm enjoying myself fine, and may I also say it does my old heart good to see you looking so boyish-silly in your face and bearing. It makes a father happy. I believe I will be able to laugh at you all the way from now till dinnertime."

7

WITH THE FEEL that things were getting too real too fast and he was having trouble keeping up, Eli rode up the Klamath valley, the road following the river through green mountain forest country, sitting shotgun alongside Franklin in his sci-fi-army-looking black and grey Toyota FJ Cruiser, nice car but kind of hard on your ass because it was ready for the coming war between whoever. "After this today, scoot up north soon as you can," Franklin told him.

"We don't own much, we're about ready to go, just need the U-Haul." The physical move was simple and Sukey'd done the packing, he'd take care of the sound system, not that there was any deejay work in his immediate future, but the change, the change, his life speeding up, no more free state of California but the prison clang and dirty clothes of his past in of all places *Seattle*.

Eli knew it wasn't logical that everyone but him knew what the world was for, but stick around long enough and he always came to the same brick wall at the end of his understanding, where everybody had the facts and were busy in the right order but he stood there all Huh like he was staring at a sky so full of stars how could he do anything? How could anyone eyes wide do anything in the face of all that is? Sometimes it seemed to him he wasn't a solid human being like the rest of them but really an angel who took a wrong turn at Pocatella and ended up on earth by mistake and that was why he didn't know the things he was supposed to and instead knew nothing at all or maybe, it could be, knew something else that was important but he couldn't put a finger on.

"But I wanted you to see what you dealing with," Franklin continued as if Eli hadn't spoken, which maybe he hadn't. "The Rec-V, the product, the how we do." Really playing up his *black* black voice today, maybe he wants to make clear I'm working for him and who we are relative to each other bosswise racially: bor-ing.

Turned out the tannery wasn't on the Klamath proper but a mile up a feeder stream running south out of the Salmon Mountains, a rocky downhill pour of rapids and pools and finally, as they reached it, a big faded red barn-thing made of weathery old wood alongside the stream on a bend of dirt road where the valley widened to make room for it to have been built there. Eli saw the big offwhite RV parked up to it, forty feet long? Fifty? A whitish roadboat with a fat orange stripe running its side and he guessed that must be the one.

"Smell that piney-woods air," Franklin advised him once they pulled up to the barn, got out and stood there while the dirt-road dirt caught up with them in a reddish sand-colored cloud.

But there was another smell to the place that turned out to be a couple smells mixed together once they went inside the big high old dark wood barn structure almost walking into a pile of heavy hides still stinking of dead animal, peeled off creatures that'd been living meat with eyes and senses and some kind of picture of the world in their heads. But he wore Justin calfskin Ropers and had a Fossil wallet. The other smell was a harsh chemical thing Eli supposed must be coming from that amazing huge planked-together wooden wheel twenty thirty feet across and a few feet thick rolling in place up against the streamside wall, waterdriven from underneath he guessed, with a closed wooden hatch in its planky side and a heavy slosh-sound coming from inside it.

"Old school artisanal shit," Franklin told him as a long thin guy came away from the turning wheel toward them through dusty sunshafts across the floor of the big old barn with little holes or something in its hightop roof.

Eli was thinking what was wrong with the world is that no one had put a wheel like that in a movie, he hadn't seen one. What a place for it, big old lumbery wheel turning and sloshing with he guessed a bunch of hides inside getting cured, whatever cured was, with dusty sunbeam shafts slanting in from gaps in the old wooden wall and way up top. Put it in the background while actors did things up front. What a thing to see. It was like being in a movie that hadn't been made yet.

"Smells great in here," Franklin told the long thin guy, not meaning it.

Big grin opened up in the guy's face. "It's *carcinogenic*," he said, pronouncing the word, *carcinogenic*, as if in the world of words it was his absolute favorite and made him happy just to say it. He was an old-school hippie unit though not that old, long light-red hair parted in the middle down to his shoulders and blue space-case eyes, the kind open on the world without much focus but taking in everything, that was their statement: I'm wide open to the whole freak show, hello universe I'm cool with wherever you're coming from. Nothing hurts me, he wanted his look to say.

"If you don't like it don't work here," Franklin told the guy.

"What *isn't* carcinogenic?" the red-haired person said, perfect stoner smile full of good teeth, because in his mind he was on top of it. That's what it was. "Where would I go?"

"Leland I want you to meet my young friend Eli, no last names, Eli this is one of my most trusted associates, Leland, shake hands you two, and Leland, give the man a tour of the works while I go downstairs to the health-food store."

Leland started walking Eli through the curing and tanning operation, explaining what went first and what was done next, and next, but wouldn't tell him about the wheel, just laughed when Eli asked, while Franklin opened a big trapdoor in the tannery-barn floor that swung up on a rope and the sound of springs and he disappeared down some stairs.

Eli was leafing through finished buckskins in browns and tans and even green, also some hides of polished leather in brown and black on the shiny side, wondering how you make a pair of pants that fit right without binding up in your ass and balls when Franklin's voice called him "*Eli!*" from downstairs and he went to the stairs and down them into the "health food store"—creepy echo of Kenny Pitcher—and the sound of the stream rushing past outside, an immaculate sorting, pressing and bagging operation, the walls and roof sealed in heavy plastic sheeting, huge rolls of plastic film on rollers in different grades of thickness including bubblepack, vacuum press machines and some industrial machines he'd never seen before and assumed must be the oil-infusion thing or how you make sheets of shatter because of tanks on top and hoses going in and coming out. Not all these works were humming but some of them was, were.

Franklin was talking to a young weedy guy in glasses with frizzy hair tied back in front of a row of tables where some nice-looking probably local women, some of them maybe Native American—Eli thought he remembered there was a small rez nearby—wearing clean white mouthmasks and goggles and wrapping and rewrapping bricks of hash in different kinds of plastic, then heat-sealing the edges under press-machines. These women did not look up from their work when he came in. They had no interest whatever. You could get ripped just on the smell in the air but Eli thought it best to try not to, try to be on your guard here. Further back in the room there were big tables with what looked like honeycolored sheets of glass and were dab, shatter, the most dangerous by-product thing he knew of. There was no sign of how they were gonna pack that up.

"Eli, this is my boy genius Arthur Double-X we call him."

"Dub," the boy genius said.

"Arthur this is our new Minister of Transportation."

"Hope he's better than the last one," Arthur Dub said.

"Because he wants to live he is," Franklin said, then slapped Eli on his back twice. "Only kidding, I've known Eli since he was sellin' on the corner, a fine honest young man, been proven, used to work for Teddy Swift."

Arthur placed his hand approximately on his heart. "Rest in peace," he said, "the asshole." The guy had a Black Muslim kind of name but wasn't black. What was up with that?

"My boy Eli was there, in the room when that guy shot Teddy." Arthur looked at Eli with fresh respect, it seemed to Eli. "Police had him overnight and got nothing outta him, tried to get Teddy's operation and people, threatened him with everything on earth and all they got was what he saw when the guy shot Teddy, a honest witness, look at him."

Eli shrugged when Arthur looked at him. He had sort of forgotten all the shit Poholek and the other cops tried to get him to give up that night, the shooting so foremost in his mind all the other interrogation slipped away, though now he wondered how come Franklin knew so much about it. Eli hadn't seen any cleaning ladies in the interrogation room, or Mexicans with brooms.

Arthur Double-X reached out and shook him by the hand and Eli hadn't realized he'd behaved so worthily, he'd just been trying to get through it and out of there. But it was true. Poholek had asked him Don't you want to say something to help us put that bad man Kennis Pitcher away and he told Poholek I can't tell you what didn't really happen and Poholek just looked at him and said Why not? Plus Poholek tried to make him narc everyone else out and threatened him with all kinds of shit. So he *had* done something good, and now he started feeling Franklin was right to trust him with this new more executive responsible job. He was Eli, a person so honest he didn't even know he was, or that it was special.

"Franklin my man," Arthur Dub had begun to say, "there will be songs, there will be ballads written about the end of Teddy Swift. Gunned down by the tobacco-company man. There will be songs written about him and they'll make him sound good, but he was an asshole and we all know it."

"If so Eli you will be in those songs," Franklin said.

Wideyed against the wall while the shit was going down, Teddy spreadlegged on top of the desk swinging his blade and then the black pistol coming out and pointing up at him, not spectacular and entertaining to look at, just death, and the boney death-look on Kenny Pitcher's face, not a human face except it was and couldn't be anything but one. Then the incredible and at the same time matter of fact flat explosion of the shot and Teddy toppling backass on the floor with his face amazed and his eyes rolling, and blood, and all Eli wanted was to get out of there. They would write songs and ballads about *that*? He wanted a drink, clearly a drink of hard hard liquor, not some Purple Martian toke, to make that picture go away, definitely not multiply in waves and colors and funny-shape variations, just please take it away and blot it out.

Eli also wanted to yell out *I am innocent*! Innocent of what he wasn't sure, and if he was, what was he doing getting deeper with these people here? Well, he liked Franklin. Franklin was good people, Franklin was all right.

No one asked him what he was thinking and feeling about any of it.

They walked him through the oiling-pressing-bagging operation, the women didn't look up and he didn't take in much because of the sense of himself he was getting from Franklin and Arthur Dub compared different to the reality of himself that he knew, but he was impressed by how much machinery there was and how clean, only it was too detailed to keep up with. Maybe the smell of unsealed hash was getting to him, but it shouldn't, right? Or the plastic smell, which was bad for you. The glassy sheets of shatter didn't smell much of anything, or were lost in the general sniff of the place. He was pretty sure he was breathing and getting high, but not in the usual way. It was confusing. Maybe all he was was a little confused, that's all.

Now they had to go outside and show him the big RV. He'd been to the Motor Vehicle office with Franklin and the papers and put his name on the title and the registration—"This way you got skin in the game," Franklin told him, "thing gets busted they come to you, so be careful, mon, this is how I do business, you don't like it say no and then goodbye"—which took time and was boring, but now that he saw the size of the thing up close it seemed impossible and who was gonna drive it? Would ordinary people be able to drive this thing? Especially, anyone he knew?

Even the trees around them, out in the open underneath the sky and alongside the rapids and smelling of pine resin, were giving him trouble. They existed and he existed, so who was who and how did it add up? There was too much of not just trees but of everything, nobody knew why it was there but he was exactly in the middle of it and couldn't get regulated.

Franklin pulled open the door in the side of the RV and climbed up the steps inside and Eli and Arthur Dub trudged up after him. It was half the size of a motel, with a double bedroom down the end, the back, the stern, narrow bunks along the middle, a kitchenette and toilet and shower closet, pinewood cabinetry that looked handbuilt like his father's work but not as good, then they showed him how the wall panels came off, you couldn't just pull them off but had to turn release handles hid under the carpet in the floor and only then if you opened a metal handle and pulled the wall would the panel come off and show the hollow space with shallow shelves level on top of level inside.

"And we can get I won't say how many hundred thousand dollars of product in this thing," Franklin told him, "even the world's champion sniffer Rintintin won't say bark one to the way we do."

Which made Arthur Double-X laugh, then Franklin was laughing with him, so Eli had to join in and hope they couldn't hear how he was starting to feel, on the general principle of there being too much to do, including especially who in Teddy's pack of idiots was going to drive this thing and could be trusted. *I don't know how to do this*, and they were expecting him to perform it like a master. He could see how he'd end up driving it himself and not tell anyone and get caught, with his name on it too, so no excuses.

It was getting to be a very whirly pressure-headed day.

"Okay Eli, look here," Franklin was telling him as if he was a real and capable other human being like the rest of them, and gave the nod to Arthur. They were over by the dining table and Arthur reached down to push aside a black iron tongue near the floor that looked to be part of the tableworks, then stood up to turn two stainless dial-things in the wall back of the table and pulled the wall panel off, fiberglass or something. There was a big rectangle of space behind that, kind of deep.

Franklin was talking to him. "This is where the sheets of dab go, quadruple sealed, which is serious bulk in terms of that special product."

Was Eli getting wrongstoned just looking at the place that crazy shit would go? Plus he was trying to price it and figure how much money was involved and it was more than he had imagined anywhere ever.

Eli started to wonder if he was being set up somehow. He was supposed to get ten grand a month and a big bonus but if it was this much money and would be all over in one move what would they be paying him for after?

After snapping the wall-piece back in place they were outside the RV and Franklin was explaining how they'd load here sometime next week, then, "Don't worry, we already got someone who'll drive it to Eureka for us."

"This thing's coming into *Eureka*?"

"I told you, half the load from here, this year's product, then into Eureka to pick up last year's stash outside town, where I stored it, didn't have a buyer at the time, safe in Eureka at the time, not so good now. It don't concern you. You won't be there. Then your drivers pick it up and take it north. You got them picked?"

"Oh, yeah, I mean I still have to choose between a couple of them."

"Straight middle-aged types. I want to meet them."

"Yeah of course, but they're coming down from up there, they're not in Eureka yet," and for a sharp guy Franklin didn't seem to pick up how far behind the curve Eli was, talking through a hat he didn't have on his head. Franklin must really respect me the way he says he does and thinks I'm a lot more solid than I feel myself to be.

Then he had to do something he definitely didn't want to do, what they called a right of passage, had to go around the barn with Franklin and clamber down the pointy grey rocks to the stream, careful not to fall, then take off all his clothes the way Franklin was taking off all *his* clothes and get down in the rapids, into the bonefreezing water rushing over the stones and get situated in among the boulderish big ones, an arm around this one and that one so as not to get pulled away, even though for a second he really wanted to get pulled away and disappear into the clear water forever, and he had to lay there naked next to Franklin of another color, which was the weirdest thing he'd done in a long time, the water pouring over their shoulders around their heads and their legs dangling down the rippling creasing bubbling flow, which was so fucking cold he didn't believe it.

"You know," Franklin had to shout over the sound of the downstream rush, the world producing water forever somehow and here they were drenching in the pour, "I was ready to laugh at your little white-boy wang-dang-doodle, but I see you a tall man all the way. Ain't this water grand, mon?"

Eli lay there as the freezing water stunned his body and his mind began to trance because of it and realized he was in a new world of trouble all over again and, good-thing bad-thing, no one around him noticed. What he felt was alone, with a world of natural law disaster pouring down from the source of all things upon him, parting his hair in the middle and getting him ready for the chop.

Nikki was excited and had something to tell Lina but wouldn't do it on the phone. Lina thought this behavior juvenile and didn't want to indulge it, but "Oh come on, you need a ferry ride" hooked her because she was in fact going stir-crazy just hanging around the house with Eli-worry. Meditating cleared it on and off while she sat, but the full condition would set back in soon after. The invitation to a ferry ride caught her with the promise of a fresh breeze across calming water, then the sight of a picture-pretty harbor with white boats in it, which couldn't happen except in an orderly world.

In the event she was physically present but so preoccupied she missed being there for the trip, didn't see the water or feel a healing breeze across it or if she did she had forgotten it one instant at a time. Similarly unconscious on the drive from Fauntleroy to Gig Harbor. So much for years of Buddhist mindfulness in which constancy is key.

Once inside the facility, the security girls didn't have as much time for her as usual, the conversation perfunctory as she was patted down and wanded, as if the world was telepathic and everyone had turned the same page as Lina to join her in the new place and share her grim foreboding of things to come, and none of these girls her special pal now. Belinda Getchek behind the u-desk told her Lina'd meet Nikki at Indoor Visiting today and Shequonda Eveningstar had restored her hair to tribal normal, a part in the middle and two braids hanging. No one offered her tea and she walked down institutional breezeblock corridors feeling more inside than usual. The message, via the world's incalculable telegraphy, seemed to be that no one gave a shit about her anymore, and Lina asked herself if that was justice and didn't know.

But Nikki, already in place in an orange plastic scoop chair at a table for four, seemed barely able to contain herself, rocking in place, practically leaping to her feet on catching sight of Lina coming in. It was a dour block room with a line of windows set too high to show anything but wire-gridded sky and Nikki seemed the only living creature in it despite the other prisoners and their family visitors, patrolling guards, and supervisors behind the security-booth window up the metal stairs. Lina hoped to be ready for whatever this was.

"Okay," she said when she got to the table and sat down across from Nikki, "what is it?"

"Work release, work release, what, they didn't call you? Work release, I'm okayed for work release, you still got that job for me and I can stay at your house?"

"Wait a minute, Nikki, no they didn't call me, and they should have called me, it's not your fault but I need time to prepare."

"Welcome to the bureauckacy, honey, state came through and I'm comin' out. Thank you Lord and thank you Lina I know you been pullin' for me, all your best efforts, here it comes."

All Lina could do was worry about Nikki running a longterm manic episode on this frequency that would whiteout the rest of the picture. Given her own current unsteady condition, she wasn't sure if she could handle Nikki if her manic state persisted, a lot of work under the best conditions and these weren't them. Note to self: check at the pharmacy on the way out and make sure they're confirming she takes her meds.

"Nikki, slow down. This is much too sudden. I have to phone the women who own the bookstore—"

"Nice two lesbian ladies with that bookstore, I know I'm gonna love them, and I will work so hard."

"Nikki, I have to call and ask, make sure they're ready. When did they say you could come out?"

"Next week! Next week and please don't tell me I have to wait," when Lina had been thinking, all right, let's get set and be ready in a month. "Four days out and three back inside, the first step on my way out of here for good, they need your signature and I can't wait I can't wait."

Nikki with eyes like pale blue lightning, no longer in touch with her purposeful, patiently constructed, scaled-down prison personality, plus the expense of providing her bookshop salary, most of it to go in escrow for her less a small allowance. Bess and Tess weren't able to pay her, lovely bookshop, better than it had to be, in the center of town in the middle of the island but under a death sentence from the internet, attacked by Amazons, add the cost of extra groceries and whatever else might come up, so that it was Lina who had promised in a carefree moment to foot the bill … while already, probably, getting ready for expenses coming from Noah's quadrant of the compass she hadn't sold enough stock for because it scared her to eat into principal.

"And do I stay in that little place you got out back or can I sleep in the guest bedroom inside the house with you?"

They had talked these alternatives through in daydream fashion, that's all. Had she missed some signals the past little while? It was true she'd been a bit preoccupied, but it must have been worse than she realized. Lina wanted to tell Nikki that she couldn't possibly do it next week, but then how could she crush the light in Nikki's eyes, this blue-grey burst of hope, the natural rush to freedom animating Nikki from inside, electrified all the way to her fingertips? Lina herself had cultivated the current and led her along.

"We can work that out in due course," she told Nikki, thinking Due Course? What kind of language is that? "First I'll have to go see Superintendent Parnell to discuss the details …"

"Superintendent Jane is waiting for you right now today. Lina my angel you made this happen, this couldn't have happened without you, please go see Superintendent Parnell right away and I will thank you forever, Lina Lina."

Lina felt rather dizzy when she stood up from her orange plastic chair.

Superintendent Parnell had so much confidence in Lina after all their planning consultations that she'd just left the papers with her secretary for Lina to sign, along with a handwritten note that said Good Luck!!

On the way back across the water she leaned into the ferry-wind at the bow hoping it would blow her clear and it was good but it was only air. When she got on the phone to them, nice grey-haired settled Bess and Tess would be absolutely delighted for Nikki to come work there for a few days next week, as long as Lina vouched for her—Lina did still vouch for her, including salary, wasn't that right?

Which meant venturing into that unattended quarter of her life, the part she didn't want to look at and simply hoped persisted like a quality of nature, available as air. In other words the presence of money.

Ray Quintana, the lawyer who administered her father's bequest and trust, was surprised to hear from her twice in one week. "You almost never call, you don't open the mail we send you, we practically have to dun you for signatures. Honey-girl, please tell me you're all right."

"Please, Ray. I've been thinking it over," she said as her stomach tightened and her free hand clenched and unclenched, "and I'm not sure I sold enough stock last week. I think it might be a good idea to free up another fifteen thousand."

"Lina," said Ray, with his professional, almost doctorish voice tuning in, as if proffering a spectral glass of old sherry to a regulation dithering soul, "it hasn't been your habit to spend principal, which has been a commendably wise policy until now. What is it you can't manage on your generous monthly allowance? I advise against selling more stock unless it's absolutely necessary, and I have to ask again: are you all right?"

Without the Honey-girl this time, since we were getting fundamental. Lina pictured him in his office high enough above Pacific and Montgomery to have swung in a six-foot arc like a metronome in the last big quake. Ray had kept doing business while the building pendled until the phones blacked out. His corner office provided imperial views of the Bay across to Berkeley and north to the Golden Gate and still more clear sky beyond the city's fiduciary obelisks. "Both my sons are expectant fathers, Ray, and they need a helping hand just now."

"Congratulations on the blessed events," Ray wished her. "That's understandable and praiseworthy, but I hope they're both making a living, because, a helping hand is okay, but I hope you're not planning to support them in the long term. I don't feel sure you're aware how big a hit your holdings have taken along with the rest of the economy in the downturn."

"I read your statements, Ray." Actually she never opened them.

"If you do, you'll know that you're in no position to start spending significant principal if you want to continue living as you do. With the Fed rate down where it is there's not enough interest for you to live on and the market's still too unstable for us to play a game with."

"I'm ready to go back to work if I have to," Lina said.

"I advise it." Ray paused for a change of key. "If you're determined to sell, may I suggest that instead of further depleting your tech stocks we sell out one of your mutual funds."

"Fine, yes, take your pick," Lina told him, alarmed at the degree to which she wished to keep her blinkers on, the downside of conceiving of money as natural air supply, and how much she was giving away to Ray to know what was up with her. Cutoff makes you panic. Since she was not yet within range of going broke Lina reminded herself unpleasantly of her bygone patient down to her last eight million trembling at the brink of perceived annihilation, though Lina didn't have that much. It wouldn't be this bad if Eli weren't shaking her faith in life working out, but a tumbleworld logic was showing her not only the prospect but the law of going under: it could always turn up and put the cuffs on you, and she could feel it. Nothing was solid in this world, said solid Buddhist principle, but she'd been counting on her inheritance as a rock-solid escape clause forever and Eli somehow lucky, getting by.

So okay, she was a phony same as everyone, with a chaos inside her that circumstances could upchuck anytime, and here it was. Thou comest when I had thee least in mind.

The funny thing, Eli was the only person in the family making a decent living at present, ten or fifteen thousand a month if Franklin Bass was to be believed. Maybe she could hit him up for a taste if things got tight, ha ha.

Ray had been going on in a blur about this fund and that fund, so to stop him Lina said, "Liberty, yes, sell that."

"So ordered," Ray said. "That'll block out as fifteen-five less fees. I certainly hope that'll be enough for any emergencies you encounter."

"I probably won't need it all but it'd be good to know it's handy."

"Honey, please tell me that if you have a real problem you'll come to me with all of it before it gets serious."

In a pig's ass, her adolescent voice said inside her. I know what, I'll marry a tall bald communist twice my age and he won't die on me till, uh oh, he does. "Count on it," she said. "I do not have an unconscious wish to put myself in jeopardy." In which case why bring it up?

"All right, honey. If there isn't anything else …"

"No, that's all."

"After we sell I'll wire the money to your local account up there as usual."

"Righto."

"All right, Lina. Don't take this the wrong way but let me say it: please be a stranger."

"Good one, Ray. So long."

Get a grip. Unclench your shoulders and your gut and make a list if you have to, start making realistic, practical, finite plans. Limit, order, fixity. You're good at that, or so I thought. At what point, for instance, do I tell Noah I can't give you any more right now because because?

What would be best of all, thought Lina, is if they could put me in a cell next to Nikki's till everything settles. I'd get along beautifully with everyone in the pokey, they'd feed me and the rest of it would work out fine.

Sic transit gloria mundi. Gloria got a tummy-ache on the Greyhound Monday.

Meaning it looked like Pitch had made his decision to talk to the media a little late. When he got down to the City Offices all the crews that had crowded the forecourt a few days back hoping for more than the sight of his hunched shoulders and lowered head coming out the door, they were gone and the only forlorn electro-presence was a small crew from a local cable outlet he had to negotiate with, first the so-called producer who doubled as sound man and then with the media-pretty face lady.

"It's an exclusive," he told the so-called producer, a curlyheaded Jewboy with glasses who thought he was too good for this town, this gig, this story, probably this world and everyone in it, typical, "so you damn well better shop it to the majors. CNN was here and hot on my trail, they'll want it."

It was a lousy conversation because all Pitch could get out of it, really, was the guy's verbal and so-bored assurance that, yeah, okay, he'd try.

Then blondie, who he tried to size up as a potential Betty-June but couldn't see it, she was pretty, but in that non-sexually-explicit way news outlets liked on camera. Something he could work with if he had time but everything was too much rush right now for him to put her in the picture he liked to paint before he started in with someone. He tried to convince her she was headed for better things in her profession via this interview, a national exclusive so please shape up and act more wide-awake please, could be your ticket if Levine over there follows through on what he promised me and shops this national. Really, make sure he does it.

"You were news a few days ago but you're an old story now," she told him.

"It's very unimaginative of you to think so," he said. "Turn the pots on and ask me good questions."

They were a sleepy bunch and he even had to tell them where to put the camera and what to use as backdrop, the City Offices' portico with logo and national and state flags drooping either end.

"Wave to the bear," he told the blondie, "on the flag, on the flag," he had to explain, and finally they were set.

Every question was routine so he just said some things he wanted to.

"I have been painted luridly in the press, but I am here in Zowie, excuse me, Eureka, as a representative of a reputable national tobacco company, Raleigh," blah blah blah, "I was assaulted by a crazed individual well-known to be in the illicit drug trade in this town, county, in fact this whole region, and this man was outraged at the intrusion of a wholly legal business operation into the criminal underworld represented by him and his kind," blah blah blah, "Raleigh would like to assist the state of California in an orderly transition to a regime in which marijuana is decriminalized, monetized for recreational purposes, taxed and properly policed, so that perpetrators of victimless crimes will no longer be incarcerated by the thousands and can return to productive," blah blah blah *blah*. He'd thought he'd come up with something less boilerplaterian than that but he hadn't, and it came to him too late that he hadn't really had a purpose, that he'd talked to her only out of frustration and vanity, and that is not how to be ol' Pitch. Same vanity had made him phone Anne Dujardin. Vanity and fuckwit brag-revenge to call her Tuesday late and start nastying about her and Marcus Q. Nigger. Don't say nothing or even think it if you ain't prepared to up and act. So let's.

But by the end of the interview he was more favorably disposed toward the blondie veezavee possible Betty-Juneing and asked her if she'd like to go with him to dine at the Belvedere this evening.

"What," she asked him. "You think shooting some stupid pothead in your office has given you an irresistible aura?"

"That's the first intelligent thing you've said all day," Pitch told her and decided fuck this, got in the car, went to the bank machine with the corporate card for money and hit the road. Shopping trip, also let's plan for the future harvest. Medium-long boring drive on the pretty coast road, which had no charm for him today, then inland on 199 and into the mountains west of Grants Pass, pretty hill and forest country, get ready for the 60s flashback.

When he pulled into Dream Camp's dirt parking lot full of old farm iron and rusting Detroit a straggling bunch of locals were carrying planks and treebranches and tools and fucking off while building some whatever that might look good stoned but likely'd fall down tomorrow and be useless if it didn't. One guy off alone was turning like a clockwork dervish on a clean patch of ground in front of a small cabin, a big-titted woman in a floral dress looking at him with a stopwatch in her hand. When Pitch got out of the Chevy a few hippie units who clearly hadn't read the papers and didn't know they'd been extincted waved stoner hellos and he scanned the patchy grass and doorsteps of the bunkhouses and sheds for sweet-looking mamas who might be laid back enough to fuck after fifteen minutes' sociable conversation and saw a couple candidates, assuming their menfolk warn't around, but that might be for later. Now he had to see the Two Dudes and they were in the main house.

Main house was the former Junior Lodge of this former children's summer camp, log-built, shambling but less decrepit than the other bunkhouses, commanding a green slope down to what he thought must be a manmade lake because it was mostly greenscummed over and the water dead still, hope y'all enjoy mosquitoes. The Two Dudes were lounging inside, old beards from the old days, the Smith Brothers off a cough-drop box, beards gone roughly halfway grey, these guys maybe sixty if you could find their faces and get a look in at them.

"Hey Dudes," he said on entering, and hey what's this? For the first time they were not all glad to see him, in fact Dude Two bent sideways in his creaking chair and rummaged behind a cabinet and came out with a chopped shotgun, looked like a Remington 12 pump with half its barrel left, lovely original walnut stock ruined with woodburned psychedelic angels and peace eyes and other crap. "Whoa, whoa, what's up with this?"

"Heyy," Dude One, without the shotgun, seated at a wooden desk full of messy papers and old bottles, drawled at him. "We were not great friends of Teddy Swift but you crossed a line, man."

Dude Two sat comfortably with the shotgun across him. There were houseflies in the room. Didn't these people believe in screens?

"You think I'm coming for you?" Pitch asked.

"Naw but better safe'n sorry," Dude Two said.

Pitch found a chair to sit in once he took the stack of old newspapers off it and dropped them on the floor. "Let me tell you how it was," he said as the chair creaked under him. "I was in *my* office, *my* space, minding *my* own business, Teddy came into it and started waving his big Bowie knife at me—"

"Yeah, we've seen Teddy act out."

"Act *out*?" Pitch asked him. "The man took a cut at me."

"Then how come you ain't cut?"

Pitch thought it best not to answer, just keep going. "I *let* him take a slash at me to make sure he intended to do damage before I formulated a response."

"So how is it you ain't slashed and damaged?"

"I must have made an evasive maneuver."

"Before formulating a response," Dude Two said. "Did you formulate it like this?" He racked the slide on the shotgun, ker-chuk. "Or did you already have one in the chamber."

"Whoa, Dude, I came up here to say hello, buy some rocket fuel and talk about harvesting the Raleigh patch, do some bidness, and you're treating me like I was a revenooer after your shine."

Dude One and Dude Two looked at each other, oh man do I have to explain even that one? "Old-time hillbilly moonshiner metaphor," he said.

"We might sell you a little rocket fuel," Dude One told him, "just to get you out of here, but no way are we doing business with you on the Raleigh patch. You have shown yourself to be an unreliable business podnah."

"Dude, Teddy was never my *partner*. I happened to buy a forest property happened to have some crop of his on it …"

To their credit, the Dudes had a laugh at that one.

"Okay, that's what made the parcel attractive," Pitch allowed.

"Attractive," Dude One said, and kept on laughing. "Nice, when you don't have to do the honorest work of it."

"When have I been unreliable with you? I come up here, I buy quality, you sell for a price, safe as safe. Man, with all I know about what you got going here, I could get you busted."

Oops. Dude Two stood up with the chopped shotgun in his hands and almost aimed it. "Busted? Maan, we can get you disappeared and buried right here on the property or burn you down to rock and takkum powder on the barbecue, traditional ceremony the whole community can take part in."

"Whoa, Dude, slip of the tongue, bad phrasing, let us put our negotiations on another footing *please*."

"What are we negotiating?"

It took twenty minutes and a stack of cash fresh from Muhrad's account but Pitch came away with some grams of coke and speed and an old-school snub-nose .38, not a Satnite Special but a true Smith & Wesson police model you could actually aim and hit something with, not too marked up with use and the serial number filed off, a dozen rounds separate and no we won't let you try it out here we ain't fools, the gun works, whynchoo shoot yourself with it when you get home. Pitch got off the property feeling that shotgun on his back the whole way they walked him down to his car and watched him get into it showing both hands on top of the wheel as he drove out.

Coke good, speed also good, not getting shotgunned and buried in the mud under the compost heap with worms eating out your eyeholes to your brain *very* good, plus he shot a roadside tree with the Smith which didn't blow up in his hand and you could sight it pretty good for what it was; but no one to work the Raleigh patch and not much time to make alternative arrangements very bad, in fact all his plans and something like half a mil or more most likely fucked. Maybe he should pay strategic house calls, once he got home and had some inspiration up his nose, on Franklin Dobbs and Elijah Chase. Get them interested in finalizing the patch or take a load off your mind with one or two erasures. Among a couple other people he could name, not now, because why complicate your perfect mind?

That evening Bob was stuck on the sofa again with Marion, watching another bad-cop show from the collection of bad-cop movies she'd been curating, which had gotten to be the oftenest form of communion they had as husband and wife outside occasional off-night semi-conscious lovemaking with a grind of despair chomping their organs: watching movies or mini-series in which bad cops illustrated what Bob had become and how she shouldn't have married him because what had happened to him was inevitable and it was her fault for not having known it in advance, though of course she never exactly said these things, sucking down vodka tonics through a straw and leaking them out of her pale eyes down her pale face, a natural hydraulic flow accompanied by none of the work of actual weeping.

Bob was drinking bourbon but he kept it to a measure.

Marion didn't cook too many dinners anymore and he had ordered ribs and such from Magnolia's again. Marion said the meat, the flesh, made her sick to look at but at least at his urging she'd eaten some yams and cornbread and blackeyed peas.

Tonight's show on DVD was one of the middle seasons of *The Wire*, where in general the street cops were mostly all right, some of them actually good, striving, but everyone captain and above were rat bastards to a man, greedy and stupid and politically compromised up to the asshole in their eyeballs.

Watching television with Marion at least he didn't have to look at her to see what she'd become, and sometimes he held her hand, complicit in what she was making herself into now, this soggy instrument of some kind of grudge revenge.

Her automatic tears of vodka overflow had begun their waterworks now, and she started speaking without taking her eyes off the screen. She sounded like someone in a movie in a trance, which Bob guessed she mostly was, unless she was playing at it to fool him.

"Don't think I don't understand what you've been through, Robert. It's not your fault. I've been thinking it through. Remember what those racist southern preachers used to say on television when rock 'n' roll came in? How if our children start listenin' to that nigra music it will corrupt our nation morally and sexually and destroy us as a country? They were talking more about Elvis but Little Richard probably scared them worse. Anyway I have come to the conclusion that despite the fact that those preachers were twisted evil shits that is what happened to the United States, the country has been Negrified, first by music, then by sex and then it spread. It's a straight line from the nigra music to everyone doing the drugs you've had to contend with all these years, poor man. Look what it has done it to you."

Bob mostly believed her up until "poor man and "done to you" but he still wasn't sure if she was putting him on or not. If so, this was some new more radical slant of attack, since originally she was left-wing and into civil rights and against the war and it was a miracle they'd fallen in love and got married. They were each other's freaky adventure into the other side and the crossover had been amazing for a time. If she was speaking what she really felt now, if she'd really changed her mind behind her washed-out face and eyes as she stared at the world through television, well, then what? "You voted for Obama," he said.

"I'll vote for him again," Marion said. "He was raised by a white woman after his feckless black African father deserted them, and he is intelligent and respectful and a good man. Bill Cosby got him elected president, and Bill Cosby is funny and loves children." Marion finished this statement with a nod, confirming it, putting on the seal.

There's a third alternative, thought Bob. She's insane, she is alcoholically deranged and I have to get her into rehab or a flat-out institution, and the second of these would fix his marriage problem basically by ending it. He wondered to what extent the institutional tab could be put on the state and would it affect his pension. This would be something to look into. It would be even simpler just to put her out of her misery. It would be a favor to her, he had no doubt, but it would be dicey for him. People might overlook a few details because of who he was but the basic forensic labwork could come up with something anyway, and most people didn't know what she'd become—she could put on a front in company while the sun was up—and they mightn't find suicide any too plausible.

"Not Richard Pryor, though, or any of the dirtymouth new ones," Marion added. "*Cosby*. It was him."

"What about modern jazz, you used to love it."

"Subtler form of the same poison."

"What about, you like Miles Davis. Or used to."

"The Serpent in the Garden."

"But you still listen to those guys sometimes, right?"

"So what. We have been overwhelmed. When I was not much more than a child, long before I met you so don't worry, I had sex with a lot of black men."

A lot? How many is that? "You don't have to tell me, because you told me before."

"It was a big mistake. I was inexperienced. Adventure—*hah*."

The scene on TV had shifted to a black dope wilderness somewhere in urban Baltimore, scenes of naked need and degradation, hordes of the sick and dying and blowjobs up the alley with dope for payment. There weren't a lot of black people in Eureka. "It's not their fault," Marion said, still in her trance voice. "They were taken from a world they were fit for and brought here, and they are not fit for it. In Africa they don't know how to organize themselves as nations. Of course there are exceptions. But these TV shows have been sent to teach us."

She was either some combination of alcoholically insane, Bob figured, or incredibly devious and intent on creeping him out. At this point he couldn't tell. There's never been any doubt that she was smarter than him. Not that he disagreed with most of what she said, which was pretty much on the money and also why he'd stopped listening to rock and mostly gone over to country music, but that was normal for him and even *he* didn't go around saying it, except of course at the office.

Coming from her it was the end of a human being, mind and body and soul too if there was any left, or she was the most devious invidious mind-invading lobsterclawed insect woman that had ever lived. The charge that this was something he'd somehow subtly done to her was bullshit.

"The Arabs are worse," she added. "Blood-crazy tribe fanatics, with the usual handful of exceptions. Don't get me started on the Jews, I'm tired."

The phone rang and before going to get it he topped up her glass from the half-gallon jug on the floor at her feet.

Long night and he was tired. "Hel-lo," he singsonged it so whoever was on the other end would know: any more shootings, any more shit going on out there, he'd delegate tonight and catch up in the morning.

It was a friend of his with State Police. "That track you had us put on a number of cellphones, Bob? I probly shoulda got this to you sooner, but you know, someone fucked up and I wasn't watching close enough—"

"Yeahh," meaning get on with it.

"Okay, Franklin Bass and Elijah Chase took a ride up the Klamath valley together yesterday," and Poholek woke up, "ending up between Happy Camp and Klamath River township, I have the coördinates if you want em."

"Oh I want em," Poholek assured this guy whose first name he was trying to remember … Russell? Russet? He couldn't risk a guess, might offend the man. "Let me find a working pen here, Russ," slurring it a little.

"Who?"

"A … working … pen, got it. Shoot me the numbers."

"And oh," not-Russ added, knowing it was a bon-bon but pretending to be casual, "Elijah Chase, according to current tracking data, has subsequently drove north out of Eureka continuing in that direction on 101. Do you wish us to apprehend him before he leaves the state, which presumably yes he will."

"No I do not, repeat do not apprehend. I know where he's going. He's runnin' to his mama in Seattle. This is a continuing investigation and do not stop or apprehend him."

"Yowsah."

"What about Kennis Pitcher."

"Hasn't budged or he's travelling without his phone."

After saying bye and thanks still without remembering the good man's name so blurring the signoff, quick fast in a hurry he phoned two old boys on the force instate, and his man Davey Booth in Klamath Valley township checked the coördinates against his map and thought he knew the property in question. "It's a leather tannery on Freefall Creek about a mile from where it feeds into the Klamath from the Salmons."

"It's a drug operation," Poholek told him. "A factory or a stash or both. Bass and Chase didn't go there to buy homemade wallets."

"We don't have probable cause but I could go up there on a house call and take an innocent look around."

"*Fuck* no don't do that, this is something in coördination with major investigations in progress, I am collaborating with Special Agent John Emigh of the DEA, among others, Dave do not repeat do not go there and upset this apple cart."

"Fine, fuck you, I'll stay away."

"Thank you. There are two things I'd appreciate it if you can do them. One, a title search on the tannery at county records and it'll come up Franklin Bass or some dummy corporation he's running and you should be able to trace. That would confirm things for us, bring us closer. Two and more important, this is just you and me, understand, for security reasons, can you just sneak up on the place through the woods, out of uniform if that's in accord with your protocol, which I respect it, and just surveille the place a few hours afternoon into evening and tell me what you see? Take a look at people coming in or out, how many and what they look like. I got a power of a hunch you'll see more of a crew than you'd expect for a working tannery."

"Can do, Bob, if it's for you."

"It is for me."

"I respect you. And if I can have a piece of glory on the production end if there is some."

"You have got it, brother. But for the moment do not intercede, do not intercept."

"Already claro, hombre."

Heading back into the living room, a happy Bob Poholek wanted to pour himself another bourbon and click glasses with his bride but she had fallen asleep on the sofa, head tipped sideways as if her neck was broken, and her glass of vodka tonic had spilled across the lap of her faded floral-print dress, including on her snatch. No ice, it had mostly melted, but even so she really should have noticed.

It would take so little.

"This place is soo beautiful," Sukey said, amazed.

"Ooh hoo hoo," was Eli's response to what he saw. Franklin's many investments, the tannery, the coffee import, not to mention the hash and bud biz, must be working really well for him to own a place like this, and on the side, besides. He didn't even live in it. Then Eli remembered Franklin saying he might sell it next year because he wasn't trucking super-bulk no more and wouldn't need a big hub up here if this year worked.

Eli and Sukey wandered through the house like enchanted children through a wonderland, a big beautiful pale blue slatted house, two storeys and an attic and many many rooms, set inside a property circled by a greystone wall with a remote-controlled iron gate at the front leading to a semicircular driveway just outside the door. Lawns, shade trees, what Sukey said was a gazebo near a big willow tree out back. And the man at the main gate, who Sukey'd called St. Pete, was a nice guy who had been called to expect them, gave them directions and a map to show them through the curving streets of the compound past the big mansions, and it was a good thing Franklin had told them to clean up and dress well before they got there, because people like them, no no no, were seldom seen in such a place. They'd stopped at a gas station south of Seattle where Sukey'd put her best dress on and given him his best shirt and jacket and brushed his hair and he hoped the car didn't look too bad. The trailer, well, it was a U-Haul.

Getting into the compound had gone smoothly and all smiles with the guy in the security booth. "I wonder if the people who run this place know what Franklin's up to and don't give a shit," said Eli as he drove through the curvy roads of the property to the house.

"Hard to believe it," Sukey said.

"I bet he had a lot of funky-lookin' people comin' in and out."

"Maybe they know. That'd be so weird, and it'd mean funny shit all over."

"I think that's it up ahead," said Sukey, pointing at a bluish house behind its own gate and lowish wall. Franklin had told them it wasn't a fortress, just something to slow people up if you know what. "Have you got the keys and the remote, honey?"

"Don't you have them?"

Sukey blew air.

"Well Franklin said he left another couple each inside anyway."

"We still have to get *in* first, dorko."

"Well *look* for them, Sukey. See that bag on the floor there? I think that's it."

The house inside was full of oversized rooms and high ceilings, lots of light through large windows and extra stairways to the upstairs and an open walkway like a bridge with a bannister between bedrooms up there, just enough furniture, all of it new-looking, plus TV and a bigass stereo—he could have left his wannabe DJ system back in Eureka, but where?—central air-conditioning that cleared the place out in minutes, a big old brushed-steel fridge that was empty except for some tubs of stuff in the freezer but they could pick up a few things tonight and fill it tomorrow. Franklin had given them a grand in starter working cash. Sukey would handle opening the bank account and he wouldn't call his mother until tomorrow even though she knew he'd be here but didn't have the number yet.

The last part of the house they looked at was the basement, its door with its own heavy deadbolt lock and key, and when they went down there with the lights on they saw that Franklin had made plans for them he hadn't told them yet: cleaned-out plastic hydroponic tubs, grow-tables sealed in black plastic for now, a disassembled set of Gro-Lights neatly stacked in a corner of the big room and covered in a clear plastic sheet with some dust on it.

"Uh *huh*," was all Sukey said.

"Well, this *is* the dope business," Eli told her, but it was a drag Franklin hadn't mentioned in-home facilities you could get busted for 24/7. Eli didn't expect Franklin telling him to let all this gear gather more dust down here. No man, you here, so use it. Or maybe Franklin was done with little indoor grows. There was no way to know till Franklin said so. "Let's go back upstairs."

The part of town this gated community was in was shaped like Manhattan with a golf course wrapped around it instead of water, and the house had views of Union Bay and Lake Washington from the upstairs bedroom and other rooms up there including the enormous bathroom with the giant golden-brown bathtub-for-two—you could fit at *least* two in there—up on a stepped wooden platform in the middle of the room as if it was on a stage. They waited for the water-heater to work up to it and did some more unpacking before climbing in. There were big pointy-top flasks of bubble-bath soap on the bathtub's deck-surround and they used the sweetest smelling one and fucked in it for about an hour with Sukey's head resting on a rolled-up towel on the smooth-bent edge of the tub. They had liked doing it in a small normal tub before but this was heaven, and he didn't know if it was the hot water on his balls or what, but he had always been able to fuck like this all day if he wanted to without coming, just a constant beat of slow sweet pleasure and here he didn't have to worry about his weight on the baby because all this water took care of it. Maybe this was how they'd do it from now on with this great tub and all, soo easy and gentle in and out. After a while they were getting hungry and thinking of where to go for dinner, so Sukey said, "Let me suck you off," and he got up on his knees in the tub and suds and let her do it, her head bobbing back and forth like a mechanical doll's and her mouth perfectly round on him, a funny almost clown-looking effect you usually didn't see because usually they did that laying on their sides. He came in her mouth, a gradual-building deep one and she drank it down making grateful noises and it was a great start in their unreal new home.

The bad thing happened after they got out of the tub and were towelling down. Sukey's body had been changing with the kid inside, her breasts getting bigger but also fuller so they weren't all hangy, which he liked, and her belly wasn't a beachball but a smooth mysterious

192

improvement it seemed to him, but not this evening: he got a look at some folds of flesh just under the sides of her breasts, which gave him a jolt, and then he saw another version of the same thing in a side view of where her belly was starting to hang. It was just folds in her flesh and skin but they scared him with how real and old it was and it made his stomach clench to look at it. Her nipples had gone darker brown and looked like big leather faucets, and the thought of everything that was going on inside her, all those tubes and things, well, it was scary.

Eli hadn't seen this coming and couldn't do anything to stop it now, but it was also, in a way, like being at the tannery with Franklin with everyone expecting him to take care of business that was too big, only this was scarier and way-way closer up. I'm not a person I'm an angel, he tried to tell himself, that old recording, only he was too tense to put it over. It was better when Sukey put clothes back on but he knew it was still there under them and he was nervous about every little thing now, like having to ask St. Pete on the way out where they could go to dinner nearby since he didn't know this part of town and asking Sukey what to buy for the fridge for tomorrow and she'd go to the bank in the morning before he returned the U-Haul, or should that be after—how would he know which thing came first? It was too complicated, was the problem.

Dinner out at the sushi place was okay, but when they got back he hurt his fingers, fuck, re-hitching the U-Haul for Sukey to take it back to them tomorrow morning, cursing and squeezing his hand in the driveway of this house he didn't know how to live in and the grow-rig in the basement, the evening darkness rising up inside these trees, the sky turning large on him and the high-rise belly shape of it accusing. No wonder his hand was fucked. He wished he was back on medication, maybe he could ask his mom but he didn't want to tell her what was going on, even though she could get stuff through her doctor friends. Unless this passed away later or tomorrow, but it didn't feel that way to the angel who didn't belong here in this life, which was his story and he was sticking to it, if he could.

8

Later Bob would work it out they had gotten into ready position in the dark and held it through dawn, waited for forward reports of picking teams vanning into the patches in the morning before moving from ready-set and going in. The switchboard at the station got jammed up early on and he found out about it only when they rang him at home to ask him if he knew. If he knew! First thing he did was try to get on the line to John Emigh but had to leave a series of call-me messages like the world's last dork, trying to keep the frustration out of his voice, the insult to him personally, not a word, they'd just gone and done it completely without him, and the first thing he wanted to do was take Marion's Ford Explorer and gun it up the mountain to the Raleigh patch to see if they'd left it for Chrissake like he'd asked, but the demand for him at the station was too great and he took the cruiser into town instead.

First thing he saw, considering the hour and the amount of reporters already clustered around the portico, was that the DEA had alerted cronies in the media, probably had crews up there filming their heroic action in the Sierra—Bob wondered how many teams and did they have a National Guard assist—the enormity of the insult sinking in, not a word, not one fucking word to him.

That fat timeserver the nominal Chief of Eureka Police Happy Sam Chasteen was fumbling it into a herd of microphones and signalled desperately for Captain Bob to save him soon as he saw him get out of his cruiser in his slant-spot at the curb. Bob came up and obliged him with a bullshitful of cover: "Due to matters of operational security we do not have a definitive statement at this time, although I can tell you this is an operation done in coördination with the federal DEA and other local forces. We expect to have an official statement for you by noon, that is all," and just as he got ready to turn on his heel to go into the station the first plume of smoke appeared like a grey ghost up the slopes east and Bob stood there waiting with everyone for more. Three helicopters hovered like insects watching. He guessed there was so much kush up there they'd control-burn most of it upslope and bring in enough baled up for show, but they hadn't asked him about the advisability of a burn this dry season.

Hippies and dippies were coming out of the woodwork from every street all gawping up into the Coastals at the end of the world as they knew it and just then his cellphone throbbed through the leather on his hip and finally it was Emigh. Bob hurried inside the station and tucked himself into a corner of the entryway to take it private, his back huddled against a front office full of people looking busy and excited but actually just answering a lot of phonecalls from the huddled masses worked up one way or another.

"Sorry I couldn't return your call earlier, Deppity Chief," rotor noise behind Emigh's voice, "but we were busy, over."

Oh were you. "Not a word to me, why is that, Major Semper Fi my ass?" No point pretending he wasn't furious at the way he'd been done.

Emigh's voice was professionally, operationally flat: "No reflection on you but we were not perfectly satisfied with the security parameters on your end, over."

"No reflection on me? How is that even possible?"

"I repeat, no reflection on you. I personally assure you no reflection on you personally but we had security concerns about your force in station that I cannot share with you at this moment but will be happy to convey later, over."

"Happy to convey later? I *gave* you all those properties up there, man. How many are you hitting?"

"You did not give me all of them, Robert. You supplemented information already in our possession and this will be credited and you will be noted and mentioned, over." Bob wanted to but did not say: *my* concept, *my* operation, *my* last roundup, all of it going right past me into federal courts, now credited to me as bullshit squared. "We are taking nine large properties down," Emigh said.

"Jesus, you got National Guard up there, ain't you."

"That is correct and you would be pleased with the speed and efficacy of the op. We have bagged not only large amounts of product and day laborers but have made inroads into management."

"Fuck's sake *who*?"

"We have Roger so-called Dodger in custody at present and we expect to apprehend Turk Windell shortly, over."

"Franklin Bass?"

"We're not ironclad on his involvement in any of these properties but we were expecting to see him and that is a disappointment, we have not."

I know something *you* don't know, Bob sang inside himself. I don't know if it's an ace, I mean an *ace of spades* up my personal sleeve, but it is definitely in the hole a distance up the Klamath. Now the question he had been dreading to ask, though if they'd bagged Roger and expected to bag Windell, who no one he knew had ever called Turk, it was maybe less important, but, "What about the Raleigh patch?"

"We are cutting now and will do a controlled burn on site within the hour aside from evidence for the lab, Bob, sorry."

And a pile for television too. "Fuck!"

"Believe me when I tell you I tried to make your case at Operational HQ but it did not go down. Please accept my personal regrets. I would have done this one for you if I could but I could not, over."

One more question that set his nerves on tippy-toe: "Is Kennis Pitcher anywhere involved? By any chance was he present at the Raleigh patch?"

"The shooter? He was not. He's not still employed by Raleigh, is he? Ain't he out of here by now?"

"I tend to doubt it, Major. I also happen to suspect that boy was planning something for himself with that patch and we could have implicated Raleigh Inc., mighta thrown a knot, something mighta impeded, mighta put a crimp into full-on legalization of this shit here if you'd asked me, Major, but too late, you've done your thing and he's scot-free for everything, thanks for all your help but I was actually thinking something there. Over."

"Perhaps we'll interview him at his home at a later time."

"If you can find the slippery piece a shit. Listen, fuck all that, brass tacks today, you coming down to the station? We got the first few of a shitload of media and I imagine there'll be more. Will you please come down so we can at least do a joint statement, I'm asking you personally for the benefit and reputation of the force, which has to keep going past this, I hope you understand." Why am I still carrying this guy's pisswater, Bob asked himself. Old habit of response to hierarchical command, and I say fuck that from now on.

"In view of what we've had to cut you out of, Bob, it may be the least and only we can do. Give me another couple hours and I will try to accommodate you at your um police station. Please repeat please stay in place and I will consider it a kindness if you would talk to those people for me until I arrive, over."

"Can I use your name?"

"Yes you can."

"You have any fire crews up there with you, Major?"

"Under control, Bob. That's who's setting the fires."

"And howbout any media with you up in the hills. Got some?"

"On three of the properties yes we do."

Son of a bitch knows how to look after himself, don't he.

Emigh made a number of other operationally peripheral requests and Bob said yes sir he would tend to that, then went outside, his guts boiling, into morning sunshine broke atop the range, made another nothing statement to the multiplying foam and raggedy-doll pods on microphone poles, about as much humiliation he'd ever had in one day, then had to stand there with the other regulation know-nothing assholes squinting up into the forested front and ridgeline at the burns on the mountain, smoke plume here, smoke plume there, most of them rising behind westerly ridges, but once or twice on forward slopes, and in the heart of the grey-on-green a glimpse, a bright red furl like the flash of a dancer, flame.

Way up top three helicopters, Major Special Agent fuck-you John Emigh no doubt his ass in one of them, hovered poisonous as Isosceles mosquitoes enjoying the big picture and gargling the air with their noise.

Fire on the mountain, run boys run, devil's in the house of the rising sun. Chicken in the bread pan pickin' out dough, let's fuck Bob Poholek and do it slow.

Even Tony himself had no respect for the way he broached the subject to Mira.

"*What?* Are you kidding me?" was her justifiable response.

"Yeah," he tried to tell her again, "what if we gave the Lama business a rest and opened a nice Italian restaurant for a while?"

"Are you out of your mind?" She was raising her voice, apart from the obvious, because she'd parked Valentino Marpa in front of the television, which Tony didn't approve of even though it was a DVD of the Dalai Lama doing a Vajrasattva ceremony and not some American crap for kids, anyway Val would stay put.

"Nah. Look, sometimes it's a strain on my moral capacity to have to be watcha call a spiritual teacher, so I thought, hey, a little break might do us all some good."

"A restaurant."

"Yeh. I got enough capital socked away, don't ask. And I know the ropes."

"You're Neapolitan."

"*And* Sicilian, *and* Pugliese …"

"You're Neapolitan when all the money's in Northern Italian."

Look, she's biting the premise. "I can cook Northern. Tuscan, Milanese, even a little Veneziano."

Mira folded her arms across her breasts, a serious move indicating all kinds of prohibitions ahead. "Not brilliantly," she said.

"I do okay."

"You do okay and you'll never do better than okay because it's not you, it's not who you are."

"Whaddayou mean?"

"Face it, you're a wop."

"Okay, so let's revive Neapolitan cuisine around here. Needs doing, fresh local seafood's fantastic quality, look what they got at Pike Street Market, we can fly in San Marzano tomatoes and local Naples cheese …"

Mira's arms stayed where they were, no tits for you in a cold world, get it? and her sharp avoidance-glances off to right and left indicating fundamental impatience with the premise. Then those Nordic eyes turned on him like searchlights of human winter. "This is about Lina Chase," she said.

"Whaad?" he said, making a hapless gesture of confession with his arms, a classic who-me? readable as a blatant lie in any Italian town including North End Boston and North Beach SF, though maybe Mira didn't speak enough hand jive to know that. "Why Lina, because she's Italian? I haven't said word one to her about the restaurant idea." Get some truth in there when you can. "I'm not asking her to invest, nothing. A free lemoncello first time she comes in for dinner, that's it."

Mira twisted her mouth sideways. "She's in it."

Well, Mira was smelling crooked, but only because he was talking a little crooked, he had to admit. Tony didn't know how but somehow Mira was on the case. Marry them old or young, they will always find you out.

"Why a restaurant all of a sudden now?"

"Why a duck?"

Mira waved Chico Marx aside. "You're about to do something so-called transgressive again, aren't you? This is your exit strategy from the life you're living. I just know it."

"Since the last big transgressive thing I did was hook up with you, Miranda, when I was still married, you shouldn't be so upset." Can you spot the flaw in the logic here? Yes but it's too late. "Even though, okay, Melissa and I were separated by then."

"And it nearly cost you this place anyway, your position, everything."

"Right." Uhh, should I chance this? "Because I loved you and I still do."

"You did it all for love of me."

"Don't be sarcastic about dat, Mira. You know I did. Do." There was a tricky bit for her here but he should not exploit it, since it did not require a man of nearly fifty, and overweight, and hairy, to be a genius to fall for a willowy twenty-seven-year-old stunner of Scandinavian descent, whereas for the aforesaid willowy stunner there were matters of material status plus a wealth of spiritual expectation in landing the Lama, and he wondered, honestly, how much he'd done for her in that regard once he'd got what he'd wanted, meanwhile she had this big house and the temple and a positional role, and even if none of it was owned it had basic human appeal for her and he'd known that going in. Her position in the world was part of this fight. She did not want to be running no pizzeria.

"So what transgressive thing are you up to now, may I ask. Because, after all," ironic ceremonial bow, "since you're an emanation of Sooba whatsisname—"

"That's just something the Rinpoche said one time, and not an emanation of him but maybe an echo, since he was a trickster emanation of the Bodhisattva Manjusri in the first place ..." He ended in a shrug at the weirdness of it, even for him.

"Hence the legend of Torrezini Lama," Mira said, picking up on it, "from Piscataway New Jersey coming to us now in an apron, bearing pizza. I can see it on a tanka. Lookin' good."

"Well," Tony attempted while appreciating the skill of her riff, "not *mainly* pizza, though of course we'd have a wood-and-coalfired brick-and-plaster oven cranking out nine hundred Fahrenheit up front on show for Napoletane pies but I'd wanna concentrate on fish and shellfish, selected meats and the finest homemade pasta in the state. Mira, for fuck's sake, Mira ..." whom he could hardly blame for turning on her heel and walking off.

—Oh help me sir, I'm in a terrible Dilemma.

—You just can't count on those fancy Italian cars, can you?

Old Groucho Marx gag.

"And I'd wait tables?" came her voice from the next room and Val started crying, means she picked him up too rough from the Dalai Lama and Val didn't want to go, he liked the colors.

"Fuck's sake no!" he called to her departing steps. "You'd run the front of the house, greet the people and ..."

That went well.

The situation, if there was one, had to be addressed seriously. If he was getting into something with Lina because he'd seen it in that special way, he had to decide: is this something that happens out of weakness and appetite or does it happen because it has to, and if it has to, why? Was it a suggestion or a warning or just the usual sexed-up sucker punch?

Plus there was always the Macbeth factor.

Anyone was eligible to be broken on the wheel: himself, Lina, Mira, even the undefended infant Valentino Marpa.

How many morally significant moments do you face in a lifetime?

Either very few or an infinite number, every breath.

Or he was simple-minded really and it was just his Catholic roots, but his basic feeling was when messages come you follow. Obedience to divine instruction, even when the divinities are provisional. The original old religious impulse was an uninstructed thing but there it was, your cross to bear. When someone is in trouble, you serve.

Eli watched the forest fires on the big bedroom flatscreen, great picture, while Sukey packed her suitcase. "What a bunch of assholes," Eli said to the screen. "Why can't they just let us live? Now look what they did."

But Sukey wasn't talking to him. Packing a suitcase she'd unpacked almost just before.

Eli wasn't used to watching places he knew on TV but here was the mountain-front east of Eureka burning, big airplanes flying past the slopes and dropping buckets of red stuff that looked thimbly in comparison to the mountains on fire. "Assholes."

The reporters nailed a DEA guy who'd been in charge but Eli noticed that Captain Bob managed to keep himself offscreen way back. The DEA guy tried to stonewall but didn't have the stuff, and the fire guys talked about control and how they hoped to have it soon. It had been an unusually dry summer and three different fires were converging but there was hope of rain overnight tonight, they said. CNN had one interview with a pair of honest country homesteaders Eli knew who grew their own for family use, mostly, and whose house had burned up with everything in it except their two kids and the dog and they talked sense to the camera. "If marijuana was legalized the right way we wouldn't have all this, you know? And the jails are full of people who don't need to be there? This is ... this is insanity and our home is gone. We plan to sue, there will be class action ... Why won't they just let us live?"

Exactly. Eli wished he could be there in the streets with all the angry people demonstrating.

Back to you in the Situation Room, Werewolf. He did look like a werewolf. He *did*.

Windell had been shot in the leg by some asshole in the National Guard while trying to "escape" and Roger didn't dodge and had been apprehended. Franklin was not answering any of his phones and Eli wondered if he was on the run, which would take some pressure off him at least. Damned if he knew someone who could drive that boatful north. Last he heard they were getting it loaded and sealed at the tannery and probly were still doing it even with Franklin not in the picture. When he thought of the tannery the image of that big sloshing wooden wheel would come up and he couldn't stop looking at it in his mind, as if it was about to tell him something important while just outside the barn that goddamn bus stood there weighing on him with all three axles. He shook his head to get rid of it but even if Franklin was on the run he, Eli, wasn't off the hook. Though maybe he'd get lucky and Franklin'd decide it was too dangerous to move the shit now. But Franklin was so sure of being clever, once he made his mind up he was right, that was it. The tannery people had their orders. Or they'd steal it from Franklin and go solo. Either whichway it did look like a good idea to get your shit out of that region soon as poss. Eli dreaded to hear his phone ring because it was sure to be bad news unless they caught Franklin and everything was off, in which case whoo. He shouldn't be thinking that, but he was.

"Don't be angry at me, Sue. Look at all the shit going down. You'll be safe and out of the way at my Mom's till it's over."

"Bullshit," Sukey said, and threw a summer dress she'd just folded at his head. "This is such bullshit and you're lying. I know because you won't touch me."

"What did we do for like an hour this morning?"

"You can always get it up for sex," Sukey told him, and he started to clasp his hands over his head in a champion gesture but Sukey wasn't having it. "What I mean is usually you can't keep your hands off me, I don't mean grabbing my ass either, I mean a million times a day, a touch here, a touch there, shoulder, cheek, top of my head, like you're making sure I'm really there."

"Sometimes I can't believe it," Eli confessed.

"Well it might come true soon. Anyhow you've been keeping away from me except when you think you have to prove something, and it's in your face, I can see it, I can tell."

What bothered him most now were not those heavy folds of flesh on the sides but how brown and gross her nipples had become. Their little outboard bumps were bigger and the main things looked like brown sores with leather nozzles in the middle. He hoped she couldn't read his mind, but she looked like she was doing it. She was the law now, she had it on her, she was coming at him with it.

Time to go. Eli turned off the burning mountains.

Sukey was silent with occasional pissed-off nearly visible fumes out her nose and ears as they said goodbye to St. Pete Two and drove along Seattle's northern edge then downhill through all the nice roofy houses to the ferry, and she was better once they were out of the car and on the water where the air was cool and smooth as it came on.

"It's beautiful," Sukey said, though you couldn't really see the island yet in all that spread of water.

"It's gonna be good for you at my mom's."

"The elevator."

"I swear to you, I swear, soon as this is over ..."

The way Sukey looked at him. "Eli, this might be it," she said. "If I'm brave enough to raise a child with someone as undependable as you I'm sure as shit ready to do it on my own. Be careful what you do, be careful not to lie, not to me and not to yourself. There will be results."

All his blood drained away somewhere. "I swear. Franklin's got this shipment, it's coming up here, I've got to get it here somehow ..."

"You're not handling it. You haven't found a driver."

"TJ and his girlfriend—"

"They might be okay for the run from here to Canada, but down in California where the security's tighter? D'you think TJ and Sherry look like happy campers in a thirty-foot bus? If you send them they'll get busted and then they'll bust *you*."

Eli didn't say anything because you also couldn't trust Teej not to bust a wall and scradulate himself some product en route. If everyone else crapped out he'd do the drive himself—way too dangerous but what else was there?—and use Jim-Bob and Placida for the Canada run even though Jim-Bob had chickened out of the Eureka leg for all the reasons Sukey'd just said.

"Eureka's on fire and they're after everyone," Sukey said.

"But I'm not there."

"I could help you with this, I'm a better manager than you and I could help you but you won't let me."

"I don't want you in the middle, that's all. I don't want you to wind up busted if I am."

"That's not what's going on here, Eli. Touch me."

"Where?"

"Just touch me."

He touched her with his fingers on her cheek but if there was supposed to be magic in it it didn't happen, he didn't feel it and it didn't show on Sukey's face, which looked like it was about to cry.

"Look, you can see the island better now," he said.

A mass of foliage looming nearer, dark solid green even though not much rain this year, wooden houses peaking out from the trees in spots, familiar, and his mother lived almost *alll* the way at the other end of the island. The drive through on the central road with town in the middle seemed to soothe Sukey a little because the woods were such a peaceful place but he knew there'd be a ton of shit to get through before goodbye.

Finally near the far end of the island they pulled off the main road that would take you to the Fauntleroy ferry if you let it, hooked a sharp left uphill and there was the house like a long wooden cabin Mom said was based on the model of a Russian dasher, and he didn't know what form the ton of shit would take but life will always come up with something. When Eli pulled the car to a stop on the dirt and gravel in front of the scrappy lawn—the garden was beautiful out back but Mom didn't seem to give a shit how the place looked when you got to it—first one out the front door was not his mother but a skinny brown woman Eli had never seen before, and if there was a race to the car between the skinny brown woman and his mother coming up behind her the skinny brown woman was going to win it. Who the hell was she exactly?

The skinny brown woman came to a stop so she could look Eli and Sukey up and down as they got out of the car. "I know all about you, Eli Chase," which how could she do that? "And you are up to two no-good things I can see from here. One criminal thing and you are dumping this nice young lady on us why exactly. I am here from prison to tell you where you're headed."

"Prison?" he asked her. She wasn't in uniform or anything, she *definitely* wasn't a cop, and he hadn't done anything, yet.

"Nikki, please." It was his mom coming past her, the words "controlled fury" came to Eli's mind and while he didn't want a lot of noise it might go better if she was in a yelling mood because he could let that roll off him like a duck, but this way maybe not. "I feel like my head is splitting," his mom not speaking to him yet, count the seconds, still to the skinny black woman, said.

"Ma," he asked her, and what he really felt like in a flash was falling into her and holding on and yelling please.

"I'll deal with you in a minute," his mother told him, and went past him to Sukey. "Hi, Sukey, come into the house. I've got the guest bedroom made up for you and I want you to know that you are completely welcome here. As for my son …" She took Sukey's suitcase from her and started toward the house, "He can stay outside for now."

So he had to stand there.

"Your mother is a saint," the skinny brown woman, uh, *Nikki*, told him. "You don't deserve her."

"Fuck, I know that. Who are you exactly?"

"I'm a friend of your mother's. I'm in prison over on the other side."

Which made no sense because, like, she's here. Unless, oh, Mom's charity projects …

"And I'm here to tell you I've seen where you're headed and you don't want to go there." She was like a missionary lady, a Jehovah's Witness, a reformed alcoholic. "I've been there, I'm there now, and I can see you coming."

"Isn't it a ladies-only prison there?"

She rolled her eyes up, then came back. "If you were mine I would hit you with a pan to get some sense into your head but I'm not licensed to do that."

"Uh, good."

His mom was coming out again, still in "controlled fury" mode. "Nikki," she said in a levelled voice, working the elevator buttons, "could you go inside and help Sukey get settled while I talk to Eli."

Nikki lowered her head in a nod that stayed there, submersive, and went to the house and inside.

"Mom I swear to you, as soon as this deal is over—"

She wasn't having it but she wasn't raising her voice either. The pointing finger, though, the narrowed eyes. "Eli, if you abandon Sukey, I was about to say I'll kill you but of course I won't. But there will be an end to something between us and an end to something inside you, and it will make me terribly sad to see you lost but I'll have to get on with my life and you'll get on with whatever's left of yours. It might be prison, it might be worse, or it could just be more random waste, which makes me very sad. I will be in grief about it but I won't be able to save you from it. I'll say it one more time: do not abandon this woman. Do that and you'll be out of reach, I won't be able to reach you. I don't think anyone will."

"I won't."

"Nothing you say has any meaning right now. She's pregnant and you're immature and I know how frightening it is but—"

"Mom, I swear, this deal is coming up and as soon—"

"When you're ready to be honest I'll be here for you, but you have to be honest with me and you're not there yet, just look at you. I don't know what it's going to take, Eli. Maybe you'll have to hit bottom, the way they say in twelve-step. But I look at you now and you're somewhere inside where you can't be reached, at least not by me and until you make a meaningful change I don't think you can even reach yourself."

That last thing almost caught and broke him because it was so, and if she'd just stayed there five seconds more he might have poured it all out of himself into her arms and heart, but she used it as her go-away line, she turned around on it and he was standing under the sun alone next to his car on an island with no one left to talk to anymore.

★

Meanwhile it was exactly like Franklin waited for him to drive back through the island deciding not to stop in and see how Jim-Bob and TJ were doing, then the ferry and the ride up through Seattle houses to Madison Park, hello St. Pete and into the house just as the land-line started ringing.

"Franklin. Man! Where are you?"

"Officially and for real I am exactly nowhere. You can not reach me at any number and I will only call you on this house phone which I have someone sweep for me every couple days."

"Cool!"

"We are getting on the move and I want to know where are my drivers."

"Hey I was just waiting to hear from you before I made the call to my ace in the hole."

"All I can say is you better be true on this one, Eli. Circumstances have compelled me to be absent for a minute, otherwise I would have been riding you closer, I'd be on your shoulder, man, so tell me you are coming through for me right now."

"Were you in the fires?"

"Let me put it this way. If you ever find yourself running down a mountain on fire with federal police on your ass, call me on the phone, because I will be able to tell you what to do. It'll cost your eyebrows and half your hair but you'll get out. What I have to do right this now present moment is be nowhere at all until I see you up by Canada. Tell me about your drivers."

"I've got my drivers. You sure I should tell you all about them on the phone?"

"Good point, mon. We talkin' too much already. Look, let's put it dis way, the mothership is sailing to the intermediate docking station, allow time for passengers to board."

"You sure this isn't this a bad time?"

"This the only time. The net is closing, there have been watchers at the wallet shop. They put a bug on the bus but we found it. We have to get this shit away from here. Also, stomp your cellphone, it's been tagged for sure."

"Right." But how would people he knew find him? He had so many calls out.

"The rendezvous is inside the edge, the place we mentioned."

"Gotcha. And the time."

"Do not leave that house landline phone for the next couple days."

"When do my drivers need to be there?"

"Now would be good."

"They have to get down there."

"Get them down there."

"If I have to stay by the phone how do I get food to eat?"

"From your woman, dork."

"I sent her away."

"What's wrong with you? Order on the telephone, man. Everything works out come see me in Jamaica for a cuppa coffee in a month or two."

"No shit?"

"Time for me to make a graceful exit for a year with lots of money. Everything *don't* work out you won't hear me coming but I'll be right behind you."

When he got off from Franklin all the shit in the world had fallen on him and after his failures to find what he was supposed to he had only one way out unless he was gonna drive it himself, which Franklin said he should absolutely not do since he would look like exactly what they're looking for. This had to be straight people with no connection that could be made to Franklin.

He had bought a half-gallon jug of Absolut because he needed clarity and put it in the freezer but it wasn't cold enough yet. He could use ice from the ice-maker in the fridge but it would build character for him to wait. The great thing about booze was how it put you in touch with the good part of yourself first thing but then got tricky after that.

I know I'm a good person but I am blowing it and I absolutely know it. Help me.

If he was a praying man like his dad or whatever it was his mom did he would have said one before punching in the number, not so much ace in the hole as last resort on earth. "Yah?" came the voice on the line, sounding so much like his own.

"Noah?"

"Hey brother, how you doing?"

"Remember what we speculated about the other day?"

"Uhh, what was that?" Noah started sounding foggy there.

"About how you could use about ten thousand dollars?" Five would come out of Eli's pocket because it was his brother, after he got his pay from Franklin. "How would that be, like, right now? The thing is happening."

"Ummm, is this for real?"

"All the way and I need to know. Will you do it for me?"

208

9

HER LITTLE HOUSE and home! There were only two strangers in it but it was as if three radios were blaring at the same time, and if Sukey wasn't talking all that much she exerted an insistent emotional pressure—the place was *crowded* and Lina's head felt ready to split.

She'd asked Nikki to stop telling Sukey what she had to do with Eli, so instead Nikki started talking about prison. "Women's D. Center where I am, eight hundred-some women, that's a paradise compared to where Eli could go because the mens, and their violence and, uhhm, the shit they do to each other, uhhmm, right. We have some fights break out too and there's a few mean people but it's small and they really try to help us, which you can do with women, but men?"

Lina hadn't really clocked Nikki's capacity for extended mania until the day the news of her work release came through, and then she'd watched the needles hit the limits on her gauges but thought this too will pass, only it hadn't yet. Maybe the prison pharmacy hadn't dosed her right, hadn't anticipated the effect of being outside. There was nothing Lina could do about it now. At least at the bookshop she was so eager to please she'd channelled her energy into the most thorough housecleaning the shelves and stock had seen in ages even though the shop usually appeared spotless, and even if Tess and Bess were a tad unnerved and uncertain they would see it through. But Nikki here at home with time on her hands?

It was a natural slide from prison back to Eli. "But you got to give young Eli credit for taking you out of the way, he's thinking of you, if you're in that house with him and it goes wrong, and it *always* can and does go wrong … All the nice things I been saying about Women's D in Gig Harbor? Forget that, girl. You don't want to be in that, specially with a child coming even though we're all babysitting champions in there …"

Lina took Sukey outside for a break. "I'm sorry," Lina told her. "I didn't exactly plan this. Can you hold up for a few days while she's here?"

Sukey's grey open-sky eyes, the kind that looked as if they could take in miles of any weather, still had that Great Plains look but the skies weren't clear. "I'm …" Lina saw that Sukey wasn't sure what to do with her body now, didn't know if Lina was huggable, Sukey didn't know whether to be more frightened of what could happen to Eli than she was about the baby dreaming itself up inside her so it could take over her whole life. Welcome to womanhood, hon.

"Okay, there's too much going on at once," Lina said, "but I want you to know that you have as much support from me as you want, how much is up to you. You're free to tell me what you want and not tell me what you don't. And if there's somewhere else you need to be, I'll take you there."

Lina watched something sharpen in Sukey's eyes, and thought there might be a phrase in the making, and hoped it didn't include that e-word again.

"You know what Eli said in his sleep last night? Out of nowhere, 'Call 1-800 Lobster, that's L-O-B-S-T-E-R.'"

Lina didn't have anything to say to that and had to try not to laugh.

"I think I must be the lobster," Sukey said.

"I'm just impressed," said Lina, "that he can spell lobster in his sleep."

When Nikki came out of the house with the phone in her hand she found them laughing together bent over, out-of-breath hysterical.

"It's, um …" she said, and gradually got Lina's attention by waving the phone.

Taking it from her and lending it her ear Lina at first mistook the voice for Eli's and thought, finally he'll let me in, he's allowing me an opening, and she was preparing her attitude and angle of address when she realized who it was. "Noah! Oh how nice it's you, I've got a lot going on here and it's a treat to hear your voice!"

"Yah," he said, "look, I have something to tell you, can this be private?"

Lina managed to indicate this to Nikki and Lina with some kind of gesture before she walked around the left end of the house and into her wonderful back garden, past the fenced-in vegetables, look at those

210

eggplants, grotesquely dark and gorgeous, totally sinister-looking but delicioso, you won't see anything like *them* in a store, and onto the impeccable emerald lawn, a world at peace but it was entirely possible that Nikki and Sukey were able to hear her from the front of the house when she exploded with "Eli asked you to do *what!*" Her volume was back down when she told Noah "I will *murder* him. One more thing, was he asking Shirine to do the drive too so you could both go to prison?" She was beginning to settle down from the shock when she came to "Okay, at least it wasn't that." By the time she got to "Noah, it's all right, I've had to sell some more stock, I'll be able to get you what you need," she was in another mood entirely, slow burn, unlikely to flare up even though the heat was palpable throughout her body.

After getting off the phone with Noah she walked in three diminishing circles three times around the lawn, gratified that her demand for privacy was still in force, and by the time she got Eli on the phone she was ready to kill again.

"Maa," he bleated.

"I will not even tell you what I think of your idea of putting your brother in jeopardy when he has a wife, an adopted daughter who is an angel and a baby on the way. You already know without me saying it. Eli, we have come to a turning point, maybe a breaking point, you and me …"

"I was gonna pay him ten thousand dollars and it's my name on the bus, all the trouble would come to me! And if someone doesn't drive it it *will* come to me, my name's the only name on it."

"Eli, *I'd* drive that load before I let Noah do it."

Silence on the line.

"Eli?"

"God, that would be so cool."

"What would."

"No one would stop *you*. You're such a …"

It was like living through a change of worlds in which the scenery atomized and scattered and the unreal became real and you walked right through the liquefied mirror. "All right, Eli," she told him, "I'm getting off the phone now because I can't believe what you just said. I can't even speak to you because I don't know what terrible and irrevocable thing I might say."

"Maa," he bleated again, and she knew her son completely helpless, completely lost.

She walked back into the house with her gaze fixed on the floor, some force pushing her head down so she'd look like a cartoon sad person, wishing she knew how to communicate with Nelson, if it were possible to go to sleep and meet with him, seriously, in a dream and talk, because it wasn't enough to simply feel his loving presence, or think she did, or hope she did, because there were no specifics in that. It felt good but it was vague.

For the moment she didn't care what Nikki or Sukey needed from her, or how much of Nikki's mania Sukey could take—Sukey Nikki Nikki Sukey, the clattering syllables sounded like a cut-rate sushi joint. "I'm going into the garden cottage for half an hour, please don't disturb me," she told them, and they stared at her.

On the way there it was still work to raise her head and once she was inside and had shut the door, simple place, table-desk, single bed, one potted miniature laurel tree, two Monet prints of blurry woods and dappled water, and sat down, she didn't know if this qualified as meditation or not and didn't much care.

"I am not willing to sacrifice my life for you, Eli," said the accomplished, professional, experienced Lina in her mind—the self she'd built up over decades of intellectual and moral effort, true and false as any other self anyhow achieved, built to protect her from what exactly? She sounded rational and grounded and assured, but some childhood-deep and sacrificial Catholic throb came back at her from the depths with Oh really? Is that all you can summon up? Is that what you're alive for? Is that the limit of your service?

There was the way of meditational wisdom and the way of unconditional love, and even if you knew the deficiencies of all that emotional identifiction it was hard to run away from your birthright, from what you'd actually given birth to. Flesh and blood Nelse and I loved into being, sometimes struggling against the current while we did it.

What's that worth under eternity's eye? Life is short and long, then gone.

This moment was less like meditation and more like taking your life in your hands and weighing its vital organs in a balance, one weight against another in a golden cup one heartbeat at a time.

At the end of the process she felt that she had arrived at a sort of ultimate grim realism, but wanted to be sure about the facts of the matter.

Meaning she needed to talk to a lawyer, not Ray Quintana with the proffered glass of old sherry implicit in his voice, a drinkie just behind the law of doom, but to an old friend who'd lived a rich irregular life, currently falling through its last timbers in a planar wooden house he'd built mostly with his own hands in the hills above Berkeley. God bless him Tim was home and verified for her in quavering voice that if she was stopped and the title was in Eli's name she could plausibly insist, given her clean life history, that she was doing her youngest son a favor without any knowledge of what was hidden in the vehicle, which obviously was his sole doing. "You'll never come to trial, much less be convicted," was his firm conclusion. "They'll try to scare you of course, but that's all they can do if you're caught."

"As long as I sell Eli down the river if it goes that far."

"That would be essential I'm afraid. There's no escaping the fact that someone must be liable, and it would have to be him."

Lina ground her teeth together, pretty sure she wouldn't be making a choice like this if she had her normal freedom of mind and her house wasn't crazy with other people's voicey lives. She phoned Eli back and explained the rules, the most important of which was, "If they stop me I tell them it's all you, all your doing, and that means you go to prison for years. You understand that, right?"

"Oh God Ma, yes, if you, if you … Oh God, Ma. Otherwise I'll have to do it myself and I'm sure to—"

"You'll get caught, with what the police already know about you, the way you look, the way you act … But listen, Eli. You have to understand this—listen closely, the elevator is stopping *exactly* at your floor—this is the last thing I can do to save you. I'll do it because you're my son and I'll always love you. I will put my life and freedom at risk for you this time but after this I won't be able to change the world for you. This is the last one. And if you're in prison I'll visit but I won't be able to do a thing for you except weep."

"Oh God, Ma."

"There's one more phone call I have to make, I'm asking one more friend about this, and listen Eli, stop sniffling, if he says no I'm not doing it. The coin is in the air and it's going to be up to what he says. I don't believe in signs but I'm going to take what he says as a sign."

"Oh God, Ma …"

"No, you can't cry all over me right now. That does not answer the situation between us. I'm going to call that person and listen to what he says, and then I'll call you back."

It really was a coin-toss in Lina's mind, fifty-fifty tumbling in the air, trust to the laws of this place and one of them is gravity, the outcome out of her hands and spinning. She fingertipped the number and listened to the ringtone as if it was a bell ringing in empty sky, a golden oldie.

Tony didn't hesitate at all. "So this is it, huh" he said. "I didn't know what it was gonna be but this is it."

"Uh huh. Wait, what do you mean? Should I do it?"

"You don't think I'm gonna let you do dis on your own, do ya?"

"*What?* No, I wasn't asking that …"

"Listen, you don't have the skill set for this and I do. Something will always fuck up and when it does you won't be ready. But you're lucky in that your Lama has a background …"

She spent a good ten minutes trying to talk him out of it but he said it was a done deal, it had pretty much already happened, he'd foreseen something and now he saw that it was this, it had to be done, he wouldn't budge and when do we start.

Three

O nobly born, when your body and mind were separating,
you must have experienced a glimpse of pure truth:
subtle, sparkling, bright, glorious, radiant and awe-inspiring,
in appearance like a mirage
moving across a landscape in springtime
in one continuous stream.
Don't be daunted or terrified or awed.
It is the radiance of your own true nature. Recognize it.

—*The Tibetan Book of the Dead*

1

SUKEY DROVE Lina to the Seattle ferry dock in the red Focus and told her she'd be okay for a couple of days. "I have Nikki to look after me," Sukey said, and tried for a laugh.

"I'll be back soon," Lina told her, thinking It's clear now, I am insane.

"*If* you're back," Sukey said, then actually bit her underlip, Lina could see her teeth do it.

It seemed that was all they were going to say to each other about Eli, whether in condemnation or profession of faith, just stand face to face with loaded looks until it was time for Lina to get on the boat when the horn blew.

Is this my last ride in the wide free world? Lina asked herself as the ferry crossed the water, greying early morning, the transcendent element in the landscape Mount Rainier with its snowtop half-socked inside cloud, felt like rain coming, maybe the same wave of rain that had finally eased the fires in the mountains above Eureka. She'd made her decision and it had seemed like granite realism and maybe brave but now doubts were coming on at least as heavy. She wished the ferry would go on and on without reaching the other shore, an endless venture across the water in the dawning world, but at length it got there and eased and bumped to dock, she walked the bridge to shore, noticing the police gals with their thick legs in shorts wandering with sniffer-dogs on the leash among the embarcaderees, smiling and nodding to people but definitely on the job. Tony was waiting for her under a tree at the edge of the parking lot offside the end of the dock just as he'd said, leaning on the car in the mottled shade, wearing what he once might have called snappy sports clothes and on his shaven head a grey snap-brim straw that looked like he might have found it at the racetrack.

"Tony, you're ridiculous," first time she'd told him anything like that, but she needed a laugh.

"You told me to disguise, you said look like a square."

"I like the duds, I meant the car."

"Long as we're doin' this might as well in style."

"A black Porsche."

"Better than a terrible Dilemma. Your friend down there promises to drive it back up here, right?"

"Yes, I think he'll want to see me."

"Ohh, it's like that."

"Not yet it isn't."

"Tryina make me jealous?"

"Maybe a little. I'm not sure what I'm doing. Let's not trade zingers."

"Okay get inna car, the clock is tickin' and the game's, y'know."

Definitely a cockpit, and the throttled under-roar of the engine as it fired up and settled into idle behind her glovelike seat. So she was something of a gearhead and idiot and enjoyed the feel of it as the car pulled smoothly out of the lot and pressed her into the tall leather bucket when Tony unleashed it just a bit on entering the road. Her one problem with the car: black body outside, fine, but the tan leather interior, a bad choice, was unpleasantly fleshtoned, not just the seats but doors and dash too. Wonderfully snug and comfortable she had to admit, and crikey even just toddling through a labyrinth of treelined neighborhood streets to the highway you could feel how fast it was and its grip on the road.

Some of this must have showed in her face. "Got a radar detector and a jammer," Tony said. "Course we could always get spotted in a speed trap but I plan on doing this quick, get there tonight."

"You could use Tibetan super-powers to intuit cops."

"I do come with that option, yeah. Now," he said, taking a small plastic box from atop the dashboard, "gimme your cellphone."

Lina dug for it in her bag while, at a stop sign with no one behind, Tony opened the box to reveal a set of tiny tools from which he took a nifty little screwdriver and opened the palm of his hand for her phone please. "I'm taking the chip card out. Anyone gets suspicious of us they can track you with it via satellite, see where we go, where we been, so," he pulled the little blue thing out and put the phone back together empty, handed the phone back to her with the chip card separate, "you don't use this till we get back here. I got us two prepaid untraceables we use on the trip in case we have to call someone or need to go walkie-talkie to each other for some reason."

"You think of everything," Lina said.

"Here's hopin."

Lina took a breath. "You can still turn it around, Tony. I plan to make that suggestion a few times on the way if you don't mind."

"Nah, go 'head. It'd mean Eli goes to jail though, right?"

"If no one picks it up his name is on the registration when the police find it."

"So there."

"What happens if we get stopped?"

"We pay the speeding ticket."

Lina did a small Bronx cheer. "I mean on the way back in the bus."

"You trust your lawyer friend we'll never come to trial if this goes bad?"

"I do, but still …"

"If we get stopped and busted with the stuff …" Tony started to say, then let it ride for a moment as he hung a left uphill and used it for a speech-break. "Well, it'd be one too many for the Rinpoche, but—"

"That's why, Tony, that's why I shouldn't let you do this."

"Lemme finish, all right? I was thinking of taking a little vocation … ignore dat, I mean *vacation* from the Lama business anyway."

Lina tried for the Laugh of Incredulity but it came out confused, as it will when you're this tense. "To do what?"

"Don't laugh, I was thinking of opening a restaurant."

But Lina did laugh, and it worked some of the rigidity out of her shoulders and eased her belly for a moment.

"Neapolitan of course," Tony continued, sounding like a voice on the radio. "Why not specialize in, you know, the fine abundant seafood of the region? They're doing good things with it at Elliott's and Acqua, and there're a coupla straight not-bad Italian joints in town but nothing first-rate along the lines that I envision."

"Good Lord."

"I wouldn't call it that. *Marpa's* I think is kind of cute under the circumstances. Vowel on the end, who's gonna know?"

"The Kagyu lineage will be pleased."

"Ehhh, maybe."

"The funny thing is I can see it," Lina said. "You'd be good at it too. You mention this to Mira yet?"

"It did not go down too well."

"I bet. And how's this little trip going down at home?"

"I won't lie to you. Even less well."

"How much does she know?"

"That we're helping Eli who is mixed up in what I didn't say but just alluded to."

"And she took it?"

"She had to. She's more upset about, you know."

"You and me."

"Yeh, which is why we have to keep it clear there's nothing doing."

"That's right," said Lina. "We are the very definition of doing nothing as we approach Interstate 5 in a jetblack Porsche heading for et cetera."

"See, that's just what I told her. This is a straight work of compassion and there's nothin to fear but fear itself. There's the on-ramp and here we go."

"I'm doing this," she told Tony, "because I'm stuck loving Eli and I'm probably going insane despite my double training. You, you're doing this for a lark, for fun, for old times' sake?"

"I'm doing this for *you*."

Up on the roadway most of the morning traffic was oncoming north to Seattle proper and its pack of clean new towers vanishing astern, but enough company on the road south to Tacoma to keep them safe five over the limit but anyway this was not the place to let the Porsche off the leash.

"Fantastic car, Tony."

"No foolin."

"One more question: why are we—"

"To help you keep your son out of prison is enough. Also, some things have to happen and I think this is one of them. Listen, tell you what I think. You and I, we know everything we can possibly say about this trip here, so let's make like we already said it and here we are so action supervenes over thought."

Tony waited while Lina reflexively washed her face with her hands.

"Plus I think you should get some sleep on the road here. You sleep much last night?"

"No."

"You look it. So here's an ancient Tibetan Jersey Turnpike passenger practice: empty your mind of thought, flow with the sound of this lovely flathead six and the great suspension—"

"The Great Suspension," Lina said.

"Because I intend to hammer it all the way to Eureka and I think you agree with me we shouldn't linger there with the whatever it is in the bus, which means can you drive the big thing late at night, two, three AM tonight, can you drive it?"

"I was born on wheels," Lina said. "I can drive anything that rolls."

"Attagirl. If we don't get enough sleep there's an old friend of mine just up the coast from Eureka and we can crash at his place, but it's better we do it in one go."

"Agreed."

"So. You want some music? Got a great sound system here, satellite radio, whatever you want. I want you to sleep if you can."

After Lina dozed off Tony looked ahead into the complicated murk of his future, his fate or destiny if there still was such a thing for him, and wondered if doing some apparently wrong shit could really demonstrate the voidness of all conditions.

This was gonna be easy as Macbeth, who got some of his info up front too, besides which it looked like Lina had blueskinned Yamantaka working the switches ahead. Of course Tony knew who it was, but the question, was the guy showing up as Death or, you know, his other aspect, the Slayer of Death. I perceive a troubling difference there. I never been set up this perfect to take a fall and play the mug in a game since the old days back in Jersey.

2

Fuckin' hell, Pitch had fallen asleep in his car parked half a block and across from Marcus Dobbs' house, hadn't he, and for how long? after following Dobbs around all day hoping to catch him together with Anne Dujardin, feeling like the king of the Schmohawks out there with nary a plan what he'd do if he got hold of them. When what he shoulda been doing was track down that rumor around town how there was a patch been harvested, one no Feds'd put a match to or a bag on. Maybe it was just one more pothead legend but the fact was he didn't know. Well, what could he do, the only people left in this burg who'd still talk to him were the street dogs and even they looked at him funny and not one tail wagging. Still, he was niggled at by the thought that Franklin Bass was the one major dealer who if he hadn't gone up in sizzling body-fat might've got away clean. But was now the invisible man. And Eli Chase was out of the picture up somewhere in Seattle.

So instead he was hunting two people he really didn't give a shit about and had been on the job so many hours he'd snarfed a bit of the Dudes' unfamiliar crystal that hit him quicker than expected, then split twice as fast and he'd fallen stupid and asleep in the street across from fuckwhat. Waking up he had no idea what time of night it was, gun under the driver's seat and still nothing definite in mind. Should probably wrap this up, no one's going anywhere now, and he wasn't gonna break and enter just to pistol-whip the jig, assuming he was even at home. Well his car was in the driveway. He'd wanted Marcus and Betty-June together but unless she'd dropped by while he was conked that hadn't happened. He trusted his warrior instincts to have woken him if it had, so no.

But hey, looky thar, wait a minute, you spoke better than you knew, howbout that, how lucky and which local gods've I got in pocket. Lights were going on and off over Dobbsie's way, that musta woke me and maybe a little birdie added a chirp, or it was my good angel, because two or three minutes later Dobbs decided which light to leave on and was heading out the door to his dark blue little 4-series Volvo Turbo Wagon. Following a darkie in the dark, that's man's work, wait for it, give him a lead wherever he's going and follow him with your lights off. Better to lose him than be seen because wherever he's going at this hour it'll to Annie's house, you could even drive ahead and wait for him, and while it was true Pitch had nothing definite in mind, the fact is that with a gun in your hand it's possible to control a situation in such a way that you could beat the shit out of two different people if that's what took your fancy.

With the Raleigh patch burnt up he'd gone through pointless rage awhile but that had burned out like the fires on the mountain when he saw there was no point to it—*shunyata*: if you're going to do something, do it cleareyed cold and cancel the background music. He was left with his local plans shot and not much to do in town but settle accounts with a few people if he couldn't refrain, Dobbs and Anne and fuck you Bob Poholek, maybe Eli Chase up north, then back to Carolina where he probably wouldn't even bother trying to keep his job with Burke and the life of a corporate asshole.

Following Dobbs's car, heyy, it looked like after one turn and was definite after two, this wasn't the way to Anne Dujardin's. Maybe he was meeting her somewhere special. You don't go out this late except for a woman, man, specially if you're a long-donged Dobbs the shade of Marcus. It was a quiet night with no other traffic in these parts—they might be meeting out of town east in the redwoods but what for?—so it was easy to lay back and not lose him, but still you had to be careful, he could hang a turn, stop someplace, switch his lights off and catch you out.

Pitch followed him east on Harris through thinning residential neighborhoods in the direction of the redwoods. A pagan sex ceremony in sacred forest moonlight majesty? The wind changed and blew a stink of burned forest down from the mountains through the windows of the Chevy, what Poholek and those assholes did, and then Dobbs started making extra turns as if he might've spotted Pitch creeping up on his ass. Pitch hung further back and took the risk of losing sight of the car while keeping track of the travelling cones of its headlights. This took attention, focus.

After a few more zigs, Dobbs turned north toward the residential pocket east of Eureka State Park and Pitch got the feeling they were back on track.

He was not disappointed.

There, Dobbs was pulling up in front of a midsize wood-and-stonework house ahead on the right on a not too thickly populous treelined street and Pitch rolled the Chevy to a stop at the start of the block in the shadow overhang of some kind of tree on the left and watched.

Up ahead Dobbs got out of his functional Volvo spiced with a blower—what does that say about a man's character?—stood there tossing his car keys in his hand and looked around, then walked the walk between the lawnsides to the front door of the house and rang the bell. There was light in one front room and the entry lamp was on and in half a tick a white guy on the large size but Pitch couldn't see much more because of how the light fell, was greeting Dobbs at the front door and it didn't look like Dobbs was going inside. Quiet talky-talk with an occasional looky-look around and then a handshake with Dobbs walking back to his car and the other guy watching him halfway to it before he shut his door. Pitch thought Dobbs might have handed off the car keys but now let's see: after bending down to look inside his car as if to check if he'd forgotten something Dobbs turned right and started walking where there would have been a sidewalk if they had sidewalks in this part of town, past the lawnfronts of the modest houses of the neighborhood, in and out of lunar patches and daubs of moonshade under trees.

Decision time, do I leave the car here, and Pitch decided that he would.

It was fun using his old tracking skills and keeping out of sight of Dobbs, who turned to look a few times and Pitch wasn't sure, as the houses thinned out and they started hitting more spaced-out rural properties, if he'd been seen, but it looked like not. Pitch moved from one pool of shade to the next behind him, hoping not to get spotted in a transition. One thing he had to hand the man, Dobbs had good bearing and a graceful walk, his spine relaxedly erect, no slouching, hear me—as if he'd been disciplined, though probably not in the army—and a general way of stepping that indicated good physical condition and confidence in how he carried himself, the fucker, on his way to whatever shady meeting with some dude out on bail, no doubt. This secrecy did not bespeak Anne, it did not.

It would have been possible in the soft sweet summer night to walk up on him and shoot him in the small of his back, but Pitch hadn't committed to anything that serious and besides was more interested to find out where this boy was going.

In fact Pitch was starting to feel so affectionate toward the son of a bitch that five or ten minutes later he nearly walked into the trap. They were on what you'd call a country lane now, only a few houses here and there with cars pulled up to them, and it was a damn good thing Pitch had been keeping extra distance because just as Dobbs walked past a big Ford Explorer on the right parked in front of nothing in particular, a head came up sideways inside the car, a man been laying low until Dobbs passed and then rose up. Right away Pitch backed himself into the lee of some monster shrubbery he was close to and squinted at the shape inside that Ford, big round head and shoulders, plus those near jug ears till he made the odds it was Bob Poholek. Not in his police cruiser but a mufti Ford, waiting.

Looking ahead to relocate Marcus Dobbs, Pitch saw what Dobbs might be headed for, in any case this was Poholek's stakeout and that was the only thing in view, a big Recreational Motherfucker pulled suggestively into the umbrella shade of a roadside willow a couple hundred feet past where Poholek was sitting in the Ford. Past the Rec-V a yellow bulb shed not much light hanging from crosswires above a T-junction with a stop sign. Some folks' hearts may leap up when they behold a rainbow but that RV was the best news Pitch had seen in a month of bone-dry Sundays, since what else could be worth staking out but a bunch of money waiting for him in the form of the legendary maybe-only dope that didn't get burned up by the federals? The only question was, whose was it, on the other hand who gave a fuck, though Pitch's first quick thought was Franklin Bass because of him and Dobbs being nig-bros together. Bass had been the seldom-seen kid since the DEA fiasco and maybe the clever jig had found a way to save the fruit of his plantation and as we know that like all the major dudes he's a client of Dobbs. So considering all the work and time I put in, that is my right and justified money on the bus, only how many other cops're holding other corners in Cap'n Poho's stakeout? It's a bitch but you got to be realistic, Pitch. Police have got the brothers surrounded.

Meanwhile he'd paid for a box seat and it wouldn't hurt to watch.

From this distance Dobbs was almost vanished in the willow-shade but still you could make out he gave the bus a once-over, then stepped up to try the door on the side and it didn't open. Stepping back from the shadow, Dobbs' posture signalled a mix of boredom and irritation, or was Pitch projecting? That's right, Dobbsy, it's too dark to see your watch, oh look at that you've got a little pocket-light on your keychain, housekey chain that'd be since you gave the car keys away, and you don't look happy, uh-uh, checking up and down the road apiece, ain't it a drag when people keep you waiting?

Pacey, pacey, Dobbs my lad, and walking in that circle will also do you lots of good when there's noplace to sit because you put your high round ass inside offwhite linen slacks, you man of style and fashion, whereas Pitch's dark blue countrypolitan suit didn't mind the bushes and went well with moonlight. No one was judging but the line of his jacket was spoiled by the .38 he'd transferred from his belt in back to his sidepocket when he sat. *Il faut souffrir pour être belle* but there's limits.

Impatient fella, Dobbs, or a nervous one, didn't give it more than a couple minutes before taking his phone out of his pocket and ringing up whoever, saying, yes, no, uh huh, checking his watch again and looking up this way for a second, didn't see me, couldn't, only thing would make this bush more perfect would be some blackberries growing on it so ol' Pitch could have a snack and appreciate the sweetness of life while he watched the show.

Over to Poholek in right field, ladies and gentleman, immobile in the driver's seat then no, as Dobbsy looked his way again Poholek tilted himself back out of sight. Is that good tactics, folks? We will have to wait and see, aaaand, it looks, batter up, Dobbs had caught the move and started ambling quasi-aimless toward the who-parked-it-there Explorer, apple-red paint Pitch now permitted himself to recognize, this could be good.

Now walking that fine athletic walk in his cool linen slacks, Dobbs approached the Explorer on the driver's side, peered in, leaned back, peered in again and knocked lightly on the window with one satirical knuckle. Took a couple seconds, what a drag for Captain Bob to rise up sideways and roll the window down.

Exchange of words, you bet, too far to catch anything but the peaks from here. "Nuh-huh," "Take them down," "What friends?" Now best of all, as Dobbs turned on his insolent heel he went into his pocket and, whoa-ho, pulled his phone out. I wouldna done that, me. This is a force that opens the doors of Fords, brings Captains out of concealment and puts the ball in play.

You had to pay close attention, though, Poholek's move was that fast when it came, Pitch almost cun't believe it.

Bob had his rear treeside window open so he'd have fresh air to breathe but occasionally a montane wind brought in the death smell of what a bunch of assholes he should have never trusted had done to his operation, his patches, his last roundup, his mountains, his beautiful tall green seaside wonder. It was a sick death smell of burned soaked forest, no trace of marijuana high, just empty devastation. How black and bitter was his anger compared to it? You don't want to know.

He'd been let down by Olaffson for years and now by that not very semper fi bastard John Emigh and by the Chief of Official Impotence himself and he had finished trusting anyone but himself. When the boys on the Seattle force wanted in on the op he knew they'd take it away from him and run it themselves and say thank you ma'am, and by now there was no one he could trust in his own precinct: it was time for everyone to climb on his back and take their turn to spit on his head. He'd never realized how little he was appreciated. So he was going to take the reins on this one in his hands and not let go till the fucker was done. Whatever it took. You want to see rogue? I'll show you rogue.

Bob had been sitting in the Ford for at most an hour since the big bus drove in from that farm outside town where probably they'd been loading it all day, we'll close that place down when this is over. His boy up the Klamath had done the law proud, put two transponders on the underchassis and Franklin's people had only found one of them. Bob had the frequency but took the chance, after the woolly-headed jerk pulled the bus in under the willow and locked up, then booked in the getaway car that had come with him, Bob took the chance of quickly-quickly getting up ahead and putting his own beeper up in the left-front wheel-well, a little low-tech one that would only distance-beep for ya but would likely be too small to find. Breaking into the bus for a look was risky, people could be coming any minute and he had no doubt the shit was packed hard to find unless you pulled the walls off and floor up.

So it was back to Marion's car for too damn long, out of uniform with his department Glock on the other seat, shotgun on the floor in back and a .32 Beretta in an ankle rig if things got hairy or he needed to drop one, a one-man operation since everyone had fucked him royally so far, though he had alerts out up north and protocols ready depending what he saw the scope of action was, and ready to follow the target out of town if, as he assumed, it didn't offer an ideal bust in Eureka. Better to go where it was going and bag everyone there. What seemed likeliest was also best, north to Seattle or environs, where Eli Chase would be there to field it along with the rest of the operation, most likely including Franklin Bass, so Bob had abstracted some operational amphetamine from an evidence locker to go the distance on if he had to. He didn't know where Bass was hiding but he should be there too and even if they only bagged the crew it wouldn't be no big trick to turn them. The material haul? Who knows how much they'd packed inside but the rest of the season's crop was burned up so this was worth extra. It was a big-ass bus. Seattle Police had been surly but cooperative once he explained they could have the glory and the photos of the haul for television assuming, that is, it came their way and please await my call, but he would not say a word more. They probly thought I was off my nut or up to nothing and they finally said okay, yes.

Pretty good setup, which is why it made him furious he'd moved at the wrong moment and let himself be spotted by Marcus fucking Dobbs, who then sashaying up knocked on the window cordial as you please.

Twenty years of eating sixteen tons of home-fried shit, right on the edge of finally getting your own back, and what do you get. One casually dressed clever jig the last thing standing in the way. This is flat-out unacceptable. Request permission to do the necessary, sir.

Well finally he had to roll his window down.

"Evening, Bob," said Marcus Dobbs, Uppity Prick, Esq.

"I suggest you leave the scene," Bob told him, "before you become party to a criminal enterprise."

Marcus affected to look around him. "I don't see anything criminal taking place here. Fancy that, finding myself unable to sleep, I took a stroll and came upon you. Small world, Eureka."

"As a professional courtesy, Marc, I'll let you walk away from this right now. You don't take it, I radio the squad and we take you in as an accessory to a narcotics offense. Might have to do that anyway, put you in custody for safety's sake."

"I don't think so," Marcus said. "I walked in here and I didn't see any backup anywhere. Workshirt and jeans are a good look for you, though."

"Get the fuck out of here," said Bob. "You waiting for a bus, Marco? There's the bus. Want to know what's in it?"

"I do not. I'm merely a happenstance passerby enjoying a stroll in the night."

"The end of everything, that's what's in there. The end of everything in a bad year. I'm not letting you get in front of this, nuh-huh. I don't figure you for the driver and let's pretend I don't know why you're here, but when your friends show up I will take them down."

"What friends?"

"I'll know soon enough."

"Will you? Well, it's been nice talking to you, Bob, but I believe I've got to mosey along." Dobbs turned to go, and as he did his hand went into his pants pocket and pulled out his flip phone.

Bob made a move to grab it from him but it slipped away.

Marcus wheeled around. "No you don't."

"Don't you do it," Bob said, thinking he has to be neutralized so he can't make that call, but then what? Trouble. Operationally unsustainable. Bob felt himself starting to boil over, and wasn't about to let Marcus grin like a coon at him like I'm stupid and he's not. "You don't know how much I've got invested in this op," Bob told him.

"I don't, nor do I care," Dobbs told him, starting to turn away but then looked shit-surprised at how fast Bob could get out of a car at him, door nearly hit him and if Dobbs thought I'm old and creaky out of a seat he's got another thing.

"Hey hey *hey*," said Dobbs, unsteady backward on his feet now and stuck his hands out to protect himself, one hand with the phone in it, hands spaced too wide to stop anything serious. This boy was not a fighter.

A fresh blow of stunk burnt mountain came down at them and that might have helped Bob out, just overadded up and he remembered doing

Eli Chase's nose but not pushing in, heard himself telling younger cops all too many tedious times how he had the training and could kill with one blow until they'd stopped listening to him, and he was pissed off enough at the whole pack of everyone fucking him over this year and every year and, a last stray thought even he knew was bullshit as it raced through, *this is for what you did to my wife, nigger,* so Bob went and crossed the line and did it, drove the heel of his hand past Dobbs' feeble self-protection and didn't choke like he thought he might, got the bridge of the nose right on target, hit it hard and drove it in, the point being to break the bone and dislodge it up into his frontal brain to finish.

Dobbs went down on the asphalt on his back but he wasn't supposed to be rolling and writhing, it was supposed to be a couple last spasms and out, fuck, so Bob had to lean down there and hit him a tight karate fist in the larynx since the moment offered it up and he felt the windpipe crush, which slowed Dobbs's wobbling down there so here we are. Bob straddled Dobbs and set his feet for stability then drove the heel of his hand in a second time where the nose had been and on the followthrough this time definitely felt the bone piece out and push far enough inside.

Bob straightened up to watch and yes, that's how it's supposed to happen, the brain-bone's connected to the nerve-bone, nerve-bone's connected to the heart-bone, heart-bone's connected to the breath-bone—he felt the thrill of evil run right through him finally—and there was Marcus Dobbs, bail bondsman licensed by the State of California, spasming out of the world so hear the Word of the Lord.

Marcus saw Poholek's big hand aimed flat between his eyes, then impact and a flash, then a blank of nothing followed by a stretch of struggle he tried to get to the other side of but couldn't and choked on something, then another impact on his blinded eyes, a jag of lightning and the sensation of being shot out a cannon through borderlines he didn't know existed, and when things slowed down he was something like the outline of Marcus Dobbs or a bottle in the shape of Marcus Dobbs, inside it a wealth of sprouting shock, shapes like blossoming starfish or anemone, orange, purple, red, oh that's pretty, a delicate bluey-green one, all on a midnight field with other shape-blossoms rising and swaying like a series of curtains, and he thought of his Dad, of the life he would have had with

229

Anne—oh, funny thing, he hadn't given much credence to the possibility but now he saw it and it was written out plain as the ink that writes the daylight, their lives together, it was real, two honeycolored children, boy and girl, beautiful, were they twins? but now they wouldn't know the sunlight or the grass of the field he saw them walking in, scrapped like a draft along with all the music that now he'd never write, the beauty he was meant to bring into the world and had been born for, the amazing human singularities he'd encountered in this world-emanation, and suddenly looming at him the truly terrible scope and size of his father's oncoming grief—I *told* him he should borrow Thor—but Dad, Poholek would have shot the dog—and Marcus saw how his death would break and just about kill his father and how he couldn't help him through it and the anguish of knowing but being unable to act was the single most destructive thing Marcus had ever felt, more than he could bear but he also knew it wouldn't last. The pain would fill his heart, insufferable and without limit, but wouldn't last, like all the lights and shapes of the bygone world, and knowing that was a blessing, if a cold one.

Then less clearly, as if in a codicil to a contract pending adjudication, he saw how Lina Chase's imminent feeling of responsibility for his death would truly damage her and he tried to reach through distances to tell her I know, I know, but let it go and move on, look at me, that's what I plan to do, look here, look here.

When Bob Poholek put the body that had been Marcus Dobbs in the rear cargo bay of his Ford Explorer there was a tremendous amount going on inside what Marcus reckoned must be his soul so he didn't notice his former weight lifted and dropped or hear the tailgate shut on it.

Amazed among the bulrushes was Kennis Pitcher at dreams he hadn't dreamed coming true. He absolutely had Poholek's balls in his hand, and if it wasn't for the near-certainty of Pitch's own money living in that big trailer he might have fiddled with the idea of walking up to Bob to make a citizen's arrest, only of course it would end in he-said he-said with law and police history on Poholek's side, or more likely a bangbang that would see both of them out of here, so maybe just walk up shoot him and take the bus. But even better, Marcus Dobbs' body lies a-moulderin' in the back of Bob Poholek's Ford Explorer with Dobbs's blood drying on Poholek's hands and under his fingernails, with Poholek, it appears, operating rogue without a team or backup. This is not law enforcement intended for daylight view. Ladies and gennamens, this is a cop fucking up on candid camera in the sight of someone who doesn't really like him anymore.

Who knew the old boy had it in him? What a show tonight gennamens, it ain't over yet and so far I ain't had to do a thing myself. Ain't it cool to be in the middle parts of fortune?

Pitch palmed his good luck charm, the littledick pistol in his pocket, and wondered how soon there'd be a moment for him. Not now but any second a door in the air could swing open and tell him to step right in.

He didn't know how long he'd have to wait and didn't count the minutes but eventually, in this quiet part of the night where the predominant sound was a now and then shushing of leaves overhead when a breeze thought to pass, there came a low thrumming engine sound and behold, a low black Porsche 911 edged cautiously into view on the right leg of the T-junction at the end of the road, turning under the hanging light to approach the Recreational Mother on watchful treads and headlights dimmed even before it slowed to a stop on the roadside about fifteen feet distant from the Mothership on the dirt.

No one got out yet and he couldn't see who was inside but the car was cool, a more recent model than his back home with the old squat shape looked like someone mated a breadbox with a shoe but it drove like a honey. This was one of the newer sleeky ones he wished he had, near as lean and bladed as a Ferrari, sculpted air-scoops astern the doors and it looked great all black, lustrous under moonlight his eyes had adjusted to by now and the edge of overhead streetlight hanging at the T.

Over to Bob Poholek in right field ladies and gennamen and he's hunkered down this time with maybe one eye topside of his dashboard, learned his lesson, no more ground-rule errors.

There you go, the Porsche's inside light went on as the door opened and a big overweight guy got out first, looked around, bent to say something inside the car and as she opened and outed Pitch was able to recognize the lady as—ooo-eee sports fans—Eli Chase's uppity bitch of a mother. Was she really in the game? Had she really been in the game all this time? No, he didn't buy it. It was something else. The two of them were dressed like jerks. The big guy, Lina's muscle, the bodyguard or whatever was big but dressed like a pissant golfer, Pitch wasn't sure but those pants might be plaid and the little hat atop his big maybe bald head made him look like an organ-grinder's monkey.

Anyway the two of them were looking around up and down the road, back to the T, over to the trailer, peering this way and that like a pair of mimes and Pitch filled in the thought-balloons above their heads: "Where's Marcus? Where is Marcus? Where the #@&*% is Marcus?"

The big guy tried the side door of the Mother to see inside but it was locked.

Poholek showed no signs of making a move and Pitch figured the odds were like the Gypsy said, everyone's going on a long voyage. One way this could work was that assuming they all took off he didn't have the tools to get through a Porsche's door but he knew how to break a window and unless the redesign was radical he could hotwire the Porsche with his Swiss Army here though he was no pro and it might take a minute.

Like Marcus before them they went through their routine looky-looky and didn't findy-find, then had a huddled confab-à-deux that ended with Mrs. Chase getting her phone out of her purse and making the call.

Pitch had to hold his breath among the bulrushes because he could just about hear Marcus's phone ringing in the back of Poholek's Ford Explorer, and for shit-sure Bob Poholek could hear Marcus's phone ringing in the back of Bob Poholek's Ford Explorer, but given the distance could Mrs. Chase and her large-size Monkey hear Marcus's phone ringing in the back of Bob Poholek's Ford Explorer?

One ring, two rings, some kind of piano music Pitch couldn't place, three rings, everything up in the air to who knows, one possible outcome everyone else dead and laid out neat and Pitch driving a Rec-V to Camp Hoo-Hah west of Grants Pass saying I know you guys have reservations about me but looky here. From the reaction shots it looked like the phone sound didn't carry the distance to Mrs. Chase and her goon despite the general quietude of this busy night.

Mrs. Chase appeared to leave a brief message, then put her phone away and sent a shrug to her big strong ape-man.

Another confab, with the Monkey shrugging too, then taking a more decisive stance and saying his piece, the practical man telling her how it is. She didn't nod yes but you could see it in her shoulders, her stance. The Monkey bent inside the car and popped the front lid, they took out a small dufflebag and an overnighter—Pitch's heart beating now so he could feel it on his breastbone—shut the lid, shut the doors, Monkey had the keys and bee-beeped the car-locks shut aand, wait for it, while Chase walked up to the Mothership's side door, took keys out of her purse, twisted and opened, her Monkey took a last looky this way and that and then—Zathena goddess of Zowie is at my side: really, it was getting hard not to feel that the gods in whom he did not believe were speeding him to his proper end—the Monkey *bent down behind the Porsche and put the keys up the ass of one of its twin tailpipes.*

The rest was history but you still had to live through it, probably took Chase and the Monkey awhile to figure out the insides of the Mothership once they were in it, get things sorted while in right field Captain Bob had reassumed the sitting position while Dobbs' phone rang again—must be a message saying where the keys were—but finally the big thing's engine stuttered on, then its lights—not headlights, just the dims for now, good move—and Pitch sat there like an angel outside time watching the slow dumb mortals go through their scripted and foreseen familiar dramas, dull as ceremony but still exciting somehow said your heartbeat, as finally the Big Mother made its first unsteady moves, and its brakes were tested, stop, start, stop, but finally the show got on the road, pulling out of the willowshade and forward into moonroad then under bulblight, slowly forward then, not sure yet about the size of the turning circle, ver-ry slowly turning right at the T and sighing itself out of sight like a white elephant that didn't know its own dignity.

After a pause, fuck, c'mon, a longer pause than Pitch would've given it, in fact it was an *intermission*—got it: Bob has a beeper on board that thing—Poholek turned his engine on, no lights, and like a little baby mothership out to follow its mom it eased on down the road and turned the corner under the hanging lightbulb out of sight.

Pitch could not afford to lose him—though cool it, there's nothing else rolling and he could follow their headlight cones, they'd turn them on before long, to 101 North or 299 East, whichever—so he ran across the asphalt to the Porsche, fingered the wrong tailpipe first, bastard really put it up there, found it then click-beep-open get in there fast and start up. The seats were deeper than in Pitch's model, set lower, the whole car lower by a palpable inch or two, with a little ridge of spoiler at the rear, but the flat-six thrum behind him was familiar and fine and the gauges lit up like old friends he hadn't seen in years but he didn't like the color of the leather. Six-speed stick, clutch smooth as butter and so's the stubby little shifter, hi-ho, hi-ho it's off to work we go.

Damn, after months of leased and paid-for Chevy Malibu it was such a pleasure, practically a sexual one, to drive so beautifully engineered and built a car.

3

Tony said he'd drive the first leg, probably take a nap later, and saw his mistake only when they were rolling. What with driving this big new thing and negotiating the little roads out of town it was hard to keep your eye on the rearview mirror steady enough to make sure they weren't being followed.

"Marcus not being there makes me worry," Lina said in the passenger seat, peering ahead through the big window at the road pearled by moonlight, then Tony switched the headlights on. "He called us from there and then left? It's not like him."

"Worries me too even though I don't know the guy," Tony said. Thinking it through, for some reason the guy either couldn't wait around and his cellphone didn't have enough bars for him to pick up when we called later, which was iffy, or he was busted at the site and bundled off. Why bust him and not us? Because there was a stakeout and he spotted it, so they had to take him off and let us come and go because the point is to follow the money. Or, best option, he went scaredy-cat at the last minute and ran away. "Maybe he had to leave to do something and he'll come back to pick up the car," he lied to her and didn't like it, also didn't want to mention Marcus maybe chickening out, she likes him and I'd get an argument, but that's the best possibility we can hope. "Do me a favor, willya? Go to the back of the bus and look out the window, see if anyone's behind us. Even a car with the lights off if you can spot it." Lina got up to go. "Also, headlights behind us from a car too far off to spot, the glow of someone back there steady. See if anything like that keeps pace with us."

"And if there is?"

"We get ahead, pull over, get out and walk away. We can't outrun anyone in this."

"Just like that?"

"We can test the situation a little before giving up, just to be sure. Go back and look. This rearview mirror's for shit."

"You're just trying to get me into bed," Lina said on parting.

Yes, Tony'd seen the bed back there and it was the one. He didn't say anything then or now but he thought Lina'd looked at it funny too when they were checking the bus out. No smell of dope in here at all. Maybe it was stuck to the underchassis or they'd bagged it very well, but if so, where? It was good not to know.

"299 to Redding," Lina called from halfway back. "Can you find it?"

"Just passed the first sign, says a mile. Don't give us much time before we get on it and I'm not doing evasive maneuvers in this thing, so please take a good look there and tell me anything you see."

"Yes Lama sir," called Lina, on the bed on her knees, parting the back curtain and steadying herself with a hand on the rear wall above it.

Tony waited maybe half a minute. "Anything?"

"It looks like night in California."

"Good, same here. Keep looking."

"I could call Marcus again."

"Do it every two minutes you'll drive yourself nuts."

"Unless he answers. The message he left said he was waiting for us. So what happened?"

"Maybe he got spooked."

"*Spooked*?"

"I tolya something always fucks up on one of these." No, she didn't like his choice of word, spooked, as if he, which he admitted was stupid. "Listen, we're coming to 299. It's pretty bendy most of the way so you probly won't see anyone behind us but watch for any headlight glow a few more minutes, oughta be enough."

Tony pulled onto well-tended two-lane state 299 east, full tank of gas, pretty long ride to Redding and the Interstate with no-fun mountains and this big thing's handling and bad uphill acceleration so he'd be completely bushed by the time they got there. He'd done most of the drive down in the Porsche and had caught an hour or two while Lina drove but that's all.

"Anything, Lina?"

"Not so far."

"Good." He drove five miles with Lina not reporting anything before he called her to come up front.

"I could keep watching, it's not hard," she said.

"Honest," he told her as she settled in the passenger seat, "look too long you'll start seeing things ain't there. Try your friend Marcus on the phone again," though he had no high hopes, "and be careful what you say in case someone else is on the line now."

He waited through the rings, looked over to see how she was holding up and couldn't tell, then her message voice: "Marcus hi, it's me. We're on a roll, sorry we missed you. Call back when you have a minute, okay? Okay?"

"He's not there," Lina said.

"I got that. What if, say, he decided not to do this," do dis, he heard himself.

"He'd call me and say so."

"Yeah, I figured from what you say about him."

"So something happened."

"The odds are something happened. Not good."

"What do we do?"

"We keep driving," Tony said, "keep looking out, we call Marcus a few more times and if at any point we decide to, we stop somewhere and walk away."

Lina took a breath before saying it, "I wish we hadn't done this."

"That's normal," Tony told her, "in a situation like this."

"Is it?"

"Yep, also normal for Plan A to fuck up, so we're on target, normal normal normal."

"What about leaving the Porsche back there?"

"Assuming we don't hear from Marcus you know anyone in Eureka you can call to get it?"

"No."

"Then at some point you call Eli and tell him to call someone he knows, we can't just leave it there, a hundred-grand car with the keys in the tailpipe. I have someone near Eureka if Eli don't, but I'd rather not involve him unless I have to."

"Oh Jesus, Tony, your friend, the Seattle guy who owns it."

"He got enough money for his next ten lives, the car's insured up the wazoo and if it happens I'll tell him losing the car's a lesson in impermanence and non-attachment."

"You'd say that?" she asked him.

"Of course not."

Lina came back to what bothered her. "It's my fault if anything bad happens to Marcus."

"All he did was show up or not show up, he didn't break any law. If they took him in they're just holding him and we're the ones in schtook."

"They could trump him up," Lina said, "and my lawyer's story doesn't sound so plausible to me now. We drove down in a day and picked this thing up for Eli without stopping. No hotel, no nice dinner, no day at the beach, no idea what was inside it because we're stupid."

"Anything happens you stick to the story and be consistent. They can't prove nothing. Your lawyer friend's right, it's good."

"And what about you?"

"Obviously I'm crazy in love with you and would follow you anywhere. That would be the cover story."

"Great for Mira."

"I'll tell her the truth."

"That'll be popular too," Lina said, and took a breath. "Okay. I want to check the rear window again."

"I think you should sit back and enjoy the ride. We're in a steady state. Next place we have to worry is the Oregon border in case State Police is on us, and that's a ways off, so like I say, lean back, enjoy."

"Ha."

"Also please pass me that water bottle there."

It was a long tiring ride, a lot of work at the wheel, the thing heavy and didn't take curves well and was down to a crawl on uphill grades, approaching Redding and the Interstate, still no answer from Marcus Dobbs and Tony's eyes starting to give out. Almost to I-5 he pulled up at a roadside rest stop to trade places with Lina, getting out for a stretch of arms and legs and especially to check the road. While waiting he checked the wheel wells and the undercoat for anything electronic but didn't find nothing. No cars came and no distant headlights showed.

"Time for you to drive, hon," Tony told her, and after some early uncertainty she managed the barge okay, the orange aurora of Redding California compromising the sky ahead, and when they reached the Interstate he asked her to take the entrance ramp ve-ry slow-ly and when he posted himself on the bed at the rear window all he saw behind them was the late night's random business, a few cars with something to do in the small hours, busy headlit corpuscles circulating north and south and nothing dangerous in view.

No one said this was gonna be easy or that Pitch would like it. Poholek had his beeper so was hanging way back but Pitch had to keep an eye almost on the cop all the way up 299, Poholek's headlight wash always in view because suppose the Mother took a rest stop and Poholek pulled aside and Pitch rolled right up on him in a car he'd recognize because how many late-model black 911s were in this small world out so late?

It could keep your nerves on edge, and he was into his second snarf of speed with some cool jazz on satellite, where some guy was heavy on Gil Evans' pastel orchestration, which eased things up a little.

Now that he was behind Poholek on the Interstate, lanes of traffic some few percent busy even at this hour, it was still no picnic. Sometimes you could see Captain Ahab and his Whale all in one go but usually Poholek kept the Mothership out of visual range, and since Poholek didn't have to look at it all the time his eye might more easily find Pitch out back, so there was a lot of careful driving to do, and because of that Pitch had pretty much forgotten what a pleasure it was to drive this fine car.

The Chase bitch and the Ape had been kind enough to supply Marcus with about half a tank but even toodling like this at sixty the flat six was no polite sipper so at some point there'd be a problem. Solution: the car was fast, so he could fall behind, gas up then catch up with his eyes on eagle since everyone knew they were all Seattle-bound unless Poholek decided to do a bust this side of the Oregon line, and they'd know that in about fifteen minutes.

Was there another way to do this ride? It'd be nice to pass Poholek two lanes over with hand covering face but one, Captain Bob would spot the car and two, though it'd be nice to get ahead of the Mothership and follow from in front, they'd know the car too. Might think it was Marcus coming with them, wonder why, and they'd pull over for a friendly chat and he'd show them the gun and take it all away from them and leave them with the 911 and no keys.

But it was no play because who would join them for the party only Bob Poholek with law and order as his armature even with a body in the back.

When he died, whether it's on this trip or the next one or the one after that, he wanted to make sure he did it bigtime enough so they'd hear it not just in the next county or downtown Chilhowie but like the shot heard round the world, and feel the impact on the boulevards of Paris where his daughters traipsing by'd register the blow, then look up to the sky and see a firework burst up there and they'd know what he'd really been all along. It almost brought him to tears to think about them doing that. He warn't going out like some goddamned bugsplat on the windshield of the world.

Really, there was nothing for him to do but hang there, wait your turn, and make like a ghost rider in the sky.

Eli woke up, then slept again, then woke, did it enough times so it didn't make a difference which, anyways he could hardly tell which from which. The living room around him was such a mess even though he'd been here all together what, hardly any time at all. What was all this shit flung on the clean floor and all over this big clean right-angled sofa?

Eli got it about alcohol though, it'd been a long time since his last real binge but what it was, your house a wreck around you, usually not a new house like this but one fucked up for months and your life collapsing on your head, booze gave you just enough edge to say You know what? *You're right.* You didn't have to blame your mother and your girlfriend or the world in general, though you could if you wanted but that was extra. You know what? *You're right.* That's enough.

He looked around the room. Even with a booze as ice-true and clear as Absolut pouring like syrup from the freezer of that super good fridge, you can't keep a house in shape, can you, because a sick animal fouls its lair and that is what you are. But you know what? *You're right.*

His mother was out there somewhere saving his ass. Was there anything worse than that? But the thing that excused him was so plain and obvious it didn't even need saying or thinking through, so he stumbled to the brushed metal fridge poured himself another measure didn't spill a drop, went down him like the pure true arctic region whole.

Sukey could take care of herself awhile.

He was happy and he flopped back across to sleep on the big corner-angled sofa. On the floor would be a different thing, would be falling down, but even that, so what. *He was right.*

He was gone awhile and next thing the phone was ringing at him and if it wasn't his mom it'd be Franklin so he'd have to get his voice straight either way.

"Yah?"

It was Franklin. "My watchers tell me the ship has left the dock. Please tell me it was your drivers and not police."

"Got to be my people," Eli told him.

"Who are they?"

"On the phone?"

"Just tell me a little something, Eli, need to know it's real."

Eli concentrated on keeping his voice together as the geometry of the room swung, the angles dipping, then slipping. "You wouldn't believe how perfect," Eli said. "Straight-up middle-class couple, dressed like squares. I got a younger pair up here for the second leg out north of here."

"Where'd you find the old folks?"

"Oh," Eli could hear the wobble in his voice, "from, like, around."

"Around, huh. Around. Man, I had planned to ride you tighter on this but I have become technically indisposed due to running through burning trees and having to hide out, so I have to trust you from a distance … Eli, tell me I'm wrong, but a bird is whispering in my ear because running through fire gave me super-powers—you got your Moms to drive the stash, din't you."

"Why would I do that?"

"Because you don't have nothing else and you got her to bail you out. Why don't I hear you talking? Jesus, it must be her, I don't know if you're a genius or a total fool doing alltime fuckup. Tell you this, if they get stopped, your name on the title and your mother at the wheel? You got no deniability atall. No way to get out from under. I wanted you to have skin in the game but this is like the whole lampshade."

"Okay."

"O-*kay*? Won't be okay if they get busted. Does your mother know my name?"

241

"No."

"I trust you not to turn on me, you a loyal nigger, but you go under for sure. Who's the guy with her?"

"You wouldn't believe me on a stack of Bibles."

"Tell me later, when we're home safe and I can laugh about it instead of worry. When the load gets there, do the change of drivers where you are, then go separate to the rendezvous short of the border, where those people come across."

"I got the map."

"Good for you. Can't tell you where I am but at least I snuck out of 'Reka and I hope to see you north. If I'm late, remember, nothing moves till I verify the money transfer on my phone."

"Got it."

"You been drinkin?"

"A little," Eli admitted, riding the room as it tilted.

"Straighten up. I need you awake for this."

"Will do. We done?"

"One last thing. If you fuck this up and you're not in prison I will come see you. You might not see me, though."

Franklin cleared his throat noisily, a machine noise more than a human noise, and clicked off. Eli headed straight for the fridge through the tossing house because he needed a dose of You're Right before the roof collapsed on him beneath an incredible weight that had been up there even before Franklin said that last thing.

4

Tony was napping in the other seat with his mouth fallen open, not a pose to emphasize one's dignity as a Lama. She'd suggested he use the bed in back but he said the thought of looking out the window for a tail would keep him up, and as for the bunk beds down the sides of the bus they were too narrow for him and all he needed was an hour or two and he could do that sitting up. He hadn't said anything about how he snored, much less the occasional catch-up honking intakes, probably an old Tibetan breathing practice meant to bring on soft summer rain. It was a long way to Tipperary and the Interstate could not have been more boring. Lina didn't bother checking the rearview for a snooper. Mile after unvarying mile of highway lanes with periodic electric signs offside for gas, motels, Denny's, the big M ... Next time let's do our dope smuggling in rural France or on the Autostrada between Roma and Firenze. Decent espresso at the rest stops, and not-too-terrible ravioli.

Tony had been out for maybe an hour with a couple of lipsmacking halfway wakeups, but he seemed deep down and she chanced turning on the radio. She lucked into the last movement of a Mozart piano concerto, twenty-two or twenty-three, ones she couldn't keep apart in memory but both of them good for what ails you even though they reminded her of Marcus, on some town's NPR out of Redding behind them or maybe Eugene ahead, but washes of static sheared across it and for fear of waking Tony she turned it off, back to lanes of road with occasional cars sailing the upright world's downtime through the dark.

Tony came awake, smacked his lips, reached for the water. "Hi." Stretched his back, legs and arms. "How long was I out?"

"Why don't you go lie down, I'm okay. You didn't get that much."

Tony rubbed his eyes with boylike fists. "M'all right. Might check the view out back in a minute."

"Stay there. Get some sleep in the bed, you might need it, I could fade."

"Nah."

But there was something in the moment, and Lina was pretty sure she knew what it was. "Avoiding that bed for some reason?" she asked him.

"So you saw it too, huh."

"Saw what?"

"You know."

Which was a conversation-killer for a few silent miles, though Lina didn't clock the distance and was imagining things instead.

"Remember how I told you," she said, "how I have trouble doing Tibetan visualization practices?"

"What you're doing now is not a visualization practice," Tony told her. "People do it everywhere, it's not specifically Tibetan."

"How do we stop it?"

"You visualize a large green triangle with golden points and I'm going back there to see if the police is on our ass, which I think if they are that could help."

Pitch was getting twitchy in his leather bucket. Seattle was a long way off and the speed he snarfed now and then got him extra impatient, plus he'd started truly hating these people he was stuck with on the highway. He wished he could blot them out along with the time between and get on with the important thing, which would happen when it could. Also, if he didn't pace the meth right, and he had no practice with this batch, he might wear it out and have to crash. It'd be one crash or the other kind if he didn't pace it right.

Now here's trouble, Poholek blinkering over to the right lane and there's a gas station coming up, an Arco, he saw its sign. Pitch couldn't see the white whale ahead and couldn't tell if it had gone in ahead of Poholek, who was easing into the service lane with the RV nowhere in sight, so it was still on the highway.

He could go past Poholek and the gas station and probably get behind the barge, but then what? Tough to manage an act of highway piracy, the Ape was big and probly armed. Poholek would still have the tracker on the thing after gassing up and catch up and would see him. Or, take out Poholek at the gas station, shoot him in the toilet and there's always a dumpster around these places you could park him for a day before anyone finds it.

Pitch slowed down and pulled into the service road as Poholek motored toward the pumps ahead, and he switched the Porsche's lights off and stopped to a near crawl to scope the scene. Sign put a McDonalds past the pumps on a turnoff, maybe the big bus went there even though it likely had a toilet onboard and Poholek who could piss in a bottle was hanging with them. So he was there for gas. At the pumps, Oregon state law you can't pump your own, two attendants worked the plexiglass booth, one of them gassing a pickup for a fat guy in a T-shirt, shorts and baseball cap, the other kid leaning out of the booth as Poholek pulled the Ford to the pumps and stopped.

Pitch waited Poholek out while he got pumped and thought about it when Poholek went to pee but didn't like the two guys at the pump and the men's room not far enough from them, plus how would I amble out witnessed by two people, not to mention how tough a customer Poholek could be up close, as he'd already seen once tonight.

Pitch waved two cars past him on the approach ramp while he waited, and let Poholek get back on the road before pulling in to top up the Porsche's tank. The amphetamine had locked his shit up tight, constipated, carrying a load, which did not make things more fun but he could deal with it and it was a plus on the practical side, at least until he slept it off, when afterwards most likely kaboom. Once the kid got pumping for him he hit the vending machines for water, chocolate and Fritos and counted on the 911 to get him back in the game, though don't be in such a rush you run up on Poholek by accident.

It took longer than he liked but then it was great to get the rocket on the road, flip on the radar detector with the windows down in a rush of air, a wee-hah moment maybe five minutes long but started going stale by ten when there was no sign of either Cap'n Bob or the white whale he was trailing. Pitch had to think twice, backchecking to see if he'd passed an exit they could've taken and he wasn't shit-sure but maybe yes.

What to do? First run it up past 100 mph just in case his sense of time was off, zoom-threading the other cars on the road which normally would have been fun but was less so every minute when neither of his targets showed. There was no way to backtrack, southbound lanes inaccessible behind a divider trough and a line of trees so he gunned ahead looking for a speed trap and, luck still with him, saw a cluster of trees where the median narrowed and he slowed for it, hoping no cop car inside—if there was one he'd claim a funny engine noise he had to check—and there it was, a gravel-covered hideaway for a radar car, empty, praise the Lord.

Pitch drove through it to the southbound lanes and peeled out, even tighter than his 911 back home, and nailed it back to the last exit where things wouldn't be easy because who knows which way anyone went? Best interpretation he could hope for: Poholek had forced the dope bus off the road and waylaid it just right for ol' Pitch to join the party and relieve everyone of their everything. Not gwine happen, suh.

He picked a right turn at the exit junction they must have used, drove up this road and that road fast as hell drawing one blank after another and getting frustrated, angry, stupid. He zeroed up a short distance on blind alleys, then put all his cards on one last road and went miles down it nowhere.

All right, all right, he had to tell himself, stop this before you lose the way back to I-5. Here's what you do. If Poholek has busted them or taken them somewhere to work his own designs it's game over, but if not you have the fastest car, a pocketful of miracle dust, you know where it's going and who it's going to—we can be sure Mother Chase is making no delivery to a buyer other than her fucked-up son unless she's in the bidness way deeper than seems likely.

He pulled to the roadside along some trees and working his iPhone quickly established there was only one gated community inside Seattle limits, up by the golf course, so that would be where Franklin Bass had put him, and one way or other he'd find Eli's house when he got there and even in a pinch he had Eli's cellphone number and could threaten him with a call and flush him out.

One regret: parting ways with Bob Poholek meant the next time Pitch saw him the cop would've gotten rid of Marcus Dobbs' remainders and Pitch wouldn't be able to nail the killing to his forehead with a hammer.

But you know what? Once he got back on the Interstate zooming north on his own a free man no longer tied to these asshole people he had to worry about, he felt better about the prospects ahead and the living moment now. There was always an opening in this land of plenty for a bright young man with a star to steer by and a vision and a dream.

Poholek wasn't expecting the RV to turn off the Interstate, and since he didn't have a screen and only the beep-tempo of the transponder to go by, he overshot the exit they must have taken and did an emergency turnaround, heading back up the highway in what was not quite a breakdown lane flashing his lights while oncoming cars expressed their anger with their brights in his face. He dug his badge out of his kit-bag just in case, out of state but still some dignity of office, and wondered what Mrs. Chase and her bodyguard might be up to. Unlikely they'd be making deals here in the boonies and what worried him was the possibility they'd spotted him somehow, though frankly he didn't see how. He'd kept good distance and there was no reason for them to put two and two together on him and decide to ditch.

Maybe they just needed to sleep and took their business off the highway. Now back to the exit road, he hairpinned it with the beeper down to almost nothing so it was not guaranteed he wouldn't lose them, one wrong supposition up a road and they'd slip off the rim. Too bad the rig Franklin's people had found back at the tannery was the GPS one and there was no way of tracking them via phone calls back to base if he lost touch. The thing he had to work with had no skyhook to a satellite.

He paused at the crossroads stop sign, the choice between right and left arbitrary except there were lights of what looked to be a small town off in the hilly dark to the west. Bob headed for it and about halfway there lost all audio contact, so gritting his teeth he muscled through a turnaround in the narrow road and left rubber on it barrelling back not to lose them east, mad enough to kill those fuckers rather than lose everything after having lost everything already and only this card left to play.

Half a mile past the Interstate junction he still didn't have them beeping again and dead Marcus Dobbs in the back was doing nothing while awaiting his role as the accomplice of these two dope smugglers, a man who had attacked a police officer during the commission of a crime and got what was coming, only problem was Bob had to find them in to get out from under an unjustifiable murder charge—he'd never met a medical examiner who wouldn't do a cop a favor on a detail or two—and with no beeps beeping he punched his GPS on and started a frantic serious search for any roads onscreen they might have taken and he would have to try a few in the bare desperate hope of finding them.

In the end it was Lina who had sealed the deal without explicitly intending to, reaching across to Tony as he drove and placing the tips of two fingers lightly on the back of his neck as if to reassure him but the deep conduit of sexual energy opened between them in an instant, and when he placed his right hand lightly on her thigh, not high, a short measure above the knee, the underthrum was conclusive. Lina's stomach pulled concave for an instant and she failed to suppress a gasp. She imagined Tony was in about the same condition.

Without a word from either of them Tony took the next exit and turned right on some two-laner heading vaguely east.

"We could just keep it like this," he said, "on the light side of tantric."

"Or we could take our hands off," doing so as she said it.

"Wouldn't make much difference now," leaving his where it lay. "We're hooked up even without the physical contact. We're linked pretty solid together on this. Because we're stupid."

"Yep."

It's good to know your Lama knows his stuff: with his hand still there, she was in shakti with the undercurrent shunting waves inside her in heavy shifts of thrum. She put her hand on his and lifted it off her leg and onto the gearshift and they rode in silence until she said, "This is worse."

"Yeah, because the energy doesn't get renewed, so it just gets in there and starts recycling—"

"Don't explain it, all right?"

"I can't turn this thing around on this little road, you know," said Tony, and she wasn't sure which thing he was talking about, "and go back to the Interstate." Oh.

"I can see that," but could also see that it made a good excuse for him to seek and find some other perhaps more suitable road, only golly-gee for what? Lina was ready to let things happen, back to the Interstate if they came upon a turnaround to the compromised but maybe halfway noble path north, and if not, then not. The other thing seemed like a good mistake to make, though maybe not so not so not so maybe not so noble just at this minute now.

Tony found a left fork over a small girdered bridge with a strong wooden roadbed that took them running alongside a stream on their right, the road sometimes rushing next to it, then the stream falling away below as the road sloped up an embankment above it. It was on one of these rises that the roadway widened on the right, not enough to turn the barge around but providing a grassy verge on which to stop, the stream through trees and shrubs down there on the right where they couldn't hear it even with the motor off, as it was now.

"A moment to consider things," Tony said.

"Right."

Mira, the prevailing peril of the trip, the certain fact that this didn't, couldn't have a future … right. Eventually they went the way of all flesh to the back of the bus. Just to work their nerves off, he guessed.

Then a brief confusion while burning up about whether to take each other's clothes off or their own first. Grappling awhile, they averaged it out. Lina had never embraced a naked man this large around and she was clumsy at it until the energy got to her, climbed her, held her, and she kissed him wanting his tongue immediately and first, and the rest of his body found the way into her quickly and close. His energy rode up the middle of everything she had, and one time when a fresh wave travelled upward from where their plumbing was active, it reached her brain and lit it up and woke it, and when her eyes snapped open to Tony in the dimness she could see that the identical or at least corresponding light had risen inside him, his head lifting from self-preoccupation, his eyes snapping awake to her, both of them startled each time the selfsame lightning struck from earth to sky inside them. How could their sex be this body-clumsy and at the same time so highly cognitive and engaged?

In this mixed heat Tony was a courteous lover aware of his weight, keeping the bulk of it off her, and he let her roll him so she could have a longish episode on top before pivoting back down.

"Stop looking at me," she told him in a hurry. "Kiss me. I want to be penetrated completely."

She had not made love to anyone since Nelson and this was vastly different, like warming up the house by setting herself on fire with a

249

friendly companion the other log in the grate, heat and energy shimmering into light as her head swam, and all at once she knew without doubt, beyond all thought of energy or kundalini or subtle-world presences or whatever other intermediate levels might be operative, that it was the Only One Ever Mercy Itself pouring through them unbarred, and just then Tony stopped moving. "Hold it a minute," he said, tense for the first time since the clothes came off, "or I'm gonna come."

"Go ahead."

"But you haven't," he said gallantly.

"Doesn't matter. Do it. I want you to. Don't hold back."

Which he did via an approach of heavy sawtoothed breaths in the depths of which she could feel him reaching for a completeness of it for himself and to pass it on to her and then he came, moaning as he crested and went over, and that much was nothing special in itself. The Mercy was larger but couldn't be seized because It did what It liked and didn't do what wasn't on Its agenda just that sec. Lina tried to wrap her legs around Tony but couldn't get them across his back and gave up, fell back, funny but heard herself say anyway, "Oh yeahh."

There seemed to be parts of her having different experiences of this.

Then it was sad to feel Tony's erection dwindle, but when he started edging back to pull out she said, "No, keep it there," and he did, a good long time before it went down to a nub, when he eased off onto his side on her right.

They did some tactful silence during which Lina noticed consciously, though the sound had been there during their lovemaking, that it had begun to rain. Rain falling on the roof filled her with memories running back to childhood, good ones, and with the thought of the world being fed by the mercy of the rain. It took her a moment to realize that she was humming.

Tony made the shift to language. "You're a Shakti, you know."

Lina stroked his arm. "Which means what."

"You're connected."

"Mobbed up?"

"Stop. To the universe and that which precedes it."

"Gosh, Lama sir."

"I'm serious. You didn't know? You're, umm, a vessel of transformation by means of you know what. I've met a couple others. Shaktis, Devis. Probly means my life's about to change."

"Guys are so romantic, calling us vessels and all. And what about *my* life? Does it get to change or am I just a vessel for the boys. Doesn't that crap ever stop, even with you?"

"The surprising thing is you stayed married to a guy for twenty-whatever years. That's not usually the way with people like you."

"What's the usual way with us wessels then."

"They get around a lot and there are a lot of guys. Usually they don't settle and in this culture it ain't easy for them."

"I loved Nelson."

"That could do it."

"And there never were a lot of guys. If I'm such a shakti why wouldn't I know it? Is it something only guys can know and we wessels don't?"

Tony sat up, possibly to attain a measure of dignity, not easy for a man that large around, as his belly pushed forward and hid his rig. "It's my field, I'm a Lama."

"You're a pizzeria. You're a pizzeria and I'm an elevator."

"See? Opposites attract."

"Umm, you do know, Tony, that there won't be a second time—"

"Huh? Hey no, we haven't even halfway finished this."

"Tony, this has to be just a one-off. You know that, right?"

Truer words were never—the air pressure in the bus whomped and slacked and the sound of rain went more treble, and Lina couldn't believe how fast Tony raced naked down the length of the trailer to where a man had stepped inside the door they apparently hadn't locked, Tony crashed into to him and backhanded him so the man lost something heavy that clattered against the front seats and fell. Naked Tony hit the man, then bearhugged him and tumbled him out the door together into the rain.

Lina herself was pretty quick wrapping herself in the topsheet and rushing up front where she had a pretty good idea what Tony had knocked to the floor, but the sheet came off her underfoot and she let it go before finding the gun where it had fallen, a chunky black automatic and drops of rainwater on the ridged rubber matting near the door. Lina checked that the safety was off before walking out naked into the rain to protect Tony with it if she had to.

Tony didn't look like needing protection, straight-arming the guy with both hands to the guy's chest again and again, explosive, and the man, it took her a couple of tries to recognize the pale blond balding head and jug ears, staggering backward each time Tony hit him. Lina could see that Tony was maneuvering him to the edge of the grassbank where it fell away toward the stream and shouting in Pollack's face, "What! The fuck! You think! You're doing! Breaking! In on us!"

"Tony," she called, hair streaming wet down her now, "he's a cop from Eureka," but she didn't think Tony heard.

More two-handed shoves. "Who! The fuck! You think! You are!"

Pollack started laughing in Tony's face and it stopped Tony shoving him for a moment. "You stopped just to fuck the bitch? I thought you spotted me and ditched. You fucking amateurs, you get no respect from me, you're *done*."

Tony pushed him again, harder, for that, had him almost to the edge now and Pollack turned his head and saw the drop, stepped closer to it, made a funny, illogical move down to grab his foot and Tony must have stopped to figure out what was going on.

A couple of confusing things happened, Pollack rising up with his mouth falling open as Tony moved in on him again, but Lina didn't think it was Tony that got his attention because very quickly she'd seen a big blue shape wave a number of arms in Pollack's face then disappear while Pollack yelled in fear and stumbled backward from it and fell over the edge and down through a clatter of branches or vines.

Lina couldn't stop herself from starting to laugh. A *deus ex machina*, for godsakes—this was comedy. She walked up to stand next to Tony, still laughing—was she hysterical? "He's a cop from Eureka," Lina managed to say.

"I heard you."

"Associate chief, I think."

"We're fucked. Only thing we can do is lock him in the trunk of his car must be around here somewhere, get away and ditch the bus someplace it won't be found so there's no proof of nothing. It's over. Hey!" Tony called over the edge.

"Fuck you!" Pollack yelled back.

Boys, boys. *Deus ex machina*. This is comedy. Lina started laughing again at the full spectacle of Tony and her naked in the outdoor night, their ridiculously shaped bodies pale as parsnips in the world's rain and one of them, the puppet with the dangly tits and flarey hips holding of all things a gun and about to yell into the abyss at a fallen clown, was her. "Did you see it, Tony?"

"See what."

Lina walked her silly naked body to the edge and looked down, couldn't see anyone down there in the dark but the rushing stream sound came through clearly. "Hey, asshole!" she called. "Give it up!"

There was a little flash and pop, and Lina heard a bullet whicketing through leaves and branches just overhead. "Oh for fuck's sake," she said before throwing a random shot down there and stepping back to Tony. She didn't have time to decide if he was looking at her funny before she heard a sick-sounding groan from down by the stream.

"Oh shit," Tony said.

"Can't be. I couldn't have hit him." But she knew her intuition and unforgotten skill had sent her shot where she'd seen the flash of Pollack's.

Tony put her in place by hand then went along the edge of the drop to the right, peeked over and pulled back, peeked again, pulled back, then stepped to the edge and tried to see. "I'm goin' down there," he told Lina. "Go get dressed and bring me some clothes."

"No."

"Do it," he said, started down looking funny fat and naked with the bottoms of his feet dirty then going out of sight and said "Fuck" as he slipped or stubbed something on the way. Lina went to the edge ready in case Pollack took a shot at Tony, and heard another sick sound at the bottom and Tony making noise as he climbed and slipped down toward it. Her life had changed, all its stagecraft had collapsed.

Time seemed to have gone on hold as well because before she knew any time had passed Tony was clambering back up through underbrush to the grassbank and her. He took the gun out of her hand, one naked parsnip to another, and held her by the shoulders. He was scratched up and had leaves and twigs clinging to him. "Okay, we're in another world. We have gone through the looking glass."

"Is he dead?"

"You gutshot him. He might have a couple minutes. I'm going back down to be with him. Get dressed and bring my stuff."

Lina decided that she must be in shock because she went through the necessary motions efficiently enough but as if tranced, wholly preoccupied with other business inside herself. If she hadn't seen the flash of blue wratful, though, she'd probably be not in shock but horror. Silly but true, true but silly. She had lost her mind.

She dressed in the bus and came back outside in shirt and jeans, hard to get into them wet, holding clothes for Tony to put on, which he did, his pants and sneakers without socks but handed his shirt back to her when it was hard to put on and he climbed back down toward the water for a while. When he came up this time he didn't say anything and it was still raining. "His car's probly back behind us." Tony showed some car keys in his hand. "Wait here."

"Where would I go?"

"Not down there."

"He was behind us the whole time."

"Looks like a solo mission. No one's here, he's out of uniform, otherwise, you know, other cops, lots of lights … Back in a flash."

Lina watched Tony, his back and shoppertops comically hairy, walk off into the diminishing rain.

Minutes later, as the rain slowed to a drizzle, Tony drove up slowly in an apple-colored four-by-four with the dims on and pulled in ahead of the dopemobile and got out. "Okay. Lina, you have to be up for this. Are you up to doing this?"

"Depends on what, I guess."

"I have to put the … his body in the back of his car and deal with it. You have to drive the big thing to Seattle alone, we can't leave it here and just ditching it somewhere, it'll land on Eli and prolly connect all of us to this shit."

"What are you going to do with Pollack?"

"Old habits, I go around all the time taking an informal survey of lakes and places you can put things. You never forget how to ride a bike."

"But you never killed anyone."

"I cleaned up a couple times."

"I'm the killer. Must try to remember that. Me, of all people."

"Wrong move. You have to forget everything except what you have to do right now. Deal with the rest of it later. Every mistake we make is the last mistake we make, anything goes wrong is fatal, and I'm sorry but I got to remind you that includes to Eli."

"Thank you for motivating me," Lina said.

"We're all each others' accessories, connected to the same bad thing. Like it or not," grim little smile, "it's all for one and one for all."

"And no mistakes."

"Especially no mistakes. You understand that."

"Yes."

"Right now I have work to do. You should get ready to go."

Tony walked around behind Poholek's—that's how his name went—four-by-four and opened the back and raised the lid. "Oh shit," Lina heard him say.

"What."

"Don't come back here," Tony said, and that was irresistible.

Lina walked the length of the car, the drizzle almost down to fog and Tony didn't step out to stop her, so her puzzled look couldn't make sense of the bundled shape in the back of the car because Tony hadn't put the cop in it yet but then, even with his face pushed in and blood dried down it she knew and it bent her double, almost broke her in half is how it felt. This is not comedy.

"Is that, ah, your friend?"

She hoped Tony could see her nod down there.

"I'm sorry. That's very, very bad and I'm sorry, but it changes things for us. Better, maybe. Not being callous just practical."

Lina straightened up and she was weeping. "Uh-hu-uh."

"You didn't kill this man. The cop killed this man, and I can maybe set it up so everyone will know that and we won't be in the picture."

"I'm glad I shot the son of a bitch. He killed Marcus."

"That's for later, right? You know what you have to do."

Lina nodded.

"Call Eli, not right away, you don't want to give him time to think and fuck things up, call him just before you get to Seattle and you've got to put the bus on him. You don't leave it somewhere for him, you don't give it to anyone he knows because you don't want them seeing you with it, you put the bus on him alone. If I was there maybe I could take charge but I won't be there."

"Uh huh."

"There are towels in there and you wipe down every surface there might be prints on."

"I know how to clean house, Tony."

"Good, get a little mad at me. Whatever works. If you have to make a stop to sleep, do the wipedown first and throw the towels away. Definitely throw the bedding out or burn it. We can't leave them easy DNA. I have to leave this car with the two of them and get out in such a way, I hopefully fuckin' hope, that no one observes me in the vicinity."

"Please, whatever you do, don't make it look like Marcus was up to something bad."

"I'll try."

"Try hard. Because he wasn't. He was only picking up a ca-ha-haar." Couldn't help it, she'd started weeping again.

"I will try. I haven't worked it out yet. Back to you, if police stop the bus for some reason and they know something, you deal with them the way we said before, you're doing a favor for your son and that's all you know, but if my prints are in it along with yours, well, that's trouble we can't have, they could put it together on us and close it."

"I'll clean it right away."

"Get out of here first, get back on the highway and cover distance. Don't go looking for me on the road, I won't be where you're going. Ready?"

Lina nodded. "Can I get a hug first?"

"Absolutely, yeah of course," and they held each other, maybe thinking to kiss but that was all wrong so it stopped them.

"I think I can do this, Tony. God help me, I can do it." She wasn't sure, though.

"Good." He kissed her hurriedly on the lips. "I gotta get my bag out of the bus. Thanks for everything, it's been great."

5

FINALLY, with the house to himself and all the booze in the world, Eli figured out in the middle of the blur that he wasn't drinking to get conventionally blotto unless you took that word all the way to passing out. Because basically he was drinking to pass out, to just not be here in this world that wasn't his and never had been and it was not his fault only he had the weight of it on him anyway. He'd spent the day passing out to sleep and waking up to drink some more, and half hidden in this lurching haze of how to live and not knowing the answer, almost buried in it was something he went looking for and was familiar with from other times. It wasn't just the twelve-steppers or his mom, but every kind of therapist and corrections officer he'd ever dealt with in the early days were all agreed on certain points in the way his life was going that he wouldn't and couldn't change until he hit bottom and knew it so he could start to turn it around and make a change. So he was looking for the bottom *again* because he didn't want to be a bad guy, and there were a couple of things that almost got him there this day, like tripping over the edge of the couch when he was headed for the fridge again and landing flat on his face on the floor thinking oooh that is good quality woodwork, because to think about how he'd fallen on his face was something he wanted to avoid noticing, so notice the wood.

Thing was he caught himself at it, and honest, tried to make a moment out of it, one where he could say, yep, that's it, just hit bottom, and then he could turn it around and slow the thing up and call Sukey to say he was sorry and he'd be true with you all the way, but the moment wasn't there yet, or he couldn't shape things to that purpose, or he was only imitating other times he'd been through it and to it, going through its motions because he knew them, but not for real enough to work yet.

When he got up from the floor he stumbled on those two little stairs and fell into the kitchen face first step by step so basically travelled on all fours to keep from landing on his tender nose again with everything around him swimming and swarming, and would that do it? He wanted it to but it would not. Eli got up on all twos and whatever you do don't drop that bottle, poured himself more frozen Absolut, first into his mouth and then into a glass he could take back to the big white right-angled couch again all slanty, where close to the telephone with its ringer set loud as possible and his cellphone likewise, he swallowed down more ice-cold wonder, feeling good and competent about everything again and slid into weaves and waves of dreamsleep, long sequences of flowing and falling past people and cities and cars and shuddering away from things—responsibilities—that threatened him with their monster shapes and faces.

Tony worked the cleanup like a robot after Lina left in the bus, trying not to think but every once so often calling himself a stoopid fuckhead while he dealt with the dead weight of the Eureka cop, also having to shove Dobbs' stiffening weight around the luggage bay to fit the cop in, both weights a judgment on him and what he'd become, one more time, despite all the spiritual input he had obviously fucking wasted, was the upshot. Which was why, as he worked in the fine mist and light rain and darkness, it was important not to think. Number one not to think about, because he had to keep going and not tear his own head off or the heart out of his chest, was how stupid he'd been to imagine he could play his little hero game with the worst possibility they'd get caught with the stuff and have to talk their way out the way Lina's lawyer said. Now he'd put everything in his life especially including his wife and innocent son's futures at risk. The easy out was to blame Lina as some kind of arch-seductress but he wasn't fraudulent enough, yet, for that. So how'd he get here? Oldschool madcap knucklehead bullshit? A fantasy that he was somehow always lucky? A dumbfuck sense of spiritual privilege now proved to be nothing flat? How could he have been so *blind*?

Whatever else had happened there was no doubt about it: on the essential plane he'd been demoted. Plus he didn't know where he was supposed to take these dead meat bodies yet.

Then had to dig in there with them showing if anyone came down the road because—slow thinking, Tones: you're too old for this on not enough sleep—because Dobbs' phone had Lina's messages on it and he had to get it. Even though the eventual investigators wouldn't be able to trace the trip-phone to him or Lina and her messages had been no-name, add them to the mix and those bodies would tell a tale other than a two-hander shootout in wherever Tony decided to dump them, "you stoopid fuck," which was when he knew where he was gonna put them. It was obvious.

Then it took Two-Gun Torrezini too long to police the ground with a flashlight until the ejected casing from Lina's shot gleamed back at him between the grassblades and he put it in his pocket. Still traces of blood on the rained-on grass in this place no one, he hoped, would ever fine-comb and would be washed away the way the rain was washing him if not clean then maybe serviceable.

The car wasn't sagging backward from the weight, the cargo top-lid was shut on the happy couple, no reason anyone should cold-stop him on the road. You didn't need a degree in advanced mobology to figure out the bodies had to go back to Eureka, only way to keep events local and unsuggest anything northerly toward home. Nothing he could do about the blood in the back compartment unless he burned the car, which would call attention to it before he could get back to the Porsche and out of there, so no. Also bad, he'd reach Eureka in daylight so he'd have to find a safe safe spot.

Tony changed into a dry shirt from his dufflebag, made sure both guns were secure under the passenger seat and started driving still in robot-mode somewhat, back to the Interstate even though he had a bad superstitious feeling about retracing any part of this trip he shouldn't have taken in the first place, but there was no avoiding the path you'd travelled, much less the inked arterial script of moral consequence and karma written on the earth like a roadmap and on high in other ink.

He reached the Interstate and was not greeted by a host of squad cars flashing the lights of hell at him because the world already knew everything. Once the heavy lifting's over call Jim Wilson in McKinleyville and crash for a couple hours no questions asked because he'd need the sleep. Would Jim connect him with bodies found in the woods not far off in a day or two? He'd have to ask Willie to keep schtumm no matter what.

He saw no other way, could not go into town even for coffee, since when the bodies turned up the question'd be Anyone see a suspicious character in town that day? Oh yes, bigass Italian-looking dude with a shaven head and I'd be happy to work with your sketch artist.

He was more than a little fried around the eyes, but here was the Interstate laid out on the earth, and although the white lines were wont to double on him he drove south under heaven a man no longer picked out by grace, not even a fool for love, just another regressive knucklehead bound to the wheel of old experience despite everything you been given, jerk.

The really unexpected thing was that Nikki changed completely after Lina left, stopped chattering and skittering and acted calm and self-controlled, okay, not exactly calm because she was so intense, but she kept it buckled in and was good to talk to. Sukey had the numbers of a couple of Eli's friends on the island but it was clear that she and Nikki would respect Lina's house rules and wouldn't get some dope and smoke it, and Sukey'd kept to Lina's beer ration rule, buying just two bottles each on the way back from picking Nikki up at the bookshop earlier that afternoon.

Nikki got seriously nervous only once on the ride, about the phone call she'd have to make soon, and even then Sukey felt it was partly because Lina's name came up.

"It's not like Lina she didn't make that call," Nikki told her, "but she left it for me to do. I understand she's in the middle of trouble and didn't want to burden me, or maybe she has some misgiving about me personally. I don't know for sure what she's into but I can guess and I wish she wasn't. It's not Lina's world and she can get caught there. I can't tell you how much I fear for her. And where would I be? She's doing it for Eli, Sukey. For your Eli."

Then Nikki sort of tucked herself back again into the seat and got quiet.

"Just don't let me not call the lady at the prison," she said after riding awhile. They had come out of treelined road with houses peeking through green, the cove with the small-boat harbor opening on their left now, picturesque. "I have to call and tell them Lina had to go away. They probly want you to take me back there right away, or they send a car to get me."

"But we have time to drink our beers, right?" Sukey asked her. They were back through forest again and for a moment the peeling red bark and naked yellow wood of the twining madrona branches creeped Sukey out. Because they were stripped like she was being stripped.

"Maybe one beer each," Nikki said. "*You* can have two. Maybe not a good idea for me, though. See, the thing about self-control …"

"But what," Sukey suggested, "what if we take a day off and get together just us girls?"

"And not call in to prison?" Nikki suppressed a guilty giggle behind her hand. "Take me to the bookstore for work tomorrow and let's you and me hide out? That might be good. There's a lot I need to tell you you need to know."

And that was how it pretty much went down, up talking late, trivially because they were just getting to know each other, and every time Nikki put on a lecturing tone Sukey got up to do something. Then a few hours sleep—Sukey worried for a minute that Nikki with her jailbird ways might want to get her into a lesbian thing but Nikki stayed bundled up on the sofa because she wouldn't sleep in Lina's bed—then an alarm-clock morning and drop Nikki at the bookstore in town, workaday work and back home, no surveillance calls from prison across the water.

Back at Lina's after work and before they had to make the prison call, Nikki had a lot she wanted to tell Sukey about how to deal with this and how to deal with that, how to deal with Eli especially, but as they drank cold Full Sail from the bottle Sukey started telling Nikki Eli stories she thought were pretty terrible and she expected Nikki to get all methodical about them and try to give her a lesson back, but they ended up laughing at all Eli's booze and dope stupidities and collapsed into each other on the couch to share how funny it was despite everything being horrible just now. "Okay, okay," said Nikki, trying to steady herself. "See, the good thing you have as compared to the way I was, I was a totally helpless addict and I was so dependent it got me in with truly bad criminal men."

"I'm worried about being Eli's enabler."

"Right, I know that word, Lina uses it sometimes, they all do, but Sukey, you can enable him bad or you can enable him good. Eli's not a hard criminal, he's a messed up guy who can't get his head straight from in front. He needs you for that, you can do that for him, and you have a baby and it can be all good, Sukey."

"What you think the odds are?"

"The odds are never good. Never ever good, this is life and we are weak people. But you have a chance because Eli is not a bad man, I've seen some true genuine really bad ones, shoot a man behind the counter of a liquor store for no good reason bad. And we both know Eli's not that. You got a chance with him and you must take it, Sukey."

Then, because Sukey had told her Eli stories, Nikki starting telling some of her own men stories and they were terrifying—men who beat her all the time, men who knifed other people, hard-drugs men who lived like angry animals in a world so full of violence Sukey had a hard time understanding it as real, as recognizably human, even, though she couldn't say that to Nikki because of the racial thing—but the surprising upshot of hearing these stories was that, much more than the preachy things Nikki wanted to tell her about being in prison and the ways Eli could get to prison or not get there, was that it showed Sukey a world Eli was living on the edge of and could fall into. It wasn't what Nikki said but that everything she said demonstrated her jail mind, the prison mind that being inside had put on her and turned her into, and Sukey saw that something like it, only worse because men's prison was worse, would be what Eli would turn into if everything went wrong. Even if Eli was big enough and strong enough not to get ass-raped all the time—he was too good-looking not to be a target, and there could be gang ass-rape he couldn't fight off—even without that he would turn into some jail-shaped Eli version of Nikki here and would have something like the form of Nikki's mind. Sukey had to make an attempt to get in the way of that and prevent it if she could. She could fail, she could see how easy it would be to fail and how tough against the odds it might be not to, but especially because the baby was coming she had to try, and started thinking how, even though she was afraid to go back to Seattle to see him because relationship-wise he'd get crazy-angry at her for showing up, which could break the camel's back. Even so, she might have to chance it even so. In fact if she believed that she and Eli had ever meant anything in life, she absolutely had to chance it. She wanted to get him out of the dope business, yes, and didn't think that'd be possible, but one thing was clear, if he was in the dope business *without her* he'd get busted and go to prison. Obviously. So there.

Of course if it wasn't for the baby coming she could walk away, but now all this was just followthrough. Should have known that Eli wouldn't make it simple. Did know. Knew.

They'd finished their beers before five o'clock, and Nikki drank some strong coffee before she made her call, the call that Lina should have made only she was so stressed out she left it, or for some other more complicated reason. Sukey listened and was afraid something terrible would come down on them, like maybe they had committed a crime. Of omission, but who knows, it could be a real crime in prison-people's world.

"Yes, Superintendent Parnell's office please ... yes ... yes ... I understand but this is Nikki Jackson on work release on Vashon Island ... yes, I'll hold ... excuse me? ... yes of course I'll talk to Miss Jane Cantrell ... okay I'll wait."

Nikki did a halfway-home relief face at Sukey and a things-are-rolling gesture with her free hand.

"Yes? Ms. Cantrell? Yes, this is Nikki Jackson ... uh huh ... I'm at her house now but there has been a family emergency and Mrs. Chase had to go somewhere urgent ... yes, at her house, not alone, I am with a friend of Mrs. Chase who is sorry she didn't have time to call you personally ... uh huh ... right ... well look, this friend of Mrs. Chase, she can take me to you in her car right now ... uh huh ... that's what I thought ... we're near the ferry here, I'm not sure I can give exact directions to the house but this friend of Mrs. Chase ... uh huh, that's the address ... GPS, yes that's where we are ... okay ... Ms. Cantrell I *am* sorry but it was not something I could ... uh huh ... I reckonize that ... the ferry schedule? Okay, I will wait here, I will be here and also I will not leave this phone if something ... uh huh ... I'm *very* sorry ... yes, we will ... Okay, good bye and thank you so much ..."

Nikki breathed out and semi-collapsed.

"What is it?" Sukey asked her.

"Like I expected they're coming over with a car and I better be here—"

"You are here."

"—and I won't be coming out to work again next week, the case has to be reviewed when Mrs. Chase, when Lina gets back and can visit at her earliest opportunity ... Lina fucked me up, Sukey, but it's okay. She is still saving my life every day to day and this'll cost me but it's all right."

263

"You still smell like beer a little."

"Hope they miss the first ferry. I better brush my teeth again and drink more coffee. It's okay if they see I'm wired, they know that one, but could you lady yourself up a bit and please Sukey put those bottles in the trash and take the trash out to wherever Lina puts it?"

It would be like seven o'clock, maybe, by the time they took Nikki away, after six at least. This whole thing with Nikki had taken a lot out of her and she didn't feel up to going out the other side of the island in Lina's car to … confront Eli, is that what she'd be doing?

But she'd do it. The thought of it gave her a puke-reflex and it was afternoon, not morning sickness. Despite all the weaknesses that had been put into her she would force herself to go. She promised herself she would, which was not a good thing because whenever she made that kind of promise it usually turned out she didn't do the thing, but this time she would, it was hard but she would, she would.

Tony wished the dark would hold out another hour or two but of course it didn't and the sun punched the clock before he got to the outskirts of Eureka. He was jumpy, though, and went to check on the Porsche and pick up its keys before taking his quiet companions into the Arcata Community Forest, and precautionate enough to get out of the car with the T-junction just in sight ahead, then make like a morning jogger just to be sure.

And nearly died on the spot when he jogged by, had a looksee down that road and David Jacklin's black beauty was 100% gone. Think fast: someone happened by and found the keys in the tailpipe or it was impounded by the police, in which case they're on to us and it is goose cooked, goodbye world. Or … some third party involved in the action? Okay, who? Some friend Marcus had left a Plan B with? Which would be wonderful, but being a stoopid fuckhead he had not questioned Lina closely enough about every aspect of the situation and every conceivable person who might be attached to it.

When he got back to Poholek's SUV, the wheels still spinning in his head, praying the Porsche hadn't been impounded by the cops, who would have ID'd the car and called David in Seattle and then the inevitable rest of doom, he phoned Jim Wilson. "Willie? Yeah, me. I know the markets are poppin' back east but look, I can't get up to your place, so can you make a million less online for a minute and pick me up at the Arcata exit on I-5? Yes I need it, yes it's serious, say in like an hour, hour and a half, I'll call?"

Let's not call David Jacklin yet. One cluster headache at a time.

It would have been bad form back in Jersey: he was in a full-body sweat driving north to Arcata in a locally known car and then following the map function on Poholek's SatNav west into the forested hills, taking it slow until he saw an unmarked dirt road forking uphill left, put the car in 4-wheel and took it into the trees. Happily there was a second, narrower fork, a marked fire road and he took that about half a mile over rough ground and branches slapping at the car until he came to a weedy patch on the right framed by fallen trees and he pulled to a stop as far into it as he could get.

The disgusting part of his morning's work was made easier by the fact that the dead cop hadn't stiffened yet, but Marcus was at least halfway there and it took all Tony's strength and some he wasn't sure of to unbend him enough to get him on the ground in a position he might have fell to on his side if he'd gone down with his nose pushed in—Tony knew one guy back in Jersey whose brag was he could kill like that but this was the first time he'd ever seen it done—and the cop posed not very convincingly on the ground below the tailgate as if Marcus's dying shot might have blown him back into it and then he fell. The blood in the back compartment wasn't going to make much sense but he couldn't burn the car so leave it.

While manhandling the bodies Tony tried not to look at their faces but the evasion was impossible: Marcus Dobbs' obviously once handsome face was losing its individuality to lustreless grey nullity, an erasure of who he'd been alive, and whatsisname, Poholek, was a pale wax doll whose lifeless accusation was going to haunt Tony for who knew how long. Poholek was clammy white washout death, his body like a bar of soap to the touch. Tony came close to throwing up a couple times but managed to hold it back.

What he could not hold back was the memory, down there in the rain by the swollen rushing stream, of Poholek dying gutshot and scared against Tony's naked wet chest and the cop's last words as his voice went weaker in what might be the last most basic human plainsong: "I tried … I tried … I … tried."

Holding him, "I know you did," Tony told him.

The man might have been looking at Tony's not exactly sculpted chest and puckered up a little when he said, "Mama, I ... *tried*," one last time, then a shudder, a twitch like your lover going to sleep. Tony would be hearing that on heavy rotation for years to come he was pretty sure.

Now he stepped back to see if he could admire his work on a technical or artistic basis and he couldn't. Bad, implausible poses. With any luck they wouldn't be found for a couple days, maybe three, so that the few hours' disparity in their times of death wouldn't be noticed and some animals had been to visit. I'm sorry I can't do any better for Marcus, Lina, I'm sorry, you don't know how sorry I am.

The last thing was the riskiest because of the noise, clasp the cop's automatic between his hand and Marcus's dead right hand and fire a shot into the great beyond to leave powder traces on Marcus. Couldn't put another one into the cop because it'd be inflicted obviously post mortem.

Tony wiped the gun clean of his prints, ditto the cop's smaller gun before placing it beside his body, wiped the casing from back at the stream and dropped it, then cleaned his prints from the car best he could and started walking downhill through the woods as it began to sort of rain, hoping he knew where he was, roughly. A burnt smell from up in the hills came down on the drizzle.

By the time he got unlost and found the true bead on where he was headed he had begun to weep on and off, not in a heaving way, just natural. If he got out of this he would beg his way back into Mira's good graces and see about the restaurant possibility because his spiritual vocation was over since he'd been revealed, again, basically, as a stoopid fuckhead who would have to do penance if God let him. Maybe if they got away with it, he saw a quick hope, the Eureka police would do a coverup to protect Poholek's reputation and their own. He would have to look after Lina awhile, coach her through the aftermath, and though they'd done some hanky they definitely would not be moving on to panky. He knew he had seduced and married Mira because of her youth and beauty, but he was going to stand by that choice, though a punchline from an old joke popped into his mind: yeah, *now*.

And if they were gonna get caught, Tony had to wonder what he really thought about suicide. Because that way he'd be the least amount of trouble to anyone. It would make an end. Though he'd probably have to go through fucking hell in the bardos. He'd earned it.

It was fucking obvious: he'd been Macbethed with one more pornographic precognition even though he'd seen it coming, and now he was trudging through rainy woods, no arrow through his neck but it could come any second. He had based his life on achieving awakened consciousness and had vowed to serve that aspiration in others travelling the way, but he was an old leopard who had climbed back into his suit of spots and was out here with the rest of the animals.

This whole level of rumination showed him he was still Italian Catholic to the core.

The drizzle mist was lifting in the forest and the light was brightening a little.

Now that he was almost in the clear and could hear what he thought must be the highway downhill on the other side of a bunch of trees, he took his phone out of his pocket. "Willie? Yeah, where I said, can you be there in twenny minutes? Come off at Arcata and I'll be there. No I can't tell you, because I would have to kill you and your entire family, uh-huh it looks like I'm still very good at dat."

Note to self: after you take a scalding vigorous shower and scrub your body, that future fat hairy corpse, remember to burn these clothes, shoes included.

Lina pulled off the road to sleep in a rest area near Eugene. She'd already damp-towelled every possible spot of the RV twice before turning in, not because she was absolutely too tired to drive this thing but in order to take refuge in sleep, if possible vanish awhile, in the last analysis take refuge in God or from God, either way, if He'd still have her or just let her hide in Him a little. The bedding and towels she'd used for cleanup were stuffed in roadside trash receptacles back up the road, she didn't know if she got to everything Tony'd touched but she racked her memory and had done her best twice over.

She wondered about other people who had passed this way or something like it. Her professional expertise, the fact that for years she had counselled people in prison, didn't give her a handle: whatever your second-hand experience, when it hit you personally everything you'd

267

lashed together unlashed itself ... *What did people do?* Her sense of moral urgency, formerly a star to steer by, was torn to shreds of no longer light, so what was left of the essential Lina Chase?

She still knew how to drive. Her eyes could still see the world other people lived in, but she was under other orders of law now and other people stood unbridgeably far from her. She had thoughts, concerns, the usual tonnage of memory, two sons and a paid-up dacha on a forest island. But she was only a functional fake-human puppet, one more moral failure in the overfed industrial world.

Marcus wouldn't have been there to be killed if she hadn't asked him for a favor. Which she knew she could get because come to the crunch she knew she could hook him to say yes, and that had made him dead.

And she was flattering herself pretending she'd thrown a casual comic shot down the ravine when she knew that her old gunrange instincts had guided her aim to where the cop's shot had come from. There was no pleading ignorance. She had meant to hit him. Kill him, she meant.

Lying in the bed in which she still smelled sex with Tony, Lina imagined her body falling through layered worlds of herself posed against the unformed unconsciousness she sought: imaged herself falling, not from a height or through distance but through stratified selfnesses, but she got distracted by everything she'd accomplished lately. Tony didn't look much like a Lama anymore, though his man-of-action moves, his speed down the length of the bus to smash into Poholek, had been impressive and might have saved them both, but it looked like his idea of getting out of professional Buddhism had come due.

He was out there driving two dead men around or he'd been caught. She had done it to him, with the same tactical knowhow she'd applied to Marcus, trading on the same, um, thing. Which one of them had had, if we're keeping score, and the other had not. Tony had a wife and a baby kid riding Mira's hip and all three lives would be beaten down.

She was going to get some sleep if it killed her. And if the police came knocking, as they might, she would get up, straighten her clothes and hair, walk to the door of the bus and say Hello officer, yes I did it.

Eli woke and slept and half woke and half slept and it looked like things were coming to the end of the day and that meant the big phone call would be coming sooner and sooner and it scared the shit out of him because then everything would get real and he'd have to be there for it and deal.

He hadn't eaten all day, made him pukey sick to think about food coming into him but now he was hungry, emptied up. Pain in the ass Sukey wouldn't buy microwave ramen noodles because the plastic was poison when things cooked in it so now he had to stand there staggering barefoot in the kitchen while the water boiled in one of the house's expensive-looking stainless steel pots while he mixed peanut butter and tamari and sriracha in a bowl trying not to stagger away from the counter and fall down backass and he mostly got it done with a few slipslops he'd sponge up after.

The noodles were brown so they weren't ramen they were … it'd come to him … bossa … it'd come to him but he did remember they cooked real quick so he had the strainer ready in the sink and he kept trying to catch a few noodles on this fork to test them but they kept sliding off though they looked about right, behaved about right, so he took a chance and poured everything to the strainer, only thing he poured some of it, noodles and boiling water together, over the back of his left hand holding the strainer ready, back of his hand and over the knuckles, and he was howling and spilling the whole mess into the sink with the strainer tipping over while he ran to the fridge to stick his hand into the plastic thingful of ice cubes the fridge kept clattering out, and it hurt so bad he wasn't slightly thinking of a twelve-step bottom but then he did hear the front door opening, someone coming in and his first thought it was Franklin angry enough to kill him, and he wished he had a scuba-diver speargun or something, but it turned out to be Sukey come to save him, never saw anyone better or more welcome in his life, and he raised his burning hand.

Sukey's answer was to walk across the distance, slap him hard in the face, but the hurt of it lost in the blur of vodka and the hot pain in his hand and the relief that she was here. He hugged and pressed his whole body so close her heavy breasts and the coming baby felt like she was pushing them inside him and he decided he would let her do just that, because that's what she meant to do, so he'd let her, he'd take it all the way in. So … this meant she was saying what?

Tony slept like the dead in Willie's guest bedroom for about three hours until he sat straight up with his heart pounding because his mind had been churning and mumbling and all of a sudden he'd figured something out in his sleep and it woke him. He couldn't call Seattle on his own phone from here because of a trace but he could use Jim Wilson's. "David," he said, his voice still groggy because he couldn't wait. "Your car's got one of those anti-theft satellite hookups on it, am I right?"

And had to hold the phone away from his ear when David Jacklin said *Whaaaat?* And nursed him back to the memory of his comprehensive insurance coverage up the car's wazoo and how even if something happened to it, which it wouldn't, he could end up with an even newer model and Tony would make up the difference, and please whatever you do, no, don't report it stolen, tell them you loaned it out and were only wondering if they could tell you where it was. I think a friend of mine has it and it's probably okay—he hated lying but had to do it—I just want to know for sure where it is.

Then had to wait entirely too long in this satellite-and-computer world for David to call back with the frightening information that his prize Carrera was heading north approaching Portland on I-5 at quite a clip. Tony told David that was fine, it was a friend bringing it back, don't worry, and hung up on him. Then tried to phone Lina on the trip-phone but got a recorded message saying not in service, which meant that Lina, good girl, had already taken it apart and junked it. He couldn't call her on her own cell because that would create an incriminating link between her and events down here. And, stoopid fuckhead, he hadn't thought to ask for Eli's phone number in Seattle, which was registered to who-knew-who so he couldn't look it up.

For a quarterbrain-asleep and wished-up instant Tony imagined it was Marcus Dobbs heading north in the Porsche repentant he hadn't made the meet and overcompensating by early redelivery of the car even though he was supposed to stay clear of the operation to protect himself and Lina … Tony was able for a refreshing helium hiatus to imagine it until the bodies came back to him deadweight heavy with a postmortem stink rising from the half-open mouth of one of them confiding its secret to him he hoped not forever.

Jim Wilson, looking good shirtless at almost seventy and his full head of hair still mostly dirty blond because he lived right, was busy in his beautiful fire-brick kitchen slicing excellent green avocados and red tomatoes in a perfect world for a lunch of some kind, and Tony had to tell him, "Willie, I don't know how to ask you this, but …"

Willie owned two cars, a forest green Beamer 540i and a blue Ford Explorer, and since Tony'd had all the Ford Explorer he could stand and because when you came down to it Willie was a soft touch he took the fast one with the radar detector north fast as he could while thinking about police. Counting the number of other people's premium-quality cars he had in circulation at present he made it two, with no idea who was rocketing north to Seattle, sleek and clad in black and way ahead of him in the game.

6

PITCH HAD BOMBED it up the Interstate, fighting to keep his fractious black thoroughbred cruising under a hundred and ten, and the radar detector had done him a solid twice at least. Now, in the early evening outside the enclosing wall of Shelbourne Estates, having circled it twice trying to get a fix on where the security cameras were hiding, Pitch was trying out a last few scenarios for the gateman. I'm here to deliver this car to Mr. Elijah Chase, it's a gift from his uncle and he'd like it to be a surprise, so if you would kindly … It didn't work better than any of his other mental tryouts. The guy wouldn't let him in without being announced, which was his job exactly, and even if Pitch got inside that way how long could he plausibly stay, holding a gun on Eli and snarfing more speed so as not to nod off—because that brain-fracking nod was starting to show signs of comin' round the mountain when she comes—while waiting for the stagecoach to come to town.

He tried Gatefella, I'm his cousin and would like to spring a surprise visit, which nope, didn't play either.

One thing was sure, Pitch couldn't do the most practical thing, sit in the car outside the gate awake and asleep as need be waiting for mama's boy Eli to come out to meet the RV when his mama brought it, since waiting within view of the gate and the gateman's box was precisely the way to get the police called on him as a suspicious character who, looky here, has a pocketful of white powder thingies and is that an old 38 Special I spy with my little eye?

Waiting to one side of the gate out of sight would lose him Eli if Eli turned the other way on leaving. Plus he might comedown-sleep right through it.

He would have to go in over the wall, suss out the security camera situation and try to find Eli's house—have to hope he doesn't garage his car, otherwise I will have to play all innocent and ask someone. Pitch did not feature holding Eli prisoner, too much time for things to fuck up, but he'd do it if there was no other way.

Pitch parked a distance from the spot he'd picked to go over—the place was very trusting, wall-wise, doing without razor wire or even old-school shards of glass, which likely meant their camera coverage was good. He had to go in anyway and didn't see much point waiting for dark, so let the chips.

When he got opposite the spot he'd picked on the wall, grey stonework with a tombstone-black granite lid set on top about five feet high, he sat quietly beside a tree for a stretch of minutes, listening to the few sedate sounds of the neighborhood and watched a couple civilians drive home from their banking gigs he supposed, and because he didn't want to stay there too long and get spotted it was time for him to brazen it out, a quick run across the street and a jump to reach the top of the wall and flip himself over into a shitload of hedges that hurt his face and hands. Then he had to lay there to listen for a flutter of response, but there was not even a birdie on his case. One dove hoo-hooing in a tree had nothing to do with him.

Pitch figured the best thing was not skulk and slink in and out of shadowy corners but take the most casual-looking honest-John stroll through the evening he could manage, hands in his pantspockets, scoping the scenery, even whistling and kicking an invisible can down the road. How many houses had they packed inside this gated piece of shit? McMansions in a row, most of them hilarious, glandular, one of them half a castleworth of mock-Tudor timber and leaded servant-dungeon windows … Somewhere between thirty and fifty crap houses inside, he guessed, a few of them not too fat and ridiculous and it was behind the wrought-iron gate and low wall of one of these where Zathena goddess of Zowie had crossed state lines and lucked him out with the sight of Eli Chase's old blue dented Saab, and easy over the ornamental stonework into the shrubbery inside. The house was a not too immodest grey and white McMac with an ovular driveway branching both ways from the gate to the Saab's spot in front of the little portico. Pitch rolled himself behind some shrubbery about halfway on the left curve and against the wall as a provisional first base.

Eli wasn't too sharp a guy and Pitch didn't expect to get spotted later on if he was safe so far. If he'd been seen someone property-official would be along and that would end it, with maybe a night in the can if I can't figure something to do with him. We'll see.

Otherwise, the RV comes in tonight, probably late, maybe toward morning, arrives with Poholek beeping up its ass or had Chase-mama lost him too? Poholek could turn up anyway: he'd know where to find Eli. That would be complicated. The bus comes here, no, Eli goes out to meet the stagecoach comin' round the mountain when she comes. He couldn't think straight when his brain and eyes got this tired now.

Thing to do was carjack Eli when he came out to make the meet, or see what happens if the Whale comes right here, so considering his current irresistible dose of speed-drop going on, should he risk a nap? He was a country boy didn't mind laying in the bushes with bugs crawling up his pants, it was like being a kid back home again. The speed still had his shit packed up solid so that wouldn't be a problem. If he slept he'd need to hear the gate open and whatever came next, and Pitch figured the best spot was near as he could to the gate, because noise and motion close to him, basic animal self-defenses kicking in and he'd hear it.

He'd left a possibility out: what if Poholek had arrested Mama on the highway even though he could have done it back in Zowie with less work, so no, unless he'd been forced to it, say, by being spotted. Then who'd win, Poholek or the Ape?

He hadn't heard the car coming, that's what you get for thinking too much, but the clunk and hum of the gate opening—which yes would be enough if he was sleeping next to it—got his attention, and the red car that drove in, Chase mama had one like it but she couldn't be here yet, soo …

He watched it pull up to the house and lurch to a stop behind Eli's car and the pregnant girlfriend whatsername got out, then went inside on the march. Definitely a non-workable hostage situation there, someone could get behind you or a big guy like Eli could feel irrationally protective of his Betty-June plus fetus and go for him gun or not. We will not have that trouble.

Pitch waited after the gate reclosed and found a spot near it where the ground looked clean enough and there was cover and he lay down on his back wishing there wasn't so much green crap over him so that in a while he could look up and see the stars.

It was like coming home. His body remembered something for him, hiding in the Smokies running away when Dad wailed on him with the belt too much, the woods and green slopes his old refuge in all this world and time. It struck him funny to recognize he'd been a child. He wondered if at the end of this he showed up in Paris with money in his pocket one of his daughters on some street would recognize him. It struck Pitch as really odd that he had been a child at one time but since then had been transfigured. He could feel his human heart beating, and with his right-hand index finger he drew a little circle in the dirt.

Eli and Sukey fought on and off for a few hours though part of that was Sukey shutting herself in the upstairs bedroom, which was fine with him so he could drink in what he had left of peace, but things were calling him and finally somehow, hard to tell the sequence because he had some memory blackout there, they were together in bed like people who had washed up by a river or on a beach, and now that he thought about it there might have been a time when he gave up and confessed to some true and awful shit and was just collapsed and weeping in her arms as he gave in and asked her, okay, okay, I give up, do you really love me, can you really take me back and help?

He kept drinking whenever he woke up anyway because he wanted to but he knew the peak of it was over so it didn't really count. Then he slept a lot, deep but rolling, and his dreams were not so bad this time, stormlike and tumbleful but less scary, and he felt Sukey near him, she was in some of the dreams and didn't yell at him so he thought they were okay again and could be for keeps, that is if he was remembering the waking things right and they had happened like he thought.

The phone tore him out of sleep like rags of himself at something like four in the morning with his brain very fucked up by being still drunk and starting to get hung over on top, like an extra lid of ashes. Or maybe like unwashed dishes in a sink. Ashes, dishes, one of those. He fumbled at his cellphone on the side table, knocked it to the floor, sprawled headfirst off the bed and clicked it on and it was the whole world on the line, everything he'd ever been and done and everything ever said about him in judgment or otherwise, in other words it was his mother.

"Yah?"

"Eli, I'm fifteen minutes south of Seattle—"

"You were supposed to call me way before to give me time—"

Sukey risen up behind him with a hand soft between his shoulder blades.

"Eli," his mother interrupted him. "I'm driving this thing to the ferry landing and I should be there, I don't know, in fifteen or twenty—"

"Don't take it there! They have sniffer-dogs and it's the middle of the night, suspicious. You can't."

"Eli, you can't order me to do anything," it was her controlled-but-full-on fury voice, right there: the elevator had landed. "In fact you have nothing left to say. Just listen. Things went wrong, things went very wrong, I'm not going to tell you how, but you need to understand—"

"Are you all right, Ma?"

"It's good you said that, because if you'd asked about the, uh, cargo first I was going to drive this fucking bus into Puget Sound somewhere, I swear. Which I might do anyway."

"Yah … You wouldn't do that."

"Don't count on it. Meet me at the ferry landing."

"Ma, don't pull all the way to the dock, hang back."

"Meet me at the ferry parking lot in twenty minutes," she told him. "I have nothing else to say to you, except obviously you're drunk, right?"

"I had a couple before but I'm okay now." Rapid calculations while the planes of the room tilted and spun: no ferry now till dawn, no way to get Jim-Bob and Placida over from the island yet to drive the thing north, I'll have to bring it here or take it and wait for them or sleep in it myself someplace between here and Canada. It was confusing.

"Eli, this is the end. This is past the end. Get to the ferry landing or I swear if you don't show up I'm driving it into the Sound."

"I'm coming!"

His mother hung up on him.

Then it was Sukey: "Eli, you're too drunk. I'll drive."

Try not to push her away physically, she'll think I'm hitting her. "I drive great drunk," he said, "and no way I'm putting you in the middle of this. No way you're going—"

276

But he had to fight her and there was yelling while he got dressed and stumbled for his shoes, falling over as he put the second one on, and more yelling bang in his throbby head as she followed him down the stairs, there were a lot of stairways in this house. So much yelling on so too many stairways when, c'mon, it all boiled down to "*I'm coming!*" and "*No you're not!*"

He turned on her at the bottom of the stairways because after all he was louder. "No way! I'm trying to keep you safe!"

But she followed him to the door with more grabbing and whining like an old movie how he wasn't okay to drive but even though the house and the night and now the black outdoors tilt-a-whirled around him and she wasn't helping he was familiar with all that, done it a million times and the fact was, "Sukey I've driven hundreds of miles worse than this and never had one accident once."

That sort of stopped her to think back and count the times to understand how he was right. Anyhow he was able to get his old blue car's door open and climb in but then had to wonder where the hell the remote was for the gate ahead because he needed it quick, then realized Oh I'm *sitting* on it, dug it out of his ass and drunk as he was he was able to get the key in the ignition in the floor hump on his third try, fucking Saabs, start the motor, the motor started, Sukey tried to open the door on the other side and get in, so he had to barrel the fuck out of there like a bat, grabbing under his ass to pull out the remote again, clicking it and hoping the gate would open in time for when he got there. The clicker worked. He saw the gate start to swing open but he might be going a little too fast for it, which uh oh might mean a crash.

He was drunk, no lie, he had to admit it as the car was a little out of control doing a getaway in this too-small yard-space, but he worked his head and eyes, squeezed his eyes shut and back open and thought he could get out okay when just then, holy shit, as he got near to the crazy gateway that was opening by some miracle maybe just in time a man in a blue uniform staggered sideways out of the bushes into the headlights waving his arms to stop Eli from getting through. Eli had no fucking idea what was happening and then of all things the guy must have had a camera because there was a flash of him taking Eli's picture, which made no sense unless it was for evidence, then something happened to the windshield and he couldn't see ahead through cracked-up glass even though he could almost make the guy out, and after that it was like one of those things that happen on the sidewalk, you try not to walk into each other but you both go the same way once, then the other way twice and that's what happened with this guy—but, you know, in one drunk compartment of his drunken mind he knew exactly what was going on, same as falling off the roof only it was happening fast this time with the windshield spiderfucked and *Thunk* he hit the guy with the left headlight area and the guy went under and what was worse *gedunk gedunk* the left-side wheels going over him front and rear, the big old car climbing up and thumping back down on him.

He heard Sukey yelling in front of the house as Eli's life was now totally fucked forever and the car ran by itself into the bushes next to the gate which softened bumping into the wall so he didn't hit his head on the steering wheel and had to climb out of the car on the other side because the bushes were in the way on his. Did he smell rosemary? Mom had a big fucking bush of it out back of her house. And those fucking eggplants.

So this was the end of everything, he had killed some guy who was probably a cop, the busful of shit was going into the harbor and everyone he knew would end up in jail, he had to get to the guy he'd hit before Sukey came and saw the horrible thing he'd done, and as he came up on the man laying on the edge of the pavement with his head pushed into the bushes Eli saw it wasn't a uniform but a blue suit he'd seen before and looking closer gradually the guy was familiar and turned into Kenny Pitcher, something Eli started grappling to understand how and why.

While he stood there with his life definitely over behind bars and imagining the every whichway it was going to collapse on top of him and Sukey and his mother too so he wouldn't be forgiven for any of it ever, God pointing his awful finger, Eli saw that the metal thing on the pavement next to Kenny Pitcher wasn't a camera, and although Pitcher was making what were probably a last few jerks with blood bubbling his lips and his head bulged with blood down it and his chest broken, because sometimes you get amazingly clear in the middle of being shitfaced Eli beheld the miracle of his destroyed life being resurrected and for all he knew redeemed around him on all sides like flowers rising up in color or the towers of a magic city thrusting out of the earth because, okay, he was driving drunk but it was on his own property where he was attacked by a known killer with a gun who had shot at him to kill—yessir I was the witness at that previous killing so probably he was worried that I—and so Eli had no other alternative, officer, than in self-defense to hit him with the car, so Sukey was the one who should phone 911 and tell them the story while he got his shit together. Man, that's coffee. Mom ain't driving the bus into the drink. We'll get hold of it. We'll deliver. Jim-Bob and Plas'll come over on the dawn ferry dressed like yuppies, or like puppies, that'd work too, Sukey can handle it while I'm talking to police and I'll be all right with Franklin, who won't have to kill me for fucking up.

Home free all, but I'll lose my driver's license and the house and there'll be police shit to deal with and other crap but it should work out, he could see the dominoes doing their thing away from his direction.

Sukey got to him crying something and he yanked her away from seeing Pitcher broken like an insect in the driveway and pulled her head into his chest telling her it's all right, it's all right, we got it covered.

There was one more something he was trying to remember he had to do but in the middle it got away from him but then like on a giant rubber band it came zooming back up close until he saw it. Remember to call your mother.

7

WHAT WAS IT, Lina wondered, about contemplating your life across the face of the waters? The Spirit of God may have moved over the face of the waters In the Beginning as related, but she wasn't Him. There was something calming in it even now that she was lost. Maybe the Spirit of God, having moved over that vast reflective face, had let fall a lasting likeness of Itself despite the infinite wavelet wrinkles on that old face, now as always, even, conceivably, for her, still, a last remnant before the blowaway of her insignificant momentary dust.

She had decided fuck it and pulled the bus into the mostly empty parking lot offside the ferry dock, let them find her, and had even walked a distance onto the bridgelet to the ferry landing just in case an advance squad of policegals were out there with soul-sniffer dogs to nose her out, but the place was deserted and presumably would remain so until a first few cars lined up for the dawn boat to the island and they turned the lights on in the ferryhouse and the world began again for those not under judgement of that selfsame Spirit of God, lastingly mirrored on the face of the waters. The one Nelson had believed in so much and she hadn't done so well with but felt His weighted presence now.

Lina walked back onshore in the empty small hours and found a way, just beyond the parking lot, alongside some houses down some rocks to the water's edge and a view across, and even if she was under judgment there was still something calming and essential in the sight of the waters that would not wash her. She tried to be logical. Pollack, she meant Poholek, hard to get that name right, had killed Marcus while waiting in ambush for her and Tony, or had somehow randomly found Marcus there, which seemed less likely. She had not tried to kill Poholek, had only, pissed off, fired a shot in his general direction to say, c'mon, give it up, this is silly, let's be fellow humans here. Or it hadn't been like that. Then when she saw dead Marcus stuffed into that back compartment, she'd said she was glad she'd killed the cop.

Emotional response. How could you be glad you'd killed another human individuality with a memory of childhood and a first then subsequent experience of the light of the world in the innocence of his eyes? How could you sit in your human body and look in the face of that face? It was as if not she but some monster were sitting there, using her body and her mind to pretend to contemplate life fallen across the face of these waters.

All sort of lofty, but then she was iced by a sudden fear that Tony had screwed up disposing the bodies—so, no, you don't really want to be caught, you just want to go through the motions of having a conscience to feel better about yourself.

And besides, *fuck* Poholek, who had been all-out to send Eli to prison. Or, since he'd already murdered Marcus, why wouldn't he kill Eli too given the least chance?

But a force drove Lina's head down. It was a cliché but her head was driven down: condemned beside the still mostly benighted face of waters. She'd been lost beneath that face one time and had wakened to another world all grey until her own face broke through it true and free. This time who knows if she comes out and if so into what.

Lina nearly jumped out of her skin when her phone rang in her pocket. It was Sukey, working a stage whisper for all she was worth, and Lina could hardly understand let alone believe what she was hearing. "Who?" she had to ascertain, and "How the hell did *he* get there?" and before she could censor herself her heart leapt up at the news that the Kenneth Pitcher she'd always figured for a greater danger to Eli than the Eureka cop Poholek had, had ... "And it really was an accident?"

"He jumped out of the bushes and took a shot at Eli in the car. With a gun. Eli was drunk and just ran into him." The next sequence of words was such a blur Lina couldn't follow them but somehow it got through to her that Pitcher's body had been examined and trundled off, the police still there so don't come up but they're kind of treating it as an accident at least for now, they don't like it but I saw it happen, we told them Pitcher killed a guy in Eureka and Eli was the witness and it checked out ... When the words came back into focus Sukey was working the stage whisper hard again. "Jim-Bob and Placida on the first ferry. Uhh, will you wait for them? Will you do it?"

"In for a dime I guess," she told Sukey somehow.

"The only thing is … "

"Out with it."

Sukey said it in a whispered rush. "I think the cops're guh-guh-goin'ta haul us in for questioning, and do I know Eli's gonna hold up under that?"

"What's the name of the officer in charge?" Lina asked.

"Benton, Benson something."

"You'll get a call in a couple of minutes. If it's not me, pass the phone to Benton-Benson."

"Wuh-what?"

"Don't ask, Sukey, it'll just slow things down. Bye."

Ray Quintana had parlayed his career insomnia into a wolf's life on the European markets overnight. She rang his private number and bless him he picked up.

"Ray, it's me. Yes, I know. I'll make it short. There's been an accident at my son's house up here … yes, absolutely an accident, not a crime, but I need you to scare a policeman for me. Come on, Ray, we both know you've got the chops for it. He's only a local. Here's the number."

Carolina and Elijah Chase, mother and son killers, a team, plus Mama knows how to work ancestral power switches. If there was a way to erase all this as the nonsense distortion it looked like … But it had the authority of manifest fact, meaning there was no escape from the wheel of law rolling alongside, orderly, patient, crushing each bug of personal protest in its false futile glossy carapace, kaput. You are less than nothing but there's still some stuff you know how to do.

Sukey rang back inside five minutes asking, "How did you what did you?"

"Sukey," Lina overspoke her, "come to the point. Are they taking you in or not?"

"They want us to stop by tomorrow afternoon, this afternoon. How did you—?"

"I'll call you after I meet the ferry. Bye."

Nicely done, master criminal, but she had tougher inside work to do, hold herself together for Eli's sake and don't plunge into destructive self-emotion in order to go under and punish, no, wait with a dog's devotion to her son since she was no longer fully human or deserved anything for herself as the dark gave up its ghost to the advancing haze of inland light and a breeze woke across the face of the waters and lights flickered on in the ferryhouse.

I cover the waterfront, unless I fall asleep.

She hardly recognized Jim-Bob and Placida when they walked landward amid cars and stray humans off the dawn ferry. She'd always liked Jim-Bob, bit of an island hippybilly, friendly guy and a good worker who'd re-roofed parts of her house and hadn't overcharged, done electrical work and fixed the plumbing, one of the few of Eli's old friends she didn't disapprove of, though here he was, embroiled in sordid criminal enterprise same as her, only with his hair fastened with a rubber band at the back and a Madras shirt and seersucker jacket, Placida likewise tricked out as an all-American girl with a regulation ponytail and smile, both of them looking like a pair of ideal and gormless squares. Maybe one touch too much?

"Mrs. Chase!" Jim-Bob said in greeting. "I can hardly believe it. *You?*"

"Let's talk about it some other time," Lina suggested.

"I mean who knew you were so cool? The Eureka run. Amazing."

"More than you know. Meanwhile I like the clothes. You and Plas look like rubes."

Jim-Bob looked honestly puzzled. "What's a rube?"

Lina decided to ignore this generational glitch. "You know, right, Eli won't be up near the border for the meeting thing. Something happened and—"

"Sukey told us. We have to wait for whatsisname, Franklin, to get in touch. It's in the works, Mrs. Chase. It's handled, it's dialled in. What happened up at the house?"

"Tell you later," Lina said.

They were walking the planks to shore and the parking lot and that force rose up again to drive Lina's head down so that Jim-Bob thought to tell her, "Mrs. Chase, relax, Plas and I, we've done this before … only not," he was seeing the RV for the first time now as they reached land and could see through the trees into the parking lot, "Jesus, not on this scale, have we, babe? Mrs. Chase, *relax*. We're on the job."

"Are you sure you know how to drive that thing?"

Jim-Bob was showing her he knew how to drive that thing, scraping some overhanging branches on the way out of the parking lot and swaying and halting into the world till Lina stood alone on the asphalt.

Sukey phoned after who knows how many minutes just standing there.

"It's all clear," Sukey said in her normal voice. "The cops are gone."

"Where's Eli?"

"He's here. He doesn't want to do this on the phone. Can you get a taxi up or do you want me to come get you?"

"Taxi? Sukey, please get real."

"I'm on my way."

We have souls and so we suffer, Lina told herself. An attractive formulation, but not enough. The oddest thing was that they had won, she and Eli had won and now she trusted Tony to have won too, so that after whatever purgatorial period the law of life demanded from them they could build on their success and maybe live, animals who had prevailed over some other animals. That would be their life, if they were lucky. That and no more than that. They'd been reduced to no more than that.

Sukey was taking her sweet time getting down to the waterfront.

Lina felt a throb of nostalgia for the end of life, one sweet day my struggles soon be over and I can rot with Nelse beneath the wildflowers or fly away home, or both, whatever. She wanted time off and a rest, but she was bound to the wheel beside the face of the waters in which every mote of light and dark accurately and minutely was reflected without exception or counterfeit.

Sukey showed up in Lina's red Ford Focus and must have seen the question in Lina's eyes because she was babbling as Lina climbed inside and tossed her bag in the back seat. "The Saab was what hit Kenny Pitcher so the police towed it away for evidence and the evidence says Pitcher shot at Eli first so there's no velicular I mean *vehicular*, you know, homicide."

"Good," Lina said. "I always like that."

"We might even get the car back. Only needs a windshield and a little bodywork in front."

284

"Good."

"This is your car. You want to drive?"

"*No.*"

Sukey steered them out of the lot and looked rigid at the wheel as she turned left, north along the waterfront before the climb.

"Sukey," Lina said. "I'm not freezing you out. I'm too tired to talk."

"Long ride, huh."

"You have no idea. And Jim-Bob and Placida picked up the RV."

"We know. They called."

And that settled it, they weren't going to talk in this freighted air, Sukey because she was afraid of the elevator landing on her and Lina because Sukey had no idea. It was a fifteen minute ride up to the gatehouse where the guard sullened at them for a good ten seconds before raising the gate to let them in.

"We're not going to be able to keep the house," Sukey said.

"No kidding."

Lina's heart rose and crested as they got out of the car and went inside to see her son. Eli was standing in the middle of the foyer as if waiting to be crucified in the oncoming daylight. His face was red and terrible with booze but he seemed to be over it.

And Lina got the picture. She and Eli had passed through a time of trial in the demon-world—Tibetan demons, Christian demons, any kind of demons, who gave a flying batwinged fuck what kind of demons?— and had emerged alive though indelibly marked with the lineaments of their passage.

Or was that just one more born-to-fail attempt to hang a frame on what had happened without remedy?

Either way, as they sat down around the white kitchen table in the white room mother and son were going to talk about it to the bottom.

Only it turned out that no one had taught either of them, or for that matter Sukey, how to do it. Sukey refilled the coffee machine on the counter, pushed its button, and it started to gurgle. She had thawed a frozen loaf of brown bread and a bar of butter and was toasting slices for them, setting out plates and rainbow-pattern cotton napkins in geometric order on the white table in the white room.

"If you're really hungry," Sukey said, "I could cook some noodles."

"Coffee and toast are fine," Lina assured her. "What I could really use is a drink."

"But it's morning," Sukey said.

"Not for me."

"Yaggh*haa*," the reddened Eli had to clear his throat so he could talk. "Yah. The police found the gro-light setup in the basement. Nothing incriminating, no dope, but what with what happened the what is it, community board's gonna want us out of here."

"Whose place is it? Franklin?"

"By some other name."

Sukey set out with frozen formality three cups of coffee, sugar, milk, two slices of toast and butter for Lina, very neat, and two more slices ticking in the thing on the counter.

"So we were thinking," Eli said, and paused while Sukey nodded him ahead, "could we, like, stay at your place until we get something going?"

"Of course."

"Because, yah, I can't be in this business right now. Too much attention on me. Maybe, because I'm like an expert, after if it goes legal next big election."

"That's in a couple of months," Lina told him. "This November."

"Really? *Cool*," Eli said.

This, thought Lina, is a bomb-shelter conversation of some kind.

Eli reached dramatically straightarm over to Sukey and seized her hand lying on the table. His chin and lips trembled as he tried to speak and not blubber. "I luh-luh-*love* Sukey."

"I know," Lina said. Sukey was still trying for impassivity in her seat and wasn't doing bad.

"She is my … real … luh-luh-luh-*life*." Tears were pouring from Eli's reddened eyes down his cheeks—he was a burst bubble, a bleating baby, and Lina hoped it was not all vodka and might last this time.

"Excellent choice," Lina said, instantaneously hating her words and tone.

Eli hadn't noticed. "So is that all right?"

"I think you're both very brave," Lina said, "and I've got your back as long as you want me." Then she was surprised to hear herself ask, "Remember Marcus, the bail bondsman?"

"Yah," Eli said. "Nice guy."

"Poholek killed him."

"*What?*" Got him staring: the lives of others registered: good. "How come?"

Lina was able to keep herself from saying Because he was helping me help you. Instead she told him, again to her surprise, "I killed Poholek. Shot him in the belly dead."

Eli stared at her with his mouth open, crumbs of toast on his coated tongue, couldn't speak. Sukey appeared to be zeroed in on the bare white wall across from her seat. Lina watched Eli's coins of conscience circulate through the pinball machine, thought she might have seen a nickel drop but still had to wait for it. "For *me*," he said at last.

"Just so you know how far down this goes," Lina told him. "Now we're all three of us going to have to live very correctly."

"Or get caught," Eli said.

"That too, but not what I mean. We'll have to live very morally now, because it's just barely possible we may have gotten away with something. We're on a short leash. Our lease on life … shaky. D'you understand me?"

"This is scary, Mom."

"It's been a tricky month."

"All because of me."

"Bingo," Lina said.

Which is when a buzzer sounded.

"The intercom from the gate," Sukey said, and all three stared at each other. They have come for us. Hello Shequonda Eveningstar, here I am in prison blues doing twenty, ain't life strange?

Eli got up like a man and went to the panel in the living room. They couldn't decipher the staticky dialogue from where they sat except for Eli's last, "Let him in."

Lina and Sukey were staring at Eli when he came through the archway back to the kitchen, the white room, the white day. "It's your guru," he told his mother.

"*Tony?*"

"Yah."

The sound of a car pulling up fast and Tony letting himself in the front door.

"In here!" Lina called, too tired to stand up and meet him.

The three of them watched Tony appear in the archway entrance sweaty and dishevelled, if you can be dishevelled with a shaven head, his clothing rumpled, face alarmed, needing a shave and some sleep. "Everyone's all right? Somebody came up here in the Porsche. It's parked right outside the walls here. Everyone all right?"

Lina was trying to formulate a one-liner. No, we ordered a hero *sandwich*, not a hero. No, we didn't order a hero, we ordered a hero *sandwich*. Either way, it both worked and didn't work. "Kennis Pitcher," Lina told him, and when he didn't get it, "the tobacco company demon. No longer among the living. We knock 'em off around here, us Chases. Sit down and have some coffee."

"He's dead," Tony said or asked.

Eli raised a grade-school hand. "Yah. Mine's. Completely legal, police approved."

They watched Tony's excited fixity loosen a little and Lina realized that since he'd burst in they'd all been staring, waiting for him to say something but they didn't know what it was. It was there, though, and it had to be said. Now they could see that he was adjusting his inner workings according to the turn of events and was looking for the thing to say but didn't have it yet. He was the messenger. The accumulated moment proclaimed him so. He would say it soon. He would say it now.

Tony cleared his throat. "If you're hungry, you got any food in the house? If you're hungry and you got some food I could cook us something for breakfast."

It wasn't what they were hoping for but it managed to almost pop the cork so that finally, hollowed out and empty, either that or overfull, at this point who could tell, they needed just one more word, maybe even a single syllable, to enter a moment's laughter that would set them free, they badly needed it even if it wouldn't last forever, which obviously it wouldn't.

They were looking at Tony so intently he had no idea what the fuck to say.

Acknowledgements

I must thank Brian Cullman first of all for telling me, essentially, "Do what you know how to do, make stuff up," when I told him that if I could get back to Eureka and ask my inside informant to aid further research I might be able to rustle up an article for *Outside* or some other magazine. Make stuff up? I'd passed about a third of a day, including a hamburger, in Eureka, so I'd have to find a lot of stuff to make up; but at least I'd lived in California for a few years and could remember some of the views and vibes. After I stopped blinking at Brian I thought of some of the things I'd learned from my source in Eureka, began to grin, added a Gila Monster to the roof of Club Rave, and watched the ideas start to multiply. Brian Cullman was, as he has been many times before, my first and best and most subtle practice reader, letting me know what worked and when I could be seen to wobble on the tightrope. Markus Hoffmann did a superb edit of *Street Legal* at the time of its composition, and made a heroic attempt to get it published. I greatly appreciated the good will of Gerald Howard at Doubleday, but that attempt turned out to be only a leaner. Henry Bean gave the manuscript a keen and helpful reading. At the last, chez Terra Nova Press, Evan Eisenberg questioned some details and made some larger, crucial editorial suggestions which, taken onboard, will surely benefit this book's prospective readers.

I would like invite all these helpers to a compensatory dinner at the Belvedere, which visitors to Eureka will seek in vain. They will likewise find it hard to obtain the excellent takeout and delivery from Magnolia's (the name is an affectionate tribute to Magnolia Thunderpussy, a chicken-delivery outfit for stoners in 1960s San Francisco). Not even Eureka's City Manager, if he existed, would be able to dine on it, and history has recorded no forest fire like the one depicted in the tale. Bob Poholek is a trumpet player I recorded with in the 1960s and John Emigh a flutist on another record I played on *à l'époque* led by the multi-instrumentalist Alan Sondheim. I remember these musicians with great affection, and have no idea why their names found their way into this book. As for Kennis Pitcher, please keep your kids away from his love life, and as for blue-skinned many-limbed Yamantaka, I encountered someone like him only once, years ago, just across Houston Street from SoHo. I hope Tibetan Buddhists will be amused by some of his antics, and forgive me for my inaccuracies re Buddhism generally.

In short, *Street Legal*'s Eureka resembles the actual Eureka only a bit more than Stendhal's Parma resembles the actual Parma, Freedonia Sylvania, and Ruritania Ultima Thule. Seattle and environs fare a little better. It's odd how inspiration strikes some people; an element of fantasy in a realistic surround has sparked me up in the past, and it may be that the present light craft will provide pleasant means of transport for those who climb aboard.

In a pinch I can always blame Cullman.

Above all and after all, I'd like to express my gratitude to David Rothenberg of Terra Nova Press for letting me know he'd like to publish a manuscript for which I have no small affection, and which I didn't even know he was considering.

Rafi Zabor was born and raised in Brooklyn and is at home there now. In between, he remembers living at various ends of his home country and in the UK and France and Turkey and Israel, amid shorter stays in other friendly harbors. He wrote about music for a number of years, playing jazz drums between paragraphs, and that work led him into his first novel, *The Bear Comes Home*, which won the PEN/Faulkner Award for Fiction. He has also been a beneficiary of grants from the National Foundation for the Arts and New York Foundation for the Arts. The novel was followed by a sort of memoir entitled *I, Wabenzi*. He completed another novel, *Downtown Loop*, before Covid came to town, and has since taken shelter in a novel set in Paris, 1966. He's older now, and seems to be speeding up as he's slowing down.